Part-Time

Gods

DFZ Book 2 of 3

RACHEL AARON

SERIES INFORMATION

Minimum Wage Magic

Part-Time Gods

Night Shift Dragons

COPYRIGHT AND PUBLISHING INFO

Aaron Bach, LLC
"Writing to Entertain and Inform."
Copyright © 2019 Rachel Aaron & Travis Bach

ISBN Paperback: 978-1-952367-01-4
ASIN eBook: B07SXVMPKP

Cover Illustration by Luisa J. Preißler
Cover Design by Rachel Aaron
Editing provided by Red Adept Editing

PROLOGUE

Seoul, Unified Korea, 21 years ago

In the Palace of the Great Dragon, on the fiftieth floor behind the seven layers of security that separated the family wing from the more public parts of the Dragon of Korea's stronghold, a five-year-old girl wearing a dress worth more than most ball gowns stood in the middle of a magical circle, staring down a line of dark-green kabocha pumpkins placed on the marble floor in front of her like a soldier on a battlefield.

"All right," her tutor said, nervously pushing his round glasses farther up his wrinkled nose as he finished adjusting the last pumpkin and resumed his position at the edge of the circle. "Do it like I showed you this time. Draw in magic to fill the circle, and then move the magic through the spellwork." He tapped his shoe against the magical equation he'd written in huge, child-friendly characters around the magic circle's edge. "The spell will tell the magic how to move the pumpkins. You don't have to touch them. Just focus on the circle. Understand?"

The little girl nodded rapidly, sending her wispy black hair flying, and the old tutor gave her a smile so forced it was almost a grimace.

"Begin."

The girl stuck her chubby little hands straight out in front of her and closed her eyes. For several seconds, nothing happened, and then magic filled the room like a whipcrack. It came on so fast that the tutor barely had time to hit the safety corollary he'd written into the spellwork with his foot, releasing the magic before it overloaded the circle and exploded. But while he made it in time to spare them from magical backlash, he was too late to stop the spell entirely. The surge of power had already raced through the spellwork, scorching the symbols into the stone floor before jumping to the pumpkins, which promptly exploded, showering the entire room in bright orange, steaming-hot squash guts.

"*Ah!*" cried the tutor, throwing up his arms to protect his face as the wave of wet, freshly boiled gourd splattered over him. The little girl wasn't nearly so quick. The flying pumpkin hit her full across the face, coating her from hair to feet in a layer of piping-hot goo.

"**No!**" the tutor shouted, flinging pumpkin off his hands as he whirled to yell at his failure of a pupil. "How many times do I have to tell you: *not that hard*! You almost—"

The rest of his tirade was drowned out as the little girl threw back her head and began to wail. Her nanny—who'd been safely out of range against the large, elegant room's far wall—ran forward at once, followed by a fleet of maids carrying towels.

"It's all right," the nanny said, her cheerful voice tinged with desperation. "You can try again."

The little girl shook her head and screamed louder, covering her pumpkin-splattered face with her hands. The move forced the maid who'd been wiping her chubby little cheeks to stop, and the nanny's eyes grew frantic. "Please stop," she begged the child. "He'll hear you."

But the girl did not stop. She just kept crying and crying until her face was bright crimson. She cried with her entire body in the way only children can, completely ignoring the adults' frantic attempts to shush her. They were still trying when the room's double doors opened with a bang.

The sound made everyone except the girl jump. The child kept on crying, oblivious, but the rest of the room went perfectly still, frozen like startled deer in a field as a tall, dark figure stepped in from the doorway.

He was shaped like a man, but he was obviously not a man. No human brought the feeling of claws with him as he entered, or smelled that strongly of smoke. Even the wet reek of cooked pumpkin was overpowered by the scent of ash as he walked into the room, sending the mortals scuttling out of his way as he approached the still-wailing child.

He paused when his shadow fell over her, waiting for the realization to hit. Waiting for the fear. But the little girl was too upset for instinct to reach. She didn't even look at him. She just kept right on screaming and screaming until, at last, even the dragon couldn't take it anymore.

"Why are you making that infernal sound?"

"*Because I can't do it!*" the girl wailed.

"Can't do what?"

Instead of answering like a sensible creature, she flopped down face-first on the sticky floor and started kicking her legs. The dragon watched for a few seconds in exasperation, and then he turned to the circle of helpless adults who were supposed to be managing this. "What is she doing?"

Her nanny looked rightfully ashamed. Beside her, the prestigious professor of Thaumaturgy he was paying through the nose to teach this noisy creature magic cleared his throat. "If you please, great dragon, the young lady is having a bit of a…control issue."

"Then teach her to fix it," the Great Yong said sharply.

"I'm trying, sir," the tutor said testily. "But it is very difficult to—"

"How can it be difficult?" the dragon demanded, pointing at the child throwing a tantrum on the floor. "She has the best genes money can buy. This should be easy for her."

"Yes, well, she is *very* young," the tutor reminded him gently. "Most children don't even know they're magical yet at this age. It could be that her brain is simply not developed enough to exert the necessary level of concentration required for—"

"I don't want excuses," the dragon growled. "My daughter is supposed to be a magical prodigy. Train her to be one, or I'll find another university to fund."

"Yes, great dragon," the professor said meekly, lowering his head.

Yong nodded and turned back to the little girl, who was still kicking her legs as if she were trying to run straight into the floor. "Stop that at once."

The child jerked at his voice, and the kicking stopped. The crying, however, did not.

"What did I say?"

"I'm *trying*," she sobbed, her voice almost unintelligible. "But I…I…"

The words dissolved into wails again, and her nanny rushed in to take her away, but the dragon raised his hand.

"Where is her mother?"

The woman bowed low. "Your consort was here until just a few minutes ago, great dragon. She had to leave to take an emergency phone call from your house in Los Angeles about the ongoing labor dispute."

Yong frowned. He hadn't known there was a labor dispute at his California property, but that was the joy of having a competent First Mortal. She took such good care of all the messy little details that he never even heard about them. But then, his consort was perfect in *every* regard: a legendary beauty of impeccable intelligence, taste, grace, and tact that surpassed even his high standards. Her offspring, though…

He scowled back down at the little creature sobbing on the floor. Her mother kept insisting that the child's beauty would blossom as she grew, but Yong had presided over uncountable generations of humans. He knew there was no saving the unfortunate squareness of the girl's jaw or the dull brown of her eyes, which were nothing at all like the rare shade of honey-tinted hazel the geneticists had promised. Her enhanced magical ability should have been her saving grace, but even that seemed beyond her stumpy grasp. While her numbers always tested off the charts, she seemed unable to comprehend even the simplest concepts of human magic.

Maybe that ineptitude would improve in time, but Yong wasn't hopeful. So far, his human daughter was a disappointment on every measurable level. A loud, dirty, stubborn, overly emotional little animal with a face that, while not technically ugly, would never achieve the beauty necessary to be worthy of a dragon. Sometimes he wondered why he kept pouring resources into such an obvious failure.

And yet…

Following what he'd seen human males do with their young, Yong leaned down to scoop the crying child off the floor. She latched on the moment his arms touched her, clinging to his chest like a monkey. This, naturally, got sticky pumpkin all over his suit front, but at least the wailing stopped. Yong sighed in relief at the blessed silence and looked down at the ridiculous little creature burrowing into his shirt front.

"Are you done howling, little dog girl?"

As always, the nickname made her laugh. The unexpected mirth drove the last of her tears away. Yong didn't see how it was possible to change emotions so quickly, but she'd always been a dramatic, changeable animal even by human standards. He was just happy she wasn't crying anymore. He couldn't think with all that noise. He was about to hand her back to the nanny when the little girl pushed back and looked at him, her face pulling into a smile that made his breath catch.

Ah, there it was.

His daughter smiled with the same intensity as she cried. The expression suffused her entire body, lighting her up from the inside until Yong felt like he was holding thirty-five pounds of pure sunshine, and all of it was for him. Not even the mortals who owed him their lives looked on him with such perfect trust, such guileless, fearless adoration. When she beamed at him like that, it didn't matter that her features were unfortunate or her eyes were the wrong color or that she was still covered in pumpkin. That look made all the mountains of trouble she caused him seem trivial. It made him feel beloved. Made him feel like a god.

And he treasured it.

"I think you've made enough mess today," he said, turning away from the nanny who'd been waiting to take her. "Why don't we leave the servants to clean up, and you can come with me until your mother's done."

It was an expensive gift to offer. Today was not a good day for playing with mortals. But any inconvenience he'd just created for himself was worth it for her gasp of unmitigated delight.

"Really?"

"I do not lie," he told her, insulted.

"Can we go look at your treasure?" she asked in a rush, bouncing in his arms.

He smiled indulgently at her excitement. Before he could reply, though, a knock sounded on the door behind them.

Scowling at the interruption, Yong turned to see his senior clerk standing in the doorway with a terrified look on his face. "Great dragon," the old human said, voice shaking. "She is here."

Yong's good mood went up in smoke. His clerk didn't even have to say *who* was here. Yong could already smell her: an acrid, bitter scent that filled his house and set his teeth on edge.

"Should I tell her to leave?"

"No," the dragon growled. "Turning someone away when they show up uninvited implies that you are afraid of them. I will give her no such advantage." He thought a moment, then nodded sharply. "Send her to the throne room. I'll deal with her there."

"Yes, great dragon," the old man said, bowing low before scurrying back down the hall to carry out his dragon's wishes.

When he was gone, Yong turned to hand the girl back to her nanny, for this was no business for a child, but the girl howled in protest. "You promised!" she cried, clinging to his neck. "You said I could go with you!"

Yong paused. He had said that, hadn't he? Not that he was bound to keep his word to such a lowly creature, but she was looking at him with those huge, hurt eyes, lip quivering as if she might start crying again at any second...

The dragon sighed in defeat. "Let it never be said that the Great Yong does not keep his word. You may come with me, but only if you promise to stay silent."

The little girl nodded frantically and pressed her mouth tight shut. When he was satisfied it would stay that way, Yong carried her out of the room and into the hall toward the elevators.

A throne room was a necessity for any ruling dragon. Typically, they were decorated with great weapons or the heads of defeated enemies, but Yong found such gratuitous displays distasteful and a sign of deep insecurity. *His* seat of power was filled with examples of his wealth and magnanimity, including a huge window overlooking the Han River whose banks he'd personally paid to reinforce against rising sea levels as a gift to the people of Korea. The other walls were covered with museum-worthy displays of his most impressive treasures, including several paintings by Renaissance masters, a seven-panel-long carving inlaid with gold showing a dragon stirring up a typhoon carved in the traditional *mokjogakjang* woodworking style, and a full wall of abacuses that was the best collection of historical counting devices anywhere in the world.

The abacuses were his daughter's current favorite. She started eying the shelves full of counting beads on wires the moment they entered the room, so Yong took her over and let her pick one out. She chose a golden frame with five racks of bone counting beads that had once belonged to a Chinese dragon who, in his human guise, had ruled as three different Tang Dynasty emperors. Naturally, it was the most valuable one on the wall, but he didn't mind letting her play with it. Unlike some young creatures who took every new object as a challenge in destruction, his daughter respected beautiful things. At the very least, clicking the bone beads back and forth kept her busy as Yong settled them down in the throne that gave the room its name, a towering chair hewn from dragon bones and crowned with rows of teeth.

It was a truly macabre sight, and one Yong no longer found pleasing. He'd had it made in his youth when such symbols were necessary. He'd often considered replacing it with something more fitting to his current style of rule, but today he was glad he hadn't. Sitting on the old bones felt very appropriate as he took off his ruined jacket and spread it over his lap so his daughter wouldn't get pumpkin on his pants as well. When she was settled, he lifted his chin and commanded, "Enter."

The word was barely out of his mouth before iron doors at the far end of the chamber burst open, and a dragoness swept into the room. As usual, she was dressed like a queen, wearing what appeared to be a modern designer's take on a traditional *hanbok* and an elaborate hairstyle that added nearly a foot to her height. Yong found the whole thing distastefully excessive, but his sister had never been one for subtlety, or for wise decisions.

"Honored elder brother," she said, sweeping into an elaborate bow so low her ridiculous hair brushed the floor. "It is a privilege to be allowed into your glorious presence once again."

"White Snake," Yong replied, acknowledging her existence. And nothing else.

His sister's jaw tightened at the cold reception. Then she was all smiles again, waving her flutter-sleeve-covered hands at the teams of perfectly matched human males bringing enormous trays covered with silk sheets into the room behind her.

"What are those?"

"Gifts," his sister replied innocently as the humans kneeled before his throne to offer up their trays. "It would be an insult to come before the richest dragon in all Asia without suitable tribute."

"You must want something very badly if you're leading with bribery," Yong replied, tapping his finger thoughtfully on the ancient bone that formed the arm of his chair. "Very well. Tell your chattel to leave the offerings and go. The affairs of dragons are no place for humans."

White Snake shot a pointed look at the mortal child on his lap. Yong responded by placing a possessive hand on his daughter's still slightly sticky hair, petting the girl like a cat while looking his sister dead in the eye.

"But of course," she said at last, clapping her hands. At the command, her human servants bowed and left, closing the doors behind them to give the dragons their privacy.

"You have one minute to tell me why I shouldn't kill you," Yong said the moment they were alone.

"Is that any way to treat your only family?" White Snake replied, lifting her chin haughtily as she abandoned her put-on innocence.

"The only thing you are to me is a trespasser. I banished you from my lands eight hundred years ago. I didn't let you back in the last ten times you petitioned. What makes you think I've changed my mind now?"

"I heard rumors," White Snake replied, her Yellow Sea-colored eyes—a perfect mirror of his own—flicking down to the girl in his lap. "True ones, apparently."

Yong said nothing. He just sat there petting the child's hair as she played with the abacus until his sister couldn't stand it any longer.

"Really, brother?" she snarled, making his daughter jump. "You adopted a *human*? Did you not stop and think for one second how that would make you appear to the rest of the world?"

"The rest of the world is not my concern."

"It should be," she said, her voice desperate, though he didn't know her well enough anymore to say if that was artifice or true emotion. "Yong, brother, you are the only dragon in the world who insists on ruling alone. Every other clan rules together, *works* together, and with good reason! A modern country as big as Korea is far too large for one dragon to manage on their own. You've made do with mortals, but they're no substitute for actual family. You need someone who understands how you think, another dragon who can assist you with the heavy burden of—"

"The last time you 'assisted' me, I ended up stabbed in the back," he reminded her.

"You were weak," his sister said, as if that excused everything. "You would have done the same to me."

"Don't compare me to you."

"But we *are* the same," she said, flashing him a red-lipped smile. "You killed Father when he was weak."

"I killed Father because he was running our territory into the ground," Yong replied crisply. "And then, when I was still bleeding from my victory, you planted a claw in my back and tried to take it from me, and I *still* won." He sneered. "That makes you a traitor *and* a failure."

"That was a thousand years ago," White Snake said dismissively. "We're both different dragons these days, and you haven't even seen what I can offer."

She reached as she finished, pulling the silken cover off the closest of the trays her humans had brought in. Beneath the silk were ten identical statues of a coiled dragon. Each one was roughly a foot tall and covered in a metal that appeared from a distance to be gold but was actually hammered bronze. Yong knew that for certain, because he had the exact same statues. They were part of the Thousand Dragons, a tribute paid to his father by the ancient Korean kingdom of Koguryo to bribe the old dragon so he wouldn't burn their fields. He still had, of course, because his father didn't understand the concept of restraint, which was why Yong had killed him. What was the point of ruling a land if you kept burning it to the ground? He had coveted the impeccably made statues, though. They'd been scattered in the chaos after his father's death, but he'd managed to find most of them in the centuries since. No matter how hard he looked, though, he'd never been able to complete the set. Now he saw why.

"You took them," he growled.

"I had to take something," his sister said, exasperated. "You claimed everything else. But look." She pulled the silk covers off the remaining three trays. "I have the last forty here, all just as perfect as the night I stole them from Father's treasury. That should complete your collection. I know how much you'd like that, because I understand you in a way no mortal ever could."

"The only thing you understand is opportunity," Yong said, forcing his eyes away from the glittering statues. "You think I can be won over by mere trinkets?"

"Why is that so wrong?" White Snake asked, nodding at the treasure-covered walls. "You seem to value your trinkets very highly."

"Not higher than my life," Yong snapped, finally losing his patience. "Did you honestly think this was going to work? You're not getting back in. I killed Father and took his land precisely so I wouldn't have to deal with creatures like you. I have worked tirelessly for a thousand years now to build a kingdom where I am the *only* dragon I have to worry about. Why would I pollute that sublime happiness with poison like you?"

"Because you *need* me," White Snake said, looking him in the eyes. "There is more to the world than Korea. The dragon clans are changing. Bethesda the Heartstriker is breeding at a monumental pace. All those young dragons are hungry for territory, and they're not making any more land. If they decide to attack, you'll be alone."

Yong sneered. "You think I'm afraid of some century-old whelps?"

"Enough of anything can be a threat," White Snake argued. "The world is full of new enemies and new fronts, far too many to face on your own. I may not be your equal in strength or fire, but I've used my years of exile to win a position at the Qilin's court in China and build inside connections with several of the major European clans. I know the current politics, what they're all plotting. I can help you."

"Nonsense," Yong said, looking down on her. "The only dragon you help is yourself."

"But I—"

"Enough," he said, standing up. "This audience is at an end. Get out of my sight, and don't come back."

His sister took a hissing breath he remembered from their youth. Sure enough, the explosion came right after. "You think you can do this without me?" she roared. "You don't even know what they say! The rest of the clans think you're mad, living in here alone with your endless collections and your hundreds of mortals. I defended you because you are flesh of my flesh, but now I think they were right." She pointed at the child in his arms. "Look at you! Coddling that stupid, filthy little creature as if she were your own blood. Madness is the only explanation. She's not even *pretty*."

White Snake finished with a nasty smirk, waiting for him to be offended. When he did not rise to her bait, she tried again. "Where is your pride, Yong?" she taunted. "You're not going to defend her? I thought she was your child."

"There is nothing to defend," Yong replied calmly, looking down at the girl, who'd gone very still. "Anyone with eyes can see that my daughter is not beautiful. I knew it from her birth. That's why I named her Opal." He reached down to slide a finger under the girl's unfortunate jaw. "She is as she is named: a pretty stone of little worth. But while she will never be a diamond or a pearl or anything that is truly rare or beautiful, I keep her for the same reason I keep every other treasure in my hoard: because she brings me joy." His lips curled into a smile as he slid his fingers up to pick a bit of pumpkin off the wide-eyed girl's chubby cheek. "She is my loud, ungainly, bumbling little puppy, and I value her brief life a thousand times more than I do yours."

"Then you truly are delusional," White Snake said scornfully. "Mortals are for viewing and eating. They are not a replacement for family. Think of your pride, Yong! If you keep this madness up, you'll be the laughingstock of the world. The others will call you pathetic and soft, a sad, old dragon filling the emptiness with his pets, and they'll be *right*. But it doesn't have to be that way. I can help you." She clutched her hands to her chest. "Take me back. Acknowledge me as your clan again, and I will go out in your name to tell the rest of the world you haven't gone senile. I will—"

"No," Yong said coldly, straightening to his full height so that he could look down on her properly. "You assume too much, little snake. We may be related by blood, but you are not my family. You are a traitorous worm, worth no more to me than the dirt you crawl in. The only reason I have not yet slaughtered you for wasting my time is because I do not wish my daughter to witness such things. Now take the life I have so graciously spared and go. I tire of you."

"You cannot banish me from my birthright!" White Snake cried, her lovely face turning ugly with rage. "I am also a dragon of Korea! These are *my* lands as much as they are—"

Yong breathed out a line of smoke, and magic slammed down on the room like a snapping jaw. The child in his arms yelped at the sensation, but he was shielding her. White Snake had no such protection. She fell to her knees, gasping for breath as Yong's magic bit into her. He let her squirm there for a full minute, giving her time to feel the difference in power all the way to her bones, to understand on a deep, animal level the true distance between someone like her, and someone like him. Only then did he speak, his voice rumbling through the building, through the very bedrock of the land he'd won in blood and fire.

"*I* am the Dragon of Korea," he said, smoke curling from his lips with every word. "I earned that name when I killed our father and took his fire, but you have earned nothing. You have done *nothing* worthy of the name dragon, and that's why nothing is all you'll ever have. Even the fact that you're still alive to bother me is due entirely to *my* magnanimity, so you'd do best to slither back out of my sight before I change my mind."

By the time he finished, the magic in the room was as thick and sharp as a forest of knives. His sister clung to the points for five more seconds, and then she turned and fled, scampering through the doors like the rat she was. Yong didn't even realize how fast she'd gone until his daughter jerked in his arms, looking around the room in confusion, her poor mortal eyes too slow to follow the panicked dragon's flight.

"Where did she go?"

"She ran," Yong said, reaching down to retrieve his abacus from her pumpkin-covered fingers. "The weak always run. That is what separates them from us."

"Because we are dragons," the girl said proudly.

"No, you are a dog face," Yong said, taking her with him as he stood up. "*I* am a dragon."

The girl pouted. "But I want to be one too. How can I be your daughter if I'm not a dragon?"

"It's because you're not a dragon that you can be my daughter," he told her, returning the abacus to the wall. "Dragons are conniving, nasty, greedy creatures who see any weakness as an invitation to attack. They have no loyalty to family or anything else save themselves. Every dragon running a clan right now got there because they murdered whoever was above them. I myself rule Korea because I killed my father and took his power. If you were my actual daughter, I'd have to constantly worry about you doing the same to me, but you're not. You're human, and that means I'm free to treasure you as much as I like."

"But you just said I'm a dog face," she said dejectedly. "I can't even do magic right."

"This is true," her father said, carrying her out of the throne room. "You are indeed a foolish puppy who will never be what I was promised. But despite your many flaws, you are still my Opal, and I take care of what is mine."

His daughter still looked worried. "Always?"

"Forever," the dragon promised, pressing a kiss to her forehead as he carried his greatest treasure back into his lair.

CHAPTER 1

DFZ, Present Day

After spending a year and a half working almost exclusively in the Underground, driving up onto the Skyways felt like entering another world. A cleaner, far better-smelling world with leafy green trees, well-maintained sidewalks, and a bright, blue sky crisscrossed by so many white commercial aircraft contrails it looked like a scratching post.

"*Ahhhhhh,*" Sibyl's voice moaned in my earpiece as she remote piloted the cheap rent-a-moving truck trundling behind Nik's car. "It's so *nice* to be back in civilization again. The Wi-Fi up here is incredible!"

"It'd better be for what they charge," I grumbled, pulling out my phone to switch us off the Skyways' premium wireless to the much slower and infinitely more annoying—but free!—advertising-supported version.

"This is your old stomping ground, right?" Nik asked beside me, leaning down to peer through his car's steeply slanted windshield at the quaintly archaic brick buildings some developer had paid through the nose to make look older than anything on the Skyways technically could be. "I recognize it from the photo on your bookshelf."

I laughed. "That's a little creepy, but yeah, this is where I lived when I was in school. The IMA main campus is five blocks that way."

I pointed down the tree-lined, pedestrian-friendly boulevard that, if not for the occasional stairway going down, you'd never know was actually suspended on a bridge eighty feet above the ground. That was entirely by design. This was College Walk—CoWa according to the developers who'd licensed the area from the city—and it had been engineered from the ground up to be exactly the sort of quirky bohemian neighborhood the trust-fund kids attending the Institute for Magical Arts dreamed of living in. Everything here was artsy and whimsical and social media ready right down to the faux-faded advertisements painted on the brick walls.

Naturally, the price of living in what was basically an art student theme park was ludicrous. I couldn't remember exactly what Heidi had charged me for my half of our two-bedroom loft, but I was pretty sure it would have covered my current expenses for a year. Hell, I could probably buy a week's worth of food just off what I used to spend every day on fancy coffee drinks.

But while it was horrifying to remember how much money I'd thrown away living up here, my wasteful old life was actually coming in useful today. A magic supplies shop I used to frequent when I was a student had shown up at this morning's Cleaning auction. It was your typical overpriced hole-in-the-wall boutique where mass-produced items were repackaged in twine and brown cardboard and sold as "artisanal" at a thousand percent markup to rich kids who didn't know better, so I wasn't surprised it had gone out of business, but the pictures had shown the place looking exactly like I remembered. I didn't know why a shopkeeper would abandon a store that was still packed full of inventory, but I wanted it. Froufrou or not, magical supplies *always* sold.

At least, that was my logic. Nik must have been convinced as well, because he'd placed our bid without a grumble. We'd ended up winning the place for ten grand, which wasn't that much by normal auction standards but a hell of a lot for me. I'd only been partnered with Nik for a week so far, and I was still getting used to the numbers he worked with. My nervousness was pretty sad considering I wouldn't have blinked twice at dropping ten thousand on a good unit six months ago, but that was before my dad had cursed me to be a walking black hole for profits.

These days, I couldn't seem to make a dollar out of five quarters, which made pushing for such an expensive unit a Big Deal. If I hadn't been so certain we'd make it all back and then some, I would have been panicking, but this was actually the safest bet I'd seen since we'd started going to auctions as a team rather than as rivals. The DFZ had the highest mage-per-capita population of any city on the planet. If we couldn't resell an entire store's inventory of casting chalk and ward tape for more than ten thousand *here*, we didn't deserve to be in business.

"It should be just around this corner," I said, pointing out my open window. "There's the wine bar where I used to go to poetry readings."

Nik snorted. "You went to poetry readings?"

"Poetry is beautiful," I said defensively. "And the best way to experience it is out loud." And while slightly drunk. It also didn't hurt that we'd had some world-class talent. IMA knew that its students—and, more importantly, their rich parents—expected a top-level cultural experience, and they'd spared no expense making sure we got it, up to and including hiring a Nobel laureate to sit around reciting poetry at us while we got blitzed on rare French wines. Ah, simpler times.

"Sounds very refined," Nik said in a monotone voice that made it hard to tell if he was making fun of me or not. "This is it. Tell your AI to stop the truck."

I relayed the command to Sibyl as Nik turned the wheel hard, whipping his sleek black sports car out of the orderly Skyways morning traffic into a brick-paved alley. There wasn't enough room for the moving truck thanks to all the planters and patio furniture put out by the café next door, so I told Sibyl to circle the block while we got out to check our purchase.

The shop we'd won was at the alley's far end next to the lattice that hid the building's dumpsters. The café and other stores that faced the main street behind us were as packed as you'd expect for a beautiful Saturday morning, but none of those people had made it back here, which was probably why the magic shop had failed. Hard to maintain an overpriced boutique without a reliable flow of gullible foot traffic.

That was good luck for us, though. Cleaning was always easier when you didn't have to explain what you were doing to a bunch of curious onlookers. It was amazing the number of people who lived in the DFZ and had no idea that Cleaners existed. I'd had the cops called on me for doing my job more times than I could count. In a nice neighborhood like this, they might actually show up. Thankfully, nobody here seemed to care as Nik and I hauled our crates of Cleaning supplies out of the trunk of his car and walked over to the door of the shop I hoped would be the smash hit that made up for all the duds.

It certainly looked promising. Just like in the picture Broker had put up at the auction this morning, I could see the shelves stacked with rows of product through the shop's glass door. There had to be thousands of items in there. Nik must have been excited, too, because he'd already pulled out his Master Key. He was going for the door handle when I grabbed his wrist.

"Wait!" I said. "You didn't announce yourself yet!"

"I don't have to," he replied, tilting his head at the glass door. "I can see inside."

"That doesn't mean there couldn't still be someone squatting in the back," I argued nervously. "We still don't know why the previous tenant abandoned a store full of inventory. He could be strung out and waiting behind one of those shelves with a shotgun."

Nik clearly thought that was far-fetched, but he didn't have to worry like I did. He had a cybernetic arm and bulletproof metal plates across half his damn body, *and* he was wearing his armored black leather bomber jacket despite the fact that the temperature was already in the eighties. I, by contrast, was dressed for the weather in shorts and a tank top. I wasn't even wearing my poncho, which was pretty stupid considering we were about to walk into a mage's shop. There were bound to be all sorts of nasty wards against intruders, even legal ones like us, but I couldn't bring myself to put my poncho on, and not just because I didn't want to wear a plastic sheet in August. I didn't want to wear it because activating my wards would hurt too much.

It had been several days since I'd backdrafted all of that roaring Gnarls magic into Kauffman's face, and my casting muscles still ached from it. I could move magic if I really had to, but even the smallest spells felt like trying to walk on a sprained leg. I couldn't afford to go to a doctor, but everything I'd read on the internet said my magic would heal if I left it alone, so I'd been avoiding casting whenever possible. You'd think that'd be more of a liability given how much magic my job usually required, but working with a partner had a lot of upsides I hadn't anticipated. Nik's ability to lift pretty much anything and bash open doors without the aid of magic was a huge plus when your casting was laid up.

But while his ability to stop bullets was a definite plus, Nik's armor wouldn't do much against an angry former magic shop owner with a quick casting circle. That required finesse, so I gently pushed him aside and pulled my goggles down over my face to get a better look inside the shop. When Sibyl's density scanner didn't turn up any human-shaped traps lying in wait for us, I stepped back to give my cameras a clear shot of the shop's street address.

"Ready when you are, Sibyl."

"I'm always ready," my AI said proudly as the red recording light appeared in the corner of my augmented-reality vision. "This is the video log for College Walk Commercial District Unit 4733, Detroit Free Zone Skyways Block 74, Receipt #145443. Cleaner IDs: Nikola Kos and Opal Yong-ae. Do you verify?"

I flipped my camera to selfie mode. "This is Opal Yong-ae, and I verify." I smiled at my own image before turning the camera on Nik, who heaved a long, put-upon sigh.

"Do we have to do this every single time? You know no one in the Cleaning Office checks these things."

I pushed up my goggles so he could see my glare, and he sighed again. "This is Nikola Kos, and I verify."

Nodding approvingly, I turned my camera back on the door. "Proceeding with occupant notification."

This was usually where I knocked and announced myself, but Nik beat me to the punch. "Cleaner!" he bellowed, banging on the glass so hard I was afraid it would shatter. "You're behind on your rent, Collections can't reach you, etcetera. We bought your stuff at auction this morning, so we're coming in. Yell if you've got a problem with that, because shooting at us will end real bad for you."

"Super professional," Sibyl grumbled.

"Good enough for me," I said, pushing my goggles back up on my head as Nik fit his Master Key into the shop's lock. "Unit has no reply. Proceeding with reclamation. Look out for wards!"

That last bit was for Nik, but he'd already opened the door. I winced as he stepped inside, bracing my poor, aching magic against whatever alarm or other nastiness was certain to go off. Even if the security wards had degraded, it was still a sealed room packed with magical stuff. There was bound to be a shock wave of some sort, but I didn't actually feel a thing. Now that it was blowing past me, the air from inside the shop actually felt markedly *less* magical than the air outside. It also smelled absolutely horrendous.

"*Ugh!*" I said, covering my face with my hand. "What *is* that? It smells like rotten hot dogs."

"It is pretty thick," Nik said with the iron stoicism of a seasoned Cleaner.

I was pretty seasoned myself, but that didn't mean I was willing to expose my nose to torture when it wasn't absolutely necessary. I had my rebreather out of my bag and over my face in three seconds flat, pulling the strap so tight that my cheeks bulged out around it. "Did something die?" I asked nervously, remembering the last stinky apartment I'd had.

Nik scowled. "Maybe. Doesn't smell like one of the usual suspects, though. And nothing looks chewed up."

That was a good point. Animals who got trapped inside units typically tore the place to shreds before they gave up the foul-smelling ghost, but as we'd seen from outside, the shop looked great. Neat, orderly, not even dusty. If I hadn't known better, I would have said this place had been closed for the night, not two months. The smell was the only sign something was off, that and the fact that it still felt like there wasn't a drop of magic in the whole place.

That was starting to seriously freak me out. Even after months on the shelves, this much magical merchandise crammed together should have been vibrating like a tuning fork. The hum was part of the magic store experience, but despite the piles of inventory I could clearly see in front of us, I didn't feel a thing. Maybe it was just my magic acting out, but I would have sworn the place was dead.

Confused and on edge, I reached into the basket by the door to pick up one of the brightly colored packages exuberantly labeled as "All Natural Chimera Feather Casting Enhancers." Before my hand could make it all the way around the vacuum-sealed tube of supposedly magical feathers, though, my fingers bumped into something soft and wiggly.

I snatched my hand back with a scream so sharp and loud that Nik pulled his gun. "What?" he demanded.

I couldn't answer. I was too busy scanning the display bin for whatever it was I'd just touched. Probably a rat. I was praying it was a *normal* rat and not one of the city's magical varieties since I wasn't keen on getting third-degree burns today, but despite what I *knew* I'd felt, I didn't see anything in the basket except packets of feathers. They didn't even have dust on them. *Everything* was clean, actually. The basket, shelves, and floor were all spotless. There was no grime or fur or rat pellets or anything you'd expect from a place that had been sealed up for eight weeks and stank like a sewer.

Stomach sinking, I pulled my goggles back down over my eyes. "Sibyl," I said quietly, propping the shop's door open behind me with my boot in case I had to make a quick exit. "Show me heat vision."

The view through my goggles flickered as my AI obeyed, overlaying a projected shot from my thermographic filter on top of my normal cameras. Sure enough, now that I was looking at heat instead of just light, I could see the too-clean shop wasn't actually clean at all. Every surface was covered with thousands of oblong shapes that stood out bright yellow and red against the cold blue background. They were all over the basket I'd just reached into, wiggling together in a seething mass that looked straight out of a horror movie.

Cursing loudly, I dug into my work bag for the rubber-and-steel-mesh gloves I *really* should have been wearing from the start. Hands properly protected this time, I reached back into the basket to grab one of the bigger glowing shapes. The thing was nearly as long as my hand when I finally pulled it free of the cluster, slug-like in shape and soft as a jelly-filled condom. It wiggled like crazy when I squeezed it, but while it looked like a bright purple and red sausage against the cool rubber of my glove in my thermographic vision, I couldn't see a thing when I switched back to my normal cameras. It didn't make any sounds, either. Or, more accurately, it didn't make a sound that I could hear. Given how it was thrashing, I was sure it was screaming its little head off, wherever its head happened to be. Being a mere mortal, though, I couldn't pick that up. I couldn't see so much as an ooze trail when I slid my goggles back up on my hair, either, even though I *knew* I was looking right at it.

"What's going on?" Nik asked, coming over to peer at my seemingly empty hand.

"The last thing we need," I muttered, opening my fist to drop the silently screaming creature back into the wiggling pile of its brethren. "This whole place is infested with dream slugs."

"Infested with what?"

"Dream slugs," I repeated furiously. "Semi-reality carrion feeders who thrive on residual magic."

"Okay," Nik said slowly, putting up his gun. "Say that again, but in a way I can understand this time."

"They're like termites," I explained. "Except they're invisible and they eat magic."

Nik looked alarmed at that last part. "Are they dangerous?"

"Not to living things," I said, shaking my head. "They're scavengers who eat the residual mana left in the corpses, usually those of magical animals, which explains why this place felt so dead. Little bastards ate the entire stock!"

Now Nik just looked confused. "But the shelves are still full."

"They didn't eat the physical objects," I explained. "Just the magic inside them. Look."

I knocked the slugs aside and grabbed a package of casting chalk. "All the stuff they sell in shops like this has a bit of magic inside it. It's not usually enough to help power the spell; it just acts as a bumper, something you can feel while casting. You don't actually *need* a bumper, of course. Technically, you can draw a circle or write out spellwork with anything, but the bit of magic inside casting markers and chalk and so forth makes it way easier to stay inside the lines you put down for your spell. Same goes for spell-ready paper and ward tape and all the other stuff people have come up with to make casting more convenient. It's all magically charged. That's what makes it valuable, and those little slimeballs have eaten it all up! They didn't even have to break the packaging. They just sat on top of the stock and slurped. And since they're invisible, we had no way of knowing the place was ruined before we bid! Now we're out ten grand for a bunch of useless *crap*!"

I was shouting by the time I finished. I knew I sounded hysterical, but I couldn't help it. Nik and I had bought a new unit every single day this week—two on Wednesday—and we'd yet to turn a profit. This was supposed to be our jackpot, but now it looked like I'd locked in our biggest loss yet. We couldn't even sell the sucked-down casting markers as normal markers because they were covered in dream slug poop. That was why this place smelled so bad. The slugs hadn't just been munching on the magical goods. They'd also been pooping all over the place while they ate. The excrement was just as invisible as the animals that had made it, but now that I knew what to search for, I could *feel* the sticky, caked-on mess all over the shelves and the floor every time I put my hand down. This whole damn place was a write-off, but we couldn't do that because we were still contractually obligated to clean it out so the city could rent the shop to a new tenant. It might take *days* to get this place clean enough for the DFZ to accept it. Days we'd never get paid for. I couldn't even calculate how much this was going to cost us.

And it was all my fault.

"It's not your fault," Nik said sharply, reading the thought right off my face. "We both looked at the same picture and agreed to bid. You couldn't have known."

"That's not what I'm mad about," I said, my voice desperate. "I don't blame myself for not seeing *invisible* slugs, but do you know what the chances are of finding a dream slug infestation in the DFZ?"

"No," Nik said. "But I didn't even know what a dream slug was before you told me, so I'm guessing low."

"It's zero!" I cried. "Because they don't live here! They're native to sub-Saharan Africa. The only reason I know about them is because I watched a ton of cryptozoology nature shows as a kid. There shouldn't even be dream slugs in this hemisphere, and yet somehow an entire colony just happened to end up trapped inside *our* unit."

I reached out to grab him before I remembered I was wearing gloves covered in invisible slug slime. "Don't you see?" I said, clenching my filthy hands into fists instead. "It's my curse! My dad's magic can't sabotage me directly now that you're doing all our buying, so it's finding new ways to keep me from making money. This is all my fault!"

"That's ridiculous," Nik said dismissively. "We only bought this unit this morning. These slugs have probably been here for weeks. How could a curse set that up?"

"Probably the same way it's been setting me up to buy bad units for the last six months," I replied angrily. "I don't know how it works! Dad never taught me the specifics of dragon magic because I'm not actually his daughter hatched from an egg, but you know as well as I do that something's going on. We're both experienced Cleaners, and we've been working our butts off all week, but we *still* haven't made a profit. Now we're ten grand in the hole!"

Nik shrugged. "Cleaning's an up-and-down business."

"Not like this!"

"Not all bad luck is magical, you know," he said stubbornly. "I get that you're cursed, but you've been blaming it for everything since you learned it was on you. You even said it caused my flat tire two days ago."

"That was *totally* the curse!" I cried. "I looked at that tire, and there was no hole. You got a flat from *nothing,* and it *just happened* to make us miss the best deal of the night!"

I'd found out later that DeSantos had been planning to hire Nik and me to help him with a glut of self-storage lockers. It would have been a straight-up hourly wage, guaranteed money, but we'd been late, so he'd given the job to someone else. That sounded like pretty obvious curse-work to me, but when I said as much to Nik, he set his jaw.

"Opal, it's *fine.* Bad things happen. Just let it go."

It was *not* fine and I was *not* going to just let it go. I hadn't told Nik yet, but one of the first things I'd done with the small amount of money he'd paid me after selling what we had managed to salvage—after taking Sibyl to a hacker to get my dad's spyware out, of course—was go to a curse breaker. I'd actually tried two, but they'd both told me the same thing: only dragons could remove dragon curses.

In hindsight, I supposed that should have been obvious. Humans couldn't even see the damn thing unless I told them it was there. Dragons could see it just fine, though, and that put me in a real bind. Just like the Heartstriker who'd first informed me that I was cursed, any dragon I went to would instantly know that I was under Yong's magic, and while there were plenty of dragons who'd love to stick it to the Dragon of Korea by setting me free, they weren't the sort I wanted to be in debt to. Being cursed by my dad sucked, but at least he wouldn't kill me. There was no guarantee of that with another dragon, especially one who hated my dad enough to directly defy him. If I couldn't get this stupid thing off, though, my life was only going to get worse.

"It's not *so* bad now, you know," Sibyl whispered in my earpiece. "I know you aren't raking it in with Nik like you'd hoped, but at least you've stopped running a loss. That's better than you were doing by yourself."

"Say that after we figure out how much this job is going to cost us," I grumbled.

"Now you're just being pessimistic," my AI scolded. "Sure, the merchandise is ruined, but the rest of the shop is still here. There's the shelving and the register and all kinds of useful retail equipment left. You can always sell that, right?"

Not if it was covered in slug shit.

Sibyl tsked at my negativity, which should have enraged me since I hadn't said it out loud this time. But I was too depressed to even care that she was reading my mind anymore. I was sinking down on the shop's front stair to brood about it when Nik caught my shoulder and dragged me back up.

"No time for that," he said, shoving a black plastic trash bag into my hands. "This place isn't a write-off yet. There could still be something good in the back. Maybe the previous owner left his safe or something."

That was so ridiculously hopeful, I actually started to laugh. "Since when are you the optimist?"

"I'm not an optimist," Nik said, pulling off his armored coat and hanging it over the railing in front of the shop, safely away from the slug slime. "I'm a realist, and the reality is we can't do anything about the stuff that's already ruined. Our best bet is to get this done as quickly as possible and move on to the next job. Now." He pointed at my trash bag. "You're the one who can see the slugs, so you're on roundup duty. I'll pull the shelving and the register. Who knows? Maybe there's something we can save."

"Maybe," I said, but I couldn't even fake being hopeful. Much as I wanted to mope, though, Nik was right. Wasting time would only deepen our losses and give my dad an even bigger win, so I forced myself to follow Nik back into the shop, huffing through my rebreather to avoid the rotten-hot-dog smell as I started grabbing the wiggly, slippery slugs off the ground and shoving them into my trash bag, stubbornly telling myself with each slimy lump I removed that things could only go up from here.

***

Surprise, surprise, they did not.

After the last six months, you'd think I'd be used to disappointment, but today was a new low even by my rock-bottom standards. It wasn't just that I was shuffling around picking up disgusting lumps of goo that wiggled like crazy and smelled like rancid lard. It was that I had to pick them off lovely handcrafted boxes with labels that said stuff like "Single Origin Kappa Water" and "Fair Trade Screaming Mandrake." Just reading all that fancy nonsense made me want to scream, because I'd been right. This place should have been a gold mine. Some of the packages I was picking slugs off had price tags in the *thousands,* but the stupid dream slugs had sucked them dry. Now all that wonderful product was just a bunch of bulky, heavy trash that smelled like death, but the real insult was the slugs.

You'd think it'd be easy to round up something with no eyes that didn't move, but you would be wrong. Even with my thermographics to help me see them, catching the dream slugs was disgusting, frustrating work. No matter how carefully I piled them into my trash bag, they always found a way to ooze back out again. I eventually caught one phasing right *through* the plastic, which made me wonder how all the slugs had ended up trapped in here in the first place. Or maybe they hadn't been trapped at all. Maybe they'd just stayed for the food.

Whatever the reason, it took me an hour to bag them all up. I'd planned to toss them in the building's dumpster, but after seeing their escape skills, tossing them into an open bin felt like inviting disaster. Also, they stank. I didn't want to be around that even with my rebreather, so I ended up dragging each bag back around to the front of the building and dumping it down the trash chute. Hopefully into the incinerator, though I was satisfied with "no longer in my sight." Once I'd chucked the last bag down the hole, I shook the slug slime off my gloves as best I could and went to see how much progress Nik had made.

As usual, the answer was "more than me." While I'd been frog-walking across the floor scooping up slugs, he'd trashed all the ruined merchandise and removed all the display racks from the store into the alley. As expected from such a high-end establishment, the shelves were lovely: big slabs of handsome, solid hardwood held together by clever nail-free joints. They even had wards carved into the sides to prolong the viability of the magical materials. It was seriously high-quality retail equipment. Under any normal circumstances, those shelves would have paid for the whole damn job right there, but these were not normal circumstances. This was my life, and from the look on Nik's face, my dad's curse was holding strong.

"They're shit," he said angrily, placing his gloved hand on the gleaming hardwood. "Literally. They look good, but there's invisible dream slug crap and casings and who knows what else all over them. I scraped one down and bleached it to see if I could save them, but the filth's seeped into the wood grain. See?"

I pulled off my glove and ran my hand over the place he was tapping before snatching it back with a grimace. He was right. The wood *looked* fine, but it felt like a grease trap, and it smelled even worse. It was so strong, I could taste it through my rebreather mask. It was enough to make my eyes water, though those might have been tears of frustration. The shelves had been our last chance at turning a profit on this job, and they were even more ruined than the shop's inventory.

"Was *anything* salvageable?" I asked, trying not to sniffle.

"I did find a couch in the back room," he said, nodding at the front of the alley, where Sibyl had finally managed to wedge in our rental truck.

I perked up. Couches were good. I could sell a couch. When I got to the truck, though, I saw why Nik hadn't exactly been enthusiastic. The couch in question was the most atrocious shade of orange I'd ever seen. I'd noticed during my killing spree that there were no worms in the shop's tiny back room, probably because there was nothing magical back there to eat, so at least it didn't stink. That put it miles above everything else we'd found, but the cushions were worn and, again, *stupidly* ugly. Now that I was closer, I saw that the hideous orange was actually covered in an equally hideous pattern of tiny deformed birds. Or maybe they were leaves? It was impossible to say.

"What do you think it's worth?" Nik asked, stepping up beside me.

I sighed. "Depends, is the buyer blind?" I gave the couch a shove. "The frame's in good shape, but no one with eyes is going to put up with that fabric."

"Could we get it recovered?"

"Not if we want to make a profit." Still, it seemed a shame to just throw it away. If you ignored how it made your eyes bleed, it was a perfectly functional couch. Good length, pretty soft, legs were in good condition. That made it infinitely better than *my* couch, which was still lying in a pile on my living room floor thanks to Kauffman's goons.

"Would you mind if I took it?" I asked Nik. "We can't sell it, and my place is kind of short of furniture right now."

"Go for it," Nik said. "We're paying for the truck whether we fill it up or not. Might as well use it for something, and the dumpster here is going to be full enough as it is."

That was the damn truth. "I guess we've got to actually start cleaning now, huh?"

Nik nodded and turned away. "You're on floors."

I groaned as I followed him back to our boxes of cleaning supplies. This was the unglamorous side of the job. Once you got all the good stuff out of a unit, you couldn't just leave it. You had to make it livable again so the DFZ could rent it out to a new tenant. That was why we were called "Cleaners" and not "Looters." Scrubbing was part of the process, and you couldn't cut corners.

The DFZ had surprisingly harsh standards about her units for such a trashy city. Units had to be spotless before she'd take them back, and you didn't know if you'd made the grade until the end of the month. When we bought a unit at auction, it became our responsibility. If we didn't clean it out to the DFZ's satisfaction, she'd just charge us rent for the next month, and she'd *keep* charging until we got it right. Having to pay rent on your units was every Cleaner's greatest fear, so we scrubbed from top to bottom. Since I was by far the shorter half of our team, I usually got the bottom.

At least the work was mindless. I just grabbed the scrub mop and bucket from Nik, turned my music to blasting, and started attacking the caked-on slug filth. While I scraped the invisible poop off the floors and walls, Nik tossed all the ruined shelves into the building's dumpster, lifting the huge, heavy wood racks one-handed with his artificial arm as if they weighed nothing.

I made sure to stick by the door while that was going on. I'd never admit it, but this was my favorite part of working with Nik. Watching him lift heavy stuff had become one of my greatest pleasures, especially on days like today when he'd taken his jacket off.

You'd think it'd be creepy since his coat hid all his artificial parts, but ironically, seeing the articulated metal moving beneath his black T-shirt actually made him look *more* human to me, not less. I think it was because I traditionally associated that sort of crazy strength with dragons, and seeing Nik's cyberware was a clear visual reminder that he wasn't one of those. Or maybe I'm just a sucker for a well-cut chest. Either way, it was a show I made sure never to miss. I never let him *catch* me looking, of course. That was what cameras were for. But watching him move was a precious highlight in what was otherwise a literal shit day.

By the time the afternoon rolled around, we were both disgusting, but at least I'd figured out how the shop had ended up filled with dream slugs. While I was scrubbing floors, Sibyl had found a folder of electronic receipts on the unit's local AI. Turned out, the previous tenant had tried to get in on last year's trend for invisible pets by purchasing a ton of dream slugs on the cheap. Too cheap, it turned out. By the time his cut-rate package had finally arrived, the craze was over, and he was stuck with a bunch of worms he couldn't sell. To make things worse, the dream slugs had bred like crazy on their trip across the sea, and since—as I'd discovered myself—it was pretty much impossible to keep the damn things contained, they'd promptly escaped and started eating his inventory. Realizing his business was ruined, the shopkeeper had skipped town without paying his rent. A month later, Collections had taken the store, and the rest was history. It was a classic DFZ story of irresponsibility, reckless greed, and, as always, someone else being left to clean up the mess. Just my luck it would be us.

"I think that's the last of it," Nik said, tossing the final soggy box of used-up inventory on top of the now very tall pile in the dumpster.

I nodded tiredly, staring bleary-eyed at the mountain of trash. "Did *anything* end up in the truck?"

"Aside from the couch? Not a bit," Nik said, clearly trying hard not to sound disappointed.

I slumped down on the shop's step. Great. Not only had we spent ten thousand dollars for the privilege of cleaning out someone else's store, I'd wasted one of the four days per month I was allowed to request a truck from my car subscription service. It was a minor loss compared to everything else, but there were only so many times you could get kicked in the same place, and for some reason, that pushed me over the edge.

"I'm so sorry," I said, burying my face in my gloved hands. I didn't even care that they were covered with slug slime. Everything was. That was the problem. "This is all my fault."

"It's not your fault," Nik said, though he didn't sound nearly as sure this time around. "And anyway, it's over now."

That much was true, at least. Cleaning the shop hadn't taken nearly as long as I'd feared, but it was still way too much. We'd gotten here at seven a.m. It was now nearly five. That was a full day of work gone to *waste*, and while it was definitely the worst we'd had so far, the others hadn't been much better. There were only three weeks left before I had to pay my dad again. If they were all going to be like this, I might as well call him and surrender right now. At least that way Nik wouldn't have to suffer another twenty-one days of this.

I must have looked pathetic, because Nik sighed and walked down the steps to his car. I heard the click of his trunk, and then he walked back up to me and set something soft on my hair. When I looked up, I saw it was a shop towel, the super-cheap kind they sold in hundred-count boxes at hardware stores. He'd gotten one for himself as well. The white cloth was draped around his neck, making him look like a boxer fresh off a championship fight. I was sure I didn't look nearly so glorious, but I was happy to have the towel.

"Thanks," I muttered, pulling off my rebreather and goggles so I could scrub the sweat and slug guts off my face and neck.

"You're welcome," Nik said, sitting down on the step beside me. Then, after a long, tired silence, he said, "Tomorrow will be better."

"But what if it isn't?" I whispered, pressing my face into the thin, rough terrycloth. "What if we just keep sinking lower and lower and—"

"Can't sink forever."

"That's called hitting rock bottom," I reminded him.

Nik was quiet for a long time after that. I just kept staring into the towel, hoping against hope that he wasn't coming to the same obvious conclusion I'd been trying to avoid all day.

"Listen, Opal…"

Crap.

"I've been thinking," he went on, squinting up at the late-afternoon sun that was streaming down like a spotlight between the buildings. "It's been a really bad day. Maybe we should—"

"Stop being partners?" I said before he could.

Nik's head jerked around in surprise, which was a surprise to me as well. I'd thought I was getting ahead of the hammer, but I must have seriously misjudged the situation, because Nik looked furious. "I was going to say 'get dinner,'" he snapped, glaring at me. "Why would you think I'd want to stop working with you?"

"I don't know. Maybe because I just cost you ten thousand and made you waste an entire day shoveling invisible worm poop?" I replied. "I mean, it's kind of obvious."

"It's not obvious at all," he said angrily. "You didn't do this!"

"Dude, *stop*," I begged. "This isn't just me being down on myself, okay? I am *literally* cursed with bad luck."

"That's not your fault. Your dad's the one who did this to you. He's to blame, not you."

That was very true. It also didn't change anything. "I'm still a walking disaster," I reminded him. "I'm not saying it's a personality flaw. I'm just saying I wouldn't be insulted if you didn't want to be tied to me anymore." Just hurt. Very hurt, because I'd really enjoyed not having to do everything by myself for once. I hadn't even realized how isolated I'd become until he'd elbowed his way into my life, but now that he was here, I didn't know how I could go back to being alone. There was no way in hell I was laying that guilt trip on Nik, though. I was determined to do the right thing and give him his out, so I was very surprised when he turned around and shoved it right back in my face.

"I'm not tied to anything," he snapped. "This partnership was my idea, remember? I'm not going to abandon you."

"You wouldn't be abandoning me," I said, striving to be reasonable. "We made that deal back when you thought I could still make money, but it's obviously not working. I appreciate you trying to help me, I really, really do, but this curse is a lot stronger than I gave it credit for. That's my fault. I underestimated my dad's magic, but there's no reason for you to get caught in my vortex of failure."

"You're not a failure," Nik said stubbornly. "I never would have bid on this store if you hadn't tipped me off, and you were right. If it hadn't been for the dream slugs, we would have hit the jackpot on this unit."

"But it's my fault that—"

"You can't just take credit for the bad things and ignore the good," he said stubbornly. "Today was pretty damn bad, I admit, but every day won't be like this. You've been cursed for the last five months, right? Were all your units this bad before?"

This was the worst unit I'd *ever* Cleaned, including the one with a dead body in it, so I was forced to shake my head.

"Exactly," Nik said, nodding sharply. "Just 'cause we pulled a bad lot this time doesn't mean that'll happen every time. Cleaning jobs are always up and down. This is just a trench. We'll be up again, and when we are, with both of us working together, I bet we'll make bank."

I pressed my face back into my towel to hide my smile. You wouldn't think being bluntly informed that I was only being used for money would make me all warm and mushy, but it was just so *nice* to hear someone say they believed in me for once. No one in my old life had believed I could do anything. My parents had always made it clear how disappointed they were in my life choices. Even my legit friends like Heidi semi-joked that I was a magical disaster area. Hell, even *I* knew I was garbage at pretty much everything that didn't involve esoteric historical trivia or evaluating treasure. But Nik was sitting there glaring at me like he was pissed I wasn't understanding how hard we were going to work this place over the moment we got our chance, and it was just…nice.

"Are you *sure* you're not an optimist?"

"Not a bit," he said solemnly. "I keep my feet firmly in reality. It just looks bright because you're so dark right now."

I had been pretty depressed lately. In my defense, learning that life's dice had been supernaturally weighted against you was pretty damn disheartening. I was already doing everything I could to fight that fight though, so maybe Nik was right. Maybe there was no point being—

"*Hey!*"

We both jumped. Down the alley, a large man wearing janitor coveralls was leaning out of a service door glaring at us. "Are you guys the ones who've been throwing all the trash bags into the chute?"

"What about it?" Nik asked, rising to his feet.

"You can't leave that stuff with us!"

"This unit's part of the building," Nik said. "We got a right to dispose of stuff here." He rolled his shoulders as he spoke, bringing his false right hand to hook his thumb on the strap of his chest holster near his gun. It was totally inappropriate, threatening behavior, but I didn't say a damn word. I didn't want to move all that trash again, either.

"The normal trash is okay, I guess," the man said, backing down at once. "But you can't leave these."

He tossed three trash bags onto the brick pavement by Nik's feet. Three *wiggling* bags.

"I don't know what the hell that is," the man said. "But all magical materials need to be warded before disposal. City ordinance!"

Now it was my turn to get mad. "There's no city ordinances in the DFZ!"

"There are in College Walk!" he yelled back. "Don't you damn Cleaners ever check the rental agreement?"

Still glaring at him, I grabbed my phone and sent Sibyl off to see if he was right. I'd never heard of any sort of trash-disposal rule before, so I was certain he was just trying to shove his work back onto us. To my enormous surprise, though, my AI came back with a ton of documents.

"He's right," she reported in my earpiece. "This is a special district. The DFZ licensed it to a private developer a decade ago, and it looks like they put in a lot of extra clauses to the leases to 'preserve the aesthetic and value of the College Walk neighborhood.'"

"They can do that?" I said, shocked.

"You can do anything in the DFZ if you have enough money," Sibyl replied. "Technically, you're also not supposed to load the dumpsters past the lids, either."

Like hell was I informing the janitor of that one. We'd stacked those suckers to the sky.

"Why do we have to obey the ordinances?" Nik asked stubbornly. "We don't live here. We're just Cleaners. Unless the DFZ herself shows up, we don't have to do bupkis except make sure the place is rentable."

I was nodding vigorously when Sibyl piped up again with my two least favorite words. "Well, actually—"

I rolled my eyes. "*Really?*"

"Hey, you took on all legal obligations for the property when you won the auction, including the special clauses. Sorry, Opal, but legally he's in the right."

She'd said all of that in my earpiece, but the man must have seen the truth on my face, because he grinned from ear to ear, which only made me wince even harder.

"What do you want us to do?"

"Just ward these so the evil doesn't leak out and stick them in the dumpster across the street," the man said, kicking the wiggling bags full of worms toward me. "Ain't my problem if it's over there, but I'm going to call the development authority on you if you leave those damn invisible stink demons on my property. They've been crawling through the walls for a month!"

By that logic, he should have been hailing us as heroes for getting them out, but I held my tongue. Calling the development authority might not sound like much of a threat, but I'd lived in College Walk. *Everything* here was rich and picky and ready to come down on you with a fleet of lawyers the second you gave them a chance. I'd ignored a parking ticket once and gotten hit with a four-thousand-dollar fine I'd never been able to contest.

There was no way I was settling us with a fine on top of everything else I'd cost us today, so I walked over and grabbed the trash bags, holding my breath against the smell as I dragged them back across the alley toward the dumpster for the adjacent building, where the janitor had instructed me to dump them.

"What are you going to do?" Nik asked, hurrying after me.

"What he said," I replied, dropping the bags beside the dumpster we hadn't filled before heading back to his car to grab a roll of blue electrical tape. "I'm going to put a ward on them and toss them in the dumpster."

"Can you cast a ward on something that eats magic?"

"I have no idea," I confessed, pulling the tape off the roll and wrapping it around the trash bags until I'd bound all three together into a nice, bright-blue circle. "I'm just going to do *something* so we can prove we tried."

That was pretty un-civic minded of me considering the damage these little guys could do, but frankly, at that point, I didn't care if dream slugs ate the entire neighborhood. I was going to do the absolute minimum required to cover our asses, emphasis on *minimum*. I hadn't even started casting yet, and my poor magic was already throbbing like an angry wound.

I put my back to Nik so he wouldn't see me wince. I hadn't actually told him about my injury yet because I didn't want to look like even more of a liability. Fortunately, Nik didn't know much about the mechanics of casting, so I didn't think he'd figured it out yet, but he'd know something was up for sure if I started moaning and groaning. To avoid this, I chose the smallest spell possible: a simple binding with less than three lines of spellwork. I didn't know if it would be enough to actually hold the slugs in, but the magic in the ward would probably keep them happily munching in one spot until the trash truck came for the dumpster tonight, which was good enough for me.

"Okay," I said when I'd double-checked my spellwork against the original Sibyl had put up in my AR. "Here we go."

"Shouldn't you put on your poncho?" Sibyl suggested. "You know, just to be safe? You don't want to take another backlash."

I was a pretty garbage mage, but there was no way even I could backlash myself on a spell this small. Also, bringing out my poncho meant I'd have to cast *another* spell to activate it, and I just didn't want to bother. One was too many already, so I shook my head and crouched, careful to keep my back to Nik so he wouldn't see my pained grimace as I started to gather magic from the surrounding air.

As always since the Gnarls, reaching outside of myself hurt like crazy. I felt like I was trying to scoop up sand with a broken hand, which *sucked*, because grabbing magic was normally the one part of casting I was actually good at. I usually had to struggle not to *over*fill my circles, and now I was barely able to grab a pinch. Frustrated, I pushed harder. That made my magic hurt even more, but dammit, I wanted to get this done today. I was sick of being here and *really* sick of these stupid slugs. I just wanted to go home and take a hot shower, so I gave my magic a shove, gritting my teeth against the pain for the short moment I needed to—

A loud *pop* sounded in my ears. Suddenly, without warning, the magic I'd been trying unsuccessfully to wrangle came together all at once. The combined force was enough to knock me down to the pavement, but the real casualty was my circle. In the space of a heartbeat, I'd gone from moving no magic to moving *all* of it, and the sudden rush of power was too much for my shoddy tape circle to handle. It snapped like a thread. The plastic bags went next, popping like water balloons and sending burning hot chunks of invisible slug flying in all directions, including all over me.

"*Ugh!*" I screamed, frantically wiping my hands across the boiled slug slime that now covered me from toes to face. "Ugh, ugh, ugh!"

"What the hell was that?" Nik yelled.

"I told you to wear your poncho!" Sibyl yelled at the same time. "Do you want me to call a medic?"

I shook my head frantically and grabbed my shirt, turning it around every which way to find a clean piece I could use to wipe the slime off my mouth before I accidentally ate any of it. Nik came to my rescue with a towel a few seconds later. I wiped the cheap terry all over my face, cursing myself for being an idiot.

"You want to tell me what just happened?" Nik asked when I finally stopped retching.

"Not really," I said, sliding my boots on the brick paving, which was now slick as an ice rink with slug guts. "Did I get any on you?"

Nik shook his head. "I ducked behind my car when I saw it blow."

I wiped my face again. "Smart move."

"It could have been worse," Sibyl said cheerfully. "You could have had your mouth open."

I almost vomited at the thought. Even though I couldn't see them, I could *feel* the cooked slug guts coating my clothes and skin in a warm, chunky layer, and the smell of rancid pig fat was so far up my nose I was *never* going to get it out. The only positive thing I could say about this entire situation was that at least it wasn't kabocha pumpkin.

"Why are you so *bad*?" I whispered in Korean, glaring down at my hands. "Why can't you just be normal?"

I wasn't sure who I was talking to, my magic or myself. Either way, it didn't make me feel any better.

"Well," Nik said, reaching down to help me up, "at least now we don't have to worry about a ticket. The slugs are all dead, and the mess is even invisible, so no one will ever know."

That was some seriously glass-half-full outlook, but I was too happy Nik wasn't cursing me out to tease him for it this time.

"Can we go home now?"

"Sure," Nik said. "Unless someone else wants to come out and yell at us."

"Let's leave before that happens," I said quickly, toweling myself off as well as I could.

We had everything packed up in ten minutes flat. Since the couch was the only thing in the truck, that was easy too. I just told Sibyl to drive it back to my apartment and flopped into Nik's car, though not before putting a towel down to guard his seat from my slime. Nik had said he was ready to stick it out with me, but I didn't want to test his resolve by carelessly getting dead slug on his baby. Seriously, he cleaned his car every damn morning. He was already giving my boots the stink eye, so I made sure to take them off and wrap them in plastic before putting them in the back seat.

"So," Nik said as he removed his own heavy Cleaning waders, revealing the sleeker pair of lace-up black combat boots underneath. "Now that hell's over, want to go back to my place for dinner before the evening auction?"

My head jerked up in surprise. Not at the invitation. I'd actually eaten at Nik's several times now, and not just because of the free food, though that was nice. I ate at Nik's because he absolutely refused to eat anywhere else. You'd think he was an emperor worried about poison the way he avoided consuming anything he didn't prepare with his own hands. But while I was starving from working all day without breaking for lunch, I had to shake my head.

"Thanks for the offer, but I already made plans tonight."

"What plans?"

"I'm taking Peter out for dinner tonight." I still owed the death priest for the stunt we'd pulled on him at the morgue. I'd been saving up all week so I could take him somewhere nice to make up for lying to him. And sending him on a wild goose chase. And stealing from his god. Honestly, it was a lot more than one dinner could cover, but I was still going to try. "I told you about it yesterday, remember?"

"Oh," Nik said, scowling at the steering wheel as he started the car.

The terse one-word reply made me wince. "Are you mad about something?"

"I'm not mad," Nik said, reaching up to rub the back of his neck. "Just tired. It's been a long day."

I winced again. We both knew whose fault that was. "You don't have to drive me home if you don't want to," I offered. "Sibyl's already driving the truck over. I can tell her to come back and pick me up, so—"

"I'm not letting you risk your life in that ad-supported death trap," he grumbled, turning around to back us out. "I'll drive you home."

"It's *really* okay."

He shook his head firmly. "You still owe me money for paying your debt last week. How am I going to get that money back if you die riding around in a plastic box they can only get away with calling a truck because it's the DFZ and no one cares?"

I didn't think my truck was *that* bad. I'd been using subscription cars since I'd started Cleaning, and while they weren't what anyone would call *safe*, I'd never had a problem that had actually led to injury. But I wasn't inclined to keep fighting when winning meant I'd have to ride home clinging to the moving truck's terrifying jump seat as opposed to Nik's sleek black sports car with actual glass windows, air conditioning, and speakers that didn't start playing advertisements at max volume the moment you sat down.

"If you insist," I said, snuggling into his passenger seat.

Nik nodded victoriously and pulled us out into traffic.

My dinner with Peter was not mentioned again. Instead, we spent the drive back to my place discussing what sort of units we wanted to buy at the next auction. We had no control over what units came up, of course, but it was fun to dream. I was telling him about the time way back at the beginning of my Cleaning career when I'd scored a hoarded apartment that had belonged to the former assistant curator of the Algonquin Corporate Museum when Nik suddenly slammed on the brakes.

I lurched against my seatbelt. Scrambling back into my seat, I whipped my head around to see a fleet of work trucks taking up my apartment building's entire parking lot.

"What the hell is going on?"

"I was about to ask you the same thing," Nik said, leaning out his window to get a better look at the gridlock. "Is it moving day for your whole place or something?"

If it was, it was news to me. The DFZ did sometimes destroy buildings instead of moving them around, but she usually gave the residents at least a month's notice. I hadn't heard anything, but I hadn't exactly been home a lot this week thanks to Nik's obsession with hitting both auctions every day so we didn't miss a good unit. I left my apartment before five most mornings and usually didn't get home again until ten, so I'd had plenty of time to miss a notice. Maybe I'd missed something important?

Having worked myself into a proper panic, I grabbed my bag and jumped out of Nik's car, sprinting between the trucks toward the renovated motel's open-air stairs. Nik parked his car on the sidewalk and caught up with me a few moments later, sticking right on my heels with his hand in his jacket pocket, which I now knew meant he was holding his gun. That seemed like super overkill to me, but it was pointless to tell him to stop. I'd long since learned that "gripping weapon" was Nik's default mode in stressful situations. He'd stop on his own eventually, so I put it out of my mind and just focused on getting up the stairs as fast as I could.

Fortunately, the further up I went, the less it looked like I was about to lose my building. There were a *lot* of people in uniforms running around, but they looked more like workers than movers, and they definitely weren't going into every apartment. In fact, there was only one door open when I reached my open-air hallway on the third floor. And, of *course*, it was mine.

My apartment—which I'd only just cleaned up from Kauffman's attack—was absolutely jam-packed with people. In addition to the aforementioned workmen, there were decorators and designers in impossibly chic suits carrying AR viewing pads. There were at least two crews of electricians, one of which seemed to be installing a security door where my wooden one had been. I was opening my mouth to demand to know what was going on here when the workers parted like a school of fish dodging a shark to reveal a woman—a staggeringly beautiful Korean woman with perfect black hair, perfect makeup, and a perfect body underneath her perfectly draped, perfectly styled designer dress.

She smiled when she spotted me standing outside, her face lighting up like a sunrise. It was so lovely that even I was frozen in my tracks, all the anger and confusion knocked clear out of my head by the jaw-dropping loveliness of the perfect woman holding out her flawlessly manicured hands to me.

"Opal."

My name hung in the air like perfume, strangling my breath and snapping me out of my stupidity. I jumped backward with a yelp, colliding with Nik's chest in my rush to get away from the trap I now knew I'd walked right into. But it was too late. The lovely woman had already grabbed my chapped hands in her iron grip, pulling me into a gentle but inescapable hug that smelled so nostalgic I started to panic. I was done for. The cage had already closed. My only hope at this point was to try to limit the damage, so I forced myself to be still, taking a deep, steadying breath in preparation for the coming battle as I said,

"Hey, Mom."

CHAPTER 2

"**W**ait," Nik said behind me, voice quivering. "That's your *mom?*"

The glare I shot him must have been one for the ages, because he began backtracking immediately.

"It's just, she doesn't look old enough," he explained quickly, stumbling over himself. "I thought maybe she was your sister or something."

My mother flashed him a dazzling smile, and I rolled my eyes. In Nik's defense, the woman standing in my doorway really didn't look a day over twenty-five. A feat achieved by religious application of moisturizer, top-notch plastic surgery, and, on occasion, literal black magic. People had been mistaking her for my sister or my cousin or pretty much anything other than my mother since I was five years old. Of course, given how I looked right now—ratty haired, big eye bags, and crispy with dried slug slime—I suppose I should have been flattered Nik saw the family resemblance at all.

"You're so *dirty*," my mother said in Korean, looking me up and down with sharp brown eyes that noted every fault. "But at least you've lost weight. Have you been following the diet I sent you?"

"No, Mom, I've been *starving*," I snapped in the same language. "That's what happens when Dad curses me so I can't make money."

"Don't be disrespectful," she chided, glaring at me as hard as she could without actually furrowing her brows and risking wrinkles. "You're the one who asked for this. Your father never wanted you to live like a rat in a hole. And speaking of rats…" She reached up to touch my head in dismay. "Your poor hair! Have you not taken care of it at all?"

"Who cares about my hair?" I yelled, smacking her hand away. "What are you doing here? And what have you done to my apartment?"

I pointed at my living room, which was so full of workmen I couldn't see past the door.

"I improved it," my mother replied without a trace of shame. "You are the Dragon's Opal. It was an insult to the Great Yong for his daughter to live in such squalor, so I flew over to fix it."

I didn't know about fixing, but my small apartment was infinitely more decorated. The ratty beige carpet had been ripped up and replaced with dark hardwood made even darker by the blindingly white silk-damask wallpaper that now covered my cement-block walls. The ceiling—which had been covered in the standard lumpy popcorn finish that was mandatory for all cheap apartments—had likewise been stripped to make way for molded plaster motifs that swirled like waves around the newly recessed lighting.

But all of that was just prepping the canvas. In addition to changing my apartment's walls, ceiling, and floor, my mother had also replaced everything inside, starting with a brand-new living room suite that consisted of a six-foot-long chaise lounge, two straight-backed armchairs, and a loveseat. I was staring right at it, and I still had no idea how she'd managed to cram all of that into my tiny living room, but the real kicker was that all of this new furniture was *white*. I was a Cleaner. If there was any color I didn't do, it was white.

"There was so much to do, it was hard to decide where to start," my mother went on, turning around to smile at the six contractors who were attempting to install granite countertops in my closet-sized kitchen. "So I decided to just rip it all out and start fresh. It made more work, of course, so we're a little behind schedule, but as you can see, it's already a vast improvement."

She turned back around with a proud smile, clearly expecting me to fall at her feet and thank her for coming all the way out here and "fixing" my life.

"Where's my stuff?" I said instead, unclenching my fist to point at the giant abstract painting of a lily hanging on the wall where the remains of my collection had been. "What did you do with my things?!"

"Don't worry, darling, they're all still here," she said, leading me into my bedroom, which was just as changed as everything else. My mattress on the floor was gone, replaced by a new queen-sized four-poster bed buried under a mountain of decorative pillows. There were also a new chest of drawers, several new mirrors, and a new vanity carpeted in acres of makeup from all of my mother's favorite brands. There was so much new stuff to look at, I didn't even notice the lit display case full of my treasures—all freshly cleaned and dusted—on the wall above my new headboard until my mother pointed it out.

"See?" she said as I sighed in relief. "It's all there." She put her perfectly manicured hands on her hips. "Really, Opal, I'm insulted you'd think I'd throw your collection away. I think it's adorable that you've started your own hoard." Her lips curved into a melting smile. "You're *so* much like your father."

The few good feelings seeing my collection had brought back went up in smoke. "I am *nothing* like him," I snarled, whirling on her. "And you had no right to do this! This is *my* apartment!"

"You are the daughter of the Great Yong," she said, as if that excused everything. Which, for my mother, I'm sure it did.

"That doesn't mean you can barge into my life and change everything!"

"Your father is showing you great favor," she lectured. "Even after you insulted and disobeyed him, he continues to care and provide for you. Who do you think paid for all of this?" She waved a willowy arm at my new bedroom. "Selfish child! How can you be so ungrateful?"

I was ungrateful because my gratitude was the objective. This wasn't the first time I'd come home to a pile of new stuff. It was my dad's standard operating procedure: if stick fails, apply carrot. But I'd grown up with this bullshit. I knew it didn't mean anything. He wasn't sorry, he was just using a resource he had in excess—money—to guilt me into going along with his whims.

It might have been more effective if my parents' lack of caring hadn't been so obvious. I'm only human. I'm not immune to gifts, and what daughter didn't want to believe that her parents were worried about her? But while the stuff my mom had crammed into my apartment was all quite nice, it showed zero consideration for my actual needs. See exhibit A: the white couch.

But while it was clear neither of my parents had taken two seconds to think about what *I* wanted, my father's priorities were on clear display. For all the "gifts" he'd packed into my apartment, I didn't miss the fact that none of it was stuff I could easily resell. There were no jewelry, no antiques, nothing that could be quickly traded for cash. The renovations were all legitimately high quality, but there was no secondary market for custom granite countertops. Even the "fancy" furniture was well below my mother's usual expensive tastes. It was still way nicer than my old stuff Kauffman's thugs had destroyed, but even if I sold the entire suite, I wouldn't get enough to make meaningful progress toward my debt.

Which was, of course, the only reason my dad had deigned to pay for it.

"I don't want it."

"*Opal!*" my mother cried, her lovely eyes shooting wide in horror. "Your father—"

"My *father* is playing me for an idiot!" I yelled at her. "But I'm not a child anymore! He can't just throw fancy stuff at me and expect me to forget that this is *all his fault*! The only reason I'm 'living in squalor' is because *he* cursed me to fail!"

"Don't you dare try to make this his fault," my mother said angrily. "Do you know how much it wounds him to see you like this? You are his daughter, his treasure! Even the curse you complain so much about is just proof of how much he cares. Do you think he would waste his magic, his very life's fire, on any other mortal? You should be thankful!"

"I refuse to be thankful for my own abuse!" I cried. "He *cursed* me, Mom! He is actively making my life worse, and you're defending him! Do you even realize how brainwashed you sound?"

"I'm not *brainwashed,*" she said, pulling herself to her full height, which was slightly taller than mine. "I am the First Mortal of the Great Yong! Cherished consort of a higher being! I've given your father everything that I am, and in return, he has lifted me to heights no other human could hope to achieve. He even recognized my daughter as his own. Do you comprehend the honor of that, Opal? The Great Yong has shared his power and protection with us, his dominion and wealth. When we are dead, he will honor our memories long after the rest of the world has forgotten our names. That is what it means to love and be loved by a dragon. *That* is what it means to be treasured. You'll understand someday."

"I don't want to understand," I said bitterly. "I don't want to be *treasured,* and you shouldn't either. We're people, not objects."

"A dragon doesn't see the difference," she said, her voice growing gentle. "I know it's hard to understand, darling, but your father is a higher being. It's only natural that his actions seem incomprehensible to us mere mortals, but he does cherish you, Opal. You know that, right?"

I glowered at her. "If he actually cherished me, he wouldn't be doing this."

"If you understood anything, you wouldn't be making him," she snapped back. "All he ever wanted was to keep you safe. Never forget that this entire situation was your idea! You deliberately tricked him into this idiotic debt. Now you're blaming him for holding you to your word? Selfish girl! You constantly accuse the Great Yong of schemes and plots, but you're the one who's so caught up in your paranoia that you can't even accept a gift for what it is. You've lost the ability to see that your father and I have only ever tried to do what is best for you!"

"Maybe if you actually *asked* what was best for me, I'd be able to tell when you were doing it! Because all I see you two doing is what's best for *you*. You're the ones who are obsessed with all this squalor nonsense. The only thing I've ever asked for is to be left *alone*."

"You are our child!" my mother cried desperately. "No matter how ungrateful or selfish you act, we will *never* leave you alone!"

She was in my face by the time she finished, her eyes on fire, and for a moment, it almost worked. I *almost* felt guilty for putting my parents through all of this. Then I remembered who I was dealing with. My mother was my dad's favorite tool, the loyal lieutenant to his evil overlord. I absolutely believed that she loved me, but her first loyalty was always to Yong. She drank the "superior being" Kool-Aid by the bucket. That was why she was First Mortal, and why I was never going back.

"Get out."

My mother stiffened. "You will not speak to me in that tone."

"I'll speak to you any way I like," I said, getting louder with each word. "This is *my* life and *my* apartment that *I* pay for. You have no rights here, so round up your people and get the hell out of my house!"

For a moment, I thought she was going to lose it. Just like her dragon, my mother couldn't stand being defied. This had been a source of friction all our lives, because I couldn't stand being dictated to. As a child, I'd had no ground to stand on, which meant I'd always had to fold, but I was no longer locked up in the Great Yong's household where she was queen. This was the DFZ: my turf, not hers. I could dig my heels down to the Gnarls if I wanted, and I did, meeting her glare for glare until, at last, my mother stepped back.

"Attention," she called, clapping her hands as she switched back to English to address her army of workers. "My ungrateful child has decreed your efforts are unwanted. Whatever you're working on, just leave it as is and go. She can finish the remaining renovations on her own since she's *so* independent."

I rolled my eyes at the editorializing. But the workers must have been as eager to get away from my mom as I was, because they grabbed their stuff and ran, flooding past Nik, who was still standing guard at the front door. My mother followed more slowly, pausing here and there to smooth a tasseled throw pillow or adjust one of the tastefully boring paintings the interior decorators had hung on my walls. I kept on her the entire time, practically walking on her heels until, at last, she too made it to the doorway.

"One more thing," she said as I was reaching out to slam my new, mostly finished security door behind her.

"*What?*"

She scowled at me, but then the anger fell away as her lovely face grew worried. "Be careful, Opal. Your father's enemies are on the move."

I shrugged. "So? They're always on the move."

"This is different," she said, voice dropping to a whisper. "You were safe until a week ago because the world still thought you were under your father's care, but thanks to your brilliant idea to call in the Peacemaker over some chickens—"

"Cockatrices, Mom. They were cockatrices."

She waved her hand dismissively. "Whatever. What matters is you made a *scene*, and now every dragon in the DFZ knows that Yong's Opal is running around loose. Even worse, they know about the curse."

"That's not my fault," I said. "I didn't even know I was cursed until that Heartstriker told me."

"Yes, well, she also told everyone *else*," my mother said testily. "Thanks to her, the whole world knows you and your father are at odds. He's already come over to deal with the fallout, but—"

"Dad's here?" I interrupted, heart pounding. "He's in the DFZ?"

"Don't be ridiculous. You know how your father feels about the Peacemaker. He'd never stoop to asking permission to enter that ridiculous dragon's territory. We've bought a house across the river in Windsor, Canada. It's nothing fancy, just a mansion on the river, but your father wanted to stay close while all this nonsense was being sorted out."

Just bought a mansion on the river. Of course. Because my dad could never do anything *normal* like stay in a hotel.

"I cannot stress how dangerous a position your defiance has put us in," my mother went on. "If it were up to me, you'd already be on a plane back home to Seoul. That would be the easiest solution, but your father's indulgence knows no bounds when it comes to you. He's already decreed that you are to be left alone until you inevitably default on your loan."

"Really?" My dad's rigid honor had been the basis of my entire debt ploy, but I hadn't expected him to be *that* hardcore about it.

"Of course," my mother said, lifting her chin. "Your father's word is his bond, but that's actually bad for you in this case. Everyone knows you're Yong's treasure, but now they also know there's a rift between you. His allies see that as a gross liability, while his enemies see an opportunity to use you as leverage. Neither can be trusted not to grab you off the street for their own purposes, and thanks to your foolish ploy, there's little your father can do to stop it."

"I'm not afraid," I told her stubbornly.

"You should be."

I scowled at the implied threat, and my mother sighed. "I know you're mad at him, darling," she said pleadingly, reaching up to cup my cheek. "But your father is trying so hard to do what's right for you. Even at great risk to himself, he tries. I wish you could see that."

I sighed against her touch. This was the side of my mom that hurt the most: the one who trusted her dragon utterly and couldn't understand why I refused to do the same. In a sad, painful way, it was comforting to know that at least my mother wasn't trying to hurt me. She was just doing what she thought was best. Too bad her worldview was completely subservient to a selfish monster who only saw us as collectibles.

"Just go," I said. "Please."

My mother stroked my face one last time, and then she turned on her ridiculously high heels and left, her perfectly shiny black hair swaying with each step as she clicked down the cement walkway.

"Do I want to know what that was about?" Nik asked when she was gone.

"Only if you want to hear about stupid family drama."

That came out more bitter than I'd intended, and Nik's dark brows pulled into a scowl. "Do you need help?"

I looked up at him in surprise. It was such a simple question, but no one had ever offered to help me with family stuff before. At least, no one who knew what my family was. But while it would have been nice to vent to someone who was actually on my side for once, I was tired of talking about my dad.

"You're already helping a ton," I told him with a warm smile. "But annoying as it was, this visit is actually a good sign. If Dad's resorted to sending Mom to meddle in my life directly, that means we're doing well."

"Or you could actually be in real danger," Sibyl pointed out.

I was waving her worries away when Nik's eyes widened in alarm, and I realized that Sibyl had just said that over my external speakers, not into my earpiece.

"*Are* you in danger?"

I shrugged. "I'm always in some kind of danger. I live in the DFZ."

"That's not what I meant."

I was too dirty to flop down on my new white furniture, so I just hunched my shoulders with a sigh. "It's complicated. By most metrics, my dad's a perfect dragon. He killed his father and took over his territory, he ruthlessly puts down anyone who opposes him, he has detailed plans to murder his enemies, all that normal tyrant stuff. But he's also famously attached to his humans, and dragons being dragons, you can't have anything you're attached to without someone else seeing it as an opportunity."

Nik nodded as if he understood that completely. "His enemies will come after you."

"They'll *try,*" I said. "But loath as I am to say anything nice about my dad, he's a pretty badass dragon. He's not the *most* powerful, but he's big, old, rich, and he has a lot of human support. He's not a beast you want to poke, in other words, which is good news for me. Everyone who's read a fairy tale knows that the fastest way to get a dragon pissed at you is to mess with his stuff, and as much as I hate it, I definitely count as 'his stuff.' I mean, my name is 'Yong-ae Opal,' which literally means 'Dragon's Opal' in Korean."

"But there must be some risk," Nik said. "Your mother wouldn't have warned you if there wasn't."

Possibly. There was always risk when dragons were involved, but I suspected Mom had played up the danger to scare me into running back to Daddy. But that was part of the family drama I wasn't burdening Nik with, so I just moved on.

"It'll be fine," I assured him. "Yong's ruled the Korean peninsula for fifteen hundred years. You can't be in power for that long without making a lot of enemies, but they've been nipping at him since way before I was born, and they'll probably still be at it long after I'm dead. He can handle himself. I'm way more concerned about how much time my mom took up. I'm supposed to meet Peter in thirty minutes, and I haven't even showered."

Nik stiffened at the mention of Peter's name. "I'll get out of your hair, then."

"I'm not trying to kick you out," I said quickly. "You can stay as long as you like. I just need to—"

"It's fine," he said, opening my door. "I have some other business to take care of, anyway."

"What business do you have on a Saturday night?" I knew he was a workaholic, but even Nik didn't usually work more than ten hours a day.

His answer was an angry shrug as he walked out of my apartment. I instinctively started after him. To do what, I wasn't sure, but I didn't like how this felt. The clash with my mom had left me angry and on edge. I couldn't handle being on the ropes with Nik too, especially since I didn't understand what I'd done to piss him off. Before I could take two steps, though, Nik suddenly whirled around.

"I almost forgot," he said, pulling an envelope out of his pocket and shoving it at me. "Here."

I took it with a frown. "What's this?"

"Your cut from yesterday's unit."

My frown grew deeper. I'd thought yesterday's unit had been breakeven. That made it a lot better than today's, but I hadn't been expecting any money. Especially not *this* much.

"Holy crap," I said, opening the envelope, which was stuffed with cash. "What's all this?"

Nik shrugged. "Sales from the salvage auction. Bidding was hot, so everything went for more than you estimated."

That didn't make sense. I didn't go with Nik to the nightly salvage auctions because my mere presence was enough to crash prices thanks to my curse, but I was *damn* good at estimating value. If I was wrong about a price, it was never by more than ten percent in either direction. To make this much on a fifty percent cut, I'd have had to have be off by a factor of ten, which simply wasn't possible. "Are you sure?"

"Are you going to make me show you the receipt?" he asked menacingly.

I backed off at once. It was clear Nik was still pissed about…whatever he was pissed about. I was starting to get pissed at him for being pissed, but I was smart enough to keep it to myself. You did not punch a gift horse in the mouth, especially when said horse was the only thing keeping you out of your father's talons.

"Thanks," I said instead, clutching the money to my chest.

"You're welcome," Nik replied, turning away again. "Should be enough to treat the death priest to something nice."

It was enough to feed Peter and cover half my rent for the month. Hell, if he could get sales this good every time, I might actually make my payment to my dad on time after all.

Just thinking about that made me forget all about being mad at Nik. "Thank you!" I called after him.

He waved my thanks away. "So what do you want me to do with the couch?"

"The what?"

"The couch from today's unit," he clarified. "We brought it back for your place, but I don't think you need it anymore now that your apartment looks like a magazine."

I'd forgotten all about that ugly orange monstrosity. I definitely didn't need it now, but it was still a perfectly good couch. I didn't want to just throw it away. "Could you use it?"

Nik looked appalled. "What the hell would I do with a couch?"

"I don't know, sit on it? I know it's not the prettiest piece of furniture, but all you've got right now are folding chairs. I'm just saying it'd be nice to have something not made of metal to sit on when I come over, you know?"

He turned his back on me again. "I'll think about it."

"I'll have Sibyl drive the truck to your place," I called after him. "I have to return it by midnight, though, so make up your mind before then."

But Nik was already jogging off down the open-air hall that ran along the outside of my apartment building, picking up speed with each step as if he couldn't wait to get away from me.

***

I was late for dinner.

It was *not* my fault. I'm not someone who takes forever in the shower, even when it's a new fancy shower with three inexplicable knobs, none of which seemed to control the hot water. I didn't even get waylaid by the wall of salon-branded bottles that had overtaken the nook where my normal shampoo and conditioner should have been. No. I took a cold shower and washed the slug gunk out of my hair with whatever floral, soap-like substance my hand landed on first. The holdup came when I wrapped my shivering, dripping body in a giant monogrammed towel so fancy and slick it didn't actually absorb water and opened my closet to discover that all of my clothes were gone.

Apparently, in addition to replacing my furniture, my mother had *also* decided to replace my entire wardrobe. With the exception of the filthy tank top, shorts, and Cleaning boots I'd been wearing when I'd come home, every piece of reasonable, practical clothing I owned had been removed. In their place, my fancy new dresser and closet were stuffed full of next-season couture from my mother's favorite designers. To add insult to injury, all of the new stuff was in the size my mother felt I should be rather than the size I actually was. The only reason I was able to squeeze into any of it was because I'd been living off Cup Ramen and coffee for the last three months.

But just because I could technically wiggle the new stuff over my butt didn't mean I wanted to wear it. Not only was my mom's taste wildly different from my own—I liked color and fun, she liked elegance and simplicity, which was a fancy way of saying *boring*—everything she'd put in my closet was so delicate and expensive I was terrified to put it on. Even the jeans clocked in at over five hundred bucks per pair when Sibyl looked them up online. A few years ago, of course, I wouldn't have blinked an eye, but now all I could think was how did anyone actually wear clothing this pricey without having a heart attack every time they touched something?

The only silver lining was that at least now I had something to sell. There was always a market for designer stuff. I could tell my mom had tried to limit herself—there were only three pairs of shoes in my new wardrobe and zero handbags, the most obvious cash cows—but she couldn't force me to wear clothes she approved of *and* avoid giving me a windfall. If I hadn't been overdue to meet Peter, I would have rushed out to sell the whole closet right then and there. But I was already late bordering on *super* late, so I forced myself to stop pricing and started looking for something I could actually use to cover my body.

After much searching, I settled on a floral skirt with a busy pattern that wouldn't show stains and a blue silk top with no sleeves so I wouldn't have to worry about sweating in it. I put some makeup on as well. Not much, but while I hated my mom's taste in clothes, her instinct for beauty products was flawless, and I'm only human. I can't resist a whole table full of brand-new shiny product in clever packaging. Also, my bare face looked incredibly out of place above the fancy clothes. Makeup was required to balance me out, so I put it on as fast as I could before shoving my feet into the lowest of my three new pairs of heels and racing out the door.

I felt better the instant I was out of my apartment. It was slightly selfish of me, but my promise to take Peter out to dinner to apologize for how horribly I'd taken advantage of him during the whole Dr. Lyle-Empty-Wind-Hand-Thing wasn't entirely for his sake. It was also an excuse for me to go out to eat, a luxury I hadn't indulged in in months. I was super excited tonight, too, because in an effort to show off, I'd told Peter to meet me in the Corkscrew, a huge shopping development near downtown that contained several of the DFZ's best Korean restaurants.

As the name implied, the Corkscrew was a massive spiral structure that ran from the Underground all the way up to the Skyways. The pedestrian ramp in the center was lined with shops and restaurants on both the inside and the outside of the spiral, though how fancy things got was determined by how high up you went. My budget being what it was, I was taking Peter to a place on the lowest loop of the spiral, but it was still delicious. Growing up, my childhood had been evenly split between my father's homes in Seoul, Las Angeles, and Hong Kong, but I'd always thought of Korean as home cooking and my absolute favorite. I didn't know if that was because most of our cooks had been Korean or because kimchi was goddamn delicious, but I ate Korean food every time I got the chance. The place I was taking Peter tonight might have been cheap, but it had the best Korean comfort food I'd found in the DFZ. Honestly, I probably would have taken him there even if money had been no object. It was that good.

Peter was waiting at the auto-taxi drop-off when I arrived. He smiled and waved when he spotted me in the cab line. Then I actually got out of the tiny car, and his expression turned to horror.

"I'm so sorry," he said, tugging self-consciously at his perfectly nice charcoal-gray button-down and dark jeans. "I didn't realize this was formal."

"It's not, I swear," I said quickly, picking at my own outfit in an effort to look less like I'd just sneaked out of a garden party on the Skyways. "It's just…um…My mom bought these for me."

For some reason, that excuse seemed to make Peter even *more* nervous. "Oh," he said, looking everywhere but me as he rubbed his hand over the back of his neck. Then, as if he'd come to a decision, he straightened up and turned to face me head-on. "Opal," he said, his voice deadly serious. "I'm honored you invited me out for dinner, but before there's any misunderstandings, I feel I should remind you that I'm a priest of the Empty Wind."

I blinked at him, thoroughly confused. "What does that have to do with anything?"

"I'm sworn in eternal service to the Forgotten Dead," he clarified, looking increasingly flustered. "There's no formal restrictions, but it's a very demanding position with long and unpredictable hours, and I wouldn't feel right… That is, I don't feel it's responsible of me to enter into a relationship—*any* relationship!—so long as I'm part of the priesthood. You see what I'm saying?"

I really didn't. It wasn't until he dropped his eyes back to his canvas shoes—and pointedly away from any part of my body—that I *finally* realized what was going on.

"Oh!" I said, cheeks burning as I looked down at my fancy outfit, which, given how I usually dressed, did indeed look exactly like something I'd wear on a first date. "Oh, no. No, no, no! I didn't ask you out with any hidden intentions! This really is the only thing I had to wear. I swear I'm not trying to put the moves on you or anything. I just wanted to thank you for your help with Dr. Lyle."

Considering how eager he'd been to tell me he wasn't available, I expected Peter to look relieved at that, but he actually seemed a little disappointed by my quick rebuttal. I was a little disappointed too, which was a surprise. I'd never even thought about Peter in that way before, but now that he'd told me it couldn't happen, it was suddenly occurring to me how good a catch he would have been. Peter was handsome with his dark skin and quick smile. He was also decent, hardworking, kind, and protected by a death god, which meant my dad couldn't bully him. He was everything I could have asked for in a boyfriend, but I'd been so busy with my own problems I hadn't even noticed. Not that I'd ever had a shot since Peter had been a priest for as long as I'd known him, but it was still a bummer. It was also just my luck. Leave it to me to get rejected before I'd even realized a guy had potential.

"I hope I didn't offend you," Peter said quietly as we climbed the steeply curving pedestrian path that channeled customers into the Corkscrew's gauntlet of restaurants, shops, and attractions. "You really do look very nice tonight."

"I'm not offended at all," I assured him, pushing my hair—which had dried beautifully shiny and maximumly voluminous thanks to my mother's PhD-level knowledge of hair products—out of my face. "Thank you for the compliment. Now let's go eat. I'm starving!"

"Where are we going?"

I immediately launched into an overly enthusiastic explanation of how I'd found this place and how good it was in a desperate attempt to make things less awkward. Fortunately, I really was eat-a-trashcan hungry, and soon the heavenly smell of frying meat banished every other thought from my head.

From the outside, Jeju's Home Cooking was your standard pan-Asian bistro. It had an enormous menu featuring everything from sushi to bulgogi to pan-fried noodles, all of which had been safely Westernized to appeal to the typical Underground dweller's palate. It all was decent enough, but if you spoke Korean, you could get the *real* menu, which was where the magic happened.

Since Peter's experience with the world's best food had previously been limited to chain Korean BBQ joints, I took my time translating the menu for him in lavish detail. It would have been much faster just to ask him what he liked, but I wasn't here for fast. I was paying for this, dammit. I was going to enjoy every bit, and there are few things I can talk about at greater length—or with more passion—than food.

After listening patiently to my dramatic reading, Peter ended up getting a bowl of knife-cut noodles with spicy pork belly. I got my usual fried chicken, which sounds dull until you remember that Korean fried chicken is in a league of its own. They did it "market style" here, too, which is where they butterfly-cut the chicken and fry the whole bird. Add in all the side-dish bowls of pickled radish, kimchi, and rice that they gave you for free and it was *heaven.* I got us beer, too, and lots of it. It was a bit more than I could afford, but you can't have fried chicken without beer. Soju would have been cheaper, but I always got way drunker than I intended when the soju came out. Given how fast I drained my beer when it arrived, going harder didn't seem like a good idea.

"Thank you again for taking me out," Peter said after the waitress left with our order. "I hope I didn't make things too awkward before."

"Don't worry about it," I said, refilling my glass from the frosty pitcher on the table. "I'm the one who overdressed. Honest mistake."

"I'm relieved I was wrong," he said, tracing patterns in the condensation of his own barely touched beer. "Not that I wouldn't have been flattered, but you seem so happy with Nik. I would have been sad to hear it was over."

I almost spit my beer in his face. "*What?*"

"You and Nik Kos," Peter said, giving me a funny look. "Aren't you dating?"

"Why would you think that?!" I cried, drawing startled looks from the nearby tables.

"Well, I mean, you two are always together at the auctions now," Peter explained. "And the other Cleaners said you were together, so I thought…Sorry, are you not dating?"

"No," I said reflexively. "We're just business partners."

"Oh," Peter said, looking sheepish. "Looks like I'm wrong about everything, then. Sorry, Opal."

I took another giant swallow of my beer, desperate to escape this conversation. In hindsight, I wasn't sure why his assumption had made me so uncomfortable. Aside from his spurts of weird grumpiness like earlier tonight, Nik and I got along pretty great these days. I didn't even flinch at his driving or gun grabbing anymore, and we were *always* together. Looking at it from an outsider's perspective, I could totally see why Peter and the other Cleaners thought we were an item, and for some reason, that filled me with panic.

I had no idea *why*. Unlike my delayed reaction to Peter, I'd had no problem noticing that Nik was handsome. He'd saved my life several times now, and—more importantly—he'd saved me from my dad. A crush would have been totally natural at this point, so why did a casual mention of us being together make me freak out? Why did I have trouble even thinking about it?

"Because everyone you like leaves."

My head shot up. Across the table, Peter was sipping his beer and studying the Korean menu with seemingly authentic interest, which meant he didn't see me slip my hand up to press Sibyl's earpiece tighter into my ear.

What the hell are you doing? I thought at her, trusting her to catch the thought through the mana-contact hidden in the tiny wireless speaker-bud.

"Being a good Mental Support AI," she whispered back, her voice so low I wasn't sure if I was interpreting the vibrations through my skin or if she'd found a way to reply in my thoughts as well. "Think about it. Every guy you've ever liked has ghosted on you. That would be heavy baggage in a normal relationship, but you need Nik to survive right now because of your curse. That's why you can't even allow yourself to imagine the two of you being together. You're afraid connecting with him will make him leave."

That's stupid, I thought angrily at her. *Stop trying to psychoanalyze me!*

"But that's what you bought me for!" Sibyl argued. "I'm a state-of-the-art companion AI programmed to support your mental health and emotional stability. I'm built to help you with this stuff! If you just wanted a yes-bot to keep track of your calendar and connect your calls, you should have gotten one of those suck-up personal-assistant AIs."

I rolled my eyes and pulled the speaker out of my ear and shoved it into my bag. It was a cheap escape, but I was here to have dinner with Peter, not a therapy session with my computer. Fortunately, our food arrived a few moments later, and I was able to lose myself in the miracle that is crunchy, spicy, Korean-style fried chicken.

After that, we talked about normal stuff: Cleaner gossip, weird things we'd seen around town, speculations about Broker's personal life. As always, Peter was a goldmine of stories. As a priest of the Empty Wind, he'd seen some wild stuff, more than enough to keep us talking well past when the waitstaff had cleaned away our plates and started blatantly ignoring our empty glasses in the hopes that we'd get the hint and leave.

The bill was a bit painful when we finally cleared out, but that was due more to me than Peter. I'd had way more beer than I'd meant to, but it had been such a happy atmosphere. I hadn't had dinner with a friend in ages, and not just because I'd been broke. Even when I'd been raking it in as a Cleaner, I'd had to cut myself off from all my old friends so my dad couldn't use them. As a protection strategy, it had worked beautifully, but it had left my social circle a single dot named Sibyl.

Really, though, the distance had been inevitable. Even if I had been willing to take a risk, none of my college buddies would have deigned to eat with me in a place like this. The Corkscrew was pretty tame by Underground standards, but Heidi still wouldn't have dared descend this far below the Skyways without a security escort. Back when I'd lived with her, I wouldn't have, either. Before my dad had put my back to the wall, I'd been just as much of a sheltered rich kid as everyone else at IMA. Now I was down here getting drunk with a death priest and happy for the privilege. Funny how life could change.

"Thanks again for coming out with me," I told Peter drunkenly as we left the restaurant. "I had a really good time. Like, really."

"Thank *you* for taking me out," he replied. "Again, though, it *really* wasn't necessary. I was just doing my job. You were the one who helped Dr. Lyle's soul find peace."

I was also the one who'd tricked him into giving me access to the morgue so I could steal Dr. Lyle's hand for my own greedy purposes. Peter didn't seem to know about that part, though, which proved the Empty Wind didn't tell his priests everything. I didn't know what I'd done to deserve such courtesy from a death god, but I was relieved Peter didn't know I was a thief, and I saw no reason to set the record straight.

"It was my pleasure," I said sincerely, leaning against the restaurant's wall so I could enjoy the happiest, most carefree stage of being drunk without having to worry about the added complication of staying upright in heels. "Let's do this again sometime."

"Sure," Peter said. Then his face grew serious. "Before you go, though, can I ask you something personal?"

When I frowned, he put up his hands. "I swear it's not about your social life this time. I was just wondering what's going on with your magic. I've been noticing it all night."

My drunken brain wasn't following. "How can you feel my magic?"

Now it was his turn to look confused. "Um, because I'm a mage?"

"You're a *mage*?" I cried, shocked.

Peter gave me a flat look. "Opal, I'm a priest. It would be kind of hard for me to do my job and talk to the Spirit of the Forgotten Dead if I wasn't magical."

That was a very good point and one I frankly had never considered before this moment. A stupid mistake in hindsight, but in my defense, I'd never seen Peter do anything magical. He never had spellwork on him, and I'd never seen him cast. How was I supposed to know he was a mage? Other than the obvious, of course.

"Wow, I feel stupid."

"Don't worry about it," Peter said. "I don't usually do my stuff where people can see. This might come as a shock, but service to the Forgotten Dead is a lot of solo work."

I snorted, and Peter flashed me a smile before his face grew grim again. "But seriously, Opal, what is going on? I don't make a habit of prodding other people's magic uninvited, but I could feel yours twitching from across the table. Doesn't it hurt?"

"Only when I use it." And at night when I was trying to fall asleep. And whenever I slowed down enough to notice. "But it's nothing serious. I just pushed too hard last week. It should calm down after a bit of rest."

Peter gave me a skeptical look. "Are you sure? I mean, did a doctor tell you that?"

No, because doctors were expensive. But all the internet searches I'd done had left me pretty sure I was suffering from an extreme version of overcasting, which made total sense when you considered how hard I'd blown Kauffman's spell back in his face. But Peter clearly didn't share my confidence.

"I think you should get it looked at," he said, pulling out his wallet and handing me a business card. "This person helped me a lot when I was in a bad place with my own magic a few years ago. I think she could do the same for you."

I took the card to be polite, but it required every bit of self-control my tipsy brain could muster to keep from rolling my eyes when I read it.

Dr. Rita Kowalski
Shamanic Healing, Soul Repair, Counseling Services.
Open 24/7 to the right people.

The address was crazy, too. There wasn't even a street name, just a set of coordinates, which did *not* make me feel confident. "You've been to this person?" I asked skeptically, handing the card back to him.

"Yes. And keep the card, please," Peter said, pushing my hand back. "It'll make me feel better just knowing you have it."

I dutifully tucked the business card into my bag, but this was seriously pinging my scam-o-meter. "I'll keep it in mind," I said. "But I'll be honest, this isn't really my thing. I mean, she's a *Shaman*."

"What does that have to do with anything?"

Sober me would have noticed the warning in his voice and bailed, but drunk me plowed right on ahead. "Because Shamans aren't real mages."

I knew I'd stepped in it the moment the words were out of my mouth. "You know I'm a Shaman, right?" Peter said in a sharp, very un-Peter-like voice.

"Crap," I breathed, covering my face. "I'm sorry, I didn't mean to—"

"No, you did," Peter said, calling me on it. "But I'm not surprised. I've seen you do magic plenty of times. You're a textbook-trained Thaumaturge. Those don't generally think well of Shamanic practice."

Considering I'd been taught that "Shamanic practice" was just another name for the lunacy people invented because they couldn't handle the logic of real magic, that was putting it mildly. Seriously, though. With the sole exception of Peter, every self-proclaimed "Shaman" I'd ever met had been one step above street-corner psychic. They didn't even use *spellwork*. They just threw magic around willy-nilly. And yeah, I threw it around too, but I was an admittedly bad mage. I *knew* I was doing it wrong. Shamans claimed their lack of proper casting protocol was due to a superior understanding of the nature of magic, which was just nonsense.

"I didn't mean to insult you," I said carefully, trying my best to be tactful without being dishonest. "I'm happy Shamanic magic works for you, but it's not for me."

"How do you know?" Peter pressed. "Have you ever tried it?"

Of course not, because I wasn't delusional. Shamanism might have been popular sixty years ago when magic was still new and people didn't know any better, but these days it was in the same boat as healing crystals and past-life regression. I didn't have money to spend on a *real* doctor. There was no way in hell I was going to Peter's faith healer, no matter how highly he recommended her.

But while my mind was made up, bickering over magical styles was not how I wanted to end what had otherwise been a very good night. Peter must have been tired of it as well, because when I opened my mouth, he put up his hands.

"Just promise me you'll do something," he pleaded. "I don't know how you're able to be out and about with your magic in that state. I hurt just looking at you."

"It's really not that bad," I assured him. "I mean, it does hurt a lot, but I've already been to two curse breakers, and they both said my magic would heal on its own if I let it rest."

I didn't realize what I'd said until Peter's eyebrows shot up. "Why did you go to curse breakers?"

Damn. Damn damn *damn*. Stupid alcohol. "It's nothing."

Peter crossed his arms over his chest. "I'm starting to wonder what your definition of 'something' is if a curse *and* your wrecked magic both count as 'nothing.'"

"All right, it's not nothing," I said angrily. "But there is nothing I can do about it. Neither of the curse breakers I went to could crack this thing, so I'm just going to have to be stuck."

"Want me to try?"

My head jerked up. "You'd do that?"

"Sure," he said, smiling. "You're a friend. Also, my god has a good opinion of you. That opens a lot of doors."

The Empty Wind's help was an angle I hadn't considered, but I still shook my head. "Thanks for the offer, but I don't think this is something human or spirit magic can handle. I was cursed by a dragon, so it's going to take a dragon to get it off."

Now Peter just looked impressed. "How do you get cursed by a *dragon?*"

"Just lucky, I guess," I said, dodging the question, but I should have known better. Like most mortals who didn't have to live with the scaly bastards, Peter's eyes had lit up the moment I said the word "dragon."

"Can I see it?" he asked excitedly. "I don't want to pry, it's just that I've never seen dragon magic up close, so…"

He trailed off with a hopeful smile. I wasn't nearly as eager, but I didn't see how he could do any harm, and this felt like a great way to make up for my foot-in-mouth Shaman comment earlier, so I held out my arm. "Knock yourself out."

Peter grabbed my hand with both of his, folding my fingers between his palms as he closed his eyes. I watched him intently, because while I was thoroughly over dragon magic, I'd never seen a priest cast. It didn't look like much, to be honest. There was no howling grave-wind or moans of the dead, but my arm did get terribly cold. I was shivering by the time he let go, which wasn't actually a bad change of pace considering how hot it was tonight. Peter, however, looked very grim.

"That is quite the curse," he said, impressed.

"Tell me about it," I grumbled.

"What does it do?"

"So far as I can tell, it makes me have bad luck," I replied. "With money, specifically. That's why I teamed up with Nik. He's doing all of my buying and selling to help me get around it."

Peter frowned thoughtfully. "Is that working?"

I started to nod. Then I shook my head. "Not really."

"I didn't think it would," he said. "Bringing another person into a curse almost never helps."

"What do you mean?" Because I'd never heard that.

"It's too obvious," he explained authoritatively. "If you're going to go through all the trouble and danger of putting a curse on someone, you're not going to leave any easy outs. A good curse thinks several moves ahead and has built-in blocks for all the obvious counters. If the target can just change their behavior to avoid the intended effect, then you took all that risk for nothing."

I looked at him in awe. "You seem to know a lot about this."

"I wasn't always a priest," Peter said with a shrug. "You're not the only person with a prejudice against Shamans, and curses are good money if you can't find other work. I did a lot of magic I'm not proud of in my youth. Fortunately for me, the Empty Wind has a soft spot for lost souls even before they die, so I didn't go *too* far down the wrong path."

"Hey, man," I said, putting up my hands. "I'm the last person who'll ever fault you for doing what you had to do." Especially considering what I'd done with Dr. Lyle's hand. "But I actually think this is great. Those other two curse breakers were just people I found online. I have no idea if they were actually good other than their positive customer reviews, but I *know* you're solid. Can you help me with this thing?"

"I can't take it off," he said apologetically. "I couldn't even *see* the spell until you told me it was there. The magic's just too different."

I sighed. That was the same thing the others had said, but Peter's words still gave me hope. "That's okay," I told him. "I've given up on getting out of it, but I'm interested in what you said about counters. If cursing someone requires the caster to think several steps ahead, that implies there *are* ways to get around curses without breaking them. Otherwise, why would you need to build in blocks? Could there be something like that in my curse? You know, a loophole?" Because if there was, I was going to abuse the hell out of it.

Peter took my hand again, his freezing magic fluttering over mine as he probed my dad's spell. Now that I knew what to look for, I could actually feel the curse twitch when he touched it, the fang-sharp magic hissing like a viper. It happened a few more times, and then Peter let me go with a sigh.

"I'm sorry," he said. "I can't make heads or tails of it."

I sighed in defeat. "Thanks for trying."

"Just because I can't find it doesn't mean there isn't one," he said quickly. "I can't see any exploits because dragon magic isn't human magic, but curses are still just spells. Dragons are incredibly powerful, far more so than any human, but if they actually had the ability to doom someone forever with no limits, all the powerful people in the world would be under their control, and humanity would have been herded into feed pens centuries ago."

That was a very good point. "So you think there's a way around?"

"There would have to be," Peter replied. "No matter how sophisticated or complex you make it, there's no such thing as a perfect spell. Even a dragon can't think of everything, right?"

Absolutely not. That was how I'd tricked my dad into agreeing to my debt plan in the first place. I'd abused his pride and his preconceptions about my abilities to make him assume I was going one way, and then I'd done something totally different. There was no reason I couldn't do that again. Honestly, I was ashamed I hadn't thought to try before now. Specific knowledge of curses aside, what Peter was saying was nothing new. I'd gone to college for magic. I knew damn well that all spells had restrictions. Hell, even Nik had realized that when he'd suggested we work together. Why was I the only one who hadn't thought of this?

The answer was immediate and damning: I hadn't found a way around the curse because I'd never actually looked. I'd fallen back into the same trap I always did of thinking my dad was infallible, an all-knowing, supernaturally superior foe that I had no hope of defeating.

In my defense, he *was* a two-thousand-year-old dragon I'd been raised to look up to as a god. That said, if my dad was really as unbeatable as he appeared, he wouldn't have needed to curse me in the first place. He'd only resorted to magic because I'd gotten so close to the finish line that he'd had to cheat and trip me. But that was all this was: a stumble, a blip. If I could just figure out how to get up again, I could get back in the race and *win.* The freedom I'd connived for was still there, still in reach. I just had to grab it.

"What do I do?"

Peter considered the question for a moment. "I'd say your first step is to figure out exactly how the curse works. You said it makes you unlucky with money, but what mechanisms does it use to achieve that result? Does it trick you into buying bad units? Do the things you try to sell inexplicably break? Does it sabotage your attempts to find good buyers? How does the magic *actually* take your money away?"

"I…I don't know," I said, cheeks flushing as I realized just how little thought I'd put into this. Everything Peter had mentioned had happened at some point, but I didn't know which ones were the curse and which were just the normal downs of a famously up-and-down job.

"Well, my advice is to find out," Peter said when I explained this. "Thaumaturges treat magic like science, right? So get scientific. Do some experiments, pin down exactly how this thing functions." He smiled at me. "I know you're no stranger to getting around the rules. Once you know what you're up against, I'd bet money you'll find a way to break it."

I perked up. "How much money?"

"Nice try," he said, laughing. "Take it as a sign of my faith that I'm not willing to risk even my meager salary betting against you."

"Thanks for the vote of confidence," I said with a grin. Then I smiled even wider. "Thanks for everything, Peter. You've been a huge help."

"I live to give comfort to others," Peter said serenely. "Usually to the dead, but I take the living when I can get them. And speaking of living, do you need help getting home?"

It was very kind of him to offer. Given how drunk I was, I probably should have taken him up on it. If I let Peter escort me home, though, politeness demanded that I invite him up, and I *really* didn't want him to see what my mom had done to my apartment. I'd die if he thought the reason I was broke all the time was because I wasted my money on stupid white furniture, so I told him I'd be fine, and we said our goodbyes, both getting into separate auto-cabs from the long line that was always waiting at the bottom of the Corkscrew.

The moment I shut my door, I called Nik.

As always when I called him, he picked up by the second ring, his voice sharp and gruff over the speaker. "What's wrong?"

"Nothing's wrong," I said excitedly. "Believe it or not, things might actually be going right! Are you busy?"

"I am."

My soaring hopes plummeted. "Oh."

"But that doesn't mean I can't get *un*busy," he said quickly. "What's up?"

"I need your help with an experiment," I said, reeling from the ups and downs. "Peter gave me an idea for a new angle on my curse, and I want to try it out."

"Right now?"

"It's only nine," I said flippantly. "That's just getting started for a Saturday night! And there's no auctions on Sunday, so we've got tomorrow off."

"*You've* got tomorrow off," he grumbled. But then, just when I was sure he was about to tell me to go to bed, Nik said, "Where should I meet you?"

I broke into a triumphant grin. "Can you pick me up at my place?"

"I'll be there in fifteen minutes."

I nodded excitedly at the phone, which was stupid because he couldn't see me. But hey, drunk. "Meet you out front."

Nik made an affirmative noise and hung up, leaving me free to close my eyes and dream of all the ways I was going to stick it to my dad.

CHAPTER 3

When Nik's sleek black sports car pulled into my apartment's parking lot exactly fifteen minutes later, I was ready and waiting at the curb with a giant black trash bag slung over my shoulder like a low-rent Santa Claus. I jumped in the moment he rolled to a stop. Since he normally started driving again the second I sat down, the first thing I did after tossing my bag into the back was slam the door and buckle my seat belt. I was still pretty drunk, so it took me a few tries to get the metal clip into the buckle. By the time I got the belt arranged over my chest so it wasn't strangling me, though, we were still idling at the curb. When I looked over to see why we hadn't moved, Nik was staring at me as if I was a stranger who'd gotten into the wrong car.

"What?" I asked nervously.

Nik didn't reply. He just kept staring, his face caught somewhere between shock and wonder. It was weird behavior even for him, and I waved my hand in front of his eyes. "Are you okay?"

He jumped, head whipping around as he started us forward, but his eyes kept drifting back to me.

"Is that for Peter?"

"Is what for Peter?"

"*That*," he said, waving his gloved hand in the general direction of my body. "I thought you were going out to dinner. Why do you look like you just got back from a wedding?"

"What are you talking—*Oh*!" I looked down at my designer duds, which I'd completely forgotten about in my excitement. "This isn't—I mean, I *did* wear this to dinner, but not on purpose. I'm only dressed this way because my mom threw out all my other clothes."

It was hard to tell in the dark car, but I would have sworn Nik looked relieved. "So you're *not* wearing that for Peter?"

"Pfft, no way." I plucked distastefully at my ruffled raw-silk top. "The yacht-club-wife look is *soooooo* not my style. Even if it was, I'd never wear it down here. Do you know how stressful it is to wear high-maintenance fabrics in the Underground?"

"You *do* look like you're auditioning for a chance to get mugged," Nik agreed, looking me over one last time before finally turning his attention to the road. "You look nice, though."

I smiled in surprise. "Thanks."

"Not that you don't look nice usually," Nik added quickly, looking so determinedly forward you'd think he'd added a steel bar for his neck to all his other cyberware. "I've just never seen you with makeup and stuff before. It makes you look different. You know, fancy."

I'd *better* look fancy considering I was wearing more than a thousand bucks' worth of designer clothing and a full face of product, but I told myself to shut up and enjoy the compliment. Nik wasn't the sort who said things just to be polite. If he told me I looked nice, he meant it, and that made me happy. After my mother's reminder of just how abysmally I failed to meet expectations, it was nice to know that Nik at least thought I made the cut.

"So," he said, clearing his throat. "What are we doing that couldn't wait until tomorrow?"

"Experiments!" I said excitedly, reaching back to open the trash bag so he could see all the clothes I'd stuffed inside. "I want to pin down exactly how the bad luck in my curse works. I decided to start with clothes since designer labels are always reliable sellers."

I grabbed my phone out of my purse, fumbling it into my lap before I managed to bring up the spreadsheet I'd thrown together while I was waiting for Nik.

"I've made a list of what I think all this stuff *should* be worth given the prices things are going for online," I said, leaning over so he could see the screen as well. "If I compare those prices to what I actually get tonight, I should be able to figure out exactly how much my curse is costing me.

Going by what I've experienced over the last five months, I hypothesize that the curse sinks my profits by twenty to thirty percent, but what I'm really interested in is *how* it sinks them. Will I just get a bunch of bad sales? Will I trip and drop all my clothes in a puddle? That kind of thing. I also want to try having you sell stuff for me to see if that lessens the effect."

I glanced up to make sure Nik was following all of this only to find him staring at me again. This time, though, he looked as if he was trying very hard not to laugh.

"Are you drunk?"

"Well, yeah," I said, shoving my hair—which was *so* glossy it refused to stay properly put behind my ears—out of my face. "But that doesn't mean this isn't a good idea! We've been trying to get around my stupid curse all week. But while it's obvious that *something's* happening, since I've been actually making money with you, I have no idea what or why. There's just too many variables involved when you're Cleaning a unit, but reselling clothing is a simple goods-for-money transaction. There's not too many ways bad luck can screw that up, so if we do it over and over and over again, a pattern will *have* to emerge. Once we know exactly how my bad luck functions, we can figure out a way to avoid it, and I can go back to making money again!"

I finished with a flourish, but Nik still looked skeptical. "Do you really need to do all this? You just said you were making money with me."

"Not enough," I argued, staring at him in disbelief. "Some money is better than *no* money, but that doesn't mean it's *good*. You know we're barely staying afloat. Do you really want to go through another hell-job like today's slugfest?"

Nik grimaced. "Fair point," he muttered, heaving a long sigh. "Where do you want to start?"

I beamed at him and pulled up my map, struggling to read the notes I'd made in my drunken research. "I don't want to go to one of our normal auction houses. They're technically open twenty-four hours, but professional bidders keep professional hours, which even in the DFZ means eight to five. This late on a weekend there'll be nothing but bottom feeders looking to scoop up deals from the desperate. I won't even need the curse to get screwed if I walk into that pit."

"Definitely," Nik agreed. "So you're thinking a flea market, then?"

I shook my head. "All the big markets close at ten. I don't want to be crushed for time, and end-of-day prices are always terrible. I don't want a bunch of false negatives screwing up my results."

"Then I guess we're not going anywhere," Nik grumbled. "You just eliminated all the markets in town."

"Not *all* of them," I said with a grin. "There's one place that won't just be open, it's actually doing its best business *right now*. I know because I looked it up." I turned my phone to him with a dramatic gesture. "We're going to the Night Lot!"

Nik hit the brakes so hard, I was thrown against my seatbelt.

"Ow," I groaned, rubbing my chest. "Dude, what the—"

"Are you serious?" Nik demanded, his gloved hand crushed so tight around the wheel I was surprised it wasn't dented. "You want to go to the Night Lot? The one in Rentfree?"

"Is there another?" I asked, suddenly very confused. "What's your problem? The Night Lot is perfect. It's the biggest collection of independent vendors in the city, it trades exclusively in cash, it's famous for being a place where you can buy and sell anything, and it's specifically open at *night*. We'll be getting there at prime time! Plus I've always wanted to visit, so this is great."

"No it's not," Nik said hotly, looking angrier than I'd seen him since the Gnarls. "Rentfree isn't somewhere you go for kicks. It's the worst neighborhood in the DFZ. You'd be better off selling your stuff in a war zone."

"It can't be *that* dangerous," I argued. "It has a giant, famous market. They did a whole episode about it on *DFZ Uncovered*."

"Life is not reality TV," Nik snapped, clenching the wheel even tighter. "Can't you just wait until tomorrow and sell somewhere normal?"

"No," I said angrily, crossing my arms over my chest. "This is a unique opportunity! I don't get wardrobes full of next-season fashion dropped on my head every day. If I'm going to use them up, I want to do it in the biggest market possible so I can watch the curse functioning under every conceivable condition. The Night Lot is a perfect venue, and I've already got everything together." I huffed at him. "You don't have to come if you don't want to, but I'm going."

That last part was pure drunken belligerence, but it worked.

"Fine," Nik growled.

"Really?" Because his tone said it wasn't fine at all.

"Of course not," he said, glaring at the road as we changed lanes. "It's a terrible idea, but not as terrible as letting you go alone."

"Why are you so against this?" I asked, baffled. "We go to bad neighborhoods all the time. You sound more afraid of Rentfree than you were about the Gnarls."

"Because Rentfree is scarier," he said, his face absolutely serious. "The Gnarls are just magical and weird. Rentfree's full of the sort of people who *choose* to live in Rentfree. They're way more dangerous."

That made a certain amount of sense. As the name implied, Rentfree was rent free. It was the only place in the entire city where anyone could just walk into a space and live there, no rent or lease or even walls required. You'd think this sort of limitless freedom would lead to anarchy, and it did to a certain extent, but it was also the only way a place like Rentfree could function.

If the Gnarls were the DFZ's backstage, Rentfree was her prop closet. It was where the city shoved all the buildings and roads she either wasn't using or was planning to move somewhere else but hadn't prepped a landing site for yet. Other parts of the DFZ got shuffled on a monthly basis, but the buildings in Rentfree changed every day, sometimes every hour. All that turbulence made it impossible to charge for space, because who was going to pay rent on a room that might not even be there tomorrow? So, to keep a chunk of her city from going empty, the DFZ had opened up the entire neighborhood as free living space for anyone willing to put up with the chaos.

As a result, Rentfree had become the DFZ's version of the Wild West. The free housing attracted a diverse array of people, ranging from those who couldn't afford even the few dollars a month it took to rent a room in a coffin community to those who used the chaos as cover to build their own mini-kingdoms. But despite being an infamous gangland, Rentfree was also a mecca for independent commerce. Anyone could come into the neighborhood and set up a shop, so *anyone* did, creating the city's biggest free market. There were no rules, no fees, no limits except what people were willing to pay, which made Rentfree's Night Lot one of the most "DFZ" places in the whole DFZ. It also had the highest murder, kidnapping, and drug-use rates, which was why I'd never gone there before, but I had Nik with me now. I'd watched him take down an entire mercenary team literally one-handed just last week. *Surely* he could handle a few hours of shopping for the sake of science, and he was waaaaay cheaper than the guided tourist groups with their armored buses and fleets of guards that were my alternative.

"It'll be fine," I told him, flashing him my best drunken smile. "This is going to work great! You'll see."

Nik made a noncommittal noise and focused on the road.

I kept smiling at him anyway, holding my phone up so he could see the screen. "Sibyl," I said cheerfully. "Directions to the Night Lot, please."

There was a long pause, and then my AI's voice sounded over the speaker.

"Oh, I'm sorry. Am I off mute now?"

Nik arched an eyebrow as I snatched my phone back. "Would you stop it?" I hissed into the mic.

"Why should I stop?" she asked flippantly. "I'm not the one who muted the literal *voice of reason*."

"Sorry."

"No you're not," my AI snapped. "I can read your mind, remember?"

I rolled my eyes, and Sibyl sighed, a purely dramatic sound since she had no lungs. "Opal," she said in a voice pitched just for my hearing this time. "This is a bad idea, and not just for all the very good reasons Nik just listed. It's late, and you've had a long and stressful day. You're also still drunk. Now is not the time to experiment with dragon magic in Rentfree!"

"Nonsense," I said. "Being drunk makes it less scary, and I'll sleep better when I have some answers."

"At least wait until your father goes back to Korea," she pleaded. "Seriously, he's right across the river. Do you think he won't notice you messing with his magic?"

I set my jaw stubbornly. "If he didn't want me messing, he shouldn't have put it on me."

"That doesn't mean he won't come down on you for trying," Sibyl said. "I'm actually really happy you're taking a scientific approach to a problem for once, but it's my prime directive to think about your well-being. Your mom *just* warned you that your dad's in town precisely because his enemies know that you two are having problems. Rentfree's dangerous enough for normal people, but you've got a target on your back. If someone was looking to grab you, you're giving them a perfect chance."

"What else am I supposed to do?" I said angrily. "Hide at home? I've got stuff to do, and I'm never going to get it done if I keep wasting my time being afraid. Which, by the way, is exactly what my dad wants. Why do you think he let my mom make my apartment so nice? He *wants* me to cower under all those throw pillows like a mouse in a hole until it's time for him to swoop down and scoop me up!"

"You're not wrong," Sibyl said. "But I have to say these things, Opal. Your dad compromised me once into giving you bad advice. I'm not going to let you walk into a trap again without saying something."

I smiled. "Thanks for caring, but my mind is made up."

"I know," she said sadly. "And I'm your AI. Caring about you is my prime directive."

That should have cheapened it, but I was too short on friends to worry that my best one was programmatically compelled to love me. It was good to have a voice of caution even if I did have to mute her once in a while. Right now, though, I was dead-set determined. Sibyl must have felt it in my thoughts, too, because she brought up the map to the Night Lot without another word, putting the directions on my phone's screen and turning the brightness to max so Nik could see them too.

***

The drive into Rentfree was even more interesting than I'd hoped. While the specific location jumped around, the neighborhood was always in the north of the city on the shores of Lake St. Clair directly under the Financial District, a section of the Skyways that was so dense that the elevated bridges overhead formed a complete ceiling. Two decades ago, this area had been known as the Pit and had been infamous for being the place where Algonquin's great wave had first crashed into Detroit, drowning millions and leaving a giant magical pollution zone famous for its ghosts. There were still a ton of rumors about it even now, eighty years later. If the Pit still existed, though, the DFZ had hidden it away long ago. These days, modern Rentfree was no more haunted than anywhere else in the city, but it was *definitely* crazier.

"Wow," I said, rolling down my window for a better look.

Ahead of me, the normal Underground with its practical, squat cement buildings that ended just below the Skyways gave way to a wall of pure architectural insanity. Buildings of every style, height, and stage of completion were crammed together like children's blocks. They leaned on each other like drunks, sometimes blending together halfway up to form entirely new floors. Several were way too tall to actually fit beneath the vault of the Skyways, so their bases had been sunk deep into the ground, which curved sharply downward, creating a chasm so deep it created its own microclimate. When I rolled down the window, I could feel the damp, cold wind blowing up out of it, bringing the smell of wet metal and decaying plastic from the depths.

I'd never seen anything so insane, and I'd seen some crazy shit. But just as I was getting hyped for an exciting drive down the side of an urban canyon, Nik turned us off the main road into one of the brightly lit, razor-wire-lined parking decks that clung to the edge of Rentfree like fungus on a well.

"Hold up," I said as the auto-ticket counter handed him a spot number with an absolutely ludicrous hourly rate. "*You're* paying for tourist parking? Are you sick?"

"Trust me, this is the cheapest place."

"But there's a five-dollar lot right over there," I argued, pointing at the big gravel field full of cars I could see through the gaps in the deck wall.

"Just because they don't charge a lot doesn't mean it's a deal," Nik said as we drove up the ramp toward the top deck. "They can afford to only charge five bucks because if you park there, your car's going to get robbed. The deck's expensive, but it's a lot cheaper than a new windshield."

That seemed excessive to me. There were a ton of cars in the free lot, and the few that looked busted could have been that way when they came in. But there was no advantage to starting a fight. I needed Nik if I was going to do this just like I needed him for everything else in my life these days, so I plastered a cheerful smile over my face and kept my comments to myself as he parked us at the ass end of the deck's top level, the cheapest spot.

"There," he said, getting out. "Now at least we'll have somewhere safe to run to."

"You really are afraid of this place, aren't you?" I said, grabbing my black trash bag of fashion out of the back seat.

"I'm not afraid," he said, double-checking the door he'd just locked. "I'm cautious. I used to do a lot of work in Rentfree. I know better than to underestimate it."

It was on the tip of my tongue to ask if that work had been on the stealing cars side or the protecting them side, but again, not the time. Even drunk, I knew better than to poke the bear I was riding on. I was far more excited about actually getting into Rentfree in any case.

"It looks *just* like it does on TV," I said excitedly, running to the edge of the deck, which was almost falling into Rentfree's cliff. The tilt was a bit dizzying, but it made for a great view down into the vortex of confused buildings, several of which were moving as I watched. They were all piled on top of each other, too, which was a new one on me.

With the exception of the superscrapers whose height demanded foundations that went into the bedrock, buildings in the Underground tended to stop at the actual ground to make room for all the sewers and old train lines and other stuff the DFZ kept below her surface. Apparently, though, the structures here weren't bound by such logic, or even by physics. Just like in the Gnarls, the stuff in Rentfree seemed to do whatever the hell it wanted, with buildings stacked as far down as I could see. Even the roads didn't play fair, snaking up and down and sideways between the structures like a roller coaster.

"That is so cool," I said, digging out my goggles and putting them on top of my head before leaning over the edge of the deck so Sibyl could get a picture of the chasm. "How far down does it go?"

"It varies," Nik said, pulling me away from the edge. "Come on. The Night Lot shouldn't be far."

"Does it move, too?" I asked excitedly as we started toward the stairs.

"Everything here moves," he said. "But the Night Lot's always near the entrance. Gotta make it easy on the customers."

That made sense. What was the point of a giant market if no one could find it? My map was certainly no help. The city didn't even bother updating the roads here. There was just a big circle marked "Rentfree" with a list of attractions and advertisements for the tourism companies who'd be happy to show them to you for a fee. Some of the prices they listed were positively criminal, making me even happier that Nik had agreed to come along.

"Here," he said, shrugging out of his coat.

Before I could ask what he was doing, Nik dropped the coat on my shoulders. The armored black leather was so heavy, it almost knocked me over. It was also warm from his body, which would have been pleasant if the temperature hadn't already been in the upper eighties.

"What's this for?"

"To hide your outfit," he grumbled, pulling off his gloves since there was no point hiding his artificial hand now that his entire fake right arm was on display below the short sleeve of his ubiquitous black T-shirt. "You're begging to get kidnapped walking around like that."

The ruffled designer silk *did* stand out. The sidewalk in front of the deck was packed with tourists with their DFZ merch T-shirts, fanny packs, and water bottles waiting for the next tour group to start. By contrast, I looked like I'd fallen off the Skyways, which was ironic since any one of these tourists probably had more money than I did given the price of guide tickets. Still, it was never good to look like you had money to burn when you were trying to sell things, so I dutifully put my arms through Nik's coat and zipped it up, hoping I wouldn't sweat too much as we walked under the tall arch made from welded metal scrap that was the official entrance to Rentfree.

My vision filled with pop-ups the moment we crossed the line. I wasn't even wearing my goggles, but it didn't matter. The tiny mana contacts Sibyl used to whisper into my earbud seemed to be enough for this level of weapons-grade advertising. There were so many that I actually had to stop walking and bat them all away so I wouldn't fall down a storm drain. It was mostly the usual stuff—drug bars, gambling parlors, VR sex pods, all the normal vices—but there were definitely some new ads that seemed unique to Rentfree.

"What's a brain farm?" I asked Nik as Sibyl scrambled to find an ad blocker strong enough to keep my vision clear without taking me off-line.

"Exactly what it sounds like," he replied, his eyes darting over the loud crowd of excited tourists and pushy local promoters who swarmed over them like flies. "It's a room full of beds where you lie down and go into a medically induced coma so strangers can use your brain over the internet. Same idea as cloud computing, except with people instead of servers. Really popular with cerebral-implant cyberware users."

I gaped at him in horror. "Why would anyone want to do that?"

"Because shunting your brain's repair cycles off onto someone else means you never have to sleep."

"No," I said, shaking my head. "I meant why would you sell your brain to strangers?"

"Because it pays a decent hourly wage and doesn't require you to do anything except lie there," he explained with a shrug. "It's not a bad deal if you need cash and you're not doing anything else with your brain."

I was appalled. Selling your body to strangers was one thing—people had been doing that since the beginning of humanity—but selling your *brain?* Just the thought made me feel violated but also incredibly curious. "So do you dream the stranger's dreams, or does the person paying to use your brain get yours?

"I don't know," Nik said. "Part of the contract is that you don't remember anything that happens while you're being farmed, and I don't have any implants in my brain, so I've never tried it from the buyer's side."

The way he phrased that caught my attention. "Have you tried it from the *non*buyer side?"

Nik hunched his shoulders and kept walking, leaving me scrambling behind him.

I decided to stop asking him nosy questions after that. Rentfree was plenty interesting without antagonizing my partner, anyway. Like most famous places in the Underground, the first few blocks were pure tourist trap. Everything was brightly lit with flashing signs promoting every form of entertainment, from booze to food to sex to spas where you could relax in a sensory deprivation tank.

The main difference I noticed between Rentfree and the more traditional tourist areas like the Second Renaissance Center was that all the vendors and promoters here got right in your face. Not in *my* face, thankfully, since Nik was walking practically on my heels with his hand on the gun in his shoulder holster, which was in plain sight since he'd given me his coat, but it was definitely a high-pressure atmosphere. Even if they were too intimidated to come right up to me, though, we definitely drew a lot of attention, probably because I actually looked like I had money for once. Nik's bomber jacket was pretty big on me, but it didn't hide my skirt or heels. We looked like a slumming rich lady and her bodyguard, which wasn't a bad look when you were trying to sell a bunch of designer clothes, but it definitely wasn't subtle. Nik was clearly ticked at the attention, but I actually liked the stares. It kept people from walking into me, which meant I could spend more time gawking at the scenery.

I'd been wrong before. This was *way* better than it looked on television. Cameras simply couldn't capture the depth of the city-made crevasse we were walking over on a thin crust of road that didn't even count as a bridge. It was more like an asphalt jungle vine. Around us on all sides, crazily tilted buildings stood like cliffs, their window-speckled faces rising nearly a hundred feet to the vault of the Skyways and falling for what had to be thousands of feet into the pit. The insane structures were stacked like cargo containers, but they moved like Jenga blocks, sliding in and out of the stack with a low, continuous rumble. A whole office complex actually vanished while I watched, leaving a giant hole in the wall of buildings that was eventually plugged a few minutes later by a brick tenement.

None of the buildings seemed to have power natively. Instead, a vast network of extension cords and power lines covered their faces like cobwebs, the thin orange, white, and black lines running into every window to power what had to be hundreds of thousands of residences. Even without the burden of rent, I had no idea how anyone could live in buildings that moved so constantly, but there were clearly a lot of them. Everywhere I looked, people had crammed themselves in to the empty apartments and offices, sometimes running rope ladders out the windows to create highways across the constantly moving building-canyon wall.

It was pretty crazy, but I was also pleased to see that Rentfree wasn't actually all homeless tent camps. The TV shows loved to play up the squalor and suffering, but some of the rooms I could see through the windows below had TVs and couches just like any other working-class apartment. This was especially true as you looked further down the pit toward the large circular structure taking up most of the bottom far, far below.

"What's that?" I asked Nik, leaning over the wire some kind soul had strung across the edge of the bridge to stop tourists from plummeting to their deaths. "It looks like a stadium."

"That's the Gameskeeper's Arena," Nik replied, keeping a firm hand on my coat collar. "They have big fights there for people to gamble on. Other than the Night Lot, it's the reason most outsiders come to Rentfree."

My eyes went wide. I'd heard of the arena—or, at least, I'd seen the ads for all the fights you could pay to watch on demand with live betting— but I hadn't realized it was so big. Big and popular. Now that I was looking for it, I noticed that most of the tourist groups were actually headed toward a wall of hacked-together freight elevators where promoters were waving signs advertising a fight between some dude and what appeared to be a tank covered in chainsaws.

"Looks like quite the show."

"It draws a crowd of suckers," Nik said, pulling on my collar as if he was tugging on a leash. "Can you please step away from the edge now? It's a long fall, and you're still drunk."

I sighed and let him pull me back, reminding myself that I could sightsee anytime. Tonight I was on a mission, and our target was rapidly approaching.

As its name suggested, the Night Lot was in a parking lot. A seven-story deck, to be precise. Like everything else here, it was covered in DIY electrical lines and absolutely jam-packed with people. It also smelled *amazing.* As we got closer, I saw why. The entire first level was packed with food trucks selling food so fried it could have been cardboard and you'd never have known. Since this was Rentfree, it probably *was* cardboard, but damn if it didn't smell good. I was seriously considering getting something just to try when Nik grabbed my arm and pulled me back on target.

"What's the plan?"

Turning away from the delicious carts with a sigh, I pulled out my phone to check my price list. "We'll start by getting a baseline," I told him, digging into my trash bag of fashion for the three almost identical little black dresses I'd chosen to be my controls. "I'm going to sell these and average the prices to get a solid idea for where my sales fall compared to the expected price. Once I've got a control number, I'm going to try and sell something for as much as I can possibly get. I want to really go all out and give the curse a push. I'd also like you to try selling some stuff for me to see if that changes the numbers. Finally, I'm going to give you some things to sell with the understanding that you'll be keeping the money for yourself."

Nik frowned. "Why?"

"I want to see if the curse affects *all* transactions involving me or just the ones I profit from," I explained. "I'm trying to figure out if the spell is sophisticated enough to understand intent or if it just latches on to anything I come in contact with. Either way, we should find out something we can work with."

"Sounds good," Nik said, taking my bag for me. "Lead the way."

I grinned my thanks at him and took off, walking up the ramp as fast as my heels allowed toward the parking-deck-turned-market's second floor, where I could already see a ton of used-clothes vendors lined up in what had been the handicapped spots.

Since the first three dresses were specifically meant to be my control, I sold them without haggling and got the expected meager results. Not a single one went for anything close to its listed value online, but I wasn't too disappointed yet. After all, this was a flea market. Everyone here was out to make a deal at someone else's expense. For my first real try, I picked my target much more carefully, selecting a middle-aged Chinese man whose booth was plastered with posters of impossibly gorgeous K-, J-, and C-pop idols. The song playing over his speakers was in Cantonese, too, which I was *way* better at than Mandarin, so I took a chance and stepped up.

"Hello, sir," I greeted him in the same language, fluttering my eyelashes gratuitously. "You have amazing taste in music! Do you have good taste in other things as well?"

Thank God I was drunk. I never could have managed a line like that sober, but it worked like a charm. The shopkeeper immediately abandoned the pack of teenagers he'd been eying suspiciously and came over to smile at me. We had a quick, flirtatious chat about boy bands, and then I started asking how much he'd be willing to pay for a lacy skirt that was the closest thing to sexy my mother had put in my wardrobe. I'd thought it was going really well, but the price he came back with made me do a double take.

"Are you serious?" I said, abandoning the overly girly tone I'd been laying down like tar. "That's less than half what it's worth!"

"Because it has a stain," the vendor said apologetically, turning the skirt over to show me a small black spot I *swear* hadn't been there when I'd put it in the bag. "I'm doing you a favor, baby."

I set my jaw hard. I didn't even know what that stain was, but there was no way it was coming out of the pale-pink lace. I poured the charm on even harder to try and salvage the situation, but the man wouldn't budge. In the end, I had to take what he offered, glumly shoving the money into my wallet as I stomped away.

"That was *bullshit*," I hissed at Nik once the crowds had swallowed us again. "I *know* that stain wasn't there before!"

"If you say so," he said, watching the people who elbowed past us warily. "I couldn't understand a word. How many languages do you speak, anyway?"

"Korean, English, and Cantonese fluently, Mandarin and Japanese conversationally, and French terribly." That last one was all my mom. She'd considered it refined for a young lady to speak French. I'd considered it torture.

Nik looked impressed. "How'd you learn all those?"

"My dad traveled a lot. His primary stronghold is in Seoul, but he visits the U.S. and Hong Kong for several months each year to oversee his various business interests. As his mortals, it was our job to tag along, so my mom made sure I could speak everything well enough not to embarrass him."

"You were taught by your mom?" he asked, seeming genuinely curious. "What about school?"

"What about it?" I said bitterly. "I was Yong's Opal. His possession, not his actual child. You don't send a rock to school."

"But you had to have *something*," Nik pressed, moving closer to me so the impatient crowd couldn't push us apart. "How else do you know so much?"

I shrugged. "I had tutors for magic, but my mother was in charge of my education. Of course, since I was being raised to serve a dragon, 'education' meant etiquette, dragon politics, and how to identify, pronounce, and evaluate luxury goods. All the actually useful stuff like math and history I had to teach myself."

"You taught yourself?" Nik repeated, flabbergasted.

"The internet is a wondrous invention," I said reverently.

He still looked shocked. "How did you get into college?!"

"Enough money can get you anywhere," I replied with a self-deprecating smile. "Dad bought me into the best liberal arts school in Seoul, which is funny because he was dead set against me going at first. My mom was the one who actually sold the idea. She convinced the Great Yong that I'd be less rebellious if he gave me a bit of freedom."

And *wow*, had that backfired. My parents had gambled that I'd get to college, freak out at all the new people and responsibilities, and scurry back home to never leave again. Instead, I'd lost my virginity to a K-drama star, thrown a raging party that had trashed my new Gangnam apartment, and gone on an unplanned vacation to Egypt all in the first week. I'd had an absolute blast, in other words, at least until my dad had showed up to drag me home. It was all a bit rich-kid-crazy in hindsight, but that's what happens when you keep someone locked up in a dragon hoard for their entire childhood.

"So did you and your dad ever get along?" Nik asked. "Not to prod a sore spot, but it sounds like you've always been at each other's throats."

"Not always," I said. "We got along great when I was little. Then I grew up and realized 'puppy' wasn't a compliment."

Just thinking about that made me a little sad. It was hard to believe given our current state, but there'd been a time not so long ago when I'd loved my dad with all my heart. Loved him like the daughter they all pretended I was, because I hadn't been pretending. Unfortunately, he had been. Once I figured out I was just a source of entertainment, a novelty he toyed with to distract himself from the ennui of immortality, nothing had ever been the same.

"Let's just keep going," I muttered, pulling the next item—a powder-blue ostrich-leather jacket—out of my bag. "You want to try selling?"

"Sure," Nik said, plucking the ridiculously delicate garment from my fingers. "So long as I don't have to bat my eyes at anyone."

"It might help."

He shook his head and walked over to the next stand, leaving me bobbing hopefully behind him as he started to haggle.

***

The night only went downhill from there.

Since I hated all of it equally, I'd brought my entire wardrobe, almost fifty items in total. The stuff I sold on my own went even worse than expected, which was infuriating because I was schmoozing my damn heart out. But no matter how much I flirted and wheedled and guilted the vendors, not a single item from my stack went for more than fifty percent of its estimated value. The worst part, though, was that I never lost that fifty percent in the same way.

Of the twenty-odd items I sold solo—all to different vendors—every single one flopped in its own unique fashion. One shirt had a manufacturing defect I hadn't noticed until the vendor pointed it out. My pair of black suede designer heels looked too similar to its pirated knockoff, so the vendor had refused to believe they were authentic. A guy bumped into me while eating a plate of mystery fry and got grease all over a pair of rose suede pants. One of the big tables already had five identical cream blouses that weren't selling, which meant none of the other vendors wanted to buy mine. On and on and *on*. Each failure was for a different, infuriatingly vague reason, but the end result was always the same: I was making half of what I should, and nothing I did seemed to change it.

Nik did slightly better. He suffered from the same seemingly random spread of unrelated problems, but his losses only came to about forty-five percent. Interestingly, it stayed forty-five percent whether he was selling things for me or for himself, which suggested that my mere presence was enough to bring down profits. We'd kind of figured that out already from the few times I'd tried to help Nik sell our Cleaning salvage, which was why he now went to the auction houses alone, but it was morbidly fascinating to actually observe the curse in action. Fascinating and incredibly, *incredibly* frustrating.

"I just don't understand," I said for what had to be the thousandth time. "Every time, it's something different! It's like there's no rhyme or reason at all, but that can't actually be the case. Even curses have to have rules, something that tells the magic to do X in case of Y. But I can't find any consistency at all! It's like he just bribed the universe to make my life fifty percent more miserable!"

Nik nodded absently, but he wasn't really listening anymore. He was too busy looking over his shoulder, his face set in a permanent scowl as he scanned the crowd behind us, which wasn't nearly as thick as it had been when we'd arrived. It was after midnight now, and even in the Night Lot, people were heading home. The main ramp through the converted parking deck, which had been so packed an hour earlier that going up it had felt like we were salmon swimming upstream, was now empty enough for us to walk comfortably side by side as we made our way back down to the ground floor.

The vendors were packing up as well, boxing their goods into locked containers to haul back home for safekeeping until tomorrow's market. Those items that couldn't be easily moved were being marked down for rapid sale. One seller actually slashed the price on a retro Kenmore fridge right as I walked past. The moment I saw the new price, my instincts started screaming at me to buy it. Classics like that were hot collectors' items, and I knew a guy who'd pay top dollar for that particular shade of lemon yellow. It was easy money dangling right in front of me, but I didn't dare reach for it. Now that it had bitten me so many times in a row, I could actually feel my dad's curse slithering over my magic. It was the lightest touch, no more than a shadow, but it was there and waiting. Waiting to do *what*, I had no idea. I also had no idea how to make it *stop*.

"Argh!" I groaned, stomping ahead so I wouldn't have to see someone else buy what should have been *my* fridge. "This is so stupid! How do I avoid a curse that dooms me differently every time?"

"Maybe it's the selling itself that's the problem?" Nik said, catching up with me. "You haven't tried making money in other ways. What about a salary? If I just paid you a flat rate every month, could the curse take that? Would it find a way to make me stop paying you?"

"I don't know," I said, looking up at him. "Would you do that?"

"If it got around the curse, absolutely," Nik said with a scowl. "I'm taking a forty-five percent hit from this too, don't forget."

I winced. "Sorry."

"I'm not blaming you," he said quickly. "But if I could stop losing half my money for no damn reason, that'd be great. I mean, just think how much we'd be making if we weren't losing a huge chunk of our cash every time."

"Believe me, I've thought about it," I said, scrubbing my fingers through my hair, which was now more sweaty than glossy. It was beastly hot in here even with the cold breeze blowing up from the depths, and Nik's heavy coat was absolutely roasting me. I'd also sobered up enough now to move on to the hangover portion of the night, which was definitely not helping matters.

"We could try the salary thing," I said, moving my hands down to rub my pounding head. "But I don't know if it would work. I don't know *anything*. That's why I'm so mad. All of these transactions were supposed to reveal the limits of the curse's power, but all I actually managed to do was sell a closet full of brand-new, never-worn, next-season haute couture for used-T-shirt prices!"

"I thought this wasn't about the money," Nik said.

"That doesn't mean I'm happy about losing it!" I cried, pressing my fingers into my eyes. It was either that or bawl in pure frustration. "The only thing I learned for sure tonight is that the curse is screwing us both even harder than I realized. We're both going to go bankrupt at this rate."

I paused there to let Nik say that he wasn't going to go bankrupt and everything was going to be okay like he had earlier today. He didn't say a word this time, though, which made me feel even worse. I was about to suggest we just go home before I got any more depressed when Nik grabbed my arm.

"What if money wasn't involved at all?"

I frowned at him, not following.

"Your curse takes fifty percent of all the money you make, right?" Nik said, his gray eyes flashing excitedly. "But what if you were trading for something that *wasn't* money?"

"You mean like barter?"

Nik nodded rapidly. "Say you swapped a thousand-dollar fridge for a thousand-dollar TV. How would the curse ruin that value? Would it cut the TV in half?"

"I….I have no idea," I said. Then my face split into a grin. "Let's try it."

Nik grinned back at me, and we both turned on our heels, racing through the throngs of drunks yelling rowdily for kebabs, funnel cakes, and jalapeño corn dogs in the fleet of food trucks that had taken up permanent residence on the Night Lot's bottom level. When we got back to the regular shops on the upper floors, though, I realized in dismay that I had nothing left to trade.

"I got it," Nik said, pulling out his wallet before I could even tell him what was wrong.

"Are you sure?" I asked nervously. "I've already cost you a lot."

"Exactly, I'm invested now," he said. "I want to see if this works just as much as you do. Now, what do you want to barter?"

After much discussion and looking over of tables, we settled on a thirty-dollar chef's knife. It was new in the box and the sort of thing that was always in demand, so I figured we had a good shot at convincing someone to trade for it. It was also a pretty good deal and something Nik needed anyway, so if we ended up getting stuck with it, it was no big loss. Under any normal circumstances, I would have called it a super-safe bet, but I'd been losing money on safe bets all night, so my heart was still hammering as I carried my new knife up one floor to a fresh set of vendors and started trying for a trade.

I struck out at the first booth. I didn't know if that was the curse or if the lady who ran it just didn't like my face, because I'd barely opened my mouth before she waved me away. The second table I tried was a guy who, ironically, specialized in dragon collectibles. He had books signed by Bethesda, Queen of the Heartstriker Clan, and a whole ton of DFZ-branded dragon swag at much cheaper prices than the Dragon Consulate's gift shop. There were posters of the White Witch and all her hot sisters, morbidly themed sauces that supposedly went well on humans, even a selection of shiny disks he claimed were dragon scales. They were *not* dragon scales, of course. I wasn't sure what they were actually made of, but no dragon was stupid enough to leave pieces of themselves lying around for mortals to find, especially not at those prices.

But while the scales were definitely a scam, the rest looked pretty legit. Dragon stuff was always a reliable seller, especially in the dragon-heavy DFZ. Like most of the vendors here, he sold a lot of other stuff as well, and so I made him a pitch to see if he was interested in my knife. To my surprise, he bit, and I ended up walking away with a stack of thirty-year-old dragon wanted posters issued by Algonquin's former Anti-Dragon Task Force. One was even signed by the famous dragon hunter Vann Jeger, which made it historically significant.

Total online retail value: forty-five dollars.

"Holy shit," I whispered when Sibyl came back with the number. "Holy *shit*." I looked up at Nik. "I made money."

"You made money," he agreed, grinning from ear to ear.

"I made *money*!" I cried, squealing so loud the whole crowd turned to glare at me, but I was too busy hugging Nik and jumping up and down to care. "It worked! It actually worked! We did it! We broke the—"

I froze, stopping so short I banged my forehead on Nik's metal chest. "Wait, no, it didn't work."

"What are you talking about?" Nik demanded. "You just made a profit for the first time in months."

"No, I went sideways," I said, shaking the pile of posters at him. "This isn't profit, it's just more *stuff*. I can't pay my dad in posters, and if I try to sell these, I'm only going to get twenty-two dollars and fifty cents, not forty-five. That's less than the knife, which means I still lost money."

"You could try to trade the posters for something even more valuable," Nik suggested.

"That won't work either," I said despairingly. "I got lucky and found a good deal, but I can't count on that happening every time. Even if I was the queen of hustle, I'd have to trade everything I got up to at least twice its original value just to counter the fifty percent the curse will take whenever I finally do cash out, and that's just not going to happen. It's not going to work."

Nik's face fell back into a scowl, and I suddenly felt like a jerk for yanking the rug out from under him, which was stupid because I was the one who'd fallen on her face. I'd really thought for a second there that I'd beaten this, but while it was nice to see something work for once, there was just no way I could barter my way past a fifty percent knockback on every single—

I froze, eyes going wide. "Wait," I said, clutching my posters. "Wait, wait, wait."

Nik crossed his arms patiently over his chest while I turned in a circle, scanning all the tables until I found one with the display I wanted. Hugging my precious win to my chest, I scuttled over to a booth where a heavily made-up lady was hawking makeup, secondhand jewelry, and hair accessories. It took a lot of looking, but eventually I found an unmatched earring in her discount bin that Sibyl's density scanner confirmed was what I was looking for. It took even longer to convince the lady to trade it to me, but I was in full-on saleswoman mode now, playing up the historical and monetary value of my posters to the Skyways. In the end, my passion for the DFZ's short but bizarre history won through, and I walked away with the earring clutched in my hot little hands. When I showed my prize to Nik, though, he looked unimpressed.

"What are you going to do with *one* earring?" he asked, scowling at the gleaming gold stud in my hand. "It's not even interesting. It's just a ball."

"A ball of fourteen-karat gold," I told him smugly, turning the stud over so he could see the microscopic *14k* stamped on the back. "Assuming it weighs at least two grams, that's one gram of actual gold once you subtract the weight of the other metals they added to make it hard enough to work as jewelry. And at the current market rate, one gram of gold is worth…" I paused to let Sibyl look it up. "Thirty-eight dollars."

"Okay," Nik said, looking far more interested now. "That's less than the posters but more than the knife, so we're still good."

"We're way better than good," I said, my voice quivering with anticipation. "Don't you see? You were *right*. The curse only seems to kick me when I'm trying to earn *money*, as in legal currency. But gold isn't money. It's a commodity, so it wasn't affected, but it *does* have a set value. This isn't like selling clothes or cheese boards or other random objects where we have to take whatever people are willing to pay. There's literally a price per gram that the whole world agrees on. That price goes up and down with the gold markets, of course, but it's not the sort of thing one person can change."

I shook the little earring pinched in my fingers. "According to the current listed gold price, this stud is worth at least thirty-eight dollars. By the rules of the curse we've observed tonight, that means I should only be able to sell it for fifty percent of that, or about nineteen dollars. But since it's *gold*, the only way it can sell for that little is if the price of *all* gold drops by fifty percent, which would be a total market crash."

Nik recoiled in horror. "Can your curse do that?"

"I don't know!" I said excitedly. "That's the question. Which is stronger: my dad's magic or an international commodities market? I honestly have no idea what's going to happen, but I saw a cash-for-gold guy one level up, so I'm going to find out."

With that, I whirled around and started running up the ramp. Nik followed right on my high heels, keeping pace easily since I was hobbled by my bad footwear choices. My feet were actually killing me by this point, but that didn't slow me down at all as I rushed toward the stall I'd noticed earlier this evening, sending up a prayer to anyone listening that it was still open.

For once, luck was on my side. I got to the enclosed booth marked CA$H 4 GOLD just as the man inside was lowering his security shutter.

"Wait!" I cried, sticking my hand under the metal lattice just before it closed. "I want to make a sale!"

I must have looked too crazy to deny, because the thin, birdlike man inside heaved a long-suffering sigh and rolled the shutter back up. "What you got?"

I showed him my tiny earring, and his face grew even more disgusted. "Really?"

"Your sign says 'Cash for gold,'" I told him pointedly, placing my other arm on the counter as well so he couldn't slam the shutter back down on me. "It doesn't specify a minimum."

"You do know it's two minutes to closing, right?" he griped. Then he spotted Nik standing behind me. "But I guess I can squeeze you in."

I beamed at the skinny man as he sat back down on his stool and pulled out his phone, which had exactly the same type of density scanner that mine did. Once he'd confirmed the earring was, indeed, made of actual gold, he popped it onto his digital scale.

"Two grams at fourteen k," he muttered, turning the scale's screen so I could see it too. "That's one point one seven grams of pure gold. At the current market price, that's…"

He looked over his shoulder at the enclosed booth's back wall, where a large, blindingly bright LCD displayed a real-time graph of the gold market with the current price shown prominently at the top. When he'd first put the earring on the scale, the glowing numbers had been the same ones Sibyl had shown me earlier: $38.02 per gram. The moment the clerk mentioned paying me, though, the sign went crazy.

The vendor nearly fell off his stool at the sight. He steadied himself with a curse, sweat rolling down his cheeks as the graph of the gold market started to plunge. I held my breath as well, watching the numbers go down, down, down. For five terrifying seconds, the glowing line plummeted like a falling arrow. Then, fast as it had begun, the crash stopped, and the graph stabilized, wobbling up and down before finally coming to a rest at $36.10.

"Holy crapola," the guy said, wiping his face with a paper napkin from the stack beside him. "That was a five percent drop!" He turned back to me with a shaky breath. "Did you stomp on a bunch of graves on your way over or something?"

"No more than usual," I said, nodding at the sign. "So is that the price you're going to give me? Because the market was higher when I first came in."

The man's pinched face scrunched even tighter, and he pointed over his shoulder at the handwritten sign taped above the fancy LCD one, which read *THE MARKET IS ALWAYS RIGHT.*

"Okay," I said, putting up my hands. "Thirty-six bucks it is."

Muttering sourly under his breath, the clerk opened his cash drawer to start counting out my payment, which came to only thirty-two dollars once he'd taken his fee. Not that I cared. I grabbed those thirty-two bucks like they were the goddamn Holy Grail, shuffling the bills in my shaking hands as I pulled out the three tens and handed them to Nik.

"There's for the knife," I said. Then I held up the remaining two crumpled bills. My beautiful, precious, glorious two dollars of *profit.* "And here's for me."

Nik grinned wide. I grinned back, and then I started to laugh. The guy in the gold booth looked at me as if I was nuts, but this was worth a little crazy. I'd just made *two dollars.* A sum greater than zero! It wasn't much even by my low standards, but the number didn't matter. The fact that those two dollars existed was the lever I could use to crack open the whole damn world. I was still cackling about that when my phone started vibrating wildly in my hand.

Too wildly happy to be properly cautious, I answered the call without thinking, lifting the flat slab of electronics to my ear as I answered in a sing-song voice.

"Yello!"

"What did you just do?"

My blood ran cold. The voice over my speakers was growling and warped, but I'd know it anywhere. That was my dad's voice, and he was *furious*. Just hearing the echo of his anger through the phone was enough to make me cower like he was right in front of me. My next instinct was to apologize and beg forgiveness, anything to make him stop snarling. The "sorry" was already on the tip of my tongue before my brain finally wrangled my terror into submission, and I came back to my senses.

"I don't know, *Dad*," I said angrily. "What *did* I do?"

The Great Yong hesitated, then he blew out a breath so hard I swore I could smell the smoke over the phone. "Don't do it again."

"Why not?" I demanded, my heart pounding wildly. I'd never had one up on my dad before, and the thrill of even this small victory was enough to set my whole body afire. "Did you feel it? Did I hit?"

The growling grew louder. "Don't play this game with me, Opal."

"You started it," I reminded him. "Everything was nice and fair until you decided to cheat."

"Don't you dare turn this back around on me," he snarled, his voice so angry I hoped he wasn't near anything flammable. "This entire situation is *your* fault. The debt was your idea."

"Because it was the only way to make you let me go!" I yelled at him. "You're the one who put me in this corner. If you don't like what I'm doing, feel free to stop."

"Don't flatter yourself," Yong said dismissively. "This changes nothing."

"I think it does," I said, my face splitting back into a grin. "You called *me*, remember? You just tipped your hand, so I'd say this changes a *lot.*"

My dad's response to that was a frustrated hiss and a change of subject, which made me smile even harder. "Why are you pushing so hard? You're fighting for a life you don't even want."

"You don't know what I want."

"I know you can't actually *want* to be a Cleaner," he said, his voice disgusted. "Working with a criminal and digging through garbage in that pit of a city. That's no future for you."

"You don't get to say that," I snapped. "It's not like you care enough to actually find out anything about me. You don't even know what sort of furniture I like!"

"You think I'd go through this much trouble if I didn't care?" he snapped back. "You are my Opal! I created you, raised you, taught you, and protected you. No one treasures you more than I do!"

"I'm not a rock!" I yelled at him. "I'm a person!"

"*Enough!*" Yong roared. "I'm done indulging you."

"You're not *indulging* me in anything," I reminded him nastily. "I'm *winning.* I figured out how to beat your little curse, and I'm going to pay you back so hard no one will ever be able to say you own me again."

"We'll see about that," my father growled. "The terms of your loan are now changed. I want your entire balance paid in full by the end of the month."

My heart leapt into my throat. "You can't do that."

"It was my magnanimity that allowed you to make payments in the first place," he said haughtily. "But you've made it clear how little you value my gifts, so I see no reason to keep granting them. Of course, if you come home, you won't have to pay a thing. Or you can keep flinging yourself at the wall until you fail. Your choice, but one way or another, you *will* return to me, Opal. End of discussion."

"That's not how discussions work!" I cried, but he'd already hung up, leaving me heaving at my end-call screen. "*Asshole!*"

"That sounded like it went well," Nik said dryly.

"Screw this!" I yelled, shoving my phone back into my bag. "Let's go make some money. I'm going to shove that debt down his damn throat!"

"Whoa," Nik said, grabbing my shoulders. "Opal, it's one in the morning."

I jerked out of his hold. "So? This is the DFZ. There's always work."

"Not the kind you want to do," he said, giving me a knowing look. "I understand you want to get a jump on this, but we've been going hard since dawn. You'll have a much better chance of actually making this work if you rest."

"Listen to the man!" Sibyl cried from my bag. "He speaks sense!"

I knew that, but that didn't mean I liked hearing it. The only thing I wanted right now was a briefcase full of gold to wing at my dad's stupid face. But while the spirit was definitely willing, the flesh was having issues. I was hungover, my feet felt like two branding irons, and my stomach was churning from all the alcohol and fried meat. Even my sprained magic was acting up again, which was unfair because I'd been so careful not to use it. But reality had never cared much about fair, and the cold, hard truth of the situation was that I was a wreck who needed to sit down before she fell down.

Nik knew it, too. He didn't even have to say anything. He just offered me his arm. The gesture was both gentlemanly and condescending, but I knew Nik well enough by now to understand he didn't mean to be either. It was pure practicality. Now that the drunken tunnel vision of conquering my curse had faded, I was rapidly shriveling into a husk of a human being. I needed sleep and water and to *never* drink that much beer again. I also needed a prop to keep from falling on my face, and his steady arm would do nicely.

"Sorry to be a burden," I muttered as I latched onto him with both hands.

"You're not a burden."

Given that he was currently supporting half my weight, that was demonstrably untrue, but I was too tired to bicker over semantics. I was just relieved to take the load off my feet after a full night of running around in these stupid heels. I couldn't believe I used to wear these torture devices every day. Shaking my head at the memory, I leaned harder on Nik as we hobbled down the ramp. We'd almost made it to the door when something hard and reeking of pot smoke and unwashed laundry slammed hard into my side. I grunted at the impact, and then I was shoved out of the way as a woman—the source of the smell—lunged out of the crowd to wrap her arms around Nik.

CHAPTER 4

I reacted before I could think, grabbing magic out of the air, which hurt like *crap*. The pain was so bad, I actually had to stop and breathe, which was a damn good thing, because the woman wasn't attacking Nik. She was hugging him, squeezing him around the neck while squealing, *"Nikki!"*

"Hey, Maggie," Nik said far less enthusiastically.

"It's been forever, man!" she cried, finally releasing her stranglehold so she could look him over. "When did you get back?"

"I'm not back," he replied, pointedly not looking my direction. "Just passing through."

"Ohhhhh, I see," Maggie said, turning to leer at me despite Nik's attempts. "Your new girl looks nice and expensive. How'd you afford a piece like that? I heard you were a Cleaner or some shit now."

I blinked, too shocked by the word barrage to be offended. Now that she was focused on me, I could see that Maggie was younger than I'd initially assumed. I'd pegged her in the mid-thirties, but she actually looked my age, maybe even younger. It was hard to tell with someone so strung out. Her skin was pale as a cave fish's scales, as if she'd never seen the sun, and her twiggy arms were dotted with needle marks from vending-machine upper packs. Her makeup was surprisingly on point, if a bit overdone on the red lipstick, but her dark-lined eyes were dilated and twitchy, and her hair didn't look like it had been washed in, well, *ever*. Her T-shirt and tight jeans were similarly filthy, the fabric stiff and reeking from too many days of wear. They weren't bad quality, though. All in all, she looked like your classic high-functioning DFZ druggie, but she was hanging on Nik like they were childhood friends. Or former lovers.

"Say," Maggie said, dilated eyes flashing as she whipped back around to smile at Nik. "You looking for a job? 'Cause I got work coming out my ears, and these new idiots can't handle it. I could really use my old Mad Dog back. Just got something in that's right up your alley too. Classic chop-and-bag job, super easy. So what you say? Wanna make some money?"

My ears perked up at the word "money," but Nik's glare hardened. "Thanks but no thanks," he said, prying Maggie's hands off his shirt. "I've already got a job."

"Aww, come on, Nikki, don't be like that," she pleaded, snaking her fingers out of his grasp to reattach at his shoulders. "Ain't no one left in this hole who can do what you did. Once word gets around Mad Dog's back, jobs'll be flying at our faces. We'll both be high rollin'! How can you turn that down? You're the one who says he's always for sale, right?"

"Not this time," Nik said stiffly, removing her hands from him yet again. "I'm not working for you, Maggie. Stop asking."

For a moment, she looked truly hurt by his rejection. Then her smile snapped back, and she put up her hands. "Sure, man, sure," she said, backing away. "You don't want to be rich, that's your call. I'm just happy to see you doing well for yourself. You know how to find me if you change your mind. Until then, have a nice life."

She walked off after that, vanishing back into the crowd as suddenly as she'd appeared. I was still trying to figure out how she'd done it when Nik grabbed my hand and started marching toward the exit so fast he was practically running.

"Whoa," I said, scrambling to keep up. "What's wrong?"

"We need to get out of here," Nik said, his gray eyes flicking in every direction as he dragged me out of the market and back onto the bridge.

"Why?" I asked, looking over my shoulder at where Maggie had been. "Wasn't she your friend?"

"There are no friends here," Nik said darkly. "Maggie's a fixer."

"Like Kauffman?"

"Yeah, but she has a lower level of client." He steered us to the middle of the road, plunging straight into the middle of a tourist group as if he were using their souvenir T-shirts and cargo-short-covered bodies as cover. "She was acting nice because she wanted to make money with me. Now that I've turned her down, she'll be angling to make money *off* me by selling our location, which means we need to leave."

That struck me as ridiculous. "Who'd pay money for your location?"

"Plenty of people," Nik said, glaring over his shoulder. "There's a lot of folks in Rentfree who don't like me. Why do you think I didn't want to come?"

"You could have told me that earlier," I grumbled, focusing on my feet to keep my pointy heels from getting stuck in any of the hundreds of cracks as Nik pushed us down the road.

Rentfree being Rentfree, the streets had moved while we'd been shopping, putting us several blocks further to the north and west of the gate than we'd been originally. The longer walk combined with the fast pace was murder on my poor toes, but I knew better than to complain when Nik looked like he did now. I did breathe a sigh of relief when we passed through the metal gate that marked our reentry into the normal DFZ, though.

"Not there yet," Nik warned me, but he did slow down, offering his arm again to help me hobble across the street into the brightly lit parking deck where we'd left his car.

At least it wasn't crowded. Rentfree was still kicking behind us, but most of the tourists had already gone back to their hotels, leaving the deck blissfully quiet and empty. Nik's car was the only one left when we reached the top level, gleaming like a black jewel under the security floodlights. I was already imagining flopping into the seat and yanking off my shoes when Nik suddenly stopped.

When I snapped my head up to see why, a huge guy stepped out from behind the thick metal lamppost next to Nik's car. A second later, he was joined by three other dudes who'd been squatting out of sight by the safety railing that kept people from walking off the edge. None of the newcomers were as big as the first guy, but they still looked salty as hell, and they were *all* cybered. Not in the subtle, classy way Nik was, either. These guys were your stereotypical chromeheads with giant metal muscles bulging out of their tank tops. I saw that tacky, hyper-masculine foolishness every day in the Underground, but I'd never had four giant examples of the form glaring straight at me before, and I had to admit, it was pretty intimidating.

"Hey, Mad Dog," the biggest guy said, stepping forward to put one giant boot on the coupe's rear bumper. "This your car?"

I saw Nik's jaw tic when the idiot pushed down hard enough to make the car wobble, but he kept his cool. "Who's asking?"

The big guy lifted his lip in a sneer to reveal a mouth full of shiny, sharpened silver teeth. "You killed my brother."

"That doesn't answer my question," Nik replied calmly. "You'll have to be more specif—"

Big-and-Ugly jerked his arm up, yanking a cannon of a pistol out of his waistband. His buddies did the same, but none of them actually managed to get their arms up before Nik grabbed me and lurched to the side, cramming us both behind the cement base of the giant security floodlight directly to our left.

I yelped as bullets pinged off the metal lamppost above me. Being mostly metal, Nik was less concerned but *way* more pissed off.

"Who are those guys?" I hissed, hunkering down behind the cement anchor.

"Don't know, don't care," he snarled, pulling his own gun out of its holster under his arm. "Stay there. I'll be right back."

I nodded, sliding the bulletproof coat he'd loaned me up to protect my head.

As the armored cloth came up around my face, it suddenly occurred to me that Nik was going to kill those men. I mean, I was totally cool with that since they were the ones who'd jumped us and started shooting for no damn reason, but it was still a shocking thing to realize. Recent history aside, this sort of thing didn't normally happen to me. I'd grown up in a dragon's household, so I was no stranger to conflict, but my dad had always been careful to keep the actual violence far away from us. I'd never even been shot at before the incident at Dr. Lyle's old house. Now I was caught in my second gunfight in so many weeks, and it just felt like a bridge too far.

Thankfully, Nik didn't seem to share my anxiety. He stepped out from behind the lamppost smooth as silk, lifting his gun like he'd already done this a thousand times to calmly peg the closest attacker in the knee. I didn't know how he knew the guy wasn't cybered there—if it was just a lucky shot or if Nik could read more from the fit of the man's tight jeans than I could—but the dude went down screaming. Nik had already moved on in any case, ignoring the bullets pinging off his metal chest as he turned and shot the next thug in the foot. That one, too, went down screaming, and I breathed a sigh of relief. It was starting to look as if the fight was already over when the big guy dropped his gun and charged, body-slamming Nik so hard they both went down with a *clang* that shook the pavement.

Swearing under my breath, I scrambled around the pole to get out of the way. A few feet from where I'd been hiding, Nik and the leader were rolling around on the pavement, but while Nik was clearly the superior opponent, the big guy was *big*. I didn't know if he had leg implants or what, but he was a good foot taller than Nik and at least a hundred pounds heavier. All that extra bulk made him pretty slow, but every punch Nik dodged came down hard enough to crater the parking deck's stained cement. One miss and it would all be over.

"Do you want me to call the cops?" Sibyl whispered in my ear.

I snorted. "This close to Rentfree? Only if you've got bribes to spare."

"We have to do something," my AI said frantically. "Mr. Kos's brains are going to get splattered all over the pavement!"

I actually thought Nik was doing pretty well. He was dodging the big man's blows as if he could see them coming a mile away, all the while working his body around his opponent's for a hold. It was still terrifying to watch, of course, but I'd seen Nik take down an entire professional merc team on his own before. This guy was huge and augmented to the gills, but he was amateur hour when it came to things you couldn't buy, like skill. Nik almost had him in a chokehold already. I was getting ready to make a dash for the car the moment Nik gave the signal when a huge, hairy arm wrapped around my waist from behind.

"Gotcha!"

I gasped in surprise as the arm yanked upward, lifting me bodily off the ground. My next instinct was to scream, but I didn't want to distract Nik and get him killed, so I bit it back, craning my neck back to see the grinning, gap-toothed face of the one thug Nik *hadn't* shot and I'd totally forgotten to keep track of.

"Easy, girly," the man said, pressing his gun into my back when I started to kick. I froze at the feeling of a muzzle poking my kidney, and the man grinned wider, leaning out from behind the lamppost to shout something at his boss.

I didn't hear what. I was too busy swearing up a storm in my head as Nik and the big guy both turned to see me strung up like a snared chicken. How had I been so stupid? How hadn't I seen this coming? I was going to get Nik killed. He'd already released his chokehold and put up his hands. The big guy responded by elbowing him in the face. Nik moved enough to avoid a broken nose, but he still got knocked onto his back, which was where I lost it.

"Opal!" Sibyl said sharply into my earpiece. "Don't be rash!"

"Screw that!" I yelled back. This was my fault. We'd been doing great, and then I'd let myself get grabbed like an *idiot.* But like hell was I going to be the mistake that got Nik killed. Like hell was I putting up with *any* of this. I'd just figured out how to make money despite my curse. I was closer to winning my freedom than I'd ever been, and these assholes thought they could come in here and grab me like I was actually some hapless rich girl? Screw that! I was a mage! I was a dragon's daughter! And I was not going to be defeated by something this *stupid*!

With that, I threw my magic as wide as it would go. It hurt even worse than when I'd instinctively tried to grab power after Maggie surprised me, but this time I didn't care. I was sick of this shit. Sick of feeling helpless, sick of always being the weakest link. Sick enough to ignore the dire warnings my body was giving me and grab the magic anyway.

I barely got any on my first try. The pain made me clumsy, and the whole spell fell apart before I could even begin it. My second try went a bit better, but again, I couldn't hold on.

Ironically, it wasn't because of the hurt. I could grit through that. *My* problem was with the part of me that actually grabbed the magic, the bit I thought of as my mental "hand." No matter how hard I pushed, it simply refused to work. I could feel the magic just fine, but handling it felt like trying to scoop sand with broken fingers. No matter how hard I tried, I just couldn't get it together, and that made me furious.

By this point, the guy holding me had already carried me over to his boss. At our feet, Nik had been forced onto his knees while the big guy put a gun—not even his gun, *Nik's* gun, which the boss had grabbed off the ground—to his head. He was delivering some big speech about payback and dying like a dog, but I was too mad to pay actual attention. Nik didn't seem to be listening, either. He was looking at me, his eyes flicking pointedly between my face and the guy holding me like he was trying to give me a signal, but I didn't know what it meant. All I knew was that I was failing, and if I didn't quit it, I was going to get us all killed. I was going to get *Nik* killed, specifically, which was absolutely unforgivable. He hadn't even wanted to come here tonight. He'd only done it to help me, and I'd be damned if I let him get shot in the head for that because I was a garbage mage who couldn't cast a proper spell even when she had a gun jabbed into her back.

With that final enraged thought, I shoved my magic as hard as I could. It hurt so bad I blacked out a little, but I didn't let up. I just kept pushing, forcing that damned broken hand to spread wider and wider, because if I was going to die here, I was taking these bastards with me. I grabbed more magic than I'd ever grabbed before, more than I'd known I could, and still I kept going. I didn't know what I was going to do with all that magic yet, but I knew for certain I could only do it once. I *had* to make it count, so I shoved the instincts screaming at me to step out of the way and *pushed*, sucking magic out of the air until even the chromeheads noticed. Pulled until the air itself felt thin and my skin felt tight from holding it all inside me.

Through the haze of pain and power, I could dimly see the big thug gesturing wildly between his guy and me. His big chromed mouth was moving, but I couldn't hear anything over the roar of magic in my ears. A few moments later, even the hurt went away. Magic was all I could feel now, all I could taste and smell and see. I hadn't even realized humans *could* see magic until it was dancing across my vision like the Northern Lights. There was no way I could put so much magic into a spell, especially since I hadn't even drawn a circle yet, but it had to go somewhere. It certainly couldn't stay in me. I could already feel the overwhelming power dissolving me from the inside out. If I didn't send it somewhere fast, it would eat me alive. So I did the only thing I could do at this point. The only move I had left.

I let it go.

I'm not entirely sure what happened after that. There was a flash of light and a wave of heat, and then I was lying on my back ten feet away wondering what the hell had just happened.

Oddly, the first thing I noticed was the smell of something burning. That struck me as important, so I feebly lifted my head, but it still took several seconds for my eyes to focus enough to see that all my clothes were scorched. Not burned—my silk tank top and skirt were still in one piece—but the fabric was blackened as if it had been baked under a broiler.

Wincing at the waste, I reached up to rub my throbbing head only to discover that my face was wet with blood. Really, though, that was to be expected. That was the biggest discharge I'd ever had. It was only natural something would break.

Since my shirt was ruined anyway, I used it to wipe my face clean. My nose and ears were tender enough to make me wince when I touched them, but weirdly, my magic didn't hurt nearly as bad as I'd expected. After a blast like that, I'd have thought I'd be blacking out from the agony, but my magic actually hurt less than it had all day. Curious, I reached out a tentative finger to prod the swirls of agitated magic left over from the power I'd dumped. At least, that was the plan. When I issued the mental command to move, though, nothing responded.

Trying not to panic, I did it again, but the result was the same. The signal was going out. There was just no answer at the other end. It felt like I was trying to move a limb that was no longer there, like the part of me that grabbed magic was simply…gone.

Now I started to panic. I sat up in a rush, closing my eyes as I moved through each step of the proper casting pattern my tutors had drilled into me since I was a kid. I even imagined a line of kabocha pumpkins to help myself along, but it didn't change a thing. This was even worse than when moving magic had felt like trying to force a sprained muscle. At least the pain had been *something*, but now there was no feedback at all. If I concentrated hard enough, I could actually feel the part of my soul that reached out for magic hanging loose inside me like a broken stick, and it was freaking me out. I'd never had a panic attack before, but I was pretty sure I was on the verge of one when I heard Nik groan.

The plaintive sound slapped me out of my downward spiral. I scrambled to my feet, looking around in a rush to see that everyone else in the lot was down. The guy who'd grabbed me had actually been blown all the way to the opposite side of the top deck, while Nik and the big dude were both lying on their backs in a shower of broken glass under the now-dark floodlight. They all looked horrible, their faces bloody just like mine. That should have freaked me out even more, but it was actually a relief. The emergency let me focus on something other than the existential terror of what I'd done to my magic, and I jumped on it with both feet.

"Nik!" I hissed frantically, kicking the broken glass out of the way so I could kneel beside him. "*Nik!*"

He groaned again, eyelids fluttering open, and I sagged in relief. "Are you okay?"

His unfocused gaze slid over me, completely uncomprehending, and I swore. Dude was backlashed to hell. To be expected, really, considering the shock wave I'd unleashed, but it was finally starting to hit me just how stupidly reckless I'd been. I'd been so focused on my own anger that I hadn't even considered what a blast like that would do to everyone else. My habit of doing stupid crap like this meant that I was inured to the worst of my magic's effects, but backlash always hit nonmages way harder since they had no ability to protect themselves. I could have blown Nik to bits or baked his brain.

I wasn't entirely sure I hadn't. He was still blinking drunkenly, head going from side to side like a baby's. His eyes followed my hand when I passed it over his face, but he couldn't respond to basic commands, which struck me as a very bad sign.

"Sibyl," I said, frantically using my ruined shirt to clean the blood off Nik's face so he wouldn't look so much like he was dying. "What's our chances of getting an ambulance up here?

"Slim to none," my AI replied despairingly. "I called the moment you blasted yourself, but dispatch is demanding payment upfront plus a nonrefundable security deposit for driving this close to Rentfree, and there's not enough money in your bank account to cover any of it."

I closed my eyes with a hiss. Nonrefundable security deposit for an ambulance. Sometimes I really hated this city.

Muttering under my breath about stupid capitalist dystopias, I gave Nik's face one last swipe before peeling off my ruined shirt and tossing it away. This left me in only my bralette, but while the pink fabric was obviously underwear, it covered all the important bits and wasn't soaked in blood. It was a sad commentary on my life that that was a step up, but here we were.

"Don't worry," I told Nik. "I'm going to get us out of here. You just stay put and rest. I've got this."

He was already lying still as a statue, so that last part was only for me, but saying it still made me feel better as I reached into his pockets to start searching for his keys.

It was a hairy procedure. In addition to his gun, which the big guy had dropped on the ground when he'd gone down, Nik carried a lot of other dangerous stuff. His pockets were always full of knives, cutting wire, and antipickpocket snap traps. Reaching into them felt like sticking my hand into a badger's den, but I didn't have a choice. Thanks to Nik's near-religious aversion to trusting AIs, his car was completely analogue, which meant no remote unlock. It was keys or nothing.

After a *very* cautious pat down, I found the ring in his front jeans pocket. Clutching the metal keys in my fist, I stood up and ran over to his car, unlocking the door and plopping myself down in the driver's seat. I was looking for the start button when I realized there wasn't one. This stupid antique still had a key crank. It also had three pedals and a manual gearshift in the center console, none of which I knew how to use.

"Oh, for the love of—"

"I'm on it," Sibyl said. "Get your goggles."

I did as she said, thanking my few remaining lucky stars that I hadn't blasted my goggles along with everything else. Unlike the lamps, though, my headset had been made for mages, and the quality showed. The moment I slid them over my eyes, a video called "How to Drive Stick" popped up in my AR with the player already skipped past the intro to the point where the actual instructions began.

"Bless you," I told my AI.

"I know, I know, I'm amazing," Sibyl said. "Just watch it quick. The big guy's starting to stir."

The guy who'd been trying to pound Nik into the pavement still looked flattened to me, but his eyes were open and looking around, which was a good sign for him and a terrible one for me. Shaking with nerves, I swept my hand through the air to activate the video, watching it at double speed to save time. When I felt reasonably sure I had the basic concept of shifting gears down, I hopped out again and ran back over to Nik, who was now awake enough to curl himself into a miserable ball.

"Hey," I said, picking his gun up off the ground and tucking it back into his holster before kneeling beside him. "I know you probably don't want to move, but we *really* need to go."

"Go where?" he asked, slurring the words so badly I could hardly understand.

"Just grab on to me," I said.

That command at least he had no problem with. He wrapped his arms around me in a bear hug, dragging me to the ground beside him.

This turned out to be an unexpectedly serious complication. I moved furniture for a living, so I was a lot stronger than I looked, but Nik was *heavy*. I suppose that was only to be expected of someone who was at least half metal, but even after I got my feet back under me, I couldn't lift him more than a few inches off the pavement.

"Nik, buddy," I panted. "You're going to have to work with me here."

He did not want to cooperate, but I was persistent, and eventually I got him to his feet. The walk to the car was even hairier. He kept stumbling, and I wasn't strong enough to catch him, but somehow we made it without falling. The big guy was starting to push himself up by the time I got Nik into the passenger seat and buckled in, so I didn't waste any more time. As soon as I was sure Nik wasn't going to fall out of the car, I closed the door on him and raced back to the driver's side, cranking the key in the ignition as I'd seen Nik do dozens of times before. I must have gotten the motion right, because the car started with a throaty roar that was both thrilling and intimidating.

"Okay," I said nervously, putting my feet on the clutch and the brake and my hands on the wheel and the stick shift. "Let's do this."

"You'll be fine," Sibyl assured me. "People used to do this all the time."

I nodded, lifting my foot off the clutch while tapping the gas pedal just as I'd seen the guy do in the video...

And instantly stalled.

"Dammit!" I cried, turning the car off so I could start it again. "Whose idea was it to design a car like this?!"

"Not to put more pressure on you," Sibyl said as she rewound the video to the part about first gear. "But you need to move a little faster."

She put an indicator on my vision, and I turned to see the leader pushing himself to his feet, wiping the blood from his face in angry swipes as he looked around for Nik.

"Shit, shit, shit," I muttered, getting all my limbs back into the ridiculous starting positions this stupid car demanded. "Don't mess up. Don't mess—"

I didn't. There were some alarming grinding noises, but the engine didn't stall this time as I let up on the clutch and hit the gas, shifting into second gear as I jerked us forward. And nearly hit the wall.

"*Shit!*" I cried again, cranking the wheel to the left. The resulting hard turn sent us squealing across the lot and nearly caused another stall, but I saved it at the last second, straightening out and hitting the gas to send us scooting down the ramp into the lower decks, leaving the cyber asshole screaming threats at my taillights.

Getting out of the deck was an adventure. I swear I almost hit every single support pole, but all those years of driving games must have been good for something, because I made it to the front gate without actually putting a dent in Nik's car. I stalled again when I had to stop for the turn onto the actual street outside, but thankfully all the other cars were self-driving, so no one crashed into us before I got the engine going again, scraping the transmission with a horrible sound as I frantically tried to get back into the right gear.

"I am *so* glad you're not conscious for this," I told Nik as we started down the street in fits and jerks.

"Just try not to grind the gears so hard," Sibyl suggested. "Remember: gentle touches."

I was way too panicked for gentle. The only good thing I could say about the drive was that at least I was too busy trying not to run into things to worry about my magic, which *still* wasn't responding. Fortunately, while it was farther than I would have liked, the drive to Nik's new apartment wasn't complicated. There were a lot of streetlights to get through, causing me to stall three more times, but I didn't have to deal with any on-ramps, roundabouts, or left turns before I arrived at his towering gray apartment complex.

I went straight to the empty spaces at the back of his lot. Given Nik's lack of coordination, I probably should have tried for something closer, but I didn't trust myself to slide between two cars without wrecking all three of us. The distance would be annoying, but I didn't want to draw more attention by causing a scene, and I *really* didn't want to dent Nik's car. He was going to be mad enough already over the backlash. If I damaged his baby, he might never forgive me.

"He's not going to be mad," Sibyl said as I cut the engine. "You just saved his life. Not that I approve of your methods, but that big guy was almost certainly going to blow his brains out if you hadn't intervened."

"I don't think it counts as saving if I'm the one who put him in that situation," I told her grimly. "He was doing fine before I got caught."

Sibyl wisely kept her comments to herself after that. Nodding approvingly, I walked around to the passenger side, opening the door very carefully. Nik had been leaning on it pretty hard, and seatbelt or no, I didn't want to risk dumping him on the ground. When I got it open, though, he was awake and looking around, which was a huge relief.

"Hey," I said, pushing my goggles up onto my head so I could see him without my interfaces. "You okay?"

He blinked at me in confusion, then his face split into the goofiest expression I'd ever seen him make. "Heyopal," he slurred. "What are we doing at my place?"

I winced. *Definitely* not okay.

"Let's just go slow," I said in a soothing voice, leaning down to slide my arm under his. "Stand on three. One—"

He shot straight up, knocking me off my feet. The resulting imbalance sent us both careening, but while Nik definitely wasn't firing on all cylinders yet, there was nothing wrong with his reflexes. I'd barely started to fall before he caught me, wrapping one arm around my waist while his other hand grabbed the top of his car door. The fiasco ended with my body pressed flush against Nik's. I was trying to extricate myself when the arm he'd thrown around my waist tightened.

"Wait," he said, his goofy expression transforming into one of amazed wonder. "Did I take you home?"

The excitement that crept into his voice at that prospect made my whole face burn. Even my still-pumping adrenaline wasn't enough to stop me from noticing the intimacy of our position. I'd never seen Nik smile like that before, either. He was beaming down at me like our current entanglement was the best thing that had ever happened to him, making me forget everything I'd been about to say. I actually started to smile back at him before I remembered this was all my fault.

"Actually," I replied with maximum professionalism, gently but firmly pushing myself out of his arms. "I'm taking *you* home. You need—"

"I'm so glad," Nik said over me, letting go of the car to slide his fingers into my hair. "Do you know how long I've wanted to do this?"

I frowned. "Wanted to do wha—"

Nik moved like a shot, bending down before I realized what was happening to press his lips to mine. The sudden contact shocked me so much I jumped, but he had both hands on me now, and he held me still.

Then he pulled me closer, curving his shoulders to enclose me against his chest as he kissed me with a gentle, hungry thoroughness.

I'm ashamed to say I let him. Sibyl was squawking all kinds of very appropriate-sounding warnings in my ear, but I was too distracted to pay attention. It had been a long time since I'd been kissed. Nik was doing a damn good job of it, too. His metal chest was a wall against mine, hard and immovable, but his hands were gentle on my waist and hair, and his lips were earnest, teasing mine with the promise of better things to come.

Things I absolutely could not have.

"Whoa," I said, wrenching myself away.

Nik looked at me like I'd just dumped him out of paradise. "Whoa?"

"We can't do this," I said firmly. As much for me as for him, because *whoa* was my suddenly lust-addled brain coming up with some bad suggestions. Hot, but bad. "I hit you with a lot of magic and you're not in your right mind. I'm very sorry about that, by the way, but we really need to get you to bed."

"I like bed," Nik purred, closing the distance I'd just made.

He stopped when I put a hand on his chest. "Nik, no," I said in my firmest voice. "I'm not taking advantage of you while you're drunk."

"I'm not *drunk*," he said, mortally offended. "I have a poison scrubber. I can't get drunk anymore."

I stared at him in horror. Unable to get drunk? Why would anyone do that to themselves?! I was dying to ask him, but Nik was already bending back down to nuzzle his face in my hair. Clearly, curiosity would have to wait until he could focus for more than five seconds.

"You're magic drunk," I specified, pushing him away again. "It's called backlash. I overloaded your brain, and you're going to be scrambled for a while until it can recover. Again, *really* sorry about that, but what you need most right now is rest. And water. Lots of water."

Nik didn't look pleased with this assessment, but he let me slide my shoulder back under his and steer him across the parking lot toward his apartment building.

The stairs down to his basement unit were tricky. He'd handled the flat pavement okay, but steps were another matter, and as I'd discovered earlier, dude was *heavy*. He was also surprisingly tall. Nik always kept such a low profile, walking with a slouch and keeping his arms close to his body and wearing that bulky jacket that hid his shape, it was easy to forget he was actually a pretty big guy. I didn't know why he'd want to hide that. As someone who'd been five-foot-four since she was twelve, being big seemed like an advantage you'd want to show off. Right now, though, his size was working against us.

I went down first, staying one step below him at all times with my hand firmly on the metal railing so I could—not catch him; there was no way I could manage that without one of us breaking something—but at least help control his fall. Thankfully, there was no need. Despite some wobbly moments, we made it to the bottom without serious incident.

"Here we go," I said, digging his keys out of my bag and trying them one at a time until I found the one that opened his vault of a front door. "Let's get you inside."

Just like everything else in our lives, Nik's apartment had changed a lot in the last week. It was still a barren bunker when I switched on the light but not quite as bad as it had been the first time I'd walked in. There were two plates in the drying rack by the sink now, and two folding chairs at the card table, both hard-won concessions he'd finally deemed necessary given how often I ate with him these days. I'd also gotten him a floor lamp since I couldn't stand his harsh overhead lighting, but the biggest change was the ugly orange couch pushed up against his previously bare living room wall.

"Is that the couch from the slug shop?"

Nik nodded, and I stared at him in shock. "I thought you didn't want it."

"I didn't," he said, leaning harder on my shoulder. "I hate furniture. It's just more junk to move. But you wanted somewhere to sit, so I kept it."

I went still. "You kept a couch for me?"

He shrugged and lurched forward, forcing me to scramble as we landed in a semicontrolled collapse on the couch's hideous but soft cushions. When I was sure he wasn't going to fall off onto the floor, I ran into the kitchen and grabbed one of his two glasses, filling it with water from the sink before hurrying back.

"Here," I said, pressing the cup of water into his hands. "You might not actually be drunk, but hydration will still help with the backlash hangover."

He was in for a brutal one. This was by far the worst reaction I'd ever seen to magical overload. I didn't know if that was due to some complication with Nik's cyberware or if I'd just hit him harder than I was giving myself credit for, but I felt guilty as hell about it. Whether it had saved his life or not, Nik didn't deserve this. He'd done nothing but help me tonight, but I'd been too much of a fail mage to help him in return when he needed it. He deserved so much better in a partner, but I was the one who was here now, and I was determined to do right by him in this at least.

"Drink," I ordered. "And then you need to sleep. You'll feel a lot better tomorrow."

"Will you stay with me?" he asked after he'd drained the glass dry.

I froze, unsure how to respond. Given how he'd been acting earlier, that might have been a proposition, but it didn't sound like one. Nik was no longer acting romantic. He mostly looked tired, sick, and scared, and no wonder. Backlash was terrifying even when you knew what was going on, but this was Nik's first time. He wasn't even a mage, and I'd hit him with a tidal wave.

As much as I wanted to stay by his side until the damage I'd caused was over, though, I didn't know if I could. My broken magic was still hanging loose inside me, rattling every time I moved. It still didn't hurt, but there was a growing feeling of wrongness in my gut, a sense of impending doom I couldn't ignore.

But I couldn't leave him like this.

"I'll stay until you fall asleep," I compromised. "Is that okay?"

He nodded and lay back on the couch. I was stepping away to go get him a blanket from his bedroom when Nik grabbed my hand.

"Don't leave."

I nodded and sank down on the floor instead, clutching his hand in both of mine. The pressure seemed to calm him, because he relaxed into the cushions. A few moments later, his breathing had evened out into sleep.

I kept hold of his hand anyway, clinging as hard as I dared, because I was scared, too. I'd *really* messed up this time, so much so that I didn't even know all of the consequences yet. Now that I had no more disasters to distract me, the feeling that something was incredibly, horribly, terminally wrong with me was getting more urgent by the minute. Even so, I couldn't leave yet. So long as Nik looked afraid, I stayed at his side, sitting on the cement floor until my legs were frozen and my feet were asleep.

Finally, when his face had relaxed into normal-looking slumber and my own internal problems had built too high to ignore, I rose silently to my feet. Placing his keys on the table where he could see them, I let myself out, using the small lock on the interior door handle to seal the apartment behind me as I made my way back up the stairs to the parking lot, where Sibyl already had an autocab waiting.

CHAPTER 5

The first thing I did when I got in the tiny, two-seat autocab was dig the card Peter had given me out of my wallet and show it to the camera. This early in the morning, the only taxis working were the old, cruddy ones, so it took a few tries before the image recognition kicked in, but eventually the destination light turned green and we puttered off. Since the card used coordinates rather than a street address, I had no idea where I was going. That wasn't *too* unusual—street numbers didn't mean much in a city that moved around whenever she chose—but there was normally at least a designation saying if we were going up or down. The only thing listed on this card was a string of numbers, though, so I was completely in the dark until the cab drove me out from under the Skyways into the open-air neighborhood still known as University Heights.

University Heights was one of those weird throwback parts of the DFZ. The university was long gone, as were most of the houses, but the neighborhood still retained its old Detroit name because, unlike the rest of the city, it had never been redeveloped. There were no high-efficiency apartment blocks, no superscrapers or elevated highways. Just the brick skeletons of collapsing houses listing in the shadow of the forest that had grown out of lawns left neglected for the last eighty years.

It was a peaceful, quiet, postapocalyptic mystery of a place. As one of the last stretches of land left where you could stand on the ground and see the sky, it should have been the hottest real estate in the city, but the DFZ refused to build anything out here. She also refused to open the land up to development by anyone else—quite violently, sometimes—and so far as I'd heard, no one knew why.

When I'd studied up on the history of the DFZ before I'd moved here, I'd read that this area used to be called Reclamation Land, a safe refuge for nature spirits who sympathized with Algonquin's antihuman, antidragon zealotry. Back when the city was still ruled by the Lady of the Great Lakes, no human had been allowed to set foot in this place, but that was twenty years ago. Algonquin had long since been kicked back to her lakes by the Spirit of the DFZ, and the vengeful spirits she'd gathered were gone. Without their influence, University Heights should have been no different from any other neighborhood. At least, that was what I thought until I stepped out of the cab.

The moment my foot hit the cracked pavement, a tremor went through my body. My ability to move magic might have been broken, but I could still feel it just fine, and hoo boy, there was a *lot*. It wasn't the usual soft, slightly greasy magic of the Underground either, or the slick corporate stuff you got up on the Skyways. This magic was thick and woodsy, a cool, wet, wild sort of power you normally never felt in cities. It was so different, so strange, that I was amazed I'd never heard about the phenomenon before. Since there was no development in this area, I'd never had cause to visit as a Cleaner, but it felt like an oversight that I'd never been sent out here as a student.

On second thought, though, maybe it *wasn't* so strange. The DFZ had more magical universities than any other city in the world, but they were all Thaumaturgical institutions. Even the Institute for Magical Arts insisted on spellwork for everything, and the entire purpose of spellwork was to translate bumpy, variable natural magic into stable, homogeneous power. That was hard enough to pull off in a city where the ambient magic levels could vary between blocks. In a place *this* wild, though, homogenization was virtually impossible. You'd need a heavy-duty circle just to get the power here stable enough for spellwork to process, which was a lot of work considering there was plenty of perfectly fine, normal magic just a few hundred feet away.

But while no one seemed to be tapping Reclamation Land's weird power, it was being monitored. There were magical sample collection sites and sensors scattered all over the dead-end road where the cab dropped me off. But while there were machines aplenty, there were no people here at all. Granted, it was pretty late at night—or early in the morning—but the emptiness still felt creepy. The DFZ was one of the world's densest cities.

Even with the population divided between the Skyways and the Underground, there was always *someone* around. Here, though, there was nothing. Just the chirping of crickets in the muggy summer air and the soft whir of the cab's electric engine as it drove itself away, leaving me standing alone in the dark at the edge of the woods.

Swallowing a little, I pulled my goggles back down over my face so I could use my night vision. When my AR came up, though, the feed was staticky and slow to respond, as if the mana-contacts weren't making proper contact with my skin, which couldn't be true. Between my goggles and the receiver tucked into my left ear, Sibyl had seven contact points to access my natural internal magic and create the images I saw as AR or access my surface thoughts. The contacts on my goggles were the new adaptable sort, too, capable of connecting anywhere along the band whether I was wearing them properly or not. It should have been impossible for my goggles not to create perfect AR so long as they were in physical contact with my body, and yet the lines remained.

"Don't ask me," Sibyl said when I pointed this out. "Everything's working fine. It's this place. The magic here is disruptive."

I frowned and looked again at the card Peter had given me. According to my map—which was updated by the city in real time—the Shaman's office should have been directly ahead, but there was no more road. The dot on my map was simply off in the woods, which looked like a mistake. The coordinates system was usually pretty accurate, though, and if there was anyone who was going to live in Reclamation Land, it *would* be a Shamanic soul healer.

I just hoped they were open. It was now nearly three in the morning, not exactly normal business hours, but the card in my hand said the place was "open 24/7 to the right people." I didn't know what that meant, but the growing wrongness inside me *definitely* felt like an emergency, and I had nowhere else to go. It wasn't even about cost for once. If I went to the ER at a real hospital, my dad would find out for sure, and then there'd be no amount of deals or honor that would keep him from swooping in and snapping me up. This was the only lead I had that I didn't think my dad would find out about, so I sucked it up and walked into the woods, hoping against hope that I wouldn't end up covered in ticks.

Ten minutes of hiking later, I realized I should have been more worried about my feet. My heels were utterly incompatible with Reclamation Land's soft, loamy forest floor. Eventually, I just took them off and went barefoot, carrying my muddy heels in one hand as I padded cautiously across the pine needles. My AR quit working entirely shortly after that. My phone still had signal, which meant Sibyl could send me messages and update my map on the LCD screen so I didn't get lost, but anything that depended on interaction with my internal magic to work— my AI's thought processing, my interfaces, my goggles' eye-tracking software and adaptive filters, even the bridge program that connected the tiny computer in my earbud to my phone's much more powerful processor—was completely out of commission. The whole thing was crazy. Mana-contacts were the oldest form of magic/technology integration, almost as old as modern magic itself. They were in every device, and they were so famously stable that hospitals used them for monitoring. They didn't just "short out." Whatever was here apparently didn't know that, though, because all my equipment was scrambled.

"This can't be happening," I muttered, pulling out my now-useless earpiece.

"What's that?" Sibyl said from my speakers. "I'm audio only right now, so you'll have to speak up."

I shook my head and dropped my earbud into my bag, looking back over my shoulder at the forest behind me, which was now as dark as the woods in front. The ambient light from the city behind me had already vanished, which felt way too fast to me. My phone's light also looked oddly dull. The normally blinding LED flash barely illuminated the leaf litter under my naked feet here, forcing me to go even slower as I wove my way between the trees, which were rapidly getting larger. As the trunks grew thicker, the magic floating around them swelled, filling the air until I felt like I was having to physically push my way forward.

It was like nothing I'd ever experienced before. If I'd still been able to move magic, I wouldn't even have had to reach out to cast here. This magic was so thick it was pushing into *me*, so much so that I was starting to feel crushed. It was pretty terrifying in my current condition, but according to the map on my phone, I was almost at the coordinates. The Shaman's office should have been right in front of me, but I didn't see any lights or paths or signs. Just dark woods stretching endlessly in all directions and the stars glittering between the branches overhead. An astonishing number of stars, actually, considering how close we were to the city.

By this point, it was obvious to me that this was no normal magical hot spot. Whatever was going on here, there was serious power at play. Ironically, that actually made me feel better about my current mission. I'd been worried Peter had sent me to see a quack, but anyone who could work in the middle of this much magic had to be the real deal. What *kind* of deal, or if it was one I even wanted, was yet to be determined, but the potential alone was enough to keep me going far past where any reasonable person would have turned back.

At least the journey gave me time to think about what had happened with Nik. Not that that was necessarily better than the existential fear of being trapped in an apparently endless magical forest, but there was only so much you could worry about concerning woods that never changed. Long walks always made me broody, and stupid as it was considering how many other problems I had on my plate, the incident with Nik would not get out of my head. Not the threats-to-my-life parts, either. That was something a sensible person would worry about. This was me, and my stupid brain was obsessed over what had happened in his apartment parking lot.

I pressed my fingers to my lips. I could remember every second of that kiss with vivid clarity, but my feelings about it were a chaos that careened wildly between two camps.

The first was good old-fashioned giddiness. Nik had kissed me! Not that I'd never been kissed before, but the boys who'd done so either hadn't known who my dad was (and generally vanished the moment they found out) or they'd done it *because* of my dad in the hope that seducing the Dragon's Opal would land them money or fame or whatever else they thought a dragon could provide for them. The ambitious guys usually lasted even less time than the ones who got scared off because I didn't take kindly to being used, but Nik was a new category. He knew who my dad was, how broke I was, *and* what a hot mess my life was, but he'd kissed me anyway.

Or, at least, he'd kissed me while he was drunk.

This was where my brain took a nosedive into the *second* camp, which was doom. I was screwed. Nik had kissed me while drunk, and now things were going to get super awkward, because that was what *always* happened after spontaneously drunken kisses. What if he'd only done it because he was smashed? What if he woke up tomorrow and regretted it? What if he *didn't* regret it?

That was the one that actually scared me the most, and not because I didn't like Nik. Now that I was free to think about it, I could admit I'd developed a pretty massive crush on him over the last week, and why not? Nik was hot, reliable, hardworking, honest, we got along, and he didn't judge me for having a very screwed-up family situation. That was a *way* better start than most of the guys I'd dated, but Nik wasn't someone I'd met online or a friend or even just a business partner. He was the rope keeping me out of the abyss. Even with the gold hack I'd discovered, there was no way I could earn enough to pay back my entire debt before the end of the month by myself. I didn't know if it was possible even with his help, but I absolutely could not do it on my own. I *needed* Nik, and that made this kiss a huge problem, because no guy I'd kissed had ever stuck around.

That was not hyperbole. My record with men was an unbroken line going straight down. I knew that fear of my dad had run off a lot of them back in Korea, but even after I moved to the DFZ, where I could hide the fact that I was *that* Opal Yong-ae, I'd never had a relationship that lasted longer than two weeks. I didn't know if it was the guys or me, if I was too demanding or too weird or too focused on earning money, but as Sibyl had so adroitly pointed out during my dinner with Peter, the pattern was clear: Opal likes boy, boy leaves. And while it might have been unfair to lump Nik in with all the others since he was so different, I couldn't afford to take a chance right now. Until my debt was paid, I needed everything to be smooth and drama free, which definitely didn't include reckless, magic-drunk kisses after life-threatening events.

But done was done. There was nothing for it now but to cross my fingers and hope Nik had been so drunk he wouldn't remember. That made me sad to think about—again, back to Camp One—but it'd be better for everyone if that sudden, remarkable, glorious kiss lived on only in my fantasies. For now, I had to focus on the real world, where I was still lost in an endless forest with blistered feet and broken magic. Even my cell phone was starting to give out. My map didn't seem to be updating anymore, and Sibyl hadn't piped in with helpful commentary in a suspiciously long time. I was seriously contemplating saying screw it and turning around when I spotted a light in the distance.

It was a lantern. Not an electric one either, but an old-fashioned glass-and-oil job with a bright, clear flame shining like gold in the dark forest directly ahead of me.

Hopes rising, I ran forward, ignoring the pine needles poking my bruised feet as I charged toward the only sign of progress I'd found yet. But while I was clearly covering ground, the lantern I was running toward didn't get any bigger. Like the spot on my no-longer-functioning map, it never seemed to get closer no matter how fast I went. It was like one of those awful stress dreams where you run and run and never get anywhere. After fifteen more minutes, I was ninety percent convinced that I'd fallen asleep on the cab ride over and this *was* a dream. It was the only logical explanation I could think of for what was happening, but I still didn't stop.

I should have. If this was a dream, I needed to wake up and get out of the cab before the meter sucked down what was left of my bank account. If it *wasn't* a dream, well, that was even worse. The walk before I spotted the lamp had been suspiciously long, but journeys through the woods at night always felt longer when you didn't know where you were going. This, however, was undeniable. Unlike the dot on my map, which was never a sure thing in a moving city, I could *see* that the lamp was not moving despite all my running, and I'd read enough folklore to know that forests in which you walked and walked and never got anywhere were generally *not* places you wanted to be. People scoffed when I applied fairy-tale logic to real life, but folk stories were how our ancestors passed on important magical knowledge in a world where magic had ceased to exist. Now that the drought was over and magic had come back, those tales were all relevant again.

That was what I'd argued in my graduate thesis, anyway. I didn't think I'd *actually* stumbled into an enchanted forest—this was central Michigan, not medieval Europe—but woods that went on forever were a persistent trope across multiple cultures. The fact that so many different people told the same story suggested such forests had once been a common occurrence. I didn't know why there'd be one at the edge of the DFZ, but given the crazy magic filling the air like syrup, I didn't find it unbelievable. But I was now *very* concerned with how I was going to get out.

Panting, I quit running and looked around. The idea was to get my bearings, but I was no longer certain which direction I'd come from, and the forest behind me was even darker and more foreboding than the woods ahead. At least that way had a light. Of course, that light might be a lure to get me to keep walking forever until I died—another common trope in these sorts of stories—but turning back felt like giving up, and I'd had enough failure for one night. If this was a trap, I was already neck deep in it, but if I was going to die stupidly tonight, I was determined to do it while moving forward. With that, I set my jaw and started walking again, stomping my dirty, bruised feet determinedly over the roots and pine needles until, all of a sudden, I was there.

I stopped with a jerk. There'd been no transition, no warning. The woods had simply ended, leaving me standing in a clearing beneath a wide, clear sky colored green with the first light of dawn. In front of me was a two-story brick house that looked like all the others in the University District, except this one wasn't ancient or collapsing. It was actually in beautiful repair, with gleaming white mortar, some really lovely decorative masonry patterns in the brickwork on the second story, brilliantly colored stained-glass windows, a deep-brown clay roof that didn't look to have a single broken tile, and a granite foundation that ran straight as a pin all the way around. It was an absolutely beautiful example of classic Old Detroit residential architecture from the time when "a man's home is his castle" had been taken absolutely literally. There was even a little tower sticking up out of the roof in the back, complete with a conical roof and a tiny window where a princess could have sat like a piece of prime merchandise.

But while the house was textbook Gothic Revival, the landscape surrounding it looked like a mad botanist's horticultural experiment gone out of control. Every foot of open ground between the house and the forest was jam-packed with plants that had all been meticulously labeled. Other than the signs, though, there was no discernible order. The whole thing was a jumble of greens and flowers, bushes and trees, gourds and berries. You had vegetables next to ornamentals next to fruit trees next to patches of what I would have called weeds if they hadn't been just as beautifully labeled as everything else.

Like the house they surrounded, the plants were obviously meticulously cared for. The blueberry bush on my left looked particularly inviting, its plump berries magazine perfect with their glistening coat of morning dew. I didn't dare pick one, though. I didn't touch *anything*.

Beautiful as it was, this place was giving me serious "witch's garden" vibes. I didn't want to bend so much as a blade of grass if I could avoid it. Fortunately, there was a stone path just a few feet away. A crazy one that zigzagged around the clumps of plants as if it was as desperate as I was not to touch anything, but I made do. My bare feet actually made it easier to follow the stones when the garden spilled across the walkway, and I managed not to step on anything all the way to the house's front door, which was painted a garish, glossy shade of candy-apple red. Taking a deep breath, I lifted my hand to knock, but my knuckles had barely touched the wood when a cross voice spoke behind me.

"We're closed."

I must have jumped a foot in the air. Heart pounding, I whirled around to see a squat woman standing on the path I'd just come from.

Going by her frizzy gray hair and stout, hunched body, I placed her age in the mid-sixties, maybe early seventies. Her face, however, looked *much* older: a pile of ruddy wrinkles with two beady eyes gleaming out through the folds like chips of dark glass.

Not surprisingly, considering where we were, she was dressed for gardening in high-waisted trousers with mud on the knees, green rubber boots, and a short-sleeved white T-shirt that showed off her wrinkly, heavily freckled arms. But while her look was pure Midwestern grandma, the magic rolling off her was the strangest I'd ever felt. It wasn't sharp like a dragon's or overwhelming like a spirit's, but it was definitely *there*, which was remarkable in and of itself since humans didn't usually put out enough magic for me to feel. Even more remarkable was how nice it felt. The power she radiated was as bountiful and inviting as the garden surrounding us, a stark contrast to the annoyance in her beady eyes as she glowered at me.

"Um," I said, pulling out the card Peter had given me to make sure I had the name right. "Are you Dr. Rita Kowalski?"

"Not yet," the woman replied, lifting her chin stubbornly. "We don't open until ten a.m."

I turned the card around so she could see it. "It says here you're open twenty-four hours a day."

"To the *right* people," she countered, pointing a bony, freckled finger at the line that did indeed say exactly that. "What makes you think that includes you?"

I winced. She had me there. "I was just hoping…That is…I'm having a bit of an emergency, and Peter—the priest who gave me your card—said you could help."

Her expression softened when she heard Peter's name. "I suppose you're talking about your magic?"

I nodded rapidly. "I hurt it really bad a week ago. I was trying to stay off it and let it heal, but something happened tonight where I had to use it, and it kind of…broke."

"So I see," the woman said, looking me up and down. "But what do you want me to do? If you're hurt, go to a doctor. That's what they're for."

"I can't afford a doctor."

"Then what makes you think you can afford me?" she snapped, pointing at the meticulous house with its lovely garden on an acre of land under the open sky. "Does this look cheap?"

"I'm sorry," I said, wringing my hands. "I didn't mean to imply—"

"No, you said exactly what you meant," she said crossly, folding her stubby arms. "You think I'm off-brand, a low-quality substitute good you're only using because emergency forced you here. If it were up to me, I'd kick you out for that, but I like Peter, and the woods did let you in, so I'll give you another chance. Now, tell me again why you're here. Properly, this time."

I took a silent breath, buying time as I scrambled for the right thing to say. Fortunately, I had a lot of experience dealing with powerful beings of prickly honor.

"I'm very sorry," I said, lowering my head. "I didn't mean any offense. It's just that I've never met a professional Shaman before, and I didn't know how to act. I don't think you're inferior. Quite the opposite. I kept walking because I knew anyone who lived in these woods would have to be an expert, and that's what I need. I've done something to my magic that I don't even understand, and—"

"I'll say," the woman interrupted with a snort. "I can feel it screaming from here."

"Then you know this is serious."

She shook her head. "It's well past serious. Your magic's the worst I've ever seen, and I've seen some disasters. Frankly, I'm shocked Peter didn't tell you to come to me sooner."

"Actually, he did," I said, both for the sake of transparency and to defend my friend. "Peter gave me your card well before this happened."

The old woman looked horrified. "You mean you kept using your magic *after* it got so bad Peter sent you to me? Are you stupid?"

"I didn't do it because I wanted to! I told you, I *was* trying to stay off it, but this was an emergency. I had to do something or my partner was going to die!"

"That was your bad decision," she said, shaking her head in frustration as she turned away. "I'm afraid I can't help you."

My stomach turned to ice. "You mean my magic is broken beyond repair?"

"No, I can repair it," the woman said as she shuffled down the winding path. "But there's no point, because you're just going to break it again. Your magic already told you as loudly as it could that you were abusing it, and you didn't listen. If you won't heed your own body, why would you listen to me? I don't waste my time on patients I can't trust to follow the treatment protocol."

"But I will!" I promised, running down the path after her. "I'm normally really good about taking care of my magic. I only ignored it this time because I was under so much pressure, and I didn't realize it was an emergency until tonight!"

"Then why didn't you go to an emergency facility?" she snapped, whirling around so fast I nearly smacked into her. "There's a thousand clinics in the DFZ who could have looked at your magic. Many for dirt cheap, so don't feed me that line about cost."

"But—"

"No buts," she snapped. "I'm a doctor, sworn first to do no harm. It's plain as day that you've been abusing your magic for years now. I'm not going to fix you up just so you can break yourself even worse next time." She turned away again. "When you're ready to address the underlying issues that got you to this point, we'll talk. But if you're just looking for another enabler, go somewhere else."

She turned on her heel and tromped off, leaving me gaping at her back. Honestly, I couldn't say why I'd ordered the cab to take me here instead of going to a normal clinic. She was right, there *were* plenty of doctors I could have gone to even at my price range who didn't live out in the crazy woods. I hadn't even wanted her card when Peter had given it to me, and I *still* didn't believe Shamans were real mages.

Then again, maybe that was it. I'd already been to plenty of "real" doctors. Growing up, my mother had taken me to every developmental magic expert in the world, all respected Thaumaturges from the best universities, and none of them had ever been able to tell me why I was so terrible at casting spells. They'd all just looked at my magic and told me to try harder, but I *was* trying. I'd tried and tried and *tried* for so long, and everything still blew up in my face. That was why I hadn't gone to a clinic even when using my magic had hurt so much it had brought tears to my eyes. I hadn't been willing to spend my hard-earned money on another lecture about how this was all my fault. And that, I realized suddenly, was my answer.

"I don't want to be a failure."

The words came out in a sad little girl's voice, but they were enough to make the old woman stop.

"What makes you think you're a failure?" she asked, turning around.

I shrugged helplessly. "The fact that I fail all the time? I don't know why, but I've been a terrible mage my entire life. Even when I'm copying someone else's spellwork line for line, it never works the way it's supposed to. The magic always overloads or blows up in my face. Honestly, I'm amazed I didn't break myself before now. I've been backlashed so many times I don't even feel it anymore. The doctors always told me I just need to be more careful, but other mages can go all out without wrecking themselves. I can't even fill a circle without getting it back in my face!" I scrubbed my hands through my hair. "It's just so frustrating! I'm not stupid about anything else. I did great in all my other classes, but magic just…"

"It doesn't work," the woman finished.

I nodded glumly. "I don't know what miracle I expect you to work, but you're right. I can't keep going like this, but I don't know what to do. I'm not…I can't…"

I closed my eyes and turned away. I would *not* cry in front of a stranger. I was *not* that weak person. At least, I didn't think I was until Dr. Kowalski put her gnarled hand on my shoulder.

"What can't you do?"

I scrunched my face up tight. "I can't keep being the weakest link," I said in a whisper. "There are plenty of Cleaners who aren't mages who make great money, so I thought I could get by, but Nik needed me tonight, and I just *couldn't.* I only saved him by accident, and I'm still not sure I didn't make everything worse."

"I see," she said, even though none of that could have possibly made sense out of context. "What do you want to do, then?"

"I want to stop," I said angrily. "I know being a good mage is probably too much to ask, but I'd be over the moon if I could just not be a terrible one. I want to be someone who's not a liability. Someone who can stand on her own."

Someone who could have saved Nik without blowing everything up.

"Fair enough," Dr. Kowalski said when I finally petered out. "Come with me."

I blinked my embarrassingly red-rimmed eyes at her. "You're going to treat me?"

"I'm open to trying," she said, trotting past me toward her cheery red door. "I wasn't willing to tape you back together, but if you can be that open with a stranger, I think we've got a good chance at making progress on your actual problem. Before we do anything, though, I need to look at your magic and assess the damage, and I can't do that out here."

My knees started to shake. "Thank you," I gasped, running after her. "Thank you so much!"

"Save the praise until something actually works," she cautioned. "Though I understand now why Peter took pity on you despite your prejudices. Hardly surprising for a priest of the Empty Wind, but that young man has a terminal soft spot for the lost."

I didn't think I was lost. Desperate, maybe, but I felt like I knew where I stood. I just hated it.

I wasn't about to shoot my unexpected good fortune in the foot over semantics, though, so I kept my mouth shut, following on Dr. Kowalski's heels as she opened the door and waved me inside.

***

The interior of the house looked nothing like its meticulous exterior. Outside was all perfect brick and clean lines. Inside looked like an overstocked antique store mixed with a vegetable silo.

"Don't mind the mess," Dr. Kowalski said as she stepped high over a pile of summer squash. "Brohomir of the Heartstrikers placed a produce order last week, but he hasn't been by to pick it up yet."

"Brohomir of the Heartstrikers," I repeated in a shaky voice. "You mean the Peacemaker's brother?"

She nodded.

"You sell *vegetables* to one of the three great dragon seers?!"

"I sell vegetables to anyone who'll come and take them," Dr. Kowalski said grumpily. "This clearing used to be a fecundity experiment site before I took it over. If I don't sell the produce, it'll bury me, but it's such a hassle to get it shipped to local markets. Fortunately, dragons have large appetites and don't mind flying in for a pickup."

I didn't know what to say to that. The Great Seer Brohomir was one of the most famous and feared dragons in the world. Even my dad spoke of him with respect, and he normally hated Heartstrikers. Of course, it was also well-known that Brohomir was crazy as a loon. That was pretty common for seers, though, so no one held it against him.

"Here we are," Dr. Kowalski said, leading me into a small room by the kitchen that had clearly been originally meant as a dining room but was now done up as an office, complete with a large cluttered desk, a couch for consultations, and walls decorated with framed diplomas from a world tour of respected magical universities.

"Wow," I said, looking in awe at the field of impenetrable Latin. "So which of these makes you a doctor?"

"Take your pick," Dr. Kowalski said, moving a crate of radishes off the desk chair so she could sit. "I was the leading expert in my field for years. Still am, honestly, but I got tired of university politics, and the universities got tired of Shamanism."

I shuffled my feet self-consciously, remembering my own thoughtless comments to Peter.

"Schools of thought go in and out of fashion just as much as anything else," the doctor went on. "Forty years ago, half the mages in the world were Shamans. It was quite the thing, but Shamanism's emphasis on intuition and changing casting protocols to match the needs of each individual and situation made it unappealing to corporations. They wanted magic that would work the same way every time, even if it was less powerful, less efficient, and took more resources. As a result, Thaumaturges started getting all the high-paying jobs, and Shamanism fell into decline. Simple economics, really. It also didn't help that the Archmage of the Merlin Council kept calling Thaumaturgy the only 'real' form of magic. She made the rest of us sound like quacks."

The Archmage *was* staunchly in the Thaumaturgy camp. She didn't actually have control over what magic was taught in schools, but she was arguably the most influential magical authority in the world. When she said Thaumaturgy was the only proper way to go, people listened. Even my dad thought Shamans were a waste of time, and he wasn't even human.

"I can see why you've had problems."

"It's not so bad," Dr. Kowalski said, settling into her chair with a creak. "Chairing a university was good for the ego, but Shamanism has never needed institutional approval to shine. We might have lost our edge in the general population, but every priest is a Shaman by definition, so we've always got that."

"Why do priests have to be Shamans?" I wouldn't have thought the gods cared what kind of magic you cast so long as you did your job.

"Because priests serve the Mortal Spirits, and unlike Thaumaturges, Shamans don't try to shove their gods into tiny circles."

"Oh." I'd expected something grander, but that actually made a lot of sense.

"But enough about the decline of my once-great discipline," Dr. Kowalski said, pointing at the couch under the window, which was covered in books rather than vegetables for a change. "Sit down, and let's have a look at your magic."

I nodded and scooted the piles aside to make myself a spot. When I sat down, the doctor reached out to take my hands. She prodded my palms with her calloused fingers for about thirty seconds, and then she placed her thumbs on the insides of my wrists as if she were checking my pulse.

"Try to move some magic," she ordered. "I know you can't, but just try."

I nodded and closed my eyes, trying as hard as I could to reach out for the thick, wild power that saturated this part of the DFZ. There was so much here that I could feel it coating my skin like water, but no matter how I pushed, I couldn't move so much as a drop of it.

"Interesting," Dr. Kowalski said as she released my hands. "Has anyone ever told you that you have a high draw? Like, *really* high?"

I nodded. Draw was the measure for how much magic a mage could grab at one time, and mine was off the charts. I knew this because my mother had bragged about it every day of my childhood. Thanks to my dad's willingness to throw morals under the bus in his quest to create a perfect mage daughter, my genes had been heavily edited before I was born, resulting in a draw number that was slightly above what had been previously considered the human limit. All that ability was *supposed* to make me a prodigy, but like everything else involving me and magic, it had flopped. My outsized draw had allowed me to sense and move magic years before other kids even knew they were mages, but it hadn't made me any better at handling or manipulating the power, which was the only part of casting that actually mattered.

I explained all of this to Dr. Kowalski. Or, rather, I told her about my high draw number and why it hadn't helped me, leaving out the draconic narcissism that had landed me in this position in the first place. It wasn't that I was ashamed of being a test-tube baby. I was just tired of my dad hanging over every aspect of my life. Seriously, I couldn't even break my magic without finding him in the wreckage. You'd think I'd be happy to lay all of my troubles at his feet, but I'd never be free if I kept blaming him for my problems, even if most of them were his fault.

"I think I see your problem," Dr. Kowalski said when I finished my story. "Two problems, really, but they're interrelated."

"That was fast," I said eagerly. "So can you fix me?"

"Fix isn't really the word," she said, leaning back in her chair with a thoughtful scowl. "Humans move magic by reaching out with the innermost part of ourselves. Officially, that's the mana-connecting prehensile self-perspective appendage, but it's better known by its colloquial name, the *soul*. Human souls are what give us our unique ability to move and process magic outside of ourselves, both the ambient stuff that rises naturally from the ground and power contained in other vessels, including spirits and other living creatures. The ability to do this consciously and deliberately is what makes a person a mage, but all humans' souls move magic to some degree whether they're mages or not. As with any appendage, though, the soul can be damaged by overuse, resulting in a sprain or a tear."

"Is that what happened to me?" Because a torn soul sounded *bad*.

The doctor shook her head. "You managed to go even further. A sprained soul hurts, but if you can't feel *anything*, that means you pushed your soul past its limit, causing it to become dislocated."

The look on my face must have been horrific, because she rushed to reassure me. "Don't worry, your soul's not broken. It's still in your body, just not in the right position. Unfortunately, there's nothing I can do to reattach it."

"So I'll be like this forever?" I asked, panic rising.

"Not *forever*," she said. "It'll reconnect on its own eventually, but the bonds you broke will take time to reform. You'll need to take it easy on the casting until your magic is fully healed. If this happens again, the damage could become permanent."

"And then my magic really will be broken forever?"

"No," she said flatly. "If you permanently disconnect your soul from your body, it'll get sucked into the Sea of Magic, and you'll die."

"Oh," I said, biting my lip. "But it *will* heal if I don't use it, right?"

The doctor nodded. "It felt close when I examined it earlier, so you should be getting some feeling back soon. But the injury isn't actually what I'm most concerned about."

I stared at her in horror. "What's worse than dislocating my soul?"

"The fact that you were able to do it at all."

Dr. Kowalski leaned forward in her chair, studying me with her small, bright eyes as if I was an interesting but very dangerous insect. "Dislocating your soul isn't a normal sort of injury. The human soul and body are tightly connected, so much so that some consider them to be one and the same. It takes an *enormous* amount of energy to split that bond. Frankly, I'm amazed you didn't blow yourself to pieces."

"I'm pretty tough," I said with stubborn pride. "Things have been blowing up in my face since I was a kid, so I'm used to it."

"That's precisely the problem," the old woman said crossly. "Backlashing yourself is an inevitable part of learning to control your magic, but you're not supposed to do it all the time. That much repeated injury over a long period can cause serious damage." She frowned. "Is casting normally painful for you?"

"Only when I mess it up." Which, admittedly, was more often than not. "But I don't normally push this hard. I've just had a lot of emergencies lately."

"You shouldn't be pushing at all," Dr. Kowalski snapped. "That's not a healthy or effective way to do magic, especially for someone with a draw as high as yours. You almost blasted your soul clean out of your body."

"But I didn't have a choice! My friend and I were about to die."

"I'm not talking about what you were forced to do in an emergency," she said sternly, poking her calloused fingers hard into my palms. "This sort of injury doesn't happen from one wild spell. What you're suffering from is the result of a lifetime of terrible casting habits. If you don't want it to happen again, you *have* to get better at regulating your draw."

I stared at her blankly. "What are you talking about? Draw is unconscious. You can't regulate it."

Now it was Dr. Kowalski's turn to stare. "Are you serious?"

I *was*. I'd always been taught that draw was something you were born with, like hair. Every mage's was a little different, which was why all Thaumaturgical spells began by drawing a circle. Not only did the circle serve as the spell's fuel tank, holding all the magic until it was needed for casting, it also acted like a transformer, converting whatever random magic the mage happened to grab into a homogeneous form the spell could use.

Other than spellwork, the shorthand language used to write out exactly what you wanted a spell to do through a series of logical statements much like computer code, magical circles were why every serious mage was a Thaumaturge. In a world where each caster and magical source was different, circles were the great equalizer. Without them, you'd have to adjust every spell individually to take into account all of the different strengths and flavors and concentrations of magic. Put it in a circle, though, and all that weirdness evened out, becoming a nice, level pool of power that flowed through spellwork smooth as silk. Circles also negated problems caused by differences in individual mages' draws, since, if it was all going into the same pot anyway, it didn't matter how fast or how hard you poured it in.

Or, at least, that was what I'd been taught.

"No, you're correct," Dr. Kowalski said when I explained this. "That is exactly how Thaumaturgy is *supposed* to work. Remember, though: Thaumaturgy, like all the casting styles, is merely a construct. It's a system created by people to help our brains manage the incredible act of grabbing the raw power of the universe and bending it into a usable shape. But like everything humans make, Thaumaturgy is not without its limitations. It was created to be a universal magical system. That's why all the spellwork languages share a common vocabulary of variables, logical operators, and constants. There's notable differences between the styles, but generally speaking, every Thaumaturge can read, understand, and cast any spell provided it's written out in spellwork. That's what Thaumaturgy was created to do. It's standardized magic."

"That's good, though," I said.

"It's fantastic," Dr. Kowalski agreed. "Thaumaturgy's universality is its great strength, particularly if you're a corporation that makes its money selling preprinted, preoptimized spells written by committee so that any idiot can cast them. But while Thaumaturgy is fantastic at being magic for the masses, it's garbage at dealing with exceptions. That's the trouble with 'universal' systems: you can't actually plan for everything. Even if your spellwork works as expected ninety-nine percent of the time, there's always that last one percent the precalculated equations just can't handle. And as someone with a draw number above what's supposed to be the natural human limit, you are *definitely* not part of the standard."

I gave her a skeptical look. "So you're saying my magic's too crazy for Thaumaturgy?"

"That's exactly what I'm saying," the doctor replied with a confident nod. "You were taught a system that's balanced for the average mage, but you're *not* the average mage. That's why spells you look up on the internet blow up in your face. It's not that you're bad at copying spellwork, you're just shoving magic into it at a rate it was never designed to handle. Of *course* it's going to break."

Dr. Kowalski said this as if it was obvious, but I felt like she'd just turned my universe upside down and put it in a paint shaker. "So it's not me?" I whispered, body trembling.

"Oh, it's definitely you," she said. "The spells are fine. You're the one pushing them beyond their limits."

"But only because my draw is crazy," I said desperately. "Not because I'm..."

Terrible, my father's voice whispered in my head. *Flawed.*

"It's not a fault in your skills," Dr. Kowalski assured me. "I mean, I've never seen you design a spell, so I have no idea if you're good at spellwork or not, but the whole point of Thaumaturgy is that you don't have to be. You don't need to be a genius to be an effective mage. You just need to be able to read and copy spellwork, which any idiot can do."

"Any idiot except me."

"Honestly, it would be easier if you were an idiot," the doctor said. "Bad spellwork and sloppy casting can be fixed with study and discipline, but your problem is baked into one of the core assumptions underpinning the entire Thaumaturgical system. You could be a spellwork genius and things would *still* blow up in your face because Thaumaturgical spellwork simply isn't designed to handle an exception like you."

I clutched my hands in my lap. You'd think after all the times I'd been told—all the times I'd told *myself*—that I was a terrible, hopeless, no-good, garbage excuse for a mage, I'd be delighted to hear that it wasn't actually my fault. That I *wasn't* a failure, at least not in the way I'd assumed. And I *was* delighted. Provisionally. Because while I was pretty sure I'd understood everything Dr. Kowalski had just said, I was still having trouble believing it could possibly be true.

"If that's what's really going on," I said hesitantly, "why did no one else see it? My draw number has been off the charts since I was born. I've had my magic poked at by hundreds, maybe *thousands* of experts, and every one of them agreed that it was my fault. They always said I wasn't listening or that I wasn't trying hard enough."

Dr. Kowalski shrugged. "Were you?"

"Of course I was!" I said angrily. "I didn't want to be a failure! I tried as hard as I could for years! But if the problem was actually my draw this whole time, why am I only learning about it *now?*"

"I don't know," Dr. Kowalski said. "I don't know why I'm the first to point out something that should have been obvious to anyone who understands how spellwork constants are calculated, but I bet it has something to do with the fact that they were all Thaumaturges." She smiled. "Experts, especially highly respected ones, fall victim to the same fallacies as everyone else. If a system always works for you, it's only natural to assume it must be that way for everyone. If a spell doesn't work, it must be an error on the caster's part. The spellwork itself is never suspect. How can it be? It always works when you do it."

She leaned forward with a wink. "That's the danger of thinking yours is the 'only' way to do magic. It leaves you blind to the fact that Thaumaturgical spellwork is as flawed as anything else humans create. I, however, am a Shaman. Unlike your respected experts, I've *always* thought Thaumaturgy was a flawed, overly rigid system destined to topple under the weight of its own hubris, which makes spotting problems like this much, much easier.”

I was shaking by the time she finished. Thinking back to all the pompous variations of “if you’d only apply yourself” or “maybe you just don’t have the mind for Thaumaturgy” I’d sat through as a child, Dr. Kowalski’s explanation made *perfect* sense to me. Hearing it made me feel both vindicated and furious. How dare they make me think this was all my fault? Didn’t they know how much I’d beaten myself up over this? How hard I’d pushed to use a system that was never going to work for me?! But freeing as it was to know that I wasn’t actually a lazy, worthless failure, there was still a problem.

“So what do I do?” I asked desperately. “It’s great to hear that I’m not actually a terrible mage, but how do I cast magic if spellwork fundamentally doesn’t work for me? And before you say ‘become a Shaman,’ I’ve already been doing my own version of no-spellwork casting where I mash the magic together, and it blows up in my face just as often as the stuff I write out. That’s how I hurt my magic this time, so what do I do? How do I cast without hurting myself?”

Dr. Kowalski gave me a biting look. “First of all, Shamanism is *not* just ‘mashing magic together.’ Just because our rules are more flexible than Thaumaturgy’s doesn’t mean we don’t have them. In fact, our rules are actually *more* important because we don’t have circles acting as a safety rail. Thaumaturges are always trying to find new ways to bottle lightning so that anyone can touch it without getting zapped. To be a Shaman, though, you have to learn to ride it. It’s an inherently more dangerous form of casting, but I’d argue it’s the only one that can truly be called *magic*. There’s nothing magical about feeding sanitized, homogenized power through a logic statement to achieve an expected result. But to take the essence of gods between your hands and weave it, to reach out and bend the power of the universe to your will using only your naked *soul*…” She took a shuddering breath. “That is power. *That* is what it means to be a mage. Everything else is just more monkey tool making.”

I didn't know if I'd go quite that far, but she did make Shamanism sound romantic. And a bit crazy. But I'd just walked out of the city to a legit witch's garden in the middle of the night through an endlessly shifting wood to find out why my soul was broken, so who was I to judge? Dr. Kowalski had already taught me more about my magic in twenty minutes than all of my dad's experts combined, and the casting she described sounded way more fun than writing out spellwork. Even when it wasn't blowing up in my face, I'd always been rubbish at spellwork. Maybe it was time to try something new?

"Could you teach me?"

After selling it so hard, I'd thought for sure Dr. Kowalski would jump all over that, but she just shook her wizened old head. "No."

"Why not?!"

"Because Shamanic casting requires an enormous level of control over your magic," she huffed. "You didn't even know regulating your draw was a *thing* before this conversation. Forget learning how to free-cast. I'm worried you won't learn how to tone down your magic fast enough to avoid breaking it again."

"Then teach me that," I said determinedly. "It's great to know I wasn't actually too stupid for Thaumaturgy all these years, but I'm still a mage who can't cast, and what good is that?" I clenched my hands into fists. "I'm sick and tired of being a failure. Whatever you've got, I can take it. Just tell me what to do."

Dr. Kowalski looked at me for a long time, her small eyes gleaming through her wrinkles, and then she started rummaging in the bags beneath her desk. "Reducing your draw is a simple process," she said. "That's not to say it's *easy*. It's never easy to change a habit so intuitive you've never had to be aware of it before, but the method itself is relatively straightforward. I just need to find the right associative device to help you—ah ha!"

She straightened back up and thrust something brown and oblong into my hands. "There. That should work nicely."

I looked down at the object in trepidation. "This is a russet potato."

"Exactly," she said excitedly. "That potato is the perfect size to help you visualize the amount of magic you should be moving. When your soul reconnects and you can cast again without hurting yourself, I want you to practice grabbing only one potato's worth of magic at a time."

"*This* potato?" I said, holding up the spud, which was no bigger than my hand. "But this is nothing! The smallest circle I use is the one that recharges my poncho, and it's four feet in diameter. Do you know how long that'll take to fill using only a potato?"

"I do," said Dr. Kowalski. "Because that potato is a good spatial representation of the size of the average mage's draw, which also happens to be *my* draw."

"But—"

"Millions of mages get through life only being able to draw that much magic or less at a time," she said sternly. "I'm sure you'll survive. In fact, it might be the *only* way you survive. Just because you were born with the ability to grab freakishly huge amounts of magic doesn't mean the rest of your body can handle it. You already dislocated your soul, and if you keep recklessly snatching as much power as possible, the next time will be worse. You said you were ready to do anything, so it's time to decide. Are you going to put in the work it takes to actually change yourself? Or are you going to keep asking me for help and then complaining when I tell you what you need to do?"

"Sorry," I muttered, clutching my potato. "I'll do it."

"Good," she said, glancing out the window behind me, where the sky had turned a lovely pinkish teal. "The sun's coming up now, so you should get going. Grand plans aside, you can't actually do anything until your soul reattaches, and that's never going to happen if you don't get some sleep."

I was *definitely* ready for sleep. My phone wasn't working at all anymore, so I didn't know what time it was, but if the sun was rising, I'd been up for at least twenty-four hours straight. "Sleep sounds great," I said, rising from the sofa with a creak. "How much do I owe you?"

Given her comment about not being cheap before we'd started this, I was braced for the worst, but the elderly doctor shook her head. "No charge today."

"You're joking."

"Why would I joke about this?" she asked. "You made it clear earlier that you were short on money, so I decided to be charitable. It's not a big thing. Other than my time, the only thing you've cost me this morning is a potato, and I have plenty of those."

I shook my head hard. "I have to pay."

"Why?"

"Because I'm up to my neck in debts already, and I don't want any more," I said bluntly. "If this works, and you actually fix my magic, I'll pretty much owe you my life. But the whole reason I'm doing this is to get my life *back*, so please just let me pay an exorbitant fee so we can call it done."

The old woman tilted her head at me. "Why is it so hard to believe I'd give you something for free?"

"Because this is the DFZ!" I cried. "*Nothing's* free here except trouble."

She looked offended. "Is that all you think the DFZ is about? Money?"

I stared at her, trying to determine if that was a serious question or not. "Um, yes? We live in a shrine to reckless capitalism, the place where nothing is illegal and everything is for sale. What else could it be about?"

"The thing all that money is trying to buy," the old woman said, her hooded brown eyes shining with a strange amber glow in the morning sunlight. "Money is just a tool. It's the means, not the end. The DFZ has always understood that."

"Could have fooled me," I grumbled.

"I don't know why this is so hard for you to grasp," she said testily. "The DFZ uses money for the same things you do."

"To pay debts?"

The old woman stared me down. "To buy freedom."

As she finished, I became aware of a pressure rising in the room. It felt like the wild magic I'd noticed on my way here, but bigger. Heavier, like a press crushing me flat. Within seconds, I was having trouble staying on my feet, but Dr. Kowalski didn't seem to notice it. She just sat in her chair, watching me with those strangely bright eyes and her weirdly prominent magic. The power rolling off her now was even stronger than it had been back in the garden. Way stronger than a human's should be. Stronger than anything I'd ever felt outside of the Gnarls when the dark had risen up to catch me...

I dropped my potato on the floor as it all came together. "You're a spirit."

The wrinkled old woman smiled.

I sank back down to the couch, not that I had much of a choice. The magic was so heavy now that I could actually feel it pushing my poor dislocated soul around inside me. It was a horrible, unnatural sensation, but I didn't have the worry to waste on it. I was too busy trying to figure out *which* spirit I was facing before I said something that got me killed.

It wasn't the Empty Wind's voice. I wasn't sure how much that mattered, since gods could probably change their voices whenever they wanted to, but there were no dead here, forgotten or otherwise, which I was pretty sure ruled him out.

It couldn't be Algonquin. I'd seen the Lady of the Lakes on TV plenty of times, and though she often donned a human form because people freaked out when they realized they were talking to a woman made of water, it was usually pretty obvious. More importantly, she was a Spirit of the Land. That still made her a god compared to a puny mortal like me, but Spirits of the Land were the oldest and smallest spirits. The really big, really dangerous gods were the ones humans made, the Mortal Spirits.

Unlike Spirits of the Land, the Mortal Spirits weren't limited to physical structures. They were as big as the human fear of death, as powerful as the ability to love, and they wore as many faces as we gave them. I was certain the thing sitting in front of me wearing the old woman's body was one of those, but which? There were so many gods these days. Which one would dare to live out here on land the city refused to—

I stopped, feeling like an idiot. Then I felt terrified, because if I was right, I was in the company of a god that scared me way more than the Shepherd of the Forgotten Dead.

"You're the DFZ."

"Took you long enough," the spirit said in a voice that no longer matched the old wrinkled face it spoke from.

I sank a bit further into the sofa. "Have you been in there the whole time or…"

"I'm always here," the city replied, flashing me a smile that looked like the sort a puppet would give if you pulled the right string. "This is just one of my faces. A city has to have a lot, but Dr. Kowalski is one of my favorites. She died ten years ago, but we made a deal that I'd take her soul in as part of mine in exchange for her knowledge. And her help with the garden. I'm terrible with plants."

She looked sad about that. I had no idea why a god cared about being a good gardener, but it struck me as important. "So was I actually talking to the doctor?"

"Oh yes," the DFZ said. "She was completely in control until just a few moments ago. I was only eavesdropping, but our offer was legitimate. I didn't order Dr. Kowalski to treat you for free, and I'm not trying to get you in my debt. We both just want to help you recover your magic."

She sounded sincere, but as someone who'd grown up in a dragon's shadow, that statement set off warning bells like nothing else could. "Why?" I asked, clutching the cushions. "I don't mean to be rude, but you're a god. Gods don't do things for free."

"Don't pen me in with your dragon morals and your anthropology," the DFZ said angrily. "I'm the DFZ. I do whatever I want! And what I want is for you to succeed."

I blinked, more confused than ever. "What?"

"I want you to win," the god clarified, sitting up straighter than the stooped old doctor ever could have managed. Her face looked younger, too, her eyes—which were now closer to the orange color of streetlights than anything human—sharp and hungry. "You came to my city to start a new life. You came to be free, to escape the domineering power who wanted to keep you as his amusement. When your father tried to crush you with his magic, you used your cleverness and ingenuity to turn that weapon back on him. You leveraged and hustled and found new ways to hold your own. That makes you one of mine."

I flinched at the word *mine*. "I'm not a possession."

"I never said you were. It's actually the opposite. You're my person because I'm *your* city. I can raise whatever buildings I want, but they're just structures. It's what lives inside that matters, and for me, that's you."

"That still doesn't tell me why," I pressed, voice shaking. Challenging an immortal spirit felt like a *really* stupid thing to do, but this conversation was throwing up every red flag I had. Whether they were gods, dragons, or people, powerful beings didn't single you out for favor without expecting something in return. "You said you want me to win, by which I presume you mean beat my dad and get free, but I don't get why you care."

"I care because you are me," the city said, frustrated. "I'm the spirit of a city. I don't get to wake up and choose who I'll be each day. You decide that. You and everyone else who calls me home. You're the ones who define me, so if I want to change, I have to start with you."

I scowled. The face of the woman sitting in the chair now looked even younger than I was, reminding me that the DFZ was not an old god. Unlike the Empty Wind, who was as ancient as the human need to be remembered, the DFZ had only risen from the ashes of Old Detroit eighty years ago, and it hadn't been born with its spirit, either. It had taken a long time for the idea of the DFZ to come together, decades before people stopped thinking of the city as merely Algonquin's conquered territory and started seeing it as its own place where anything was possible and everyone was free. The first recorded sighting of the Spirit of the DFZ was only twenty years ago, which meant that I, being twenty-six, might actually be *older* than she was, which was a strange thing to realize about a god.

"You said you have to start with me," I repeated slowly. "What does that entail? What do you need me to do?"

The spirit's hands—still Dr. Kowalski's wrinkled claws, a sharp contrast to her new young face—tightened on the arms of her chair. "You're not the only one who wants to change herself, Opal Yong-ae. I am the city of dragons and mages, multibillionaires and superscrapers. I'm the richest place in the world, and yet I have the highest murder, child poverty, addiction, and suicide rates on the planet. You had a shootout on top of one of my parking decks just hours ago, and the ambulance wouldn't even come unless you bribed it." She shook her head. "You clean my abandoned places, so you know how ugly I can be, but that's not what I want. I want to be better, to push out the things that make me toxic. If I were any other city, I could just pass laws to fix my problems, but I'm the Detroit *Free* Zone. I'm defined by my lack of restrictions, but that doesn't mean I want to be the pit where everyone goes to do their terrible things. I want to be a good city. A place people *want* to live, not just somewhere they go to do the stuff they can't get away with anywhere else. But I can't become that without good people living in me. It's a catch-22, which is why, whenever I find someone who *does* match the city I want to become, I do my best to keep them around."

I pressed my lips together. There it was. "You want me to stay in the DFZ."

The god nodded. "One person in a city of nine million might not seem important, but pile up enough, help them succeed and put down roots, and the city itself will change. *I* will change. You're an important part of that process. Honestly, though, I'm here talking to you now because I hope you'll be even more."

Once again, my alarm bells went off. "What does that mean?"

"Exactly what it sounds like," she replied. "You're precisely the sort of person I want to attract to my city: young, driven, entrepreneurial yet unwilling to sell your morals. But I'd be a fool to overlook the fact that you're also a genetically engineered super-mage with a draw that's off the charts who might also be a natural-born Shaman."

That last part caught me off guard. "What?"

"Come on," the god chided, grinning at me. "Do you think everyone can grab magic and shape it at will? I know you have a low opinion of Shamans, but it's actually incredibly difficult for most people to gather and hold enough magic to cast even a small spell without the assistance of a circle. At least, that's what world-renowned Shaman Dr. Rita Kowalski is frantically telling me." Her grin grew wider. "Just as there are people who grasp the logic of spellwork intuitively, there are people who just *get* Shamanic shaping. We won't know for sure if that includes you until you start practicing, but Dr. Kowalski thinks it looks good. If you can learn to handle the enormous amounts of magic you're capable of pulling down without killing yourself, it might be *very* good."

For someone who'd been called a failure her whole life, those were heady words. But while I couldn't stop myself from grinning like one, I wasn't *actually* an idiot. "That sounds a lot like a sales pitch."

"You *are* sharp," the spirit said approvingly. "As expected from the Dragon's Opal. I want you even more now."

"Want me for what?"

She grinned so wide her face no longer looked human. "My priesthood."

I recoiled. "You mean like that blind priest in the Wandering Cathedral?"

"Nameless is one of mine, yes," the spirit said. "But I have many others. I think you'd be a fantastic addition, and it would be a good deal for you as well." Her face grew sly. "I know you're looking for a way to escape the Dragon of Korea."

I went still.

"I'm very familiar with dragons," she went on. "I'm full of them, after all. I've seen how stubbornly they cling to what they consider theirs. But as powerful as he might be on his own land, we're a long way from Korea, and Yong is not a god. I am. If you were under my protection, he wouldn't be able to touch you."

I took a shuddering breath. Tonight's victory with the gold markets had given me hope, but two dollars was a far cry from the hundreds of thousands I owed my dad. I was a damn good Cleaner when the curse wasn't holding me back, but even at my best, earning enough to pay back my entire debt before the end of the month—a mere three weeks away—was going to be nigh impossible. There was no getting around those hard truths, but the DFZ was offering me a whole new road. As powerful and terrible as my dad was, even the Great Yong couldn't take a god. The DFZ also wasn't another dragon, which meant running to her wouldn't spark a clan war or get me pinned under yet another set of claws. I didn't particularly want to be a priest, but those were both factors I couldn't ignore. I was trying to think of something clever I could say that would count as neither a no nor a yes when the DFZ raised her hand.

"You don't have to decide now," she said. "Unlike your father, I have no interest in owning people. I want willing followers I can count on to do their jobs without me having to babysit them, and I'll let Dr. Kowalski train you no matter what. She's been bugging me to get her an apprentice since before she died, and having a powerful Shaman who isn't psycho or corrupt is a win for my city whether you decide to become my priest or not. But do please keep my offer in mind." She reached out to touch my hand with Dr. Kowalski's calloused fingers. "I've heard you say you hate me sometimes, Opal, but what you don't know is how much I hate those parts of me, too. We both want to break free of who we were, but unlike you humans, I can't do it alone. A city is only as good as those who call her home, so I hope you'll be proud to call me your city someday."

That was her best pitch yet. Looking at the DFZ, I could actually see a way out for once. One that didn't involve dragons or betrayals or once-in-a-lifetime feats of money grubbing. It did, however, require bowing my head to yet another unbeatable power, and while I was feeling a lot more kindly toward the DFZ than toward my father right now, I didn't know if I could ever do that again.

"I—"

"Ah," the spirit said, covering my mouth with her hand, which smelled faintly of wet pavement. "Not yet. Go home and think about it. When you're ready, I'll appear, just like a god should."

I couldn't decide if that was comforting or terrifying, but the spirit in front of me was already vanishing, her gaunt, hungry face crumpling back into the prodigious wrinkles of the old lady gardener.

"My, my," Dr. Kowalski said in her creaky, mortal voice. "She hasn't come on that hard in a while. She must really like you."

I nodded absently, staring down at my potato on the floor. "What's it like?" I asked quietly. "Being hers?"

"Like most things," the doctor said as she pushed herself out of her chair. "Little good, little bad. I didn't get much of a choice, of course. When she made that pitch to me, I was already dead. It was go with her or be lost forever in the black swells of the Sea of Magic, which made the decision pretty easy." She chuckled, and then her face grew serious. "For what it's worth, she's been a good god to me. She's preserved my knowledge and listened to my advice, and she lets me plant whatever I want here. Like all deities, she demands to be put first, so you won't be able to have much of a life outside her. But she's fair, and the work is interesting. You could do a lot worse."

She gave me a smile, but I couldn't work up the energy to return it. Now that the DFZ's crushing magic had faded, I was suddenly too overwhelmed and exhausted to speak.

"Go home," Dr. Kowalski ordered. "There's a cab waiting at the edge of the woods, and I promise the hike will be shorter this time. Make sure you get at least eight hours of sleep, or your soul might not reattach."

The terror of that was enough to finally get me moving. I thanked her and left, picking up my potato and clutching it to my chest like a talisman as I walked out of the house and into the woods, which were now drenched in bright morning sunlight.

As promised, the walk was *much* shorter this time. The garden had barely vanished into the trees behind me before I spotted the autocab waiting on the same tiny stretch of pavement where the previous one had dropped me off. Moving in a rush, I stumbled past the clusters of magic monitors and threw myself inside the tiny vehicle, collapsing into the bucket seat as I punched in my address. When we started rolling, I pulled out my phone to check the time and see why Sibyl was so quiet. The answer turned out to be seven a.m. and because my internet was still reconnecting. I could almost feel my AI's curiosity building to a crescendo as the little connection wheel spun, but I didn't feel like answering questions, so I went ahead and put her on mute, leaning my head against the cool plastic window as I waited for the cab to take me home.

CHAPTER 6

I woke up much later to the sound of my phone buzzing on my nightstand.

I reached out groggily, worming my hand through the hazard course of pillows, duvets, and other tassel-covered gewgaws that carpeted my ridiculous new bed. I'd meant to throw it all on the floor, but I'd been so tired when I got home that I'd just collapsed right on top of the pile. I hadn't even gotten undressed. I must have made it under the covers at some point, though, because I was buried now. That was a state I had no interest in changing as I tugged my phone under the covers with me.

"'lo?"

"Where are you?"

I frowned. That was Nik's voice, and he sounded…Not panicked—Nik never panicked—but whatever the next step down was. "At home?"

There was a hiss over the speakers as he let out a sharp breath of relief. "Are you okay?"

My body felt like I'd been hit by a truck, my eyes were gummy, my head was on fire, and I wanted to sleep for another month. Other than that… "I'm fine," I said around a giant yawn. "What time is it?"

"One in the afternoon."

Ah, that explained it. I'd only been asleep for five, maybe six hours. That was two short of the eight Dr. Kowalski had ordered and definitely not enough to recover from a full day of Cleaning, a hangover, and an all-nighter. I was about to ask Nik if I could go back to sleep now that he'd verified my status when the almost-panic returned to his voice.

"What happened last night?

That woke me up. "You don't remember?"

"Not a damn thing," he said, clearly furious. "Last I remember, the idiot with the bad implants was trying to use you as a hostage. Next thing I know, I'm waking up on my couch with the mother of all headaches."

I sank into my pillows with a giddy sigh of relief. He didn't remember what had happened in the parking lot. Finally, a stroke of luck. Maybe I *wasn't* doomed after all! But while I was celebrating my unexpected good fortune, Nik was sounding more and more freaked out.

"How did I get here?" he demanded. "How did we escape the roof? Why do I feel like I went on a giant bender? I don't even drink!"

"That was me, I'm afraid," I said, trying to sound properly contrite and not as if I'd just dodged a bullet. "I kinda blasted everyone on the roof with magic. You got hit with hard backlash and blacked out, but so did the bad guys."

"But not you?"

"Oh no, I ate it too," I said. "I'm used to things blowing up on me, though, so I recovered fast. I grabbed you while the others were still down, and we GTFOed."

Nik let out another relieved breath. "Thank you."

I was really hoping he'd leave it there, but I should have known better. Nik was what my mother would have called "detail oriented." If something didn't make sense, he was fundamentally unable to let it go until he'd picked out all the inconsistencies, even for his own miraculous rescue.

"*How* did you get us out, though?" he pressed. "I've never seen you lift two hundred pounds, so there's no way you carried me. How did you get me back to my apartment?"

"You weren't *totally* out," I said, feeding him the truth in carefully sanitized bites. "You could walk if you leaned on me, so I helped you into your car and then drove you back to your place."

There was a horrified silence. "You drove my car?"

"It's still in one piece!" I assured him. "I parked it at the back of your lot far away from other cars."

"Thanks," he muttered, clearly trying to sound gracious. Trying and failing. "Is the transmission on the ground?"

"I don't think so," I said, refusing to take offense. If the only thing Nik freaked out about in this was his car, that was fine with me. "It made some grinding sounds, but I don't think any permanent damage was done. You can go out and check if you want."

"I will later," he said. "I haven't actually managed to get off the couch yet. Every time I stand up, I get so dizzy I go right back down."

I winced. "I'm *really* sorry about that."

"Better dizzy than dead," he said. "But how long does this usually last?"

"It varies from person to person, but it should pass quickly now that you're awake." I frowned, trying to remember all the tricks I'd developed my first year of grad school when I'd been making my final, hardest push to not suck and was backlashing myself nearly every day as a result. "Eat something salty. That usually works for me."

"I don't even want to think about food right now," Nik said, sounding queasy. "Is this how you feel every time?"

I'd *never* had backlash like Nik was experiencing now, but I didn't think that would be helpful information. "It'll pass," I said instead. "Just take it easy, get your electrolytes, and you'll be fine."

There was a long silence. I was wondering if he'd fallen asleep on me when Nik suddenly spoke.

"We need to talk."

I cringed. Nothing good ever came from those words. "Why?"

"That's part of what we need to talk about," he replied cryptically. "Can you come over? I'd go to you, but I can't stand up right now."

"Sure," I said, trying not to sound like I was bracing for a firing squad. "I'll be right there."

He hung up, and I hauled myself out of bed, not even bothering to look at my burned, bloody skirt and bra-turned-shirt before I threw them both into the trash. My underwear followed, and then I walked into my bathroom to clean up, hoping against hope there was something left in my apartment that I could wear.

There was not.

Thanks to yesterday's zeal for experimentation, the only clothes I had left were the ones I'd worn to Clean the slug shop yesterday. They didn't look too bad thanks to the invisible nature of the slime, but the slug guts had hardened overnight, leaving the fabric stiff as cardboard. Fortunately for me, I lived in the DFZ. I wasn't quite bold enough to stroll down to the corner store in the buff, but I could throw on a blanket and scuttle to the row of vending machines just down the hall from my door.

I didn't live in one of the supercomplexes, so my selection was limited, but there were still machines selling at least one of every sort of home good, toiletry, and basic sundry you could need, including clothes. It was all single-wear garbage that was barely thicker than toilet paper, but it was clean and, more importantly, it was what I had. The styling was very "I'm a sixteen-year-old girl sneaking out to go clubbing," but I actually preferred that to my mom's conservative couture. At least I didn't look boring in my new glittery skin-tight leggings and slashed up, asymmetrical T-shirt for a band I'd never heard of, and I was able to scrape the slug grime off my Cleaning boots, which meant my feet wouldn't get tortured again. That was as good as I could ask, so I grabbed my shoulder bag and ordered up my subscription car for the day.

While I waited for it to arrive, I noticed Sibyl was still on mute. I took her off at once, apology already on my lips for forgetting her. When her speaker came back on line, though, the first words over my earpiece were, "Do you have your potato?"

I blinked in surprise. "How do you know about that? I thought you were off-line."

"*I* was off-line," she said smugly. "But your phone and goggles were still on your person. I keep both of them recording by default just in case I miss something. Good thing, too. They caught the whole night for me. I've been parsing the tape for you while you slept, and I've got some great links about regulating draw that you should—"

"Wait, you've been recording me this whole time?" I cried. "*Sibyl!*"

"What?" she said. "I'm your AI! My programming requires me to keep up with everything that goes on in your life. And I *would* have asked, but you muted me before I could reload myself from the cloud!"

I ran a hand over my face. I supposed it was too much to expect privacy from an AI who read my thoughts whenever possible, but I still felt invaded. Not that I'd said anything to Dr. Kowalski I didn't want Sibyl to hear, but it had still been a deeply personal experience, like a therapy session. And anyway, who *liked* discovering they'd been secretly recorded?

"Isn't this against your EULA?"

"I don't know," Sibyl said innocently. "Did you read my EULA?"

We both knew I hadn't, and I looked away with a huff.

"I did it for you, you know," she said. "I was worried someone would take advantage of you during your time of emotional vulnerability. But I ran your whole conversation with Dr. Kowalski through four psychology analysis programs, and they all agree that you had a breakthrough! That's fantastic, Opal!"

"I also met a god," I said casually. "That was pretty intense."

"You met a god last week, too," Sibyl reminded me. "But who cares about that? This is progress on your *magic*! Your inability to cast has been your number-one source of negative self-image for years. Improvements here could be huge for your emotional well-being!"

I did feel a lot better. I was still short of the eight hours of rest the doctor had ordered, but now that I was awake and moving around, I'd noticed my magic was aching again. You wouldn't think I'd welcome the return of pain, but after feeling that terrifying nothing last night, the throbbing felt like a blessing. It meant my soul had reconnected, just as Dr. Kowalski had said. I definitely didn't want to try moving magic, potato-sized or otherwise, anytime soon, but I was more hopeful than I'd felt in years, maybe *ever*. That was not to be discounted, but excited as I was, I had bigger problems right now.

"What's bigger than your magic?" Sibyl asked.

I didn't know, which was one of the problems. I'd thought I was saved when Nik had said he didn't remember, but you didn't wake someone up and ask them to drive across town to chat about nothing. Granted, most guys who dumped me did so without bothering to invite me over, and Nik wasn't even supposed to remember all the stuff that would lead us down the doom path, but I'd never had a "We need to talk" that had ended well for me, and that was a problem. The DFZ's offer notwithstanding, I was still set on using the gold-market trick to get around my dad's curse. I actually already had a plan to ramp us up to the kind of money I needed to hit my dad's deadline, but it required Nik to work. If this talk went the way all my others had, I might be crawling back to the DFZ this afternoon.

But while I was definitely worried about money, my true fears were much simpler. I didn't want things to blow up because I *liked* Nik. I hadn't realized it until after he'd kissed me and thrown everything into chaos, but I'd come to rely on him for a lot more than just work. For example, Peter should have been the one I asked to come with me to the Night Lot. He was the mage, and experimenting with my curse had been his idea to begin with. He was the obvious choice, but I hadn't even considered asking him to help. I'd gone straight for Nik and guilted him into coming instead. He was the one I trusted, the one I turned to. I'd never had that with a guy before, and if I'd screwed everything up because of one stupid drunken kiss, I was going to be so freaking *mad*.

But there was no way to know without talking to him, so I sat nervously on the edge of the subscription car's cheap seat, staring out the window at the passing city until it turned into the drop-off zone for Nik's building.

I got out slowly, tugging at my cheap clothes in an effort to make them look less like I'd pulled them out of a plastic tube. When my teenybopper ensemble was as decent as I could manage, I tromped down the stairs to his basement apartment.

Since Nik tended to answer his door with a gun, I'd made a policy of announcing myself. I did so this time out of habit, knocking on the metal door as I called out, "It's me."

There was a soft shuffle inside, and then the door opened a crack, but I didn't see Nik. My first paranoid thought was that he was avoiding me, then I spotted him lying on the couch, one long leg stretched out to open the door handle with his bare foot.

"Sorry," he muttered, covering his eyes with his hand. "I can't get up."

"Oh my god," I said, rushing inside. "Have you been there the whole time?"

"Not the whole time," Nik said, adding his other hand so he could grind his eyeballs with both palms at once. "I took a shower after I called you, but standing made me dizzy, so I laid back down."

That explained why his short black hair looked wet. "You could have moved to the bed, though," I said, glancing at his legs propped up on the couch arm. "You'd fit better."

He shook his head. "If I lay down in bed, I'd just have to get up again when you arrived. This was easier."

"I could have talked to you there," I argued, biting my lip. "Seriously, you look terrible. Can I help you with anything? Do you need food or water or…"

"Some water would be good."

I nodded and grabbed the glass I'd given him last night off the floor. By the time I'd filled it and come back, Nik had managed to push himself into a sitting position. He drank three cups of water in rapid succession and then flopped back against the ugly cushions with a sigh. "Maybe having a couch isn't so bad after all."

If things had been normal, this was where I would have said "I told you so," but all I could think of now was him telling me last night that he'd kept the couch because I'd asked him to, so I said nothing. Instead, I grabbed the folding chair by the wall—which I'd come to think of as *my* folding chair—and brought it over. It wasn't really necessary, but if we were going to have A Talk, I wanted to be sitting down for it.

"Do you need anything else?" I asked hopefully.

Nik shook his head and pushed himself up again, but he didn't look at me. He just sat there staring at his hands, one human, one articulated metal. Both were clenched, digging in my certainty that this was going to be bad.

"We need to talk about last night."

I'd known it was coming, but hearing it still made my stomach drop. "Okay," I said, trying not to let my voice shake. "What do you—"

"I owe you an apology," Nik interrupted, speaking quickly and clearly, as if he'd rehearsed this. "I told you I didn't want to go to Rentfree, but I didn't tell you the real reason why. That was my bad judgment, and it almost got you killed. I didn't know the attack on the roof was coming, but I knew there was bound to be something. I should have warned you, but I thought I could handle it. Obviously, I was wrong. This whole thing was my fault, and I'm sorry."

Nik looked at me then as if he expected me to hit him, but I was sitting with my jaw open. "Wait," I said at last, barely believing my ears. "*That's* what you called me here for? To apologize about what happened on the roof?"

Nik scowled. "What else would there be?"

"Nothing," I said. Way too fast, but I couldn't help it. I was just *so* relieved he'd wanted to talk about the fighting and not the kissing, which told me something about my screwed-up priorities. Still, it was *such* a relief to see that he really, honestly didn't remember. For once in my life, the worst hadn't happened. I *hadn't* screwed everything up, and it felt so much like a miracle, I actually started to laugh.

"What are you doing?" Nik demanded as I collapsed into giggles.

"Nothing," I gasped, waving my hands at him. "It's nothing, really. Please don't mind me, and don't worry about what happened on the deck. It really wasn't a big deal."

Now it was Nik's turn to gape at me. "Not a big deal?" he repeated, gray eyes wide. "Opal, we got jumped by four guys with full cyber. You were nearly *shot in the back* so they could get to me. This is not a small thing! I still don't completely understand how we got out alive. *Look.*"

He lurched sideways to grab the armored leather jacket I'd been wearing last night off the arm of the couch. "There's blood all over the shoulder here." He held out the coat so I could see. "It's not mine, so unless you got it near one of the guys I shot, it has to be yours. You got hurt because of me, and then you had to rescue me from my own mess, and I don't even know what happened!"

The almost-panic crept back into his voice as he spoke, snapping me out of my stupid giggle fit. "Let's not jump to conclusions," I said, calmly now. "First of all, that is my blood on your coat, but it's not because you got me hurt. I did that to myself, but I'll pay for all the dry cleaning—"

"*I don't care about the dry cleaning!*" Nik yelled, clutching the jacket as he looked me over, clearly searching for hidden bandages. "How bad were you hurt?"

"Not as bad as you were," I said, setting my jaw stubbornly. "And again, it was *my fault.* I was the idiot who was too busy gawking at what was in front of her to watch her back. I got grabbed, and then I got all pissed off and blasted the roof with way too much magic. It was prideful and shortsighted, and while it did get us out, it's a miracle I didn't cook your brains. Really, you should be yelling at me. You were handling things just fine until I messed you up."

"You shouldn't have been in that situation to begin with," Nik said, seething. "I never should have gone with you to Rentfree. You would have been fine on your own. Tourists go to the Night Lot all the time. Me being there just complicated things, but I didn't want to let you—" He cut off, snapping his mouth shut as if he'd just realized what he was about to say. "I didn't want to say no when you asked me for help," he finished carefully. "But I should have. As you saw, Rentfree and me don't mix."

"Why not?"

Nik flinched at the question, and I started to scramble. "You don't have to tell me if you don't want! I was just curious."

"It's okay," he said, slumping back into the cushions again. "You faced a gun for it, so you deserve to know." He took a deep breath and looked me in the eyes. "You've probably guessed I did some…questionable things before I became a Cleaner."

I shrugged. "Being a Cleaner's pretty questionable by itself."

"Not like this."

He said that like he expected me to gasp and faint, and I rolled my eyes. "Nik," I said, frustrated. "I grew up in a dragon's household. I discovered a *dead body* in an apartment just last week. I'm not a fragile flower." I pointed at his false right arm. "I know you don't get cyberware like that from an office job, but whatever you did in the past, I'm the last person in the world who's going to jump down your throat about it now. People do what they've gotta do, and you've done more for me than anyone. It's okay. You can tell me. I mean, were you in a gang or—"

"Not in a gang," he said, shaking his head. "But I did work for several. I worked for everyone. I was a freelancer. I did whatever people paid me to do, mostly in Rentfree."

That explained Maggie's interest when he showed up, but, "Why Rentfree?" I asked. "It's the definition of 'low rent.' Doesn't seem like a good place to look for work."

Nik shrugged. "It was good for the sort of work I did, and it was familiar. I grew up there."

He spat that last bit out like a pulled tooth, but I sat straight up in my chair. "Wait, really? You grew up in *Rentfree?*"

That was clearly not the response he'd expected. "Yeah," he said, looking at me warily. "You don't think that's scary?"

"It's rough, sure," I said excitedly. "But Rentfree's always in the movies, and it looks damn cool with the bridges and the crazy stacked buildings and everything moving all the time. So did you live in that insane pit area with all the electrical wires or..."

I trailed off, eyes going wide. Crap. *Craaaaap.* I was being a total tourist. Nik had just told me he'd grown up in the poorest part of the Underground, a place that was famous for murder, drug use, and gangs, and I'd responded by talking about how cool it looked. Talk about insensitive.

"I'm sorry," I said, covering my face with my hands. "Let me try that again."

"It's okay," Nik said quickly. "I prefer the way you talk about it. I've always thought of Rentfree as a cesspool. It's the bottom of the DFZ, the place where all the trash settles." His lips pressed into a flat line. "I fit right in."

"I don't think so."

"You didn't know me back then," Nik said darkly. "Trust me, I was right at home. I did whatever work people needed, didn't matter how dirty. Hits, robberies, drive-bys, arson, kidnapping, it was all game. I had no limits so long as people had cash, and as you saw from Maggie, there's always work to be had if you don't care what you're doing."

I nodded slowly, trying to imagine it. Then I remembered something. "Wait, does that mean you *did* kill that guy's brother?"

Nik shrugged. "Maybe? I honestly don't remember. I've killed a lot of people, and I was on a lot of drugs back then. It all kind of runs together."

He said this like a confession, but I was more shocked than anything else. Nik was so disciplined and together, I couldn't imagine him as a druggie. That would explain the liver scrubber, though. I'd known plenty of addicts during my trust-fund-kid days, and the ones who got clean tended to be super hardcore about staying that way. A device that automatically scrubbed intoxicants out of your system sounded like it would be a real help in that fight, but it was still so strange. I just couldn't see the Nik I knew getting involved with anything that messy.

"How did you end up in that situation?"

"Just sort of fell into it," he said, eyes locked on his hands again. "My mom was a chiphead who spent all her time lying in flop houses plugged into whatever VR fantasy she could afford. I couldn't wake her up most of the time, so it was learn to fend for myself or starve."

I stared at him in shock. "That's *horrible*."

Nik shrugged. "It was pretty common for the neighborhood."

"That doesn't make it right," I said angrily. "How old were you?"

"For which part?" he asked. "It was that way for all I can remember. I'm not actually sure if I really am twenty-eight. That's just my best guess. I was basically alone for most of my childhood."

He said this as if it was nothing, just a normal sort of hardship, but I couldn't even imagine. "How did you survive?"

"Stealing mostly," Nik said casually. "Sometimes people would give me food when they wanted me to do something, but mostly I just took what I could. There's always food in the DFZ if you're not too picky."

I nodded numbly.

"That's why I'm so picky about my food now," he went on. "I don't ever want to have to eat trash again. Really, though, it could have been worse. Rentfree moves so much there's always somewhere to hide, so I never got scooped up by traffickers or sold into one of the kill arenas. I got tall early and learned to use a gun, which helped me get my first real job. Things just kind of snowballed from there."

I looked down at my hands in my lap as I tried to process all of that. I'd always known the DFZ was a city of personal tragedies. You didn't get to be that reckless with your capitalism without someone getting wrecked. There was a whole genre of movies about the mean streets of places like Rentfree. I'd been a sucker for all of them, but watching a sob story and sitting across from someone who'd actually lived one were two very different experiences. I had nothing in my life I could relate to Nik's hardship, nothing I could give. Saying "sorry" felt like a cop-out, but I *was* sorry. Heartbreakingly, tragically sorry for everything that had happened to him. The idea of Nik as a kid trying desperately to wake up his blissed-out mother because he was hungry made me want to sob, but that felt selfish when Nik wasn't reacting at all.

It would have been easier if he *had* broken down. At least then I could have comforted him. But he'd told me all of this the same way he told me salvage prices had dropped again: just repeating unhappy facts. I couldn't be calm, though. It must have shown, too, because Nik sighed.

"I didn't tell you all this to make you feel sorry for me," he said bitterly. "I know you thought I was a criminal when we first met, and you weren't wrong. I got into Cleaning because I was tired of getting shot at, and I was running out of body parts to replace, but as you saw last night, you never really get out. I've got so many people who want revenge on me that I can't keep track of them all. Staying out of Rentfree and moving to a new apartment every few months avoids most of the trouble, but I can't dodge it all. What happened on that parking deck was bigger than it should have been because I got reckless, but it wasn't that unusual, and it'll probably happen again. You shouldn't have to deal with that."

I shook my head. "It's not—"

"You're here to make money, not take a bullet because of some shit I did years ago," Nik said, finally lifting his head to look at me again. "This was my screwup. I should have told you what you were in for at the beginning, but I didn't want to scare you away, and I thought I could handle it. I couldn't, though, and I can't guarantee it won't happen again, so if you want out, now's the time."

A chill crept over me. "Why would I want out?"

"I don't know," he said angrily, glaring at his fisted hands. "Maybe because you don't want to get shot at for stupid crap?"

"I get you shot at, too," I reminded him. "We got jumped by a whole merc team in the Gnarls just last week because of me."

"That's different."

"How is it different?"

"Because I knew it was going to happen!" he yelled at me. "Kauffman's a fixer, and I've worked with him before. I knew what we were in for better than you did! Everything I've done with you I've done eyes open, but this is different. I didn't lie to your face, but there's so much I didn't tell you that I might as well have. If someone gave me a job and told me as little about the potential dangers as I've told you, I'd have killed them!"

"I don't see what that has to do with anything," I said, getting angry too now. "You keep trying to make me jump, but I'm not doing it, Nik. Maybe it was wrong of you not to tell me the risks, but I totally understand why you hid them, and I don't care! You told me yesterday when I was feeding you these same lines that it was your choice to stay. Well, shoe's on the other foot. You can give me all the logic you want, but I'm not going to leave you. If you want to end our partnership, you're going to have to be the one who stands up and walks out, because I'm not budging."

To prove my point, I crossed my arms over my chest and sat back in my chair with my feet flat on the ground, daring him to try and move me. For his part, Nik just stared at me as if I was crazy, and then he dropped his head into his hands.

"Why are you being so stubborn?" he whispered.

"Because I need you."

I regretted the words the moment they were out of my mouth. They sounded so cold and transactional, like I was only here because of my debt. But at least Nik was looking at me again, so I kept going.

"You're the only one I trust to help me," I went on, angling for brutal honesty since tact was dead and buried. "You want to talk about lies? I didn't tell you my dad was a dragon. You had to find out the hard way, but you didn't abandon me. Even when you found out I was cursed, you still stayed and helped bail me out. I can't replace that. I appreciate everything you've told me, and I understand why it took you so long, but none of it changes what you are to me. You're my hope. You're my ally and my trusted partner in a city where those things are very rare. We've got an amazing thing going here, and if you think I'm going to let some chromed-out idiots ruin that for me, you're insane."

That might have been a bit *too* much honesty. Nik certainly looked stunned, and then he let out a long breath.

"Okay."

"Okay what?" I asked nervously.

"Okay, I'm insane," he said, flashing me a helpless smile.

"Well is it a temporary madness? Because I don't want to have to go through this again."

He laughed at that. I laughed, too. Not because I thought any of this was funny—it had been terrifying—but because I was so relieved. "So we're good now?"

"We're good," Nik said, rubbing a nervous hand through his damp hair. "Sorry I made such a big deal about it, but in my defense, most people freak out over being shot."

I snorted. "What part of our interactions made you think I have a normal reaction to anything?"

"None," he admitted. Then his smile grew warm. "After all, you didn't leave."

I froze, mind whirling back to last night when I'd been sitting in this exact spot except on the floor instead of a chair, holding his hand to show him I was still here. "I thought you didn't remember that?"

"I remember the roof," he said. "When those guys jumped us, you didn't leave me behind."

"Oh," I said, slumping over in my chair. Then I snapped right back up. "Of course I didn't leave you! What kind of person would just run off and leave you to die?"

"Most of them," he said, completely seriously.

I harrumphed. "You must know some shitty people."

"That's why I'm happy to be partnered with you," he said, that warm smile still on his face.

I actually leaned into it before I caught myself and jerked away. *Stupid, stupid.* I'd been handed a Hail Mary by Nik's loss of memory, but it was all for nothing if I screwed up my end by getting mushy. Fortunately, I knew just the thing to keep myself safely distracted. Or obsessed, depending on how you looked at it.

"So," I said, rising from my chair. "If we're back to normal…" I paused until he nodded. "I have a new proposition for you."

He arched an eyebrow. "Proposition for what?"

"Work," I said, pulling out my phone to show him the price of gold, which had rebounded slightly from the dip I'd caused last night. "We know how to get around my dad's curse now, but I've still got to make three hundred thousand dollars by the end of the month."

"Wait," Nik said, eyes wide. "Three *hundred* thousand? By the end of the month? *Why?*"

I blinked at him. "Because my dad threw a fit when he called and demanded I pay the full amount. Didn't I tell you?"

"*No!*"

"Oh," I said, frowning. "Sorry. Anyway, them's the breaks. But I know we can do it."

"By what logic?" Nik demanded. "DeSantos can't pull that kind of money in a month, and he's got a ten-man crew. *I* didn't even get paid that much when I was working freelance."

Wow. Apparently hiring someone to kill people you didn't like was a lot cheaper than I'd thought. But that was neither here nor there. "I've got a plan," I told him. "It'll take a lot of work and no small amount of luck, but if we hit the morning and evening auctions every day, it should be doable. Just. Unfortunately, if we keep dividing our income fifty-fifty—"

"I see the problem." Nik said. "You need to change the profit split."

"Just for this month," I promised. "Here's my deal: if you let me keep all our earnings for the next three weeks, I'll give you *all* my money I make for the next three months minus what I need for rent and food.

Everything over what I need for survival will be yours to keep, and since I'll be uncursed by then, it should be a *lot*."

Nik scowled, thinking that over. I held my breath, waiting. I was giving him a hell of a deal, but giving up a month's worth of income was a pretty big ask. I didn't even know if Nik had that much ready money on hand, but pulling this off was already one hell of a push. If I had to split profits even a little, the chances of making my goal by the deadline were pretty much zero. I was about to sweeten the deal by telling him he could keep all the money if we didn't make it since I wouldn't need it trapped in Korea when Nik suddenly nodded.

"Deal."

"You sure?"

"Absolutely." He flashed me a greedy smile. "I saw how much money you were making before the curse, and I know how much you make now. With this bargain, I'll be giving up fifty percent of your worst-performing weeks for nearly a hundred percent on twelve of your best. That's a three hundred percent return on investment."

"And you're sure you can make it for a month?" I asked nervously. "Because I'm going to need everything."

"I'm fine. I've made plenty of months on no income before."

He said that casually, but the reminder of his poverty-stricken childhood still made my heart go out to him. Even at my hungriest, I'd always known in the back of my head that I could run back to my dad if things got unbearable. Nik hadn't had a safety net like that. He hadn't had anyone.

"Can I ask you a personal question?"

"Depends on the question," he said. "But go for it."

"You said you grew up alone on the streets of Rentfree," I said quietly. "But how did you do it? I get that you found jobs, but in between that, how did you go for weeks on end with no money?"

Nik shrugged. "This and that. A lot of it was learning how not to spend money so I'd have cash to cover the lean times. Also, if I got really desperate, I could always find work at the arena."

"The arena?" I frowned. "You mean that big place at the bottom of the pit?"

He nodded. "The guy who owns it, the Gameskeeper, will give anyone a job if they ask. He's the biggest employer in the neighborhood. Everyone in Rentfree's worked for him at some point, though not always in the same way."

That sounded like a decent, community-minded thing to do, but something in the way Nik said it made me wince. "What kind of work does he have people do?"

"Stuff you gotta be desperate to take," Nik said grimly. "He's the one who taught me that some jobs aren't worth the money."

The fingers on his mechanical right hand closed into a fist as he finished. The curious idiot in me was dying to ask if this "Gameskeeper" was the guy he'd said he'd never work for again when he'd turned down Kauffman's final offer on the cockatrices, but this was definitely not the time. I had Nik on my side and a very limited span of days to put my plans into motion, which meant it was time to get to work.

"So," I said, flashing him a smile. "Ready to make some money?"

"I'd hoped for more sleep," Nik said, leaning back on the couch. "But you're the boss this month, so what do you have in mind?"

My body ached at the word "sleep," but I fiercely ignored it. I could sleep when this was over. Right now, time was money, and everything was against us.

"Next Cleaning auction isn't until tomorrow morning," I said, waving my hand over my phone's screen. "But Sunday afternoons are prime shopping time, and I've still got an apartment full of brand-new, overpriced furniture I don't want."

Nik gave me a skeptical look. "You can only empty that apartment so many times, you know."

"I know," I said. "But you work with what you've got."

"Fair enough," he said, standing up. "Better get moving, then. I'll drive, you get the truck."

"Already on it," I said, ordering Sibyl to scramble our last moving truck rental of the month and to find out where we could get more trucks on the cheap, because we were going to need a *lot*.

CHAPTER 7

We grabbed everything in my apartment. Ev. Re. Thing. We took the furniture, the pillows, the appliances. We grabbed all the makeup and the toiletries, the vanity and the hairbrushes. We got the curtains and the paintings and the bulbs out of the recessed lights. Nik showed me how to remove countertops, so we ripped the granite out, too, as well as the plates, silverware, and the fancy laser faucet my mom had stuck in my kitchen sink.

In the end, the only parts of my new apartment that didn't get shoved into the truck were the hardwood flooring (only because it would have been more work than it was worth), my mattress (I needed somewhere to sleep), and the dry food in my pantry (supplies). Everything else we hauled away to sell, though not to the flea market this time. Selling to individual vendors was usually the best money, but as I'd found last night, most tables didn't keep gold on hand, and I didn't want to have to run every single item in the truck through a web of barter until I found one that did. If I was going to use this trick to pay my whole debt, I needed a scalable solution. Somewhere with a lot of gold on hand and an insatiable appetite for secondhand goods, which is how Nik and I ended up rolling to a stop in front of a squat brick building with iron bars in the windows and a blindingly bright sign that read *Martin's Tailor and Pawn*.

"A pawn shop?" Nik said, looking at the flashing neon in disgust. "Seriously? Are you *trying* to get ripped off?"

"No, I want to be paid in gold," I said, getting out of his car. "Pawn shops always have gold. And yeah, they'll try to cheat you hard, but when you consider I'd be making fifty percent less at places that only pay in cash, getting ripped off for ten to twenty suddenly isn't so bad. Also, they're everywhere. The DFZ Underground has more pawn shops than banks and credit unions combined, so if we buy up all the gold at one place, we can just move on. It's perfect!"

"It's embarrassing," Nik snapped. "We're Cleaners. *Professionals.* Pawn shops cater to the desperate and idiots who don't know any better."

"Or people who want to be able to get their stuff back someday," I said defensively, motioning for Sibyl to pull our moving truck into the side alley. "Are you coming in or not?"

Nik rolled his eyes and climbed out of the car, shoving his gloved hands into his pockets as he followed me through the jingle-belled door into a shop filled with the usual DFZ Underground assortment. There were guns on the wall and jewelry in long glass cases. A double-layered rack in the middle displayed all manner of scandalous clothing, and there was a cabinet in the back corner filled with hookahs and pipes in every shape, color, and suggestive theme. There were more practical items, too, like power tools and winter coats, but nothing really stood out. Honestly, the only things in the shop that were worth a second look were the items on the shelf behind the register.

Now *these* were good. First in line was a taxidermy pangolin that still had most of its scales. Next to that was a religious icon painted on a folding wood panel depicting the martyrdom of St. Sebastian. That wasn't too unusual—Sebastian was a very popular saint—but this painting was remarkable because he actually looked like he was dying, not just sitting there being hunky with a few arrows jabbed artistically into his rippling abs. Next up was a pair of opera glasses decorated with scenes from Swan Lake that had been used at the Bolshoi Theatre before the first Russian revolution. That was a *really* good piece, actually. So rare to find one that wasn't cracked. I was rising up on my toes to get a better look when a middle-aged man with a bald head, a protruding gut, and a bushy beard came out of the curtained back room.

"Ophelia!" he cried, holding out his arms when he spotted me. "It's been an age! Are you here to pay up and get your stuff back?"

"It's Opal, and hey, Martin," I said, ignoring Nik's startled look. "I'm here to sell today. You still buying furniture?"

"I buy anything," Martin said, giving me a wink. "I don't have enough room for the big stuff here, but my brother and I have a warehouse under the freeway that sells furniture exclusively. What you got?"

I smirked and crooked my finger. "Quality."

He followed me delightedly, giving Nik a wide berth as we went outside to inspect the truck. As expected, Martin's eyes lit up when he saw all the pricey crap my mom liked. With so many flea markets and the big auction houses, pawn shops usually got the scraps. A haul like mine was a rare event on his calendar, and I knew it.

"I want three thousand for the whole thing."

"That's crazy," he said. "I can't sell it for that much."

He could get five thousand easy, but you never opened a negotiation with what you actually wanted. "Twenty-eight hundred," I countered, lifting my chin. "But I'll drop it to twenty-five if you pay me in gold."

Martin did a double take. "Pay you in what?"

"Gold," I said again. "Watches, jewelry, coins. I don't care so long as the weight's there."

"Why do you want gold?" he asked, giving me a funny look. "Is this more of your witchcraft stuff?"

Nik's head whipped around. "Witchcraft? What year do you think this is? She's a *mage*."

Martin snorted. "You haven't seen the things she's sold me."

I *had* sold him some pretty awesome stuff over the last few months. Stuff I absolutely intended to get back once my current state of magically induced poverty finally came to an end. "I'm just in a gold mood right now," I said, giving him an innocent smile. "Twenty-five hundred. We'll trade by weight."

"Two thousand and I'll give you back your stuffed armadillo."

"It's a *pangolin*, and no," I said firmly, clenching my hands to keep them from reaching out for my armored darling. "Twenty-five hundred is fair and you know it. Do you want this stuff or not? Because we can go somewhere else."

Martin looked hungrily at the white-quilted bed frame. "Twenty-two hundred?"

I pulled out my phone and started typing a command to Sibyl to close up the truck.

"Okay, twenty-five!" Martin said angrily. "But you have to unload it."

I glanced at Nik, who shrugged. "Deal," I said. "Where do you want it?"

"Put it in the garage," he said, pointing at the rolling door set in the rear wall of his shop. "I'll go see if I can scrape together twenty-five hundred in gold."

"Pleasure doing business with you," I said cheerfully as he shuffled inside, muttering under his breath about witches and gold and cursed furniture. When he was gone, I turned to find Nik glowering at me.

"How much stuff have you pawned in the last five months?"

"All of it?" I said with a shrug, walking up the ramp into the truck to grab a box. "Hard to say exactly. I pawned it off in bits and pieces whenever I needed to cover a bill. The stuff you helped me save was the last dregs. Trust me, my collection used to be *amazing*."

"Why didn't you just sell it?" Nik asked, tromping up to grab my couch. "You would have gotten a lot more."

"Because I'm one of the people who wanted to get her stuff back someday," I said grouchily. "If I'd sold, I probably could have made double, but it would have been bought by an actual collector, and then I'd never see it again. If I pawn it here, though, no one cares. Did you see the prices he's charging? No one in this neighborhood is going to pay that much for a 'stuffed armadillo.'" I smiled. "Way I see it, he's paying me to store my stuff. And yeah, there's a chance it'll get sold before I can buy it back, but I'll take the risk and the price cut if it means a chance to buy my treasures back."

And I *would* get them back. I'd scattered my collection to pawn shops all across the city to limit my losses in case another collector walked in one day and realized what he was looking at. Ironically, a lot of it was stuff I'd bought with my dad while he'd been teaching me how to auction. A mutual love of beautiful and interesting stuff was the only thing we'd had in common there at the end. He'd been so proud of me when I'd spotted the one actual antique in a sea of fakes, or when I'd scored what had looked like a dirty length of cloth at a salvage auction that turned out to be a previously unknown portrait by John Singer Sargent. That oil painting was still on display in the entrance hall of my dad's art museum in Seoul. We both knew it wasn't one of Sargent's best and probably didn't deserve the front billing, but my dad had refused to move it.

It was stuff like that that used to give me hope. All through my first four years of undergrad, I'd thought Yong could be reasoned with if I could just find the right argument. Every time I tried, though, we ended up yelling at each other, until eventually I'd accepted that I was wrong. There was no reasoning with a tyrant who refused to change his mind.

"Come on," I said angrily, glaring at my mother's over-priced ecru pillows and embroidered throws. "Let's dump this junk and go."

Thanks to Nik's ability to carry five boxes at a time and lift couches one-handed, it took us barely twenty minutes to empty the truck into the dirty garage. When we walked back into the shop, Martin had my gold all laid out on the counter. He'd even put it on a black velvet cloth, as if I actually cared about the craftsmanship of the watches and rings. I could already tell the Rolex was fake from the doorway, but the label didn't matter. All I cared about was if the gold plating was legit. Fortunately, my goggles had a density sensor that was even better than the one on my phone. I normally used it for checking the thickness of doors and seeing what was on the other side of box piles, but the interface had a whole menu for testing metals. Gold, being so dense, showed up great, which was how I knew just how badly I was being cheated.

"I said gold, not yellow-tinted aluminum," I growled, tossing the watch back at him.

Martin was completely unapologetic. "What do I look like, Dubai? Real gold's hard to get here. Everything's fake in the DFZ."

"Well, keep looking," I ordered.

He held up his phone. "I can trade you cryptos."

"No one wants your imaginary money."

"All money is imaginary," he said stoically, then he ruined it by adding. "I can also give you real money."

I planted my finger on his counter hard enough to make the glass squeak. "I said *gold*."

"All right, all right, geeze. What are you, a dragon?" He bent down and came back up with a huge bucket of gold jewelry. "Find it yourself, you're so picky."

I dug into the box greedily, holding up each ring, earring, chain, and tennis bracelet so my scanner could get a good shot. As Martin had warned, almost all of them were fakes, which made me feel very sorry for anyone who didn't have a scanner, because this bastard was pricing them as if they were the real deal. Fortunately for me, twenty-five hundred dollars isn't actually that much gold. Only seventy-eight grams according to the current market price Sibyl looked up for me. I had to piece it together bit by bit, but in the end, I got what I was looking for.

"Thank you for doing business," I said as I scraped my *actual* gold into a pile.

"Yeah, yeah," Martin said, clearly eager to be rid of me, but I wasn't done yet. "Before I go," I said, holding my ground when he tried to lead me to the door, "it said outside that you also buy gold here."

"So?" he said. "Every pawn shop does. Where do you think all that stuff you pocketed came from?"

"Not gold jewelry," I clarified. "Scrap gold. You know, bought by the ounce for the commodity price."

"Oh yeah, I do that, too," he said. "Profit's not as good as jewelry, so I haven't been pushing it, but I buy gold and silver on the market, yeah."

"Great," I said, shoving all the gold I'd just meticulously picked out back across his counter. "I want to sell this."

He stared at me for a good thirty seconds. "Are you serious?"

"As a heart attack," I said, staring right back at him. "And before you ask why I didn't just ask for money in the first place, it's complicated. You don't want me to talk about it."

Martin shook his head and walked back to his register, muttering under his breath about why the DFZ attracted so many crazies. "How many grams did you weigh out?"

"Seventy eight," I told him, placing my gold on his digital scale so he could see.

He double-checked the number and punched it in. "Okay, looks like the current price is thirty dollars per gram."

I shook my head. "That can't be right. It was thirty-five when I looked it up a minute ago."

"Yeah, well, the market went down, see?" He turned his monitor around to show me the graph, which was indeed plunging toward the bottom of the screen. "Sorry, Ophelia. Your bad luck, eh?"

I didn't bother to correct him on my name this time. I just waved for him to finish the transaction before the price fell any lower. After the exchange fee, my total came to just under twenty-two hundred dollars. A terrible take for an entire apartment's worth of brand-new furniture and luxury beauty products, but a lot better than I normally did.

"It dropped a lot more this time," Nik noted when we finally left the store. "I bet it's because you exchanged so much."

"I was thinking the same thing," I said as we walked to his car. "If the market drop depends on how much we're selling, then we should make sure to sell as often as possible to limit how much we get screwed. It would suck to save up a hundred thousand in gold only to trade it in for fifty grand."

"You still made a profit, though!" Sibyl said encouragingly.

"Hard not to make a profit selling stuff you got for free," I quipped, checking my bank account. "But we've got enough to buy some good units tomorrow. Now we just need to do this a hundred and thirty-six more times in the next twenty days and we're set."

"Oh sure, easy," Nik said as he climbed into the driver's seat. "So is there anything else you want to sell, or are you done?"

I didn't want to be done, but until the auction tomorrow morning, there wasn't anything else for me to do. "I think I'm good for tonight."

"Great," Nik said, cranking the engine. "I'm starving. Want to get dinner?"

I was sorely tempted, but "getting dinner" with Nik meant him cooking, and I didn't want to eat Nik's food while I was also taking all his money.

"No thanks."

He stared at me as if I was a pod person, which was fair since the real Opal never turned down food. "Are you feeling okay?"

"I'm fine," I said. "Just tired." Which was the goddamn truth. I was so exhausted I was about to fall asleep in his car, but Nik kept pushing.

"Are you sick?" he asked, looking me up and down. "Wait, you're not planning to eat that potato in your bag, are you? 'Cause we just sold your microwave and your convection oven."

"It's not for eating!" I cried. "That's my magic potato!"

I knew how bad that sounded as soon as it came out of my mouth. Unfortunately, everything I could have said to explain it made even less sense. What was I supposed to tell him? That I'd gone on a journey of self-discovery through a never-ending forest and received a magical potato from a dead Shaman who was also a satellite body for the god of the DFZ? Even I thought that story sounded fishy, and I'd been there.

"It's complicated," I said instead, pressing a hand over my tired eyes. "Can you just take me home, please?"

Nik stared suspiciously at me for a good thirty seconds, and then he shook his head and cranked the car, sliding us into the evening traffic like a fish jumping back into a stream.

***

"Okay, how much do we have?"

We were sitting in the auditorium-turned-auction-room at the DFZ Cleaner's headquarters. It was five fifty-five am on Monday, five minutes before the week's first bids opened, and the place was packed. Nik had picked me up early so we could get good seats, but the front seats had already been taken when we'd arrived, so we'd had to settle for second row middle. It was still a good spot, but I knew from the crowd that bidding was going to be fierce.

"Three thousand twenty-four dollars and eighty-seven cents," Sibyl replied, covering my AR interface with the accounting spreadsheets she'd put together for me while I slept. "I went through all the records of your previous units, and your best average rate of return is when you buy a two-bedroom apartment on the first floor of a mid-sized building in a middle-class neighborhood for under a thousand dollars. I'd recommend getting three of those to maximize yield."

I sighed. "You know I don't control what comes up for auction, right?"

"Hey, I'm just telling you what the algorithms told me," my AI said. "I ran ten thousand simulations using data from the past five months, and even applying the loss from selling at pawn shops and converting profits to gold, I estimate you have at least a forty percent chance of success. That's not too bad! It's just a simulation, of course. You're the one who has to actually pull it off in meatspace. But if you avoid wasting your money on the long shots, you should have a slightly less than a coin flip's chance of making your goal."

I would have preferred better than a coin flip, but forty percent wouldn't take *too* much luck. "Thanks for the number crunch, Sib."

"Always a pleasure," Sibyl replied warmly. "I know how happy good numbers make you!"

They did. I'd say I was easy to please, but it was actually really hard to get good numbers these days.

"So what's the plan?" Nik asked, handing me back my cup of vending-machine coffee when I pushed my goggles off my face.

"Same as always," I said, ignoring the taste of cheap chemicals as I sipped my lukewarm beverage in a desperate quest for caffeine. "I'm still cursed, so you're going to have to bid. I'll tell you maxes like usual, but I want to buy a lot of units, so get ready to go crazy."

"How many units are we talking?" Nik asked. "There's still only two of us."

"Trust me, I've got a plan," I told him confidently, draining the last of my cup and pulling my goggles back down. "Just bid on everything I tell you."

Nik still looked suspicious when his face popped up on my goggles' cameras, but Broker was already walking in, so we both turned to face the short stage with its ancient red velvet curtain.

"Happy Monday, kiddos!" Broker said cheerfully, his surgically perfected face grinning as he took his place at the podium. "There's a lot of you and a lot of units, so let's do this quick-like."

He ran his fingers over the glass touchscreen on his podium, and an image popped up in my AR. It was also projected on the actual screen up on the stage, but my shot was much bigger, clearer, and—most important of all—ready to be digitally searched by Sibyl's photo-recognition software.

Not that it was necessary for this one. As always, Broker led with the big tickets, starting with an entire abandoned factory. No one raised their hand on that one. There was almost certainly profit hidden in there somewhere, but even the shot of the front showed a lot of broken windows, and who had time to dig through three hundred thousand square feet of broken factory equipment that had probably already been picked over by looters? Broker went all the way down to one dollar before shucking the factory into the shred pile, which was basically the end of it. If even Cleaners didn't want a property, the DFZ considered it dead. Shreds were sometimes remodeled, but the city spirit usually just sucked them back down into the ground and replaced them with something new. That was the way of the DFZ: if you weren't valuable, you were waste.

Not always.

I jumped a foot in my chair.

"What?" Nik said, whipping around.

"Nothing," I lied, rubbing my temples as I tried to get the ghostly voice out of my head.

I'm a spirit, not a ghost, the DFZ's voice said huffily. *Totally different phenomena.*

I don't recall allowing you into my head, I thought back at her testily.

"Yes you did," Sibyl said defensively. "I showed you how to turn off surface thought reading in the options, but you said to leave it alone, so—"

"Not you," I told my AI.

"Not me what?" Nik said.

I shook my head and closed my eyes, trying to shut out the crowd I'd built up.

Don't worry, I'm not here all the time, the DFZ assured me. *I just popped in to say that my offer is still open. Oh, and Dr. Kowalski wants you to practice your potato.*

I rolled my eyes. Great, now I had people badgering me to practice again.

"I'm not badgering you," Sibyl said, sounding hurt.

Think of it as a friendly reminder, the DFZ said cheerfully. *Next auction's up, by the way.*

Broker was indeed putting the next unit on the screen, so I put the spirit's voice out of my mind and focused on paying attention.

The second place was an apartment on the Skyways. That should have made it stupid expensive by default, but the picture from the doorway showed a living room that was waist-deep in trash. I grinned at the disgusting spectacle. Hoarding always brought the price down, and I'd already spotted several good signs. Enough to make me lean over to Nik.

"Go up to one thousand," I whispered.

He blinked at me. "Really? It's a trash heap."

"A trash heap with a pile of takeout boxes from *Le Palais,*" I said smugly. "That place is three hundred bucks a plate."

Nik still didn't look convinced, but he dutifully raised his hand for the hundred-dollar starting bid. There were a few other contenders, but everyone hated hoarded units, and we ended up winning it for eight hundred bucks.

"Right on the money," I said as the unit address flashed up on my screen next to our names. "Okay, next."

"Next?" Nik said. "You just bought a full day's worth of work."

"Relax," I said. "I told you, I've got a plan."

"Does it involve a bulldozer?"

"We're not going to make three hundred grand in three weeks if we stick to the same old routine," I reminded him. "Just keep bidding. I got this."

Nik scowled, clearly unhappy. I let him grump, mostly because I had nothing to say that would cheer him up. But uncomfortable as it was, I was committed, eyes locked on the screen as the next unit popped up.

We ended up buying four units before our money ran out, all apartments, and, with the exception of the first, all in the Underground. Nik's posture got tighter with every new property I picked up, but he was a good Cleaner, so he didn't say anything until we got back to the car.

"Are you out of your damn mind?" he demanded the moment the doors closed. "Why did you buy *four* units at one auction? They do these things twice a day! Were you afraid they were going to run out or something? Because we can't clean that many in one day."

"I know," I said, pulling my goggles off my head. "But it's okay, because we're not going to clean them. We're going to raid them."

Nik looked shocked. Then his face grew angry. "Are you shitting me?"

"It's the only way," I argued, pulling up the sheets Sibyl had prepared for my phone. "I woke up extra early this morning to look at the numbers, and they're clear. If we actually Clean every unit we buy, we're never going to make it in time. Not unless we hit a jackpot unit. We can't count on that, though, so my plan is to buy as many units as possible, pillage them for valuables, and leave the actual cleaning for later."

"We can't do that."

"Sure we can," I said. "I mean, technically, we don't have to clean them at all. We just won four leases. The DFZ doesn't care what we do with the places so long as the rent's being paid."

"And who's going to pay all that rent?" Nik demanded, and then his eyes went wide. "Wait, is this what you meant when you said you'd give me all your cash for the next three months *except* rent? Are you planning on sticking me with hundreds of apartments you already pillaged for valuables?"

"*No!*" I cried, horrified. "I'd never do you like that! This month is just the big push. Once I've paid my dad off, I'll get all those places Cleaned and back into the system before next month's rent comes due."

"But what about this month?" Nik asked. "Who's going to pay when everything ticks over on the thirty-first? You won't have the money. That's the same day you have to pay off your dad."

"It'll be fine," I said stubbornly. "We'll just put all the units in my name only, and I'll let them go into Collections. My credit's already in the toilet, so it won't matter if I default on a few hundred rent payments. And if I make sure they're all move-in ready before they get repossessed, I won't technically be in violation of my Cleaning agreement with the city. Even if I *do* get in trouble, your name won't be on the leases, so you'll be safe."

I thought that covered everything nicely, but Nik was shaking his head. "This is a *bad* idea, Opal. You're abusing the Cleaning system. If the other Cleaners find out you're raiding, they'll never let you win another unit."

"I'll burn that bridge when I get there," I grumbled, slumping in my seat. "I'm not doing this because I want to. My back's against the wall here, and this is the only way I've found to get out. I'll make it work."

"I hope you do," Nik said, turning around in his seat to look over his shoulder as he put the car in reverse. "Because you're screwed if you don't."

I was a lot more than screwed if that happened, but there was no point worrying about failure now. I'd cry when I crashed and burned. Until then, I was going to focus on flying as high and fast as possible. That was my mantra as I pulled up the first address on my map, reading the directions to Nik as we started our trek across the DFZ's nightmarish morning traffic.

***

It's amazing how fast you can go through an apartment when you don't have to worry about cleaning up after yourself. On a typical day, Nik and I could process two mid-sized apartments before we broke for dinner. This time, we did all four by two in the afternoon.

We went through the units like thieves, ripping out drawers, emptying closets, throwing stuff on the ground when it wasn't what we wanted. Even with our new not caring, the hoarded unit still took the longest, but my instinct about it had been right on the money. Like most Skyways hoarders, the lady who'd owned this place had had a shopping problem. We found tons of electronics, clothes, and glassware all new in box with tags mixed in with the trash. Some of the stuff had never even made it out of the shopping bags, which made it all the easier to toss into the bin for resale.

We had to go to three pawn shops to sell it all. It took forever since I had to check every piece of gold, but by five o'clock, we'd cleared it all, bringing in a gross profit of six thousand dollars.

"Not enough," I grumbled, poking at the spreadsheet floating in the AR in front of me. "That's only three thousand once you subtract what we spent on the units. I need to be making fifteen thousand in actual profit per day if I'm going to reach three hundred thousand in twenty days."

"Nineteen now," Sibyl said.

I shot her icon a nasty look.

"It's still double your money," Nik said, showing my supposedly emotionally sensitive AI how to *actually* be encouraging. "That's damn good, and now you've got six thousand to spend on the evening auction. If we can pull this off again, you'll end the day at twelve grand. Still not enough, but it's a good direction."

It was, but, "I thought you hated this plan?"

"Oh, I still think raiding's a terrible idea," Nik said as he pulled us out. "But it's pretty nice not to have to actually clean stuff for once. We're basically just doing the fun treasure-hunting part of the job. If it wasn't for the giant pile of work we're building up, I could do this all day." He smiled, then his eyes went hard as they flicked to me. "I'm not helping you Clean all that crap we threw on the ground when this is over, though."

"Wasn't even going to ask," I assured him. "This is all on me."

And *wow*, was I not looking forward to that. Nik and I had trashed all four places digging for salables, and now we were headed to the evening auction to pick up even more. It was starting to hit me just how much work I was piling up for myself at the end of this, and that was on top of my promise to Clean with Nik for the next three months to pay him back. I was going to have to work days and nights just to get it all done, assuming getting it all done was even possible. We were piling up units way faster than I could process them, but if I won an apartment at auction only to let it go right back into collections two months later still not

Cleaned, I'd be in violation of my agreement with the city. I could lose my Cleaning license and my Master Key, which meant I'd lose my livelihood.

"You could hire someone to help," Sibyl suggested. "It'll be expensive, but this was always an emergency scramble. Better to go into debt again than lose your only source of income."

I didn't even want to think about it.

"Really, though, right now you should be more concerned with the price of gold," my AI went on. "I've been keeping an eye on it since you made your first transaction, and it looks like the market doesn't just drop when you sell. It also goes down whenever gold comes into your possession. It's like the curse knows what you're about to do and is bracing for impact. At this rate, gold will be worth less than dirt by the end of the month."

"So long as people pay me in equivalent value, I don't care," I said. "Gold tanking is actually great for me. If the market's in free fall, vendors will start throwing gold at me to unload their supply before it becomes even more worthless." I pursed my lips in thought. "I should start asking for more."

"You need to find a way to make it faster first," Nik suggested. "You want to buy more units, but it took us three hours just to sell the haul from these. We can't scale up if we're losing a fourth of our day to pawn shops."

"What if we save all our selling for Sunday?" I suggested. "We'll still need to sell some stuff to get capital for buying units, but we can stash the rest in my apartment since it's empty now. Or in any of the units we're not using since we've still got them all. It'll be a risk with gold dropping, but it's only going down a few percentage points at a time, and only when I have or sell gold. Our time's worth more than that right now. If we save all our selling for the day when there are no auctions, we'll be much more efficient."

"Worth a try," Nik said. "We'll hit up the evening auction, eat dinner, and then get back to work. When we're done grabbing the valuables, we'll sell enough to get money for tomorrow and stash the rest in your place. Sound good?"

It sounded like an eighteen-hour day. Nik worked those on the regular, but he was half machine. I was all human. A very, very tired human, but I didn't dare complain. This was my idea, so I wiped the look of horror off my face. "Sounds like a plan."

He nodded and focused on the road, leaving me frantically researching new pawn shops to make sure we hit the best ones in the most efficient manner.

***

And so it went for a week. We woke up, auctioned, raided, sold just enough to cover the next auction, and then did it all again. By the third day, I didn't know why I'd bothered to keep my mattress. I lived on coffee and energy shots, ignoring Sibyl's increasingly pointed remarks about what this schedule was doing to my health. When I did sleep, I slept on Nik's couch so we wouldn't have to waste time on the drive to pick me up.

I gave up finding my own food around day four and just ate whatever Nik put in front of me. I showered when I remembered and bought new clothes out of the vending machines whenever mine got too ripped or dirty because disposables were easier than taking the half-hour necessary to purchase something actually decent or do laundry.

Honestly, I was amazed Nik put up with it. Sure he was going to get paid a lot if we made it through this, but I'd basically turned from a functional human to a dirty little goblin squatting in his living room. I still didn't know if his attraction to me that night in the parking lot had been a real thing or just a drunken impulse, but if Nik *had* liked me before, I didn't think it was possible he could keep those feelings alive after this, because I was a mess. One night, I actually fell asleep in my chair while eating. Literally facedown in my plate. I only woke up when Nik lifted me out of the seat to carry me to the couch. I apologized profusely, of course, but he claimed he didn't mind. He just sat there untangling my hair—which I hadn't brushed since my dinner with Peter, just washed and put back up in a ponytail—until I passed out again, which took about fifteen seconds.

Like I said, *total* mess.

Really, the only thing I did during this time aside from work, sleep, and crash the gold market was practice my magic. I would have skipped that too if I could, but the DFZ had apparently taken my agreement to consider her offer as an open invitation to hang out in my head. Between her and Sibyl, I was guilted into practicing multiple times a day, typically whenever I needed magic to bust through a ward on one of the units we were shaking down for valuables. The moment I reached for my power, the DFZ popped up to play telephone between me and Dr. Kowalski, relaying my new mentor's annoyingly detailed instructions as I struggled to learn how to grab only one potato's worth of magic.

It was so *hard*. I'd never actually realized just how much magic my typical handful contained until I tried to fit it into a tuber. Apparently I'd been grabbing bathtubs of the stuff my whole life, which explained a lot. Learning to limit myself to only one potato's worth was like trying to change how I breathed. It took serious effort just to be aware of something that had always been subconscious. Effort I did *not* appreciate considering how overworked I was already, especially since I had to do it in front of Nik.

I'm sure he thought I was crazy. Whenever we encountered a magically sealed safe, we'd have to stand there for twenty minutes while I clutched my potato and acted like I'd never cast magic before. It got to the point where I started actively trying to move the magic in my mind to block the DFZ's voice just so we could get through things faster, which was how I learned that you don't play those games with a god. The moment I tried, she locked me inside the day's first unit—a horrifying closet of an apartment tucked up under the new M-8—until I apologized and dropped my barrier.

But while I absolutely hated the infringement on my *very* limited time, I had to admit it was working. Despite using it constantly, my magic stopped hurting almost immediately, probably because I was no longer stretching it to the absolute limit every time I cast. I still shorted out spellwork, but it no longer exploded on me, and the backlashes stopped all together, which was a miracle. I'd never gone this long without popping myself in the face with my own magic. If I hadn't been so exhausted, I'm sure I would have felt amazing.

I was very much looking forward to enjoying that once everything was over, actually. For now, though, it was work. Work, work, work, and more work. I'd almost forgotten what the sun looked like when I got a sudden, unexpected, and extremely unwelcome visit from my mother.

In hindsight, I should have seen it coming. I didn't go back to my apartment anymore except to drop things off, but we were at the Cleaning auctions every day like clockwork, and that was where she caught me. I walked in to find her sitting in the front row, no security detail, no servants, nothing. Just my mom wearing one of her typical six-figure white dresses that she somehow managed to make look pure and elegant rather than boring, which was how they always looked on me.

It was a testament to her power that no one was sitting next to her despite the fact that she was unbelievably beautiful and alone in a prime seat. There was nothing about her that screamed DRAGON, STAY BACK, but no one seemed to want to get close. Even I was a bit intimidated as I walked up to ask what the hell she was doing here. When she turned to look at me, though, that was when I really got my shock.

"Holy crap, Mom," I whispered, sitting down next to her. "What's wrong?"

My whole life, I'd never seen my mother be anything but perfect. Perfectly mad, perfectly smug, perfectly victorious, but *always* perfect. The woman sitting in front of me now, though, looked like she'd gotten even less sleep than I had. There were dark circles under her eyes that even the best makeup couldn't hide, and her face was pinched with worry, making her look a decade closer to her actual age.

"Mom," I said again, in Korean this time as I reached out to grab her cold hands. "What happened?"

"Daughter," she said in the same language, looking warily at the room full of Cleaners watching us as if we were the drama of the century. "Is there somewhere we could talk?"

Normally, I would have suspected a trap. This time, though, I just nodded and helped her up, linking my arm through hers as I led her out of the auditorium. Nik caught my eye at the door, but I just shook my head, motioning for him to get us seats as I led my mom down the former elementary school's yellow-tiled hall toward the bathrooms.

"Okay," I said when we were safely locked inside the women's restroom. "What the hell is going on?"

"Language," my mother said, but the scold was clearly reflexive. My mom looked like she was about to cry, and while we weren't on the best terms right now, I was still human, and she was still my mother.

"Mom, tell me what's wrong," I pleaded. "What are you doing here? Did Dad make you come?"

"No," she said, pulling a handkerchief from her purse to dab her eyes. "He thinks I'm on my way to the airport to fly back to Seoul. He doesn't know that I'm—"

She cut off, crushing the lace handkerchief in her fist as she stared at me with a terrifying look in her eyes. "Opal, you have to stop."

"Stop what?"

"I don't know," she said angrily. "Your father won't tell me, but whatever you're doing, you have to stop *right now*. You're killing him!"

I jerked back in alarm. That sounded hysterical, except my mother didn't get hysterical.

"Ever since the day I redid your apartment, something's been wrong with him," she went on, speaking so fast I had trouble keeping up.

"He hides it well, but I know him, Opal! I can see he's getting weaker, and I think it has to do with you. You have to stop!"

I stared at her in shock for several seconds. Then I got mad. "*I* have to stop?" I cried. "*He's* the one who put a curse on me! If he doesn't like what I'm doing with it, he's free to remove it at any time."

"You know it's not that simple!" my mother shouted, her face truly afraid. "He is the Dragon of Korea! His weakness makes us all less safe, including you! You're free to be angry with him all you like on your own time, but this affects us all. His enemies were already circling, but now White Snake herself is in the DFZ!"

I pressed my mouth tight. White Snake was my father's younger sister, only surviving relative, and most persistent annoyance. She was also an even greater enemy of the Peacemaker's than Dad. "What's she doing here?"

"Oh, some excuse about considering the Peacemaker's offer of mutual accord," my mother said furiously. "It's all lies, of course. The Peacemaker forces all of his dragons to swear they won't kill each other, and killing your father is the only way she'll ever get what she wants. But the Great Yong is no fool. He's wisely kept to the house since he arrived, so I don't think she knows about his condition. Still, her presence here means no good for anyone."

That was definitely true. White Snake was everything I accused Dad of being, only without the moderately redeeming feature of Yong's honor and sense of fairness. If she was in the DFZ, my mother was absolutely right to panic. I just didn't see how any of this was my fault.

"Again," I growled. "Not. My. Problem. If Dad doesn't want to deal with his sister, he can go home. He can remove my curse. He can do any *number of things* to repair the situation. Why should I take a hit to fix his shit? He's the damn dragon!"

"He is your father!" my mother cried.

"He's not my father," I snapped. "And he's not your husband, either. He's our *owner.* We're his mortals, his stupid little pets! If he's in a bind because I'm yanking the leash *he* put on me, then maybe he should do the decent thing and *let me go.*"

"I don't know why I thought I could come to you!" my mother cried. "You are an ignorant, selfish child who would rather pull the most beautiful creature in the world down with her than admit she's wrong!"

"I'm not wrong!" I yelled back. "I'm the victim! He's the one doing this to *me!*"

"We'll see how far that pity takes you," my mother snarled, baring her teeth as if she was the dragon. "I'm going home now, Opal. You may have abandoned him, but the rest of us have not forgotten what we owe our dragon. We will keep his home safe at any cost. I just hope you realize how hard your father is fighting for you before it's too late."

"Oh my *god*, Mom!" I cried. "This is not my fault!"

But my mother was already storming out, tears streaming down her face as she marched into the hallway, slamming the bathroom door in my face. I'd already bashed it open again to chase after her when my phone buzzed.

Auction's starting, Nik texted me. *You coming?*

I took one last look at my mom's back as she stomped down the hall, high heels clicking like knives on the tile floor, and then I sighed.

Be right there.

CHAPTER 8

The second week was even more insane than the first. Now that Nik and I had worked out the kinks, it wasn't uncommon for us to push ten units a day. Other Cleaners were starting to notice, and the grumbling was getting fierce. DeSantos actually got in Nik's face at one point, which was a bad decision on his part. Nik did better on five hours of sleep a night than I did, but he was starting to fray at the edges too now, and he damn near took the older man's head off.

I'm pretty sure people were trying to start shit with me as well. I know I got cornered on more than one occasion, but I was honestly too tired to be intimidated. I just wanted this to be over. We were so close now, just a few days away. But even though I woke up already counting the hours until I could go back to bed, I dreaded the passing of time, because now that we'd entered the third week, I was no longer able to deny that we were falling farther and farther behind.

I couldn't have told you why. When I looked back at everything we'd done, all the stuff we'd sold, there were no obvious failures. Overall we'd done well, sometimes *very* well, but while the graph of our income was a line going straight up, the arc still wasn't high enough to hit my target. Unless we got lucky, we were going to fall short, and the more days passed, the luckier we had to get.

"Just one chance," I muttered to Sibyl as I flopped down on the dog-chewed couch in the latest apartment we'd picked up in downtown. Or maybe we were in the Financial District? I didn't even know anymore. "Just *one* lucky break, that's all we need."

"You've had plenty of lucky breaks," my AI reminded me. "Statistically speaking, you're still doing better than the average."

"Not good enough," I said, burying my face in my hands. "My dad doesn't care about 'almost.' If I don't have that money, I lose."

"You haven't lost yet."

That was sweet of her, but I wasn't in the mood for affirmations. I was exhausted and hungry and so beaten down I wanted to cry. If Nik hadn't been in the next room over, I probably would have, but I still had my pride. I'd chosen this death march, dammit. I was going to see it through to the end. I was telling myself this over and over when my phone buzzed in my pocket.

"Ooooh," Sibyl said. "Opal, look at this!"

"You look at it," I grumbled, rubbing my tired eyes. "That's why I have you."

"Listen then," she said. "You just got an email on your old college account."

"So? I get emails there all the time. That's why I don't check it."

"This one isn't spam, though," Sibyl said. "It's a request for a consultation. Some guy wants you to have a look at his dragon statue."

I sighed. I'd done jobs like that all the time back in college. It was a good way to find hidden gems before they went to auction, but mostly I'd just liked showing off my vast and esoteric knowledge of weird historic trivia, which was why I usually hadn't charged. I still liked showing off, but I didn't do that "work for free" thing anymore. I also had no time.

"Tell him to take it to one of the auction houses."

"You sure?" Sybil asked. "He says he'll pay you a thousand bucks."

My eyes popped back open. "Really?" I said, sitting up. "A thousand bucks for one valuation?"

"That's what the email says."

I frowned, thinking it over. "Can he do a VR call?"

"Messaging him now..." Sibyl hummed to herself for a moment, and then my phone vibrated again. "He says that's fine."

"Great," I said, sitting up. "I'll do it now."

While my AI dutifully carried the message, I got up and went in search of Nik. I found him in the bedroom emptying drawers of men's clothing onto the floor for sorting. "Hey," I said. "I'm going to take a phone call real quick. Some idiot's offering me a thousand bucks to ID a statue."

"Can you do that over the phone?" Nik asked without looking up.

"I can in VR."

He nodded tiredly, kicking the piled clothes with a sneer. "An extra thousand would be good, because this place is looking like a whole lotta we got suckered. I don't know how many dogs this dude had before he bailed, but they ruined everything."

He held up a dress shirt that was stained and chewed at the sleeves, and I winced. "Living room furniture's the same story," I said. "Just save what you can, and we'll move on when I'm done. I could use ten minutes on a couch anyway."

Nik nodded, and I went back to the living room to put on my goggles. "Ready?" I asked when they were over my face.

"Got him on the line now," Sibyl replied. "But I'm not connecting the call until you sit down."

Using VR while standing was normally a bad idea. It was easy to break your toe or knock your shin when the world your eyes saw didn't match the reality your legs were in. Not that I needed safety as an excuse to sit back down. I flopped before she could finish, resting my head on the sharp edge of the wooden frame the previous owner's demon dogs had chewed bare in hopes the discomfort would keep me from falling asleep.

"Good to go."

"Connecting you now," Sibyl said, and then the view through my cameras fell away, replacing the world beyond my AR with a shot of a pretty cafe somewhere on the Lake St. Clair waterfront. From the tiny sliver of hotel balcony I could see at the shot's edge, I was pretty sure it was the big pier at the New Regency, but I couldn't say for certain. All the ritzy hotels looked the same, and it didn't matter anyway. I was far more interested in the incredibly handsome dark-skinned man sitting at the wicker cafe table.

The moment I saw him, I knew he was rich. Not only was he lounging by one of the city's nicest hotels in the middle of a work day, he was wearing a tan summer-weight suit I recognized from last year's

Paradise collection by Y23, a super-hot brand. His watch was similarly pricey, and he was wearing a set of AR sunglasses so thin and light they looked almost exactly like normal sunglasses, which meant they had to cost a fortune. Even his delicious-looking iced coffee drink was from a famously overpriced shop. Put it all together and you had the sort of travel magazine–worthy shot that simply couldn't be accomplished by the non–jet set crowd without hours of preparation. For this guy, though, it looked like just another Tuesday, and that made me salivate. This was going to be *money*.

Thankfully, Sibyl had had the good foresight to use a recorded picture of me for his end rather than an actual camera shot. There'd been a time when I could have matched his "I'm so rich I don't even have to try" aesthetic, but those days were long gone. I didn't know what fire was under this dude's butt to make him offer a thousand dollars for an emergency antique consultation, but if he saw me the way I looked right now, he'd hang up before I could get a word in.

"Is this Opal Yong-ae?" he asked, flashing me—or, rather, the infinitely more-fashionable picture of me from my college profile three years ago—a perfect white-toothed smile. "Famous daughter of the Great Yong?"

"It is," I said, silently signaling Sibyl to make sure this call wasn't being traced. "Whom do I have the pleasure of speaking with?"

"You can call me Ainsley," he replied with the pointed stress at the end that told me my next question better not be "Ainsley what?"

"What can I do for you, Ainsley?"

"I heard you know your stuff when it comes to dragon art, and you're a peach about doing quick evaluations," he said, reaching under the table for his bag. "I'm a bit of an impulse buyer, and I just picked up a piece from a rather…unorthodox supplier. I really should have been more careful, but I've been after one of these for so long I'm afraid I got carried away. Naturally, I don't want anyone to know I got suckered—a man has to maintain his reputation, after all—so I asked around for someone discreet, and your name came up. Thank you for responding so quickly."

"I've been in your shoes before," I said, which wasn't technically true since I always made a point to look *before* I shelled out cash, but I understood the general sentiment. "My assistant mentioned a payment?"

The quick pivot to cash made him jerk a little, but I was too tired to be coy. I needed my money, dammit. "I'll need fifteen hundred."

"I thought we agreed on a thousand?"

"No, you offered a thousand," I replied in my sweetest voice. "I'm asking for fifteen hundred. Up front."

His brilliant smile faltered a little. "Up front?"

"Rush jobs cost more."

Considering my curse was almost certainly going to take half of whatever he paid me, I really should have demanded double, but two thousand was too much even for my current gouging mood. Good for me, Ainsley must have been in one hell of a hurry, because he agreed.

"Sending it to you now."

I waved my hand to bring up my digital wallet. Sure enough, a payment of fifteen hundred dollars from a private account popped up just a few seconds later, though it was now seven hundred and fifty thanks to transfer fees and a previously unmentioned fine. A month ago, that would have made me rage. Now I just rolled my eyes and added the loss to my mile-long list of grievances against my father.

"Payment received. Let's see the statue."

Ainsley grinned wide and pulled a wrapped object out of his tooled-leather bag. It was about the size of a football—an American football, not a real football—and heavily protected in bubble wrap. When all the wrapping finally came off, Ainsley leaned down to give me a full shot of a very old-looking dragon statue covered in what appeared to be gold but I knew was hammered bronze. It was so well-done that I could see every little scale. Just to be sure, though, I wanted to check one more thing.

"Turn it upside down?"

He dutifully flipped the statue over, giving me a view of the inscription underneath. The Korean was a much older form than I could read without a dictionary, but I knew what it said just fine because I'd seen hundreds of others just like it in my dad's hoard.

"That's one of the Thousand Dragons cast by the ancient Kingdom of Koguryo," I said. "It dates from the Three Kingdoms period of Korea, most likely around the fifth century C.E."

Ainsley let out a relieved breath. "So it's real, then?"

"If it's not, it's the best forgery I've ever seen," I told him honestly. "The dragons were cast to bribe the first Great Yong into not eating the peasants. He took the gift and ate them anyway, of course, because dragon, but it's still a great historical piece and a fantastic example of metal-covered wooden sculpture from the time. Good condition, too, considering how old it is. Nice find."

"Thank you," he said with the warm appreciation of a true collector. "I don't suppose you know where I could find more of these?"

"Not outside of the Korean peninsula." My dad had all but forty of them. I dimly remembered his sister having the others, but I couldn't recall for certain. Honestly, I wouldn't have been surprised if White Snake had sold them. Clanless dragons who had no lands to milk for cash always needed money, and selling the treasures he needed to complete his set would spite my dad like nothing else.

"Such a shame," Ainsley said with a sigh. "If you *do* see one, though, be sure to let me know. I pay top dollar, and I don't ask questions, which I hear is important to you these days."

I did *not* like that he'd heard that about me, but I supposed he must have heard something or this call wouldn't be happening, so I let it go. "I'll drop you a line," I promised.

He gave me a final charming smile and hung up. I was taking the deep breath to prepare for the exit from VR when my bank account pinged again.

"What the—"

There was another transfer of seven hundred and fifty dollars in my account. I poked it to make sure I wasn't seeing the same entry twice, but the total confirmed it. I'd lost half to fees again, but this Ainsley guy had just tipped me fifteen hundred bucks.

"Nice," I said, breaking into a grin. I'd forgotten what life was like when you had money. I used to do stuff like that, too. It always made people *so* happy when you called back. It certainly encouraged me to save his number. It never hurt to know a buyer with deep pockets and tight lips. I was still smiling like an idiot when I pushed my headset up to see Nik standing over me.

"How did it go?"

"I just made fifteen hundred bucks!" I told him proudly.

"Great," he said, reaching down to pull me up. "Because this place is a loss. And speaking of, when you come back to clean next month, make sure you save the bathroom for last."

I blanched. "What's in there?"

"We're eating in the next few hours, so I'm not going to say," Nik replied. "Let's just say I see now why the previous tenant bailed on this apartment."

I groaned at the thought. But that problem—like so many of my problems—was an issue for next month. Right now, we had to hit the evening auction and pick up the next round.

"Can we stop for coffee?" I asked Nik as we walked out the door.

"Isn't your blood coffee by now?" he quipped. "And what did I tell you about coffee shops? There's no point working this hard if you're going to waste your money buying fancy hot water with bean dust in it for five bucks a cup."

"Just leave me this one joy," I begged him.

Nik sighed and started down the stairs. "Where do you want to go?"

"Tim Horton's," I said instantly, pulling out my phone to see where the closest source of life-giving sustenance was.

***

Thirty minutes later, I carried two giant paper cups of fresh coffee into the evening auction.

"You know," Nik said as we snagged our usual front-row seats. "You should probably just switch to buying the gallon carafe box at this point. The price per ounce would be cheaper."

"I don't like drinking out of a box," I said, taking a huge gulp off the cup in my left hand. "It makes me feel like I have a problem."

"And double-fisting two twenty-four ounce cups doesn't?"

I didn't like his logic, so I took another sip and turned in my chair to study the room. I'd lost track of what day it was, but it must have been closing in on Saturday, because the place was dead. Like most of humanity, Cleaners were very diligent at the start of the week but tended to fall off as the days stacked up, which was fine with me. Fewer people meant less competition. I was looking forward to scooping up some choice units when Broker came into the room.

"Blessed city, you two are persistent," he said when he spotted Nik and me. "When do you sleep?"

I wiggled my coffees at him, and he shook his head. "It's your adrenal failure, darling," he said, hopping up on the stage. "Let's get this started!"

I handed the cup in my right hand to Nik so I could pull down my goggles.

The first several units were worthless. There was a house that looked interesting. Actual, freestanding residential buildings were rare in the city and usually had good stuff, but this one had been inhabited by an elderly shut-in with dementia. Not only had the building been horribly neglected, but the furniture I could see in the interior pictures was so hideously ugly I would have paid *not* to look at it, so that was a pass. The rest of the stack were a bunch of samey cheap apartments that I already knew wouldn't be worth the effort. I was starting to worry we wouldn't find anything to buy tonight when a picture popped up on the screen that made my heart skip.

It was another apartment. A small, dirty two-bedroom that was virtually identical to the others we'd been plagued with all night. But on the ratty secondhand bookshelf in *this* unit was a statue of a dragon. Not one of the mass-produced factory-stamped ones that was riddled with production errors, either. This was a perfectly made, shiny bronze figure that looked identical to the one I'd just IDed less than an hour ago. It was even lying on its side so I could see the inscription on the bottom, almost like the universe wanted me to have it.

I grabbed Nik's arm so hard he jumped. "*Bid!*" I hissed at him.

"On this one?"

I nodded frantically, drawing a square in the air with my fingers to zoom in on the picture in my AR. The closer I got, the more convinced I became that this was another of the thousand Koguryo dragons my stylish collector friend had just promised to pay through the nose for. It certainly looked absolutely identical. If it hadn't been extremely unlikely, I'd have said it was the same statue, but the whole point of a matched set like this one was that you couldn't tell them apart. It had to be a different statue, which meant we were about to make *bank*.

Schooling my face to hide my excitement, I leaned in to whisper in Nik's ear, holding up my coffee to shield my lips from DeSantos, who was sitting right behind us specifically to vulture tip-offs. "We have to get this. Sky's the limit."

Not long ago, saying that about an apartment this shabby would have gotten me a serious side-eye, but after three weeks of frantic buying, Nik and I were a well-oiled machine. He didn't even ask what I'd seen. He just raised his hand, face carefully neutral as he put in a bid so reasonable no one could ever suspect it.

The ploy worked like a charm. We won the unit outright with zero competition. The moment Broker said "Sold" and the unit's info appeared in my inbox, I was out of my chair like a shot.

"Where are you going?" Nik hissed. "The auction's only half over!"

"We don't need that other stuff," I whispered back, grabbing his arm to tug him up with me. "This is the big score!"

"What big score?" DeSantos asked, leaning on the back of my abandoned chair.

I flipped him off and yanked harder on Nik's arm. Shrugging apologetically at Broker, who was giving us a stern "settle down" glare, Nik rose from his seat and followed me out of the auditorium. "What did you see?" he asked when we reached the hall.

"I'll tell you when we get there," I said, hurrying toward the fire door that opened into the former school's tiny parking lot. "I don't want someone to overhear and steal it."

"That has literally never happened."

He was right, but my lips stayed shut. This was the big break I'd been waiting for. I wasn't taking *any* chances. I didn't even finish my coffees, just dumped them in the trash can by the door as we walked into the parking lot.

Thankfully, our new apartment wasn't far. It was actually just a few blocks from Nik's place. The ugly cement brick of a building it was nestled in looked exactly like Nik's, too. Honestly, I'd never understand why a living city who could create anything she wanted made so many ugly apartments, but I guess you had to have something for everyone, and this place was certainly cheap. It didn't even have an elevator, just a metal stairwell that ran up the outside of the building all the way to the top floor just below the Skyways, where our unit was located.

"Video log for wherever this place is," I said, activating my cameras with a flick of my hand as I jogged down the dimly lit hall. "Receipt number..."

"12297," Sibyl supplied.

"12297," I repeated, yanking my Master Key out from under my cheap baggy shirt. "Cleaner IDs: Nikola Kos and Opal Yong-ae. I verify. Proceeding with resident notification."

I lifted my fist and banged on the door. When no one answered in the next five seconds, I stuck my key in the lock. It slid in beautifully, and I breathed a sigh of relief.

"Going in!"

I opened the door and rushed inside. Nik came in right behind me, hand on his gun, which felt both unnecessary and entirely justified, because I'd come into this place like a SWAT team on a bust. For all my excitement, though, it looked exactly like it had in the picture. Just a sad little two-room apartment that smelled of instant noodles and mold. And there on the shelf in front of me, glittering like a forbidden idol in the harsh white glare of the naked bulb in the ceiling light, was my prize.

"Gotcha!" I cried, snatching the dragon statue off the shelf.

I knew it was the real deal the moment I touched it. Old bronze made in the traditional way had an entirely different feel from the modern metal. Holding it up to the light, I could see the tick marks where some long-dead artist had pressed the shiny metal into the dragon's eyes and mouth, forming each tiny tooth to a perfect, needle-sharp point. The scales on his snaking, wingless body were likewise works of art, and the craftsmanship on the flowing mane that ringed his head was so well done it looked like real hair. It was a thing of absolute beauty, and any other time, it would have been the new crown jewel of my collection. Today, though, it was something even better: my ticket to freedom.

"I'm guessing that's an expensive statue?" Nik said as I clutched the thing with shaking hands.

"Oh yeah," I said, flashing him a victorious grin before turning my attention back to the task at hand. "Sibyl, call Ainsley."

Nik scowled. "Who's Ainsley?"

I was about to launch into a gushing monologue about obsessive collectors and their famously fat wallets, but my soon-to-be buyer was a lot faster off the block than I expected. Sibyl had barely started the call before Ainsley picked up.

"I hope this is important," he said, his refined voice irritated. "I'm in the middle of dinner."

I replied by sending him a picture of the shiny dragon in my hands. There was a pregnant pause, and when he spoke again, his voice was entirely different.

"How much?"

"A hundred thousand," I said without missing a beat. "And I want it in gold."

I was fully expecting him to balk at that. It wasn't a crazy price given the age of the artifact and his professed rabid desire, but it was definitely high. You always started high, though. It set the right tone, and it gave you somewhere to come down from without going too low. I was still building my negotiation strategy in my head when Ainsley said, "Done."

I blinked. "Wait, really?"

"I don't bother haggling over such small sums," he said haughtily, reminding me sharply of my dad. "Will Swiss bank–issued bullion work, or do you want another format?"

"Bullion is fine," I said when I'd recovered from my shock. "Where do you want to meet?"

He sent me the address of a merchant bank in the Financial District that specialized in high-touch wealthy clients. I told him we'd be there in thirty minutes and hung up, lowering my phone to stare blankly through the apartment's tiny window.

One hundred thousand. I'd just sold a statue for one hundred *thousand* dollars in gold. Even if the curse found a way to take a chunk out of that, I'd still have way more than the forty thousand I needed to reach three hundred grand and pay off my dad, which meant...

"I did it."

I turned to Nik, who was staring at me as if he wasn't sure if I was going to scream or faint. To be fair, in that moment, I could have done both. "I did it!"

His lips quirked in a smile. "You did it."

I did scream then, a high-pitched wail of pure delight as I threw myself at him, wrapping my arms around his neck as I jumped up and down. "I did it! I did it! I paid him off! IdiditIdiditIdiditI—"

"It's not done until the money's in his hands," Nik said, though I noticed he didn't peel me off him. "Let's go get that gold."

I nodded frantically, racing for the door so fast my foot slipped. I caught myself at the last second, clutching the dragon I'd just nearly crushed to my chest. *Oh no,* I thought with a snarl. The curse wasn't getting me now. Not when I was so close.

Panting, I grabbed one of the stained bath towels off the floor of the abandoned apartment and wrapped it around my precious prize. When it was swaddled like an infant, I walked into the hall, taking every step as if it were my last while Nik led the way down the stairs to the parking deck.

***

The drive to the bank was the most harrowing of my life. Nothing actually went wrong. There were no near misses or even bad traffic, but knowing the universe had been magically bribed to bring me down was a killer for paranoia. I spent the whole ride in Nik's back seat clutching my statue the way you saw refugee mothers holding their babies in pictures on charity brochures.

Nik wasn't immune, either. When we reached the Financial District, he didn't even cruise to find the cheapest parking. He just turned us into the first deck we passed, paying the exorbitant fee without so much as a grumble.

As its name implied, the Financial District was one of the ritziest parts of the Skyways. It was also one of the tallest. There were more superscrapers here than anywhere else in the city, turning the streets into a maze of canyons that channeled the wind off nearby Lake St. Clair into hurricane-force gales. This wasn't normally a problem, since no one who frequented the Financial District would be caught dead on foot outside, but it made getting to the meeting spot hairy.

By the time we reached the elegant paved square lined with fountains and corporate art where Ainsley had said he'd be waiting, I looked like a crazed homeless lady who'd just escaped a wind tunnel, and Nik…well, he still looked like Nik, which was pretty intimidating. All the snappy Skyways office workers waiting in line at the trendy coffee carts gave us a wide berth as we walked past, and the doormen working the front entrance of the merchant bank preemptively signaled for backup. If I hadn't been so preoccupied, I would have been insulted. Right now, though, I don't think I'd have noticed if a dragon had landed on top of me. I only had eyes for the dark-skinned man in the designer suit and classy AR sunglasses—which he was still wearing despite the long shadows of the buildings and the approaching evening—sitting on the edge of the fountain with a briefcase in his lap.

"Miss Yong-ae!" he said cheerfully when he spotted us. "Delighted to finally meet you in person. Do you have it?"

I wasn't here for pleasantries, so I just nodded and unwrapped the towel, showing him the goods as if I was one of those evil antique dealers in an Indiana Jones movie. The whole thing was so sketchy I was amazed security wasn't coming over, but the guys watching the door hadn't budged. That might have been because Ainsley had already paid them off, but I suspected the real reason was because this was the DFZ. Even up here on the Skyways, suspicious stuff happened all the time, *especially* with super-rich people. This little trade-off probably didn't even register on their weird-shit-o-meter, for which I was very grateful. What we were doing wasn't illegal, but I was so twitchy right now I didn't trust myself not to be stupid. I just wanted to get my money before I got hit by a meteor or killed by an out-of-control bus or whatever other heavy-handed tool the universe came up with to ruin it all.

"Oh my," Ainsley said when he saw the dragon. "And it's the real thing?"

"As real as the one you showed me this afternoon," I said, trying desperately not to sound as nervous as I felt. "I can't give you a certificate of authenticity or anything, but we can go to an independent appraiser if you really—"

"No, no, I believe you," he said, grinning wide. "It looks perfect. I'll take it."

He reached out to grab the statue, but I snatched it back. "Payment first."

"Of course," he said, holding out the briefcase. I couldn't grab it since I was still clutching the statue, so I nodded at Nik, who took it instead, setting it down on the edge of the fountain as he clicked open the top to reveal the most beautiful glittering pile of gold bars I'd ever seen outside a dragon's hoard.

"Sorry it's so heavy," Ainsley said. "You don't normally get a whole briefcase for a hundred thousand, but the price of gold's been crashing for weeks now, so the bank clerks had to pack it tight."

I didn't know what kind of person complained that their briefcase full of gold was too heavy, but it wasn't me. I was already hovering at Nik's shoulder as he lifted the first layer of certified one-ounce bars so we could see how many were actually in the case.

"That's a hundred thousand," Sibyl said cheerfully when her photo-recognition software had checked all the serial numbers. "At least it was five minutes ago. Gold market's falling fast."

"How fast?"

"Let's just say that if you want the stuff in that briefcase to be more than a pretty paperweight, you'd better start running."

I nodded and turned back to Ainsley. "Here," I said, practically shoving the dragon at him. "It'll look great next to your other one."

"We have several, actually," he replied with a smile that was slightly too sharp. "Pleasure doing business with you, Dragon's Opal."

I didn't even say goodbye. I just grabbed the briefcase in one hand, grabbed Nik with the other, and marched straight across the square to the merchant bank.

"I'm here to make a transaction," I said when the security guards stepped in front of me. "You guys cash gold, right?"

The two men looked at each other, and I held my breath. They'd *just* watched me get a briefcase full of gold, though, so even though I looked crazy, they let me inside, opening the bank's sleek tinted doors with a whoosh to reveal a posh marble foyer full of frantic people.

Too harried to care, I pushed through the chaos to the nearest teller, who was sitting behind a beautiful old-fashioned wooden bank window surrounded with shiny brass fittings. The thin, balding man was fidgeting at his desk like a nervous bird, his long, spindly fingers shooting through a complicated AR interface only he could see.

"Excuse me," I said, placing the heavy briefcase on his counter with a thunk. "I'd like to cash this gold and transfer the money to my account."

"I'm sorry, ma'am," the man replied, his voice so polite I was certain he hadn't actually looked at me yet. "We're having a bit of an issue at the moment. If you don't mind waiting a—"

"I do mind," I said sharply. "I know gold is crashing, which is why I need this cashed *now*."

That got his attention. "Madam," he said, much less politely this time. "It's not just gold. Gold merely started the panic. *All* the markets are in free fall now, and I'm very busy dealing with concerns from actual clients."

"It was one of your clients who gave me this," I snapped, opening the case of gold so he could see. His eyes went wide when he saw the glittering pile, and I took my chance. "Come on, Andy," I pleaded, glancing at his fancy name tag. "I just got the most important payment of my life, but it's going to be worth nothing if you don't cash me out. I know the bank doesn't want to take on more gold while it's falling, but it always goes up again. This is your chance to buy at the bottom."

He still didn't look convinced, and I gave him my best sad eyes. "Please," I pleaded. "A hundred thousand is nothing to a big place like this, but it's everything to me. Help me out, and I'll write you an amazing customer service review."

The teller sighed and reached for the briefcase. "You'd better mention me by name."

"Absolutely," I promised as he started transferring the shiny one-ounce bars one by one to his desk.

It was a harrowing wait while he weighed and recorded golden brick. By the time he'd done the whole briefcase, the price of gold was dire. But unlike all the other places I'd been to this month, this wasn't a shady Ca$h 4 Gold operation or a pawn shop. It was a legit commercial bank with branches in other countries that actually had consumer protection laws, which meant I got paid the price gold was when he started my transaction, not the one ten minutes later when he finally finished weighing everything.

That turned out to be a difference of several thousand dollars, most of which was eaten up by the merchant bank's multiple and exorbitant fees for transferring money to my cheap online bank. There were so many hidden gotchas, I didn't even know the final amount until I saw it appear in the account app at the top of my AR. When it finally updated, the sight almost made me faint.

"You okay?" Nik asked, putting a hand on my back when I wobbled.

I nodded, then shook my head, reaching out a trembling hand to poke my fingers through the glowing number floating in the air in front of me.

Total Funds: $323,924.53

"I made it," I whispered, my voice so hoarse I hardly recognized it. "I got to three hundred thousand."

I'd actually gotten a lot more. Even with gold in free fall, that briefcase had been way in excess of what I'd needed to pay my dad. Considering how many units Nik and I had raided, and how much rent I was about to owe, I needed it all, but I was too shocked to think that far ahead. The only fact my poor, exhausted, over-caffeinated brain could process right now was that after years of fighting tooth and nail, fleeing my home and moving to a terrifying city I knew nothing about, and working myself to a husk, I'd finally done it. I'd *won.*

The joy that came next was so sharp it hurt. Other emotions followed, coming at me so fast, I couldn't process them all. I wanted to laugh and sob at the same time. In the end I did both, burying my face in Nik's shirt as the whole confused mess rolled through me.

He let me do it. It had to be embarrassing, holding me in the middle of that fancy bank lobby while everyone watched. I was embarrassed *for* him, but when I tried to pull away, he didn't let me go. He just stood there with his human arm draped over my shoulders, whispering that it was okay. He never specified *what* was okay, but it didn't matter. The fact that he was there—had been there the whole time, through all my craziness—was the kindest thing anyone had ever done for me.

That thought set me off all over again. I probably could have stood there hysterically laugh-crying the rest of the night, but every time I looked up, that three hundred thousand was staring me in the face, reminding me it wasn't over yet. Nothing was final until I actually paid my dad. I could have done it with a transfer right now, but I didn't trust sending the funds remotely while my curse was still in play, and I wanted to see his face. He thought he'd beaten me. He thought he'd won like he always did, but not this time. This time, this one time, *I* was victorious, and I was going to shove that money down his scaly dragon throat.

"I have to get to Canada," I said, pushing away from Nik's chest.

"Why Canada?"

"My dad's staying across the river in Windsor to avoid the Peacekeeper," I explained as we finally left the frantic merchant bank. "I have to go pay him before something else happens."

Being familiar with my curse, Nik nodded as if that made perfect sense. "I can drive you."

"No," I said firmly. "I don't want you in the blast radius when Yong finds out I beat him."

I also wanted to do this alone. That wasn't really fair since I couldn't have done any of it without Nik, but he didn't care about this like I did. No one could. He'd come along for the money, but this victory was my future, my *freedom.* I was selfish enough to want that all to myself, but I wasn't going to be a total jerk.

"Here," I said, waving my fingers through my AR to pick ten thousand dollars out of my pot and pass it to Nik's picture on my contact list. "There's the money I owe you for bailing me out last time."

Nik's face normally lit up at the mention of money, but he looked put out by the idea this time. "You don't have to pay me right now," he said. "You're acting like you're leaving."

"I'm not leaving," I assured him. "I'm just making sure you get paid first in case something stupid happens. You know, 'cause curse."

Nik's scowl deepened. "Are you *sure* I can't drive you?"

"Positive. I'm about to super piss off an ancient dragon. You do *not* want to be around for that, especially since I couldn't have done it without you. Honestly, you should probably spend the rest of the evening hiding out in your bunker of an apartment."

He nodded, but the scowl was still here. "Will you come back when it's done?"

"Couldn't keep me away," I promised with a wide grin. "When this is over, we're going to party like this city's never seen and then sleep for a week."

That made him chuckle. "Looking forward to it, then," he said as I walked over to the taxi stand where a line of autocabs was waiting for the evening rush. "Good luck."

"I've already got it," I told him, and it was true. For the first time in months, I felt lucky. Like I was back on top. "I'll call you when I'm done," I said as I climbed into the first car. "And thanks. You know, for everything."

Nik smiled and shut my door for me, standing back to watch from the curb as the little autocab rolled away with a smooth electric purr, joining the traffic that was already jockeying for position on the artery roads that fed into the New Ambassador Bridge.

CHAPTER 9

Twenty years ago, when Algonquin, Spirit of the Great Lakes, had ruled the DFZ and dragons were banned on pain of death, the neighboring city of Windsor, Canada, had had the highest dragon-per-capita population in the world. Being right across the river from Detroit, it was an easy jaunt for any dragons who felt like taking their lives into their own claws. Even those who hadn't wanted to risk it couldn't bear to be farther than necessary from all that power and money. They'd piled onto Windsor's riverbanks, building their mansions and strongholds as close to the DFZ border as possible without actually touching it.

These days, of course, there was no need for such tricks. Now that the DFZ ruled herself, dragons flew over the city on a daily basis, and most clans had relocated across the river to build new strongholds in the city they actually wanted to live in. But while going into the DFZ wasn't a death sentence anymore, it *was* the Peacemaker's territory. Any dragon who entered had to abide by his rules, which included no killing each other, no burning buildings, and no eating humans off the street. That all sounded pretty reasonable to me, but dragons weren't reasonable creatures. Most clans were willing to swallow their pride in order to get access to the world's most magical city, but there were still many dragons who considered the restrictions absurd and insulting, and for these tyrants, there was still Windsor.

Naturally, my dad was one of the holdouts. He'd actually avoided this part of North America for decades, but he'd changed his policy in order to corner me, purchasing a sprawling Gothic mansion on the river to use as his stronghold while he was in the area. I suppose I should have been flattered he'd gone through so much trouble and expense for my sake, but like everything my dad did, this was all for him. The Great Yong would never deign to stay in a hotel with mortals who weren't his, so he'd bought himself a multimillion-dollar house that looked like Wayne Manor to use as a temporary base of operations. You know, as you do.

I rolled my eyes so hard when my autocab stopped at the wrought iron gates for a security check that I hurt myself. At least he'd gotten a nice chunk of land for his wasted money. The house's lush green lawn stretched all the way down to the muddy bank of the Detroit River with an excellent view of the cliff of the DFZ across the water, its multiple layers lit up like a slice of neon birthday cake. It was actually a lovely picture with the setting sun painting the superscrapers gold and fiery red above the sprawling mansion's steep-pitched slate roof and gabled windows. If I'd come under any other circumstances, I would have loved it. But I wasn't here for a vacation, so I forced myself to stop appreciating the perfectly manicured rose garden and the row of willow trees elegantly trailing their branches in the water and focus on the task at hand.

By the time my little autocab finally finished the ridiculously long drive to the house, a servant was waiting on the stairs to greet me. It was the really old guy with the bushy mustache who'd worked as my dad's clerk for forever, which was odd because I thought he never left the main compound in Seoul. Even stranger was the fact that he'd come out to meet me himself. Menial jobs like doorman were usually shoved off on the low-ranking staff, but the stooped clerk opened my car door with his own hands, bowing low as I stepped out onto the driveway.

"Young Mistress," he said, his voice impossible to read behind the iron wall of professional decorum. "The Great Yong has been expecting you."

I was sure he had been. Gripping my bag, I motioned for the clerk to lead the way. He did so in a stately fashion, guiding me up the stone stairs of the mansion's ridiculously wide front porch into a grand vaulted entry full of furniture that had been shoved up against the wall and covered in dust cloths.

That made me do a double take. Temporary or not, my mom would *never* allow a house to look like this while my father was in residence. "Why is everything put up?"

"It couldn't be helped," the clerk said, raising his feeble voice over the echoing booms of our footsteps. "The Great Yong ordered your lady mother and the rest of the household back to Korea weeks ago. Only a handful of us were allowed to stay behind with him, but this house is so large we couldn't keep the place clean with so few, so we had to close most of it up."

That sounded perfectly practical, but "Why didn't he just hire local workers?"

"I would never question the Great Yong," the old man said, giving me a look over his shoulder to add the unspoken, *And neither should you.*

I rolled my eyes and decided to focus on the house, which was definitely worth the attention. Whatever other feelings I had about him, my dad's good taste was undeniable. Even in a temporary residence like this, the walls had been covered in art from a wide range of cultures and time periods. He had Old Masters, modern mixed-media pieces, Chinese calligraphy, Korean textiles, Egyptian artifacts, Japanese Noh masks all thoughtfully positioned to show each piece at its best.

Even with the lights off and the furniture stacked in the corners, walking through my dad's house felt like a trip through an amazingly well-curated museum. He even had some stuff from DFZ artists that had to be new purchases. I was pretty sure I spotted a Barklay three-dimensional watercolor—*highly* collectible—on one of the stairway landings.

Alas, we didn't get close enough for me to tell for certain before the servant led me through a heavy wooden door into what must have once been a library but now looked like the modern version of a king's receiving room. There was a couch for waiting, a carpet in the middle for kneeling and begging, and a towering, ornately carved wooden bishop's chair where my dad could sit and look down on those who'd dared to seek his attention.

It was all very oppressive and draconic with lots of allegorical oil paintings of humans prostrating themselves before various monsters and gods, but at least it was well lit thanks to the wide, west-facing windows looking out over the mansion's emerald-green back lawn. Beyond that was the wide expanse of the Detroit River and the DFZ rising out of the brown water like a steel-and-concrete glacier. Being able to see the familiar, glittering chaos of the city made me feel a bit less like I was stranded in enemy territory. Enough that I was actually able to summon up a smile when the old servant bowed and left, presumably to get my dad.

I pulled out my phone the moment the door clicked closed, checking and rechecking my accounts. I preauthorized the transfer I was about to make at least six times, even going so far as to make Sibyl get a certified response from my bank's customer service AI that yes, they knew I was about to make a payment to a private account, and no, they would not hold up the transfer of funds for any reason. I was still fussing with settings when the door opened again, and my father came into the room.

I dropped my phone when I saw him. Not because of dragon-induced terror; I was used to that. No. I jumped because my dad looked *horrible*.

My entire life, I'd never seen Yong look anything less than what he was: a great and terrible immortal, beautiful and deadly and inhumanly mesmerizing. Now, though, his mortal form looked as if it had been through the wringer. His normally immaculate face was gaunt and pinched. His blue, green, and golden eyes were red rimmed and sunken, leaving huge, bruise-like dark circles in the hollows above his high cheekbones. Even the glossy black waterfall of his hair looked stringy and dull, and he was *so* thin. What I could see of his body beneath his designer suit looked positively skeletal, the lean muscles I'd never seen him work for wasted away to nothing.

It was shocking to see and honestly pretty terrifying. My father was as timeless as the treasures he collected, the definition of unchanging, unshakable power. Seeing him gaunt and gripping the door frame to stay upright felt like a constant of the universe had been violated. It didn't seem possible that something like this could happen to a force as great as the

Dragon of Korea, but as I watched him shuffle into the room and take his place in the throne-like chair, I came to a clear and sudden understanding.

I'd done this.

Realization came in a rush as all the clues I'd been too angry and distracted to care about before now suddenly clicked into place. This was my doing. I'd hacked Dad's curse, but the magic that stole my money had to come from somewhere. *Something* was powering all of that unrelenting bad luck, and looking at the husk my dad had become, I knew it had to be him. That was why he'd gone nuclear on the phone the first time I'd slammed his curse against the gold market and discovered something too big for it to break. That was why Mom had come to the Cleaner auction without his knowledge to try and make me stop. Because it was doing *this.*

In hindsight, I didn't know why I hadn't realized the truth earlier. Unlike humans, who grabbed their magic from whatever was nearby, dragons powered their spells with their own fire. I knew that. *Everyone* who studied magic knew that, but it had never occurred to me before this moment that my father's fire was not infinite. I'd never even heard of a dragon spending himself dry, but it was the only explanation for the husk of a dragon sitting where my glorious father should have been.

For a crazy, stupid moment, that made me feel crushingly guilty. I'd just wanted to get free. I hadn't wanted to hurt him, hadn't wanted *this.* As horrible as he'd acted, he was still my dad. I'd loved him with all my heart once. Part of me still must have, because I actually got up from the couch to run to him before I remembered the truth.

This wasn't my fault.

Yes, my actions had drained him, but he was the one who'd put the curse on me. He could have stopped and saved himself at any time, but he hadn't. From the stony glare in his sunken eyes, he *still* wasn't going to let go, and with that realization, all of my sympathy evaporated.

"You look terrible," I told him, crossing my arms over my chest.

"I could say the same of you," the Great Yong replied, his inhuman eyes looking me up and down as his scowl deepened. "You've lost weight again."

I'd thought my vending-machine clothes had felt even baggier than usual, but I refused to let him change the subject. "I'm here to pay my debt."

"What makes you think I'll accept it?" he said, leaning on the arm of his throne-like chair as if it was merely a comfortable position and not the only thing holding him upright. "It's not due for a few more days."

"It doesn't matter if you accept it or not," I growled, bending over to snatch my dropped phone off the thick carpet. "I pay you back for my college tuition, you let me go do whatever I want with my life. That was the deal."

He flashed his teeth. "*Your* deal."

"That you agreed to," I reminded him.

"Only because you deliberately misled me," he snarled back. "You hid that you were a Cleaner. I never would have given my word if I'd thought there was a chance you'd actually succeed."

"Yeah, well, maybe you should have thought about that before you assumed I was stupid enough to bet it all on a bargain I couldn't win," I said in a nasty voice, looking him straight in the eyes as I mashed the Send Payment icon on my phone screen. A second later, a message beeped up telling me that payment had been received.

"There," I said in a shaking voice. "It's done. I've paid it. *All* of it, as demanded. I've fulfilled my end of the bargain. Now remove this curse!"

I braced as I finished, planting my scuffed Cleaner boots on the carpet as I waited for him to rage, but my father just turned his gaunt face away.

"No."

My eyes went wide. "W-what?" I sputtered. "You don't get to say no. I won! We had an *agreement!*"

"We did," my father said, his deep voice haggard and tired. "But the curse was never part of it. I promised that if you paid the debt on your own, I'd allow you to live as you chose. I never said anything about magic."

"Because there was no magic involved then!" I shouted. "You only cursed me because you were *losing*! But I can't live as I choose with you dragging me down, so take this stupid thing off me!"

Yong's eyes narrowed. "No," he said again. Then he bared his teeth. "*Never.*"

That hissed word ripped the bottom right out of me. From the moment I'd come up with this plan almost five years ago, my father's famous integrity had been my hope. The Dragon of Korea would stomp you under his boot and grind you into the dirt, but he *always* kept his promises.

But apparently not for me.

"You can't do this!"

"I can do whatever I want!" he roared, all his usual decorum vanishing as he lurched to his feet. "You are my Opal! I *made* you!"

"I am a *human being*!" I yelled back, stomping forward until I was right in front of him. "No one owns me!"

"You have no idea what I've sacrificed for you!" Yong snarled, his wasted hands clenching into pale, bony fists. "I have tried and tried and *tried* to give you what you wanted, but every time I grant you freedom, you use it to hurt what I hold most dear." He grabbed me by the shoulder and whipped me around to face the large gilt mirror across from the window. "Look at what you've done to yourself!"

Angry as I was, the sight of the two of us in the mirror stopped me cold. I hadn't actually taken the time to look at myself in more than glances since the final push had started. Staring at my reflection now, I didn't even recognize the gaunt, used-up girl staring back at me. My skin was dry and scaly from my terrible diet and weeks of bad sleep. My bony limbs were covered in cuts and bruises from all the Cleaning, and my face looked like a skull. I didn't even look human anymore. I looked like a ghost. An exhausted, used-up shadow. Which, ironically, meant that for the first time in my life, I actually looked like my dad.

"Look at what you've done to her," my father whispered in Korean, reaching out to brush my dirty hair away from my face. "I would kill anyone who did this to my puppy, but what do I do when that person is you?"

"I didn't do this," I said through clenched teeth as I turned back around to face him. "You did. This only happened because *you* forced me into a corner. You could have saved both of us at any time by taking a hint and *letting me go!*"

My father's face grew hard as iron. "I will never let you go."

"Why?" I demanded, my voice cracking like thin ice. "Why are you holding on so tight? You're the one who's always calling me a dog face and a failure. My earliest memories are all of you telling people how much of a disappointment I was. You even named me after a worthless gem so everyone would know I wasn't the genetically perfect supermage you'd intended me to be." Tears began building up at the corners of my eyes. "You've always made it perfectly clear how little you value me, so why are you doing this? Am I part of some scheme? A cog in some long-running dragon plot too convoluted for mortals to follow? Why won't you just let me be?!"

I hadn't intended to get so emotional. My father despised weakness of any sort. Tears especially did nothing but earn his disdain, but I was just so hopeless. Even when Kauffman had put a gun to my head, I'd never felt this trapped, and I didn't even understand...*"Why?"*

"You gave me no choice," my father said in a low, ragged voice. "I told you years ago, puppy, I take care of what is mine, but you made that impossible. From the moment you arrived in this cursed city, you've done nothing but throw yourself into danger and poverty. You consort with criminals and risk your fragile, mortal body going into the houses of strangers to sort through their trash. Your mother and I have tried and tried to talk sense into you, but you refuse to listen. You're still that foolish child throwing a tantrum on the floor, but I can no longer afford to indulge you." His face grew stern. "If you won't do what's best for yourself, then I must. That's what fathers do."

"That's what *tyrants* do," I snarled, ripping out of his hold. "My life is *mine*! I'm not another treasure for you to hoard!"

"You are my greatest treasure," Yong said, reaching out to grab my arm. "And I am taking you back."

My eyes went wide as his bony fingers wrapped around my bicep. "What are you—"

The dragon didn't listen. He just turned and started toward the door, dragging me behind him across the carpet like a petulant puppy.

"You can't do this!" I yelled at him, struggling with all my might, but it was hopeless. Even gaunt and weakened, he was still a dragon, and I wasn't exactly in the best shape myself. "I paid you back!" I cried, trying another angle. "That still means you have to let me go, curse or no curse. What about your promise?"

"I'm breaking it," Yong said bitterly, dragging me into the hall. "And before you start in with threats against my reputation, I've none left to lose. The whole world knows what I'm willing to do for your sake now. Oath breaking is nothing next to that, but done is done. I've paid the price for both of us, and now you're coming home."

My booted feet scrambled on the hardwood as I fought him. "I'm not going anywhere with you!"

"I've already sent word to ready the plane for our flight back to Seoul," he went on, completely ignoring me. "The servants will pack up the house, but I still have to attend to a few things myself before we go. It should only take a few minutes, but until I'm finished—" He stopped to yank on a door just down the hallway from the library. When it opened, he jerked me forward, flinging me onto the floor inside. "Stay here and think on what you've done."

I shot back to my feet in an instant, but my father had already slammed the heavy door and turned the key in the old-fashioned metal lock, sealing me inside.

"You *asshole!*" I screamed, pounding my fists on the wood.

My father's answer was a bestial growl as he stomped away down the hall, shouting orders to his few remaining servants to pack his things. The Dragon of Korea and his daughter were going home.

I beat on the door a few more times for good measure, then I turned around to examine my prison. Now that I was no longer blind with rage, I recognized the room. It was a shooting closet, a room commonly found in wealthy nineteenth-century homes for the safe storage of sporting rifles. There were no guns now, though. Just dusty racks, a whole lot of windowless stone walls, and a heavy door that locked from the outside. So a prison, basically.

"He can't keep me in here!" I yelled at the servants I could hear rushing by in the hall. "I do *not* consent! This is kidnapping!"

No one answered, of course. Maybe a newer servant would have been swayed, but Yong had pared his retinue down to just the loyalists. Some of the people outside had been working for my dad for generations. Every one of them would have happily gutted me if it pleased their dragon, the brainwashed bastards.

"I'd offer to call someone," Sibyl said while I kicked the door. "But the security AI on this house is amazing. I'm already on total lockdown, zero connectivity for every network. He's even blocked the emergency radio frequencies, and no one remembers those! I can't even be mad I'm so impressed."

"That's fine," I said through clenched teeth as I turned around to try bashing the heel of my boot into the door since the steel toe wasn't doing shit. "I'm mad enough for both of us."

Mad wasn't even the word. There was no language for the murderous fury building up inside me. I'd *won*. I'd paid my debt. I was supposed to be free! What was the point of killing myself for weeks if my dad dragged me home anyway?

Cursing loudly, I turned to glare at the door that was still standing strong despite my best efforts. Damn solid oak construction. Why couldn't my dad have bought a cheap McMansion full of hollow doors and gypsum walls you could punch through?

"What are you going to do?" Sibyl whispered.

"I don't know," I muttered, covering my face with my hands. "Just let me think."

My AI dutifully went silent, but that actually made things worse. Without Sibyl's chatter, I could hear my father walking on the floors above me, his instantly identifiable footsteps sharp and efficient. It wouldn't take him long to get his things together. If I was going to get out before he dragged me onto a plane, it had to be now, but unless I found another hundred pounds of force somewhere, there was no way I was getting through that door. I couldn't even blast my way out. Like every place my dad deigned to sleep, the house was warded inside and out. I couldn't see any spellwork locked up in here, but I could feel the orderly hum of magic flowing through the floor like an electrical current. It zapped me when I poked it, and I snatched my mental hand back, shaking my head furiously. What the hell was I going to do?

You could ask for help.

At this point, the DFZ's voice didn't even make me jump anymore. I was confused what she was doing here, though. "How are you talking to me?" I asked out loud since I no longer gave a shit what my dad's servants thought. "I'm not even in the DFZ."

We have a good connection, the god replied. *Your high draw makes you easy to reach for from my end, if that makes sense. Also, you're currently leasing four hundred twenty-three of my properties. That puts us in bed together pretty solid.*

I winced. Oh yeah. I'd almost forgotten about all the apartments I was going to have to pay rent on in just a few days. Considering it hadn't changed a damn thing, I was really wishing I hadn't transferred all that money to my dad now.

It still wouldn't have been enough. The DFZ informed me. *Your total bill is going to be over six hundred thousand, but that's what you get for abusing my Cleaning system.*

My stomach dropped. That was a lot more than I'd realized, but it did give me an idea. "You should bust me out of here, then," I said sweetly. "Because I can't pay you back if I'm locked up in Korea."

I could, you know.

I froze. "Really?"

I am a god, she reminded me huffily. *I think I can manage freeing someone from a closet even if it is across the river. But breaking that door would make me a powerful enemy, so I'm not going to do it for free.*

I sighed. Should have known. "You still want me to be your priestess, don't you?"

Of course! the DFZ said excitedly. *Dr. Kowalski and I have been most impressed with your progress controlling your draw. You'd be absolutely wasted as a dragon's pet mortal.*

"I agree with you there," I said. "But I already told you I'm not trading one master for another."

You're not going to have much of a choice in a few minutes, the spirit said. *Windsor is still just barely inside my reach, but once your father takes you over the sea, you'll be out of my power. If I'm going to help you, it has to be now.*

I couldn't let it be now. I understood what she was saying, I could even admit that she was right, but I hadn't fought this hard to turn around and sell myself to someone new. All I wanted was to be free for once in my life. Why was that so difficult? What did I have to do?

Serve, the DFZ whispered.

"No," I growled back. "I don't bow. Not to anyone. Not anymore."

Then I guess you're on your own, the spirit said sadly. *And I'm not saying that just to hard sell you. I'm the god of a city. My powers are defined by my borders, and those don't extend into Canada. I can't help you in Windsor unless you're part of me. For a still-living mortal, that means priesthood.*

I sighed and sank down to the floor, burying my face in the canvas fabric of my bag. On the other side of the door, the house had gone still, probably because everyone was packing up the cars outside. Soon they'd be coming to pack *me* in, and then it'd all be over. I'd be over. I was finished, done for, completely and totally de—

I stopped suddenly, blinking the tears out of my eyes. Sitting up again, I opened my bag and dug around until I found the lump that had been pressing into my cheek. The slightly soft, dusty-brown lump of my potato.

The spirit in my head went quiet as I pulled the tuber out and stared at it. A few of the eyes had sprouted over the weeks I'd been carrying it everywhere, but it was still mostly the same as when Dr. Kowalski had handed it to me. I knew its shape by heart at this point, the size and weight of it in my hand. I knew how to take just that much magic, no more, no less. I hadn't tried to cast anything serious with it yet because things had been so busy, but I'd refilled my poncho's wards and pried open magical safes and done tons of other stuff without blasting myself in the face. Maybe I could do this.

Mind spinning, I got on my knees and pressed the hand that wasn't holding the potato against the floor to check the wards again. The magic flowing through them felt smooth as silk, definitely high grade. I couldn't tell exactly what it did without seeing the spellwork, but that didn't really matter. I wasn't skilled enough to hack any spell, let alone one this expensive, and blowing it would probably kill me. But while I still wasn't and likely would never be the sort of wiz who could disarm a ward blind, I *did* know my dad. He trusted his people, and he didn't make a habit of taking prisoners. His threats were all external, which meant his magical security was likely balanced toward defending against attacks from the outside. There was no reason the Great Yong would want to block magic cast *inside* his own property, and while it would be foolish to lock a mage in a room she could blast her way out of, I wasn't a mage to him. I was his bumbling, hopeless little Opal, and if there was one thing my dad would never expect, it would be me casting magic that actually worked.

I jumped back to my feet, scrambling to dig the casting chalk out of my bag as I raced to the door. When I started to draw a ring around the door knob, though, I paused. If there *was* anything in that ward to stop casting inside the house, it would be triggered by circles. Wards, like all spells, needed specifics to work, and what better specific to look for than the first thing every Thaumaturge—which at this point meant every employable mage—did. Just drawing one could set off the alarm, and then my dad would rush in, and the jig would be up.

Shaking my head, I tossed my chalk back into my bag and put my hand on the door instead. I could do this. I'd cast without circles plenty of times, but this time I was going to do it right. I just needed to—
Dr. Kowalski says remember to ride the lightning.

I twitched a bit at the interjection, but there was no point complaining. My head was a highway whether I liked it or not, so I might as well accept the help with good grace. So, with that, I took a deep breath and focused on my hands—one on the door, one holding the potato. When I had both sensations firmly in mind, I reached for the magic.

As usual, my first handful was way too much. But I'd learned now that magic could be put back as well as picked up, so I let go and tried again, pinching the free-floating magic like I was trying to pluck a single frond from a dandelion until I had exactly one potato's worth.

Cupping my seemingly tiny sip of magic, I turned my focus to the hand I'd placed on the door and thought about what I wanted the magic to do. I didn't try to order it or bend it as I would with spellwork. Instead, I created an image in my head, a picture of a knife thin enough to slide between the door and the frame but sharp and strong enough to cut through a steel bolt. I imagined how it would slice, the way the metal would part soundlessly beneath it like butter. Then, when the picture in my mind felt so real I could have picked it up, I poured my magic into it like molten metal into a mold. It hardened instantly, forming a knife that felt as real as I was. Real enough to grasp as I slid it into the door crack and pressed it down.

The rest happened in an instant. The magic sliced the bolt in half exactly as I'd envisioned, cutting through the steel with no more sound than a sigh. I didn't even realize I'd done it until it was over and the door, cut free of its moorings, swung open under its own weight. Swung open for *me*.

"Wow," I said, sitting back in amazement. "It actually worked."

"Of course it worked," Sibyl said proudly. "You've been practicing."

If practicing was all it took to make a good mage, I'd have been a world champion ten years ago. But while Sibyl wasn't right, she wasn't wrong, either. I *had* been practicing. The difference was that this time I'd been practicing the right thing.

Dr. Kowalski says congratulations, the DFZ relayed. *Actually, she's saying a lot more than that, but I don't think you've got the time right now.*

I did not. I was already peeking my head out the door, heart pounding as I glanced down the dark hallway. Everyone must have still been outside, though, because I didn't see a soul. I didn't hear anyone either, and I took that as my sign to make a break for it.

Can you get me a cab?

"No," Sibyl replied.

Sure, the DFZ whispered. *Where do you want it?*

I pictured the closest intersection and hurried into the hall, my sneaking steps breaking into a quiet run as I darted in the opposite direction from the library where I'd screamed at my father toward the patio that let out onto the mansion's expansive back lawn. I opened the glass doors with a soft click, slipping out onto the flagstone paving with barely a—

"*Opal!*" my father bellowed.

Shit.

"You'd better have that cab ready!" I hissed at the god in my head as I broke into a sprint. Above me, I could hear my father running down the upstairs hall, but either he didn't want to risk going full dragon and harming his art or he was even weaker than I'd realized, because no giant shadow appeared behind me. There were plenty of shouts and running, but the people running after me were all nice, fancy mortals who served a dragon. They were fine chasing me across the grass, but when we reached the muddy bamboo grove that separated my father's stretch of river from the neighboring yard, they stopped and looked for a path. I, being a grubby Cleaner, dove straight in. River mud was nothing compared to what Nik and I had to wade through every day, so I barely noticed the greasy, reeking dirt trying to suck my boots off my feet as I shoved my body through the woody bamboo pipes until, at last, I fell out into the springy, well-manicured grass of the adjacent mansion's yard.

I was back on my feet in a heartbeat, legs pumping as I sprinted across the lawn into the cherub-filled rose garden of the Italianate villa. Behind me, my father's roar shook the ground, spurring me to run even faster toward the road where I prayed to god—or at least to the DFZ— there was a car waiting to catch me.

Don't worry, the DFZ whispered into my fight-or-flight–driven mind. *I'm a very good god. Keep this prayer stuff up and you'll see! You might just end up a priest the old-fashioned way.*

If she got me out of this, I might. But I tried to keep that thought to myself as I sprinted into the boxwood hedge my dad's neighbors had planted like a wall around their property. Getting through cost me several inches of my cheap shirt, but I fought my way free in the end, wiggling out of its green, leafy clutches to burst out onto the actual sidewalk.

Panting and sticking close to the hedge to make it harder for my dad's people to spot me, I turned and looked frantically at the intersection on the corner. Like any street in a major city, it was full of parked cars, but wedged in between the perfectly nice Canadian sedans was a beat-up DFZ autocab. The door was even open for me, creating a perfect bolt hole for me to jump inside.

See what faith provides?

I thanked the god profusely as I started to run. I nearly caused an accident as I sprinted across the intersection and dove into the car, slamming the door and dropping my body to the floor just in time as my father burst out of the wall of bushes I'd just come from. I didn't know if he'd followed my footprints or traced my scent like a bloodhound—as a dragon, it could have been either—but whatever had gotten him this far wasn't enough to catch the cab. Even in Windsor, the cheap little autotaxis were common as dirt. Dad didn't even spare mine a glance as it puttered past him, humming down the elegant street at its top speed of about thirty miles per hour.

"Welcome to Val-U Cab, Val-U customer!" the cab's AI said cheerfully, her computer-generated face beaming down at me where I was still cowering on the floor. "Where would you like to travel today?"

That was a damn good question. There were several places I *wanted* to go, but only one that could actually help. It was a place I usually avoided like the plague, but after the epic hornet's nest kick I'd just delivered, it was the only place in the world I could think of where my dad couldn't get me.

"Take me to the Dragon Consulate," I ordered, still too afraid to get off the floor.

"Right away, Val-U customer!" the taxi chirped, slowing its meager speed as we turned a corner and entered the squall of traffic headed for the bridge.

*****

As the nexus for all official dragon activity in the city and home of the Peacemaker, the Dragon Consulate was one of the biggest—and strangest—buildings in town. Though shorter than some of the newer superscrapers, it was so wide it took up two entire blocks, mostly to create more surface area for the landing balconies that covered its upper levels.

Given how big some dragons got, though, those weren't always enough. When one of the giants like Conrad, Champion of the

Heartstrikers, flew in, he had to wrap his enormous body around the asymmetrical steel-and-glass building just to get enough footing. I'm sure that made for some pretty interesting viewing from the upper levels, but the Skyways portion of the consulate was reserved for dragons and the world leaders who were constantly coming over to negotiate with them. Unimportant mortals like myself came in through the building's far less glamorous Underground entrance.

As usual, the square out front was packed with tourists and dragon fanatics hoping to catch a glimpse of someone famous. Around that was the ring of ever-present vendor carts that always appeared wherever people gathered. My little cab couldn't even make it to the drop-off zone thanks to all the congestion, so I ended up getting out a block away and jogging the final distance, pushing past all the hopeful foreigners lining up for the official Dragon Consulate tour to the small, unassuming door off to the side marked "Official Consulate Business Only."

"Not to be a nag," Sibyl whispered nervously in my earpiece as we walked through the security scanners and threat-detection wards. "But seeing as we're entering the point of no return, I have to ask: are you *sure* you want to do this? I know you and your dad aren't on the best terms right now, but the Peacemaker is *not* his friend. This isn't a safe space for you."

"Nowhere's a safe space for me anymore," I said as the door lights turned green, allowing me to proceed through the security cage to the row of clerk windows inside. "But if there's one dragon Yong won't mess with casually, it's the Peacemaker. Dad may not be part of his big dragon alliance, but one of the reasons the Peacemaker built this place was to improve human/dragon relations, and mine *definitely* need improving. Also, he's called the 'Peacemaker' for pity's sake. If I'm going to run to another dragon, I might as well go for the one who's famous for talking rather than biting."

"I can't fault your logic," Sibyl said. "But your father is *not* going to like this."

"Good thing I don't have to care about what he likes anymore," I snapped, stepping up to the window to show the worker my ID. The human clerk inside did a double take when she saw my name, but I must have checked out with their records, because she didn't ask questions. She just buzzed the door open and told me to follow the signs to Mortal Services on the third floor. I thanked her and stepped through, walking past a security window overlooking the crowded tourist lobby with its velvet ropes, augmented-reality displays of dragons in flight, and expansive gift shop into the actual business part of the building.

The inside of the Dragon Consulate was just as confusing now as the last time I'd been here. I didn't know if that was because it had been designed to make sense to twisty dragon minds or if the excessive complication was the natural result of trying to cram so many different offices into one enormous building, but the hallways snaked on forever. Fortunately for me, the lower levels all were mortal turf, and not even the sort you usually found near dragons. No one down here was remarkably beautiful or impeccably dressed. Other than the interesting job titles on the doors like "Treasure Hoard Tax Assistance," "Modern Life Integration Counseling," and "Accidental Municipal Arson Mitigation Unit," everyone down here seemed to be perfectly normal office workers of the sort you'd see at any corporate HQ in the DFZ.

Ironically, the Dragon Consulate actually looked *more* like a municipal building than any of the actual municipal buildings I'd been to in the city so far. I didn't know how a dragon managed to out-bureaucracy the spirit of a city, but this place was pure social services right down to the fluorescent lights, beige carpet, and plastic racks of free informational pamphlets. I felt like I was coming to file a zoning complaint as I walked through the glass doors marked "Mortal Services" and approached the wrap-around desk staffed with middle-aged women all wearing the same "don't even try it" expressions.

They all seemed equally unhappy to see me, so I went for the closest one, flashing the lady my best beleaguered expression as I walked up to the desk. "Hello," I said. "I need help. I'm stuck under a dragon curse."

She looked unimpressed. "Is the dragon part of the Peacekeeper's Accord?"

"No."

The lady gave me a "then what do you want me to do about it?" look, but she'd clearly been at this for a long time, so she kept any actual comments to herself. "Fill this out, and we'll see what we can do," she said instead, handing me an old-fashioned touchscreen tablet from the pile beside her.

I smiled politely as I took it, walking over to the couch with a sinking feeling. I knew my dad wasn't one of the Peacemaker's buddies, but I'd hoped for better than a standard form. I'd thought mentioning the curse would at least get me a meeting with an actual dragon of some sort, but the bar for concern in this place must have been damn high, because the woman at the counter hadn't even blinked. Still, the waiting room was nice enough, and, more importantly, there were no dragons. The Dragon Consulate was famously riddled with spies. Every clan in the world had someone in the building listening for gossip, but they all seemed to be up top where the dragon intrigue happened. Down here in the bureaucratic bowels of the Peacemaker's great social experiment, there was no one important, and while that didn't help my emergency, at least I was free to fill out my form in peace.

It took me five minutes to fill out the electronic questionnaire with all my important information. When I was done, I handed the tablet back to the lady and settled in to wait. There was no one else on the couches, so I was hoping it wouldn't be long, but I'd barely pulled out my phone to play a round of *Candy Crush 2099* when someone yelled my name.

"*Opal!*"

I jumped a foot off the beige cushions. I didn't even have to look up to know that wasn't the staff calling me back. My ears already knew that voice wasn't human. Nothing mortal could sound that pretty while inspiring instinctive terror. Sure enough, when I raised my head, there was a dragon standing in the office doorway. But while she clearly recognized me, I couldn't say the same for her.

She was beautiful, of course. Every dragon, even the young, scrubby ones, looked like a supermodel in their human form. My mother claimed it was just their natural superiority showing through, but I'd always suspected it was a hunting adaptation. Tasty humans let you get a lot closer when you were dazzlingly gorgeous.

This one's mortal mask looked ethnically Korean. That meant her territory must have been near my father's since dragons tended to adopt the guise of whatever mortals lived in their area, but I didn't recognize her from any of my father's parties, which made me even more nervous. There was only one Asian dragon my father never invited to view his collections, and that was the one who hated him the most.

"White Snake," I said softly, pressing my back into the couch's hard cushions in the hope I could vanish between their cracks. "What are you doing here?"

The dragoness's blood-red lips curled in a predatory smile. "It's *Lady* White Snake to you, little girl," she said, walking into the waiting room. Now that she was inside, I could see that she had her mortals in tow, a pair of handsome, impeccably dressed young men wearing the same ludicrously expensive AR sunglasses Ainsley had sported. It should have looked ridiculous in a fluorescent-lit room with no windows, but nothing looked stupid when you were that good-looking and standing in the shadow of your dragon. I, however, was alone and on the wrong side of the power balance. A fact White Snake did everything she could to drive home.

"I'm surprised you remember me," she said, stalking closer. "The last time we met, you were still just a little puppy." She brushed her razor-sharp nails over my cheek, waiting for me to flinch. When I didn't, she moved on.

"What are you doing here?" she asked, her lovely voice perfectly casual, as if she'd just happened to bump into me in a place she had absolutely no conceivable business being. Even the ladies behind the counter had lost their seen-everything expressions. Two had stopped their work to watch, while a third was frantically whispering into a phone. If I'd had sense, I would have run behind the counter to join them, but I was at the end of a very peculiar day, and—ironic, given where I was—I'd had enough of dragon bullshit.

"I could ask you the same question," I said, glaring up at her. "Did you finally give in and join the Peacemaker's social club?"

"Never," White Snake said with a laugh. "The Peacemaker has forgotten what it means to be a dragon, if he ever knew in the first place. I'm just here to take advantage of his declared neutrality while I negotiate a contract. Routine business, nothing special."

I fought not to roll my eyes.

"So how's your father?" she went on, moving her hand up to play with my unwashed hair. "I hear he's been feeling poorly."

"He's fine."

"How can that be if you're here?" she cooed. "Aren't you the treasure he'll do anything to protect?"

When that failed to get a rise, White Snake leaned down, dropping her voice to a stage whisper as she pressed her red lips to my ear. "If you're here about Yong, I can help you far more than the Peacemaker's lackeys. I understand my brother better than these outsiders ever could, and unlike them, I won't make you wait in the foyer like a common peasant. I'll treat you like the elevated mortal you are, and if you show proper respect, I might even take that curse off just for the pleasure of watching Yong squirm. So what do you say, Dragon's Opal? Want to trade up?"

It was a sign of how mad I was at my dad right now that I actually considered it. I trusted White Snake even less than I'd trust a normal dragon, but it would have been so *satisfying* to let her remove my curse knowing my dad couldn't do anything to stop her. As tempting as that mental image was, though, it was a pipe dream. No matter what she promised, White Snake would never remove my curse. Not if she could use it against my father instead. She would absolutely put me under her claws, though, and I wasn't about to trade my pain-in-the-ass dragon for one that was even worse.

"No thank you."

I leaned back as I spoke, giving myself room for when she inevitably went nuclear, since that was what dragons did when you told them no. To my astonishment, though, White Snake just smiled.

"You should really reconsider, little pumpkin," she told me sweetly. "Your father's good at hiding weakness, but we both know he's in a bad way. This is a rare opportunity for both of us. Don't you want to make him pay for what he's done to you?"

My breath hitched, not in temptation but in fury. I might be super mad at my dad right now, but I was no traitor. Yong was an overbearing ass who deserved everything he'd done to himself and more, but like hell was I going to sell him out to his sleazy sister. The snakes could fight each other all they wanted, but I refused to be a weapon in their war. I was done being a dragon's possession, just like I was done with this conversation.

"Piss off," I told her.

The dragoness above me went so still, I swore her cells stopped moving. "What did you say to me?"

I looked her right in the face so she wouldn't miss it this time. "Piss. Off."

As they left my mouth, I knew there was a strong chance those rude words would be my last, but it felt *so* good to finally tell one of these power-mad tyrants where to shove it. The shocked fury on White Snake's face was definitely worth the risk so far. I was telling myself to enjoy it thoroughly just in case it was the last thing I saw when a hand landed on my shoulder.

I jumped even higher this time. I'd been so focused on the dragon in front of me that I hadn't noticed the one sneaking in from the side. This felt ridiculous, because even my feeble mortal senses could tell that the newcomer was *much* bigger. He was ridiculously tall and pretty even for a dragon, with his sharp cheekbones, light bronzed skin, bright-green eyes, and straight black hair even longer than my father's, which he wore in a messy bun held in place by paintbrushes, many of which still had fresh paint on them. He was dressed equally haphazardly in an untucked white tuxedo shirt, paint-covered jeans so old they'd turned white, and a pair of leather moccasins that looked like they'd been made by actual Native Americans from before the white man's invasion.

And if all that wasn't strange enough, there was a pigeon on his shoulder. Not a turtledove or some other genteel variety, but the same gray city pigeon you normally saw eating dropped french fries off the street. It was nesting happily in the dragon's long hair, turning its rainbow-sheened head from side to side to look at me with each of its beady, black eyes as the dragon sat down next to me like we were old friends.

"I'm sorry," I said after a long, awkward silence. "Do I know you?"

"Not a bit," the new dragon assured me, pointing a paint-stained finger at White Snake. "But she does."

White Snake looked as if she'd seen a ghost. She'd already backed away from us, but when the dragon called her out, she jumped like a frightened mouse. It was shocking to see. My father had always said his sister was a coward, but I'd assumed he was just being insulting. There must have been some truth to it, though, because I'd never seen a dragon act in such a blatantly undraconic fashion. White Snake knew she'd been caught out, too, because when she finally managed to look the new dragon in the eyes, her lovely face was pinched with rage and shame.

"Who gave you the right to interrupt us?"

"Oh, I'm sorry," the green-eyed dragon replied, not sounding sorry in the slightest. "I was unaware there was an application process." He looked at me. "You don't mind if I butt in, do you?"

I shook my head frantically, and the dragon turned back to White Snake with a charming smile. "See? She doesn't mind."

"Her opinion is not important," White Snake snarled. "I am—"

"A guest in my little brother's home, I *know*," the new dragon replied. "And so soon to be leaving us, alas! I'm sure I will be heartbroken by the loss of your company as soon as someone reminds me who you are."

In any other situation, I would have laughed out loud at that. But even in my current state of near-suicidal recklessness, I didn't dare laugh at White Snake now. Her face was red and blotchy with fury, and there was black smoke pouring from her nose and mouth. The dragon sitting next to me might have been able to weather that fire, but I'd be burned to a cinder if she decided to let loose. Terrifying as she was to behold, though, the balance of power had already shifted, because for all her smoke, White Snake was the one who dropped her eyes first, retreating to the hallway where her mortal entourage had already run for cover. She cast me a final nasty look over her shoulder, but all the parting threats I'm sure she would have loved to lob at me were cut short by a raised eyebrow from the dragon next to me. After that, she gave up all pretense and fled, striding away down the beige corridor at a speed mortals would have considered a flat-out run.

When she was gone, I turned to my unexpected savior with a bow. "Thank you."

"Don't mention it," the strange dragon said, patting me on the head like a dog. "I was just down here to buy some sunflower seeds for my lady love"—he stroked the pigeon on his shoulder, who cooed happily—"when I saw your predicament and decided to have some fun at someone else's expense."

I stared at him in horror. "You—you mean you weren't sent to save me?"

"Sorry to bruise your ego, but I'm not actually entirely sure who you are," the dragon said cheerfully. "I was just cutting through because the vending machine in the employee lounge next door is the only one in the building that sells the right brand of sunflower seeds. I keep telling my brother to stock more, but he's all 'Bob, you are the greatest, most powerful, most handsome dragon in the world! Go buy your own sunflower seeds!' Can you believe it?"

I could not, but not for reasons that had anything to do with sunflower seeds or snack machines. I'd *finally* realized which dragon I was talking to, and I was no longer sure it was a good thing he'd chased off White Snake. At least I'd known how she would act. This dragon was something altogether more terrifying, because between the pigeon and the stupid nickname he'd just let slip, I now knew that I was sitting beside Brohomir, eldest son of the Heartstriker dragon clan and one of only three dragon seers left in the world. He was also the Peacemaker's brother and rumored to be stark raving mad. Rumors I now *definitely* believed.

"Well," I said, scooting down the sofa. "Thank you so much for the save. I don't want to take up any more of your extremely valuable time, so why don't you go ahead and get those sunflower seeds? Your lady, who is very beautiful by the way, looks, um, hungry."

"My consort is quite *peckish*," the Great Brohomir said, wiggling his dark eyebrows. "But you're surprisingly polite for a lesser creature." His face lit up in a beatific smile. "You should come with us!"

"Oh no, I couldn't," I said quickly, waving my hands. "I wouldn't want to be a third wheel, and I'm waiting for an appointment with a—"

"Nonsense," Bob said, wrapping a long arm around my shoulder and lifting me physically off the couch. "It doesn't take a seer to see where *you* need to go. I could smell that curse on you from three floors away. What in the world did you do to make Yong so mad? The Dragon of Korea normally *loves* mortals. Seriously, last I heard, he had *two hundred* of you death-bound critters scampering around his lair! That's the dragon equivalent of being a crazy cat lady, you know."

I laughed nervously, frantically scrambling to figure out how I was going to escape this horrifying new situation I'd landed in. Dammit, I should have known better than to go to the Peacemaker for help! Dragons *always* made things worse. Now I was probably going to end up being fed to this cheerful lunatic's pigeon girlfriend.

"At least he's taking us up the ranks," Sibyl whispered in my ear as we got on the elevator.

Brohomir did indeed hit the button for a *very* high floor. The elevator shot up at a terrifying speed, making my stomach flip-flop as we rocketed toward the top of the building. Finally, the elevator slowed, and the doors opened to reveal a beautiful hallway that was worlds apart from the drab, fluorescent-lit rooms downstairs. Here, at last, the Dragon Consulate was the proper level of opulent. There were soaring windows looking out over the ever-shifting DFZ skyline, a lovely polished marble floor with real fossils inside each slab, and wood-paneled walls covered in a staggeringly lovely series of Chinese watercolor paintings of dragons in flight from an artist I didn't recognize, which was the biggest shock of all. My dad had taught me to recognize every major painter in China from the last two thousand years on sight. How was it possible I'd missed someone this good? I was still puzzling over it when Brohomir shoved me out of the elevator.

"Hey!" I cried, stumbling forward.

"Don't worry," he replied, hitting the button to close the doors again. "You can't miss it."

"Can't miss what?" I said frantically. "I don't even know why you brought me here!"

"I have to get my darling her seeds," he said, ignoring me. "Take care, little mortal!"

He waved cheerfully as the elevator doors closed, leaving me crouched in a panic in the lovely hallway. The lovely *dragon* hallway in a part of the *Dragon* Consulate I'd never been to.

"I'm going to get eaten," I whispered to Sibyl.

"It'll be fine," my AI replied in the soothing voice she used when it was absolutely not going to be fine. "Brohomir's one of the three dragon seers. That means he sees the future, right? He must have brought you here for a reason."

"That doesn't mean it's a good reason for *me*," I hissed back. "The Peacemaker is Dad's enemy, remember? This could all be a plot to—"

"Miss Yong-ae?"

I jumped with a squeak and looked over my shoulder to see a young man poking his head through the double doors at the end of the hall. He looked so unassuming with his boyishly cropped black hair and quick smile, I didn't realize he was a dragon as well until I noticed his eyes were that tell-tale insane shade of neon green that was the mark of the Heartstriker clan. Not that that told me anything, of course. The Heartstrikers were the dragons of the Americas, and there were a million of them. Well, maybe not a million, but there were a *lot*. This Heartstriker looked pretty young, too, maybe even younger than the one who'd taken my report in the Gnarls. I was trying to decide if he was actually employed here or if he was just hanging around listening for gossip when he hurried forward to greet me.

"Sorry for the wait," he said, holding out his hand. "I've heard about your problem with your father, and I'd like to help."

"Really?" Because that was the last thing I'd ever expected a dragon to say. "Thank you very much, um…"

I trailed off, embarrassed. This dragon clearly expected me to know who he was, but I had no idea. I was mentally nudging Sibyl to help me out when the young dragon laughed.

"I'm not surprised you don't recognize me," he said, giving me a wide smile. "Everyone says I look different on television." He pointed at his face.

"I'm the Peacemaker."

CHAPTER 10

I stared at him, speechless. Then I blurted out, "*You're* the Peacemaker?"

I was horrified at my own rudeness, but I was just so shocked. The Peacemaker was one of the most powerful forces in the world, the only dragon *ever* to create and sustain a coalition of multiple clans for more than one conflict. He didn't just rule all the dragons in the DFZ. He and his allies controlled fully two-thirds of all the dragons in *existence*. I'd heard he was young, but the dragon in front of me barely looked old enough to drink. He didn't even radiate a predatory menace. If it wasn't for his eyes, I'd have sworn he was human, which was not a mistake I normally made with dragons.

"I—I'm sorry," I stuttered at last, dropping to my knees in a desperate attempt to salvage what I'd just ruined. "Forgive me, great dragon. I did not know."

"That's fine. Everyone does it," the Peacemaker said, waving at me to stand up. "And Bob always throws people off. I wouldn't have sent him down to get you, but the only other dragon I trusted for the job with White Snake in the building was Justin, and I didn't want to start a war."

I didn't know who Justin was, but if the Peacemaker considered the Great Seer Brohomir to be the safer choice, then I was terrified of him.

"Please come in," the dragon said, waving me toward the double doors he'd come out of. "My office is a mess, but it's the only room in the building where I know we won't be overheard. Dragons are horrible gossips, and we're full to the rafters right now."

I nodded slowly, creeping after the Peacemaker down the hall and into a room that was indeed quite messy but in a way that made me feel at home.

It wasn't nearly as grand as you'd expect from the hall outside. The ceilings were very high, and the walls were decorated with more of the beautiful watercolor paintings I'd seen outside. Aside from staggeringly lovely masterpieces from an unknown genius, though, the Peacemaker's office looked astonishingly normal. There were no heads of his enemies mounted on the walls, no storied treasures or piles of gold stacked in the corners, no famous weapons of war. Just a few comfortable chairs, a bunch of potted plants, and a desk covered with vacation photos of him and his mortal wife. It was so relentlessly undraconic that I was starting to wonder if Brohomir's madness might not be shared among all the Heartstrikers when the Peacemaker motioned for me to sit.

"We need to talk about your father."

That, at least, was expected, and I sat down with a sigh. The Peacemaker did the same, flopping into the worn leather chair behind his desk and folding his hands on the blotter. "I understand you and the Dragon of Korea are having a problem right now."

"*He's* having the problem," I said bitterly. "He cursed me."

"I know," the Peacemaker replied. "My sister, the dragon who helped you in the Gnarls, told me all about it."

From what my mom had said, she'd told *everyone* about it, but that wasn't my concern. "If you know that, then you know this is not my fault," I said angrily. "We had a bargain! If I paid off all the money I owed him, he'd let me go free. That was our deal, but when I started to win, my dad cursed me with bad luck that made it impossible for me to earn money. I managed to pay off my debt anyway, but now he refuses to remove the curse. He even tried to kidnap me back to Korea! I had to break out and flee here in a cab."

"The DFZ told me," the dragon said, nodding.

I stared at him. "The DFZ told *you?*"

He smiled. "She's my city, too."

Huh. Apparently all those rumors about the city being close to her dragon weren't just rumors. Another time, I would have asked him how the hell he'd ended up on a first-gossip basis with a god, but right now I had bigger dragons to fry.

"If you know the story, then you have to help me," I said. "I know my dad's not a member of your peace club, but I live in your territory, and you and the DFZ both have rules prohibiting holding mortals against their will."

"I know my own laws," the Peacemaker said, though not crossly. He sounded more sad than anything, which was why I wasn't surprised when he added, "But I can't help you."

"Why not?" I demanded, shooting to my feet. "A dragon cursed me against my will! I'm not asking you to go to war with him. I just need someone to get his magic off me!"

"Those are one and the same, I'm afraid," the Peacemaker said, steepling his fingers on his desk. "I've actually known about you and your father's unique situation for some time. When you first wanted to move here four years ago, Yong came to me personally to request permission."

I blinked. "He did?"

The Peacemaker nodded. "It was a big deal. As you said, Yong's not part of my 'peace club,' and that was a problem. I'm the Dragon of Detroit. Living in my territory is a privilege extended only to those dragons who've sworn to abide by my rules. I can't just let any dragon's mortals live here. There's an application process, and your father applied for you. Quite forcefully, actually."

I'd...I'd never known that. I'd always thought I'd moved to the DFZ against my father's will. I hadn't realized he'd gone to bat for me. I wasn't entirely sure I believed it, to be honest. Not that I thought the Peacemaker would lie about something so easily confirmed; I just couldn't imagine my dad swallowing his pride and asking a favor of a dragon he so famously despised.

"I couldn't believe it either at first," the Peacemaker said when he saw my expression. "But it was clear to me that your father cared about you very much. He wanted you to be able to go to the school you'd chosen, and I allowed him to send you here."

"That was very generous of you."

The dragon's lips quirked in a smile. "It wasn't *entirely* selfless. I was hoping to convince him to join us. Korea is one of the last great unallied territories, and Yong is famous for being an honorable, stand-up sort of dragon. He's a prime target, in other words. I was hoping to tempt him with generosity, but he's a stubborn dragon who values his independence."

"Sounds like someone else I know," Sibyl whispered in my ear.

I gave her a mental shove and returned my attention to the Peacemaker, who was still talking.

"Obviously, relations with Yong have deteriorated in the years since," he went on. "But I'm afraid I still can't allow any of my dragons to take his curse off you."

"Why not?" I demanded. "I read the declaration you made to the people of the DFZ when you founded this place. It's printed on all the brochures downstairs. You *promised* you wouldn't allow your dragons to abuse humans anymore." And I was *definitely* being abused.

"I did promise," the Peacemaker said. "But, as I keep trying to tell you, Yong is not my dragon. He's a power in his own right, and three weeks ago, he declared that any interference with the magic he'd placed on you would be considered an act of war."

I stared at him in disbelief. "He told you that?"

"He told *everyone*," the Peacemaker said grimly. "Rumors of your curse hadn't even finished spreading before he came to address our assembly and laid down the law. And since Yong has a reputation for keeping his word, we all believed him. That's why I can't do as you ask. I have great sympathy for your plight, Miss Yong-ae, but the whole point of the Peacemaker's Accord is to end the constant warring that has plagued the dragon clans for so long. We're finally on the brink of real worldwide peace for the first time in our bloody history. I can't jeopardize that for you."

"So what am I supposed to do?" I cried. "I can't break this thing on my own!"

"Well, if it makes you feel better, it can't go on for much longer," the Peacemaker said. "You're the one who's cursed, but Yong's taking the brunt." He tilted his head at me. "Do you know how dragon magic works?"

I nodded. "I know Dad's been spending his own fire to keep me in check."

"He's been spending more than that." The young dragon placed a hand on his chest. "Our fire is more than fuel for our spells. It's our life, the thing that makes us *dragons.* Yong's curse on you is so strong because he's been pouring his fire into it. Old as he is, he has a lot to give. But no dragon's fire is infinite, and when you made him use it to crash the gold markets, you took more than he was wise to spend."

I stared at him in surprise. "How did you know about the gold markets?"

"There are few things dragons pay attention to more than gold," he said with a chuckle. "Add in the flares of Yong's magic at the same time as every dip plus his bizarre warning about your curse, and most of us were able to put two and two together. It's earned him a lot of new enemies. My mother in particular wants his head on a platter. She has a *lot* of gold."

She wasn't the only one. I'd seen the piles dragons slept on. I'd been too busy to think about it at the time, but I could absolutely see now how crashing the gold market would step on a lot of tails. That was honestly a bonus, though. Anything that put more pressure on my dad was A-OK in my book. What I didn't understand was why the Peacemaker was telling me this as if I cared.

"His enemies are not my concern," I said coldly. "I did what I had to do. If he didn't like it, he could have stopped the curse at any time."

"But he didn't," the Peacemaker said. "And now we've all got a problem."

I arched an eyebrow at that, and the dragon leaned forward with a grim expression. "Whether he was right or wrong to do so, your father has spent an enormous amount of his fire trying to force you back under his control. It's left him weak and vulnerable, and that's not good for anyone.

The Dragon of Korea isn't part of my Accord, but he has his own alliances with several dragons who are. If one of his enemies sees his weakness as a chance, it could plunge the whole region into war and threaten the peace I've been building for twenty years. That's a lot of unnecessary damage for what is essentially a family problem."

My hopes sank with every word. "So you're just going to throw me under the bus?" I said. "Give me back to my dad to placate him just so you can keep your peace?"

"I'm not giving you to anyone," the Peacemaker said patiently. "But I think you need to ask yourself why your father is willing to go this far."

"Because he's a narcissist who can't let go," I snapped.

"Narcissists don't hurt themselves for others," he argued. "There's no question Yong is going about this in entirely the wrong way, but I believe that, deep inside, he's a good person."

"Don't you mean a good dragon?"

The Peacemaker shook his head. "Those are two very different things. Funny enough, I believe Yong's problem is that he's both. The Dragon of Korea is famous for his ruthlessness, cunning, and honor. He is feared by his enemies, respected by his neighbors, and worshiped by his people. With the exception of his excessive exuberance for mortal collecting, his reputation as a dragon has always been flawless. And then you came along."

"Are you going to tell me I ruined him?" I asked bitterly.

"Not at all," the Peacemaker said. "If anything, this turn of events only makes me want him more. No properly prideful, selfish dragon puts himself in this much peril for a mortal. It's clear to me that, no matter what he might claim, the Great Yong loves you very, *very* much, and it would be the greatest tragedy to go to war over something as beautiful as that."

I looked down at my hands. Hearing him say it like that made me want to believe it. I was only human, after all. Of course I wanted to believe my father loved me. But I'd been down that dead-end road too many times already, and I refused to be tricked again.

"You're wrong."

The Peacemaker sat back in his chair. "How so?"

"My father doesn't love me," I said, fists tightening on my cheap, dirty leggings. "He covets me. I'm his Opal—a thing, not a person. He isn't doing all this because he misses me or wants me around. He's doing it because I'm the only one who's ever had the guts to reject him, and he can't stand it."

"Well," the dragon said slowly. "He's your father. I suppose you'd know him best."

I nodded approvingly, but the dragon wasn't finished yet.

"Sometimes, though, the people we're closest to are the hardest to see truthfully. Our own feelings can get in the way, making it difficult to see what's right in front of our noses."

My fists clenched in rage. Who did he think he was, saying that to me? This wasn't some little family spat that could be cleared up with a good long talk and a hug. My father had tried to *kidnap* me! But before I could figure out how to tell him how wrong he was without being directly insulting, the Peacemaker lifted his hands.

"I know, I know," he said, smiling. "But before you dismiss me entirely, can I ask you a question?"

It couldn't be worse than what he'd just said, so I nodded.

"Do you hate your father?"

I blinked in surprise. I'd never actually thought about that before. Now that someone had asked me directly, though, the answer was obvious. "No," I said. "I'm mad at him, and I want him to stop, but I don't *hate* him."

"Why not?" the Peacemaker asked. "You just said he's done horrible things to you. I can't take that curse off of you, but there are plenty of other dragons who will. Why not sell him out to one of his enemies and be done with it?"

I opened my mouth to tell him my usual line about how I didn't want to trade one master for another, but the words felt like ash in my mouth. The situations were entirely different, but the simple, straightforward way he'd asked the question reminded me of Dr. Kowalski when she'd demanded I tell her the truth. Then as now, I'd thought I was, but when I stopped and asked myself for the truth—the *real* reason I'd stuck so hard to our bargain instead of selling my dad out to any of the powers who would gladly have bought his weakness—the answer that came back was very different.

"Because he's my dad."

Even as I said it, I knew my answer was indefensible. Parenthood didn't excuse anything. There were plenty of people who hated their dads with good reason. *I* had good reason, and yet, despite everything he'd done, all the times he'd stomped all over my life and called me a dog-girl and a disappointment, I couldn't do it. I wasn't sure if I loved him anymore, but I couldn't bring myself to hate him. Not even to save my own neck, which was probably the stupidest decision I'd ever made. I fully expected the Peacemaker to tell me so, but to my surprise, the dragon just nodded, his young face made older by deep, deep sympathy, as if he knew exactly what I was feeling.

"It gives me hope to hear you say that," he said. "And for what it's worth, I don't believe Yong sees you only as a thing."

"But he does," I argued. "He told me so."

"I'm sure he did," the Peacemaker replied. "But you should know by now that what a dragon says and what he feels are often two entirely different things. He might *tell* you you're a possession, but in every interaction I've had with him—from the first time we met when he asked me to let you live here to his declaration that anyone who touched you would be his sworn enemy—Yong has constantly and consistently referred to you as his child. You might not be his by nature, but in his actions, you are his beloved daughter, more important than fire or gold."

"If that's true," I whispered, voice shaking, "why is he doing this to me?"

"I don't know," the Peacemaker said. "But I think you had the right of it when you said he coveted you. I can see how that would be intolerable from your perspective. No one wants to be owned. But for a proper old dragon who's been taught since birth that affection was a weakness that would get him killed, coveting a gem is a lot safer than loving a daughter. That's his problem he's going to have to get over on his own, of course, and I'm not asking you to forgive him. I'd just…I think it would be good if the two of you could talk."

"I've tried that," I said angrily. "I've tried and tried a hundred times, but he doesn't listen! He just yells."

The Peacemaker's mouth twitched. "Do you yell back?"

I looked down at my hands. I…might have yelled at my dad a bit. Or a lot. But it wasn't my fault! He was just so unreasonable, and it made me so mad. Before I could think of how to explain this to the Peacemaker in a way that didn't make me sound like part of the problem, though, the dragon stood up from his desk.

"I can't fix what's broken between you and your father," he said. "You're the only ones who can build that bridge, but you're going to have to find a way to do it soon. The whole dragon world is in uproar over the gold markets, and they're blaming Yong for it. I'm sure you don't have a lot of sympathy for him right now, but a weak dragon is a volatile thing. Yong has spent his magic nearly dry trying to keep you on a leash, but unlike you, he can't just reach out and get more. All he's got is the fire inside him. When that's gone, so is he."

"It won't come to that," I promised. "My dad's stubborn as a pig, but he's not going to kill himself over my curse."

"Maybe not on purpose," the Peacemaker said. "But even prudent dragons are capable of doing amazingly stupid, reckless things when they're desperate to win."

My eyes dropped. I knew all about that.

"Just talk to him," the dragon said. "He's going about it all wrong, but I'm certain that your father loves you. You've told me you don't hate him, so that's a good start. Yong's old and set in his ways. He's not going to be the first to come around, but you're young and human. Your kind shapes the entire world. Surely you can make one stubborn old dragon see the light."

I sighed. "It's not going to work."

The Peacemaker shrugged. "Maybe not, but I suggest you give it a try anyway, because no dragon under my command is going to remove that curse for you. I'm not kicking off a war because you two are too stubborn to work out your differences like civilized people."

That was fair enough, I guessed, but "What do I do in the meantime? Talking to my dad is great and all, but I'm here because he's trying to *kidnap* me. That doesn't give me a lot of negotiating room."

"You're welcome to stay at the Consulate as long as you like," the Peacemaker offered. "I can't take your curse off, but I can offer you sanctuary, and I promise you'll be safe here. No matter how hard he rages, your dad can't break in past all of us, especially not in his current condition."

The idea of another dragon knowing how weak my father was made me nervous, but I shook it off with a grimace. I was not responsible for what he'd done to himself or for keeping him safe. That was for his obedient mortals to worry about. I was free, and like hell was I cowering in here.

"You sure about that?" Sibyl whispered. "This place is really nice. They've got a pool and a cafeteria and everything."

It's a prison, I thought at her.

"You can't have it both ways, you know," my AI snapped. "Even if the Peacemaker was willing to snip the curse off you right now, it's not as if your dad would stop. He'd still be chasing after you, trying to make you go home. Your choices are stay here and be safe in a cushy cage or go outside and take your chances. Whatever you decide, though, this isn't going to end until you and your dad come to some kind of resolution."

The truth of those words hit me like a train. I *was* trapped, wasn't I? I'd been focused on the curse just like I'd been focused on the debt, but they were all false goalposts. Every time I crossed one, my dad would just create another. That was exactly what he'd done with the curse. I could cross all the arbitrary finish lines I wanted, but this was never going to be over until one of us gave up.

I desperately wanted to believe that wasn't me. I liked to think I was stronger than that, but I was the mortal in this conflict, and he had my back against the wall harder than ever. Now that I knew how much my gold work-around was hurting him, I couldn't even make money anymore. Not unless I wanted to risk killing my dad by accident. Even knowing it would be his own fault, I felt sick just thinking about it. But if he was willing to do whatever it took to win and I wasn't, didn't that mean I'd already lost?

That line of thought was too depressing to bear. "I'm sorry," I said, rubbing a hand over my face.

"Take all the time you need," the Peacemaker said, walking out from behind his desk. "I have to get going. There's still a lot of panic over the gold situation. I have to go make sure no one's doing anything they're not supposed to, but you're welcome to stay in my office for as long as you like. When you're ready to move to a proper room, just call the—"

"No," I said quickly. "You've been very kind, *too* kind, but I can't stay here. I didn't break out of one dragon's prison just to go live in another, no matter how nice it is. I'll manage on my own."

"Are you sure?" he said, looking sincerely worried for my well-being, which was an expression I'd never seen on a dragon before. "We have off-site housing for our human staff if you'd be more comfortable—"

"No, really, I'm fine," I assured him. "I've got somewhere to go."

"Let me walk you down, at least," he said, hurrying to get the door for me. "This place is a warren. I don't want you to get lost."

More likely he didn't want the mortal of the dragon who was currently devaluing the wealth of every other dragon in the world wandering around by herself. The Peacemaker was far too tactful to say as much directly, though. He was a lot of things I hadn't expected, actually, and horrible as I felt right now, that made me smile.

"Please don't take this the wrong way," I said as I followed him to the elevator. "But you're the nicest dragon I've ever met."

"Thank you," the Peacemaker said with a beaming smile. "Skyways entrance or Underground?"

"Underground, please," I said, holding his sunny, confident smile in my mind like a warming fire as the elevator whisked us down the building and back into the fray.

***

I went straight to Nik's house.

It was a shitty thing to do. Now that I'd left the safety of the consulate, my dad would be on my trail again for sure. Bringing that disaster to Nik's doorstep was a horrible way to treat the person who'd helped me the most, but I couldn't let this blow up without seeing him one last time. I didn't know what I was going to do about the months of wages I'd promised him in return for helping me these last three crazy weeks, but I was sure I'd come up with something. I was most likely about to go back to being a rich dragon's possession, after all. Dad would probably slip him a few million to make sure Nik kept his mouth shut.

Just thinking about that sent me to a really bad place. My thoughts got so dark at one point, I actually had to switch Sibyl off to keep her from going into emergency intervention mode. I know that sounds like a terrible idea that defeats the entire purpose of a mental health AI, but I wasn't actually suicidal. I was just defeated. More so than I'd ever been in my life.

It took me a solid five minutes after the cab dropped me off to actually make it down the stairs to Nik's door. He must have been waiting for me to arrive, because I'd barely lifted my hand to knock before he opened the door.

"You're back!" he said excitedly, his freshly shaven face grinning down at me. He'd showered and changed into fresh clothes, too, which meant he looked a million times better than I did. "Does that mean your dad let you go?"

I didn't know if I had it in me to explain how wrong that was. I opened my mouth to try anyway, but nothing came out. Even the stuff I'd practiced in the car, all the "Thank you for everything" and "I'm so sorry" speeches I'd planned out so carefully, had vanished from my head. Staring up at Nik with his bright gray eyes and his freshly washed hair sticking up in every direction, all I could see was what I was about to lose, the life that was being taken from me by a force I couldn't fight, and I…I…

"Opal?"

I couldn't help it. I started to cry. It was a horrible, childish, humiliating way to act, but my body wasn't listening to reason. It was all over. Everything I'd worked for, everything I'd built. My life here hadn't been much or pretty, but it had been mine. The *only* thing I'd ever been able to call my own in my entire existence. Now my dad was taking it just like he took everything else, and I couldn't stop him. I couldn't do *anything*.

Nik swore under his breath, looking nervously down the hallway as he pulled me into his apartment and locked the door. This turned out to be a bad move, because the privacy gave me a false sense of security, which allowed me to cry even harder. I tried to apologize for being an idiot who always cried in front of him, but I was sobbing too hard to say anything intelligible. That was a real problem, because Nik was starting to look panicked.

"What do you need me to do?" he asked, grabbing my shoulders. "Whatever it is, I'll do it. Just please stop crying."

I covered my face with my hands. That was simultaneously the most touching and most humiliating thing anyone had ever said to me. I hated myself for being the weak, weepy girl who needed that kind of support, but at the same time, I was desperate to take him up on it. I was so tired of losing. So tired of fighting and pushing and sacrificing only to have everything blow up in my face. Just tired. So, so tired down to my bones.

"Can I have a hug?"

The sad little question came out in a spasm of hiccups, but I knew Nik understood me, because he jumped. "Yeah," he said, putting his arms around me awkwardly. "Of course."

I closed my eyes guiltily as he pressed me into his chest. I had no right using him for comfort like this. I felt like I was always mooching off of Nik, but he'd said it was okay, and I'd had nothing left to say no with. Thankfully, Nik didn't seem to mind. After the initial awkwardness, he got into the swing of things pretty quickly, pulling me into his chest as I cried and cried and cried.

We must have moved at some point, because when I finally stopped sobbing long enough to pay attention to my surroundings, we were sitting on the couch. I didn't know how long it had gone on, but it must have been quite a while, because Nik's black T-shirt was soaked.

"Sorry," I whispered.

"I don't mind," he said quietly, patting my hair. "You lie on me as long as you want."

I nodded and buried my face in his neck, greedily taking all the comfort he was willing to give me, because who knew when I'd get another chance like this. Hell, I'd probably never see Nik again after today.

That thought started me crying all over again. I hadn't thought I had anything left, but for once I was being an overachiever, because I got in another solid thirty minutes of weeping before I finally managed to pull it back together.

"So," Nik said when my heaving finally faded back to sniffles. "I take it the payoff didn't go well."

I shook my head against his chest.

"You want to tell me what happened?"

Hell no. I didn't even want to think about it, but I'd been selfish enough already. Nik needed to know what was chasing me. If I let him get caught flatfooted because I'd been too gutless to warn him about what I'd brought to his door, I was no better than all the other criminals who'd screwed him over.

"I paid my dad the money," I said quietly, keeping my head against his chest so I wouldn't have to watch his face when he heard how bad I'd let myself get cornered. "But he refused to remove the curse. When I tried to make him, he locked me up. He was going to drag me home right there, but I escaped and ran to the Peacemaker."

Nik's chest hitched beneath me. "You *talked* to the Dragon of Detroit?!"

I nodded. "He couldn't help me, though. My dad already announced he'd declare war on any dragon who tries to take my curse off, which means I'm screwed. And it gets worse. I also found out that all the stuff we've been doing to get around the curse has been hurting him. Turns out forcing him to crash the gold markets over and over was burning up all his fire. He looked half dead when I saw him, and I…I…"

I trailed off with a shudder, and Nik scowled. "I don't understand," he said. "If crashing the market hurts him, can't you just use that to make him let you go?"

I shook my head frantically. "I don't want to kill him!"

"You don't have to go that far," Nik said. "Just push him a bit. You know, play chicken."

That was the obvious tactic. It was what a real dragon would have done, but I shook my head again. "I don't have the stomach for it," I told him honestly. "I'm madder at him than I've ever been, but…"

"But he's your dad."

I nodded, so grateful he understood that I didn't have words. "I'm not willing to torture him to get free, especially since I don't know how much more he can take. What if I went too far and killed him?"

"He can stop at any time."

"But I don't trust him to," I said frantically. "He's already gone farther than I ever thought he would. I'm terrified to keep pushing him. I know that makes me a wuss and that I'm playing right into his hands, but I don't care anymore. I don't have the stomach for this. I'm not a dragon, and even though he's being an ass and it would solve all my problems, I don't want to kill my dad."

There it was, the crux of all my problems. I knew what I had to do. I just couldn't do it, and that was why I'd lost. I'd always taken a stubborn sort of pride in the idea that I could out-crazy anyone, but apparently I'd finally met my match. Just my luck it'd be the one dragon who could ruin my entire life.

"So what are you going to do?" Nik asked.

"I'm not," I said bitterly, finally pushing myself off him. "Don't you see? It's over. I'm honestly surprised Dad hasn't kicked down your door already and dragged me out by my hair. He already knows where you live."

"Maybe he didn't think you'd come back," Nik said. "If I was him, I'd expect you to run for the airport or Canada. Not back into the Underground."

"Well, he'll figure it out eventually." And when he did, I was toast.

"What if he didn't, though?" Nik asked.

I frowned, not following, but Nik was grinning as if he'd just had a great idea. "This isn't his city," he said, leaning closer to me. "But it *is* mine. I've lived in the DFZ all my life. I know how to vanish here. I could take you with me."

He looked so sure that my hopes actually rose for a moment. Then I came to my senses. "Come on," I said, shaking my head. "The DFZ's big, but it's not infinite. He's an ancient immortal dragon who already burned up his magic for this. He's not going to let something little like not knowing where I am stop him. He's got functionally infinite time and resources to spend hunting me down. We can't beat that."

"Not with that attitude," Nik scolded. "I don't blame you for not wanting to kill your dad. That shows you're a better person than him. But losing one battle doesn't mean you've lost the war. We've been working this whole time on the assumption that we needed money to win. We haven't even tried running. Maybe it won't last forever, but he's the immortal, not you. You don't need forever. You just have to beat him for as long as you're alive, and that's a game I think we *can* win."

I stared at him in shock. "Are you serious?"

"I wouldn't have suggested it if I wasn't," Nik replied stubbornly.

I still couldn't believe it. "I can't ask you to do this. We can't be Cleaners if we vanish!"

Nik shrugged. "There's plenty of other ways of making money."

"Ones you became a Cleaner to get *away* from!" I reminded him. "I don't want you going back to that for me."

"There's lots of work between Cleaning and murder, you know," Nik said, smirking. "We could do repo, we could do renovations, we can clean stuff in the traditional sense of the word. There's tons of jobs out there if we're not too picky. It might not be the prettiest work, but you won't be beholden to your dad, and you won't have to do it alone. I'll be with you every step of the way. It'll be just like these last three weeks minus the crazy schedule, because seriously, you're going to die if you keep that up."

That was probably accurate, but I still couldn't believe what I was hearing. "But..." I whispered. "*Why?*"

"Because even I can't keep working eighteen hours a day."

"No," I said, shaking my head. "I meant, why are you offering to do this? I know how hard you've worked to build your current life. Why would you give that up for me?"

Nik dropped his eyes. "You know why."

I had my guesses. It was hard not to after what had happened in the parking lot, but that still didn't explain this. "There are other girls," I said quietly. "Less troublesome ones."

"Yeah, but I don't want them," Nik said angrily, still refusing to look at me as he scrubbed his hands through his dark hair. "You're..." He trailed off with a sigh, and then he turned to face me. "I got a couch for you. I loaned you *money*. I don't do that. Ever. Or at least I didn't used to, but you—" He cut off, searching for the words. "You make me want to have two plates," he said at last. "I used to see that stuff as overhead, just more useless crap I had to move, but you make me want to have things so that I can share them with you. I get lonely when you're not around. That's never happened to me before. I've never had someone to miss or worry about, but you make me do those things. I'd thought I'd hate it, but I don't. I like it. I like *you.* You're the only person I've ever known who hasn't screwed me over, so if you need to run, I'm coming with you, and I don't care if that means I can't Clean anymore. I can make money anywhere, but I can't get another you."

I was holding my breath by the time he finished. In fear or hope, though, I couldn't say. This day had been such a roller coaster of highs and lows I didn't know what to feel anymore. I still didn't think Nik's plan was going to work, but the fact that he was willing to try even after everything that had happened undid me completely. Enough to do something very selfish.

I kissed him.

It was more of an attack, really. There was no finesse or grace. I just lurched forward and pressed my lips to his. I definitely caught him by surprise, because Nik's body jumped beneath mine. Then, before I could think better of my actions, he kissed me back, wrapping his arms around me as his mouth slanted open under mine in welcome.

I responded by latching onto him like an octopus. It was a terrible, reckless idea on every count. We were both exhausted and emotionally vulnerable, not to mention we were *supposed* to be running, but I couldn't stop. I'd been fighting and losing on every front for so, so long, but kissing Nik—*actually* kissing him, not just taking advantage while he was blitzed on magic—felt like victory. My *only* victory. No wonder I clung to it with everything I had, reaching down to grab the hem of his shirt with desperate, shaking hands.

His breathing hitched in surprise when I pulled his shirt up, but he didn't fight me as I tugged the damp cotton over his head, revealing his metal chest. I'd only been able to look at it in stolen glances through my cameras before, so now I took my time, breaking the kiss to explore the scuffed, flesh-colored metal plates.

Nik was armored across both shoulders. His left had just a strip of metal running between his collarbone and his real arm, but the plating on the right covered his entire shoulder from the base of his neck straight down into his cyber arm. His false fingers curled just like his real ones when I stroked my hand down the metal arm to his wrist. I did it once more for good measure, and then I moved on to his chest and back. These were both completely covered in interlocking, articulated steel plates that went all the way down into the hem of his jeans. I was reaching for his fly to see just how far down they went when Nik caught my hand.

"Not here."

I looked up in surprise to see him breathing hard, his face flushed but determined. "I've thought about this a lot," he explained at my questioning look. "Not going to waste it on a couch."

Now it was my turn to blush. "Then why don't we—"

He stood up before I could finish, scooping me up and carrying me into his bedroom like a man on a mission. I clung to him happily, laughing with borderline-manic delight as he locked his door and set me down on his mattress, which was still on the floor since I hadn't been able to convince him yet that beds were worth the effort of moving. I didn't mind so much now, though. Honestly, the concrete floor felt safer when Nik knelt down beside me, his metal body crushing the soft foam mattress flat. But when he leaned forward to kiss me down to the bed, he stopped.

"Are you sure about this?"

"You mean do I think it's a good idea?" I asked, grinning at him. "No. But do I *want* to?"

I let my actions say the rest as I pulled my own shirt off. The cheap fabric, already ripped from my fight with the bushes, tore even more when

I yanked it over my head, but I was way past caring. I was too busy pulling Nik's mouth back to mine and kissing him until I couldn't breathe. He kissed me just as hard, peeling off my leggings and cheap sports bra with ruthless efficiency. Determined not to be the most naked, I went in for his jeans next, undoing the button and sliding them down his legs by touch alone. When I finally broke away to see what I was in for, I stopped cold.

"Whoa."

I'd known Nik had a lot of cyber up top, but I hadn't realized that it went down as well. It wasn't full coverage like his chest, but the armor plates on his legs still went all the way to his knees. Only on the front and back, though. The sides of his legs and what I could see of his groin under his boxer briefs were still flesh, but heavily scarred. The inner walls of his thighs in particular were a crisscross of incision marks from multiple surgeries. Painful ones from the look of it.

"What are those from?"

I didn't realize how intrusive that question was until it popped out. Fortunately, Nik didn't seem offended. "Titanium bone lacing, artificial kidney, new liver, and two fake knees," he replied matter-of-factly, pointing to each scar as he listed them off. "My dermal plating used to stop at my hips, but people like to shoot you in the legs, and I got tired of digging slugs out, so I got it extended."

He rapped his metal knuckles against his plated thighs, and my eyes went wide. "Does it hurt?"

"It did going in," he said. "Now, though." He shrugged. "It has its issues like anything else. Stuff breaks and there's filters to replace and whatnot, but the extra protection's worth it. I was saving up to get my skull armored next when I realized maybe I didn't want to do a job where I got shot in the head."

"Prudent choice," I said. Then my eyes dropped to his underwear. "So do you still have…"

Nik flashed me a wicked grin. "Want to find out?"

I grinned back and jumped him, pulling off the last of our clothes as we fell into a tangle on the mattress.

Not gonna lie, I'd imagined sex with Nik plenty of times before. It was only natural. He'd saved my life, he was hot, and we were together all the time, so of course my mind would go there. But while my fantasies had always been as rough and fast as the rest of our lives, the reality was surprisingly sweet. I was in a rush, but Nik refused to be hurried. He stubbornly took his time, touching me as if I was wondrous, making me feel treasured in a way I never had before.

I was the opposite. I held on to Nik like he was the only thing keeping me from falling, losing myself in the dichotomy of his body, the different temperatures of skin and metal and the heat of his breath in my ear. Eventually, I didn't even open my eyes anymore. I just clung to him and sank in, letting the physical sensations drive away my fear and my worries and my loss until there was nothing left but this moment where everything was beautiful and nothing hurt.

When it was over, we both flopped back panting, lying splayed out and tangled on his single mattress as if we'd fallen there from orbit. "Well," Nik said, his deep voice so content he was practically purring. "Guess I need to buy an actual bed now."

"Or at least a bigger mattress," I said, rolling over on my side to grin at him. "So does this mean I don't have to sleep on the sofa anymore?"

"Not unless we're both sleeping there."

I didn't see how that was physically possible unless I was sleeping on top of him, but sweet nothings weren't supposed to make sense.

"Let me see what time it is," Nik said, grabbing his jeans from where I'd flung them into the corner to retrieve his phone from his pocket. "Wow," he said when he saw it. "It's late. We should probably get moving if we want to stay ahead of your dad."

"Probably," I murmured, snuggling back up against him.

Nik made no effort to move me. Logically, I knew we needed to get up. My dad wouldn't follow false trails forever, and Nik and I had been operating out of this place for weeks. The moment he decided to look into the city, he'd find us, but it was difficult to be properly afraid. Nik's windowless basement bedroom felt so secret and secure. The only noises were the hum of the AC and the steady rhythm of our breaths, lulling me into thinking about things other than debts and survival.

"Can I ask you a question?"

"Shoot," Nik said.

I propped myself up on my elbow so I could see his face. "Did you like me before, or is this—" I waved at our tangled bodies "—a recent development?"

He shrugged. "Does it matter?"

"Just humor my vanity."

Nik chuckled. "It's definitely not new. I've been interested in you from the very first time I saw you at a Cleaning auction."

"Really?" I said, flattered. "Why didn't you say something earlier?"

"Didn't think it'd be appreciated," Nik said with brutal honestly. "I could tell you looked down on me."

"I didn't look down on you!"

He gave me a scathing look. "Please. I know when someone's afraid of me. You used to flinch every time I sat next to you. You thought I was a thug."

I winced at the accurate assessment.

"I'm not mad about it," Nik went on. "You weren't wrong. I *was* a criminal, and you were clearly a rich girl slumming it with the Cleaners. I didn't hold your fear against you, but I wasn't stupid. I knew I didn't have a chance, so I told myself to just enjoy the view until you got bored and left. But you didn't leave. You stuck around and stuck around, and eventually I ran out of excuses to stay away."

I laughed. "Are you saying you followed me to Dr. Lyle's house with salacious intent?"

"I don't know what that means, but I wasn't just chasing your tail," Nik said. "I legitimately wanted to know what the hell you were doing. I didn't intend for it to go anywhere, but once I fell in with you, it was hard to get out."

"My life has been a vortex of crazy," I agreed.

"That has nothing to do with it," he said, pushing up on his side to look at me. "I didn't want to go. You were beautiful and funny and a damn good Cleaner. You worked your ass off and knew all the fancy stuff I didn't. You were even better than I'd imagined, and I'd imagined pretty high." His smile turned into a grin. "You were my jackpot. Why the hell would I leave?"

I bit my lip, wiggling happily. I'd never been someone's jackpot before. Not for myself, at least. I'd had plenty of guys go after me as a way of getting to my dad, but Nik was the only person *ever* who'd wanted me for what I was now. Wanted me as Opal, dragon not included.

"Well, glad I brought something good to the table," I said, brushing my tangled hair behind my ear to hide how giddy he'd just made me. "I was worried all you'd gotten out of this partnership was trouble."

"That's okay," he said. "I liked the trouble, too."

"*Why?*" I asked, baffled. "Are you an adrenaline junkie or something else I should know about?"

"Not like that," Nik said. "It's easy enough to get in over your head in the DFZ without bringing a dragon in. I just meant that I don't mind your complications. I like helping you. It makes me feel needed."

"I tried not to use you," I said, desperate to make sure he understood.

"I know," he assured me. "I noticed that from the beginning, actually, but what really sealed it was when you volunteered to take my name off all the apartments when we went raiding. You didn't have to do that. My name was on every one of those leases automatically. You could have easily left me on there and stuck me with the bill, but I didn't even have to worry about it. You took care of every lease, every single one. You took care of *me,* even when I wasn't looking. That's when I knew I could trust you. Really trust."

The reverent way he said that went through me in warm tingles. I was still basking in the glow when I suddenly remembered.

"Oh my god, the apartments!"

Nik frowned. "What about them?"

"They're still in my name!" I said frantically, jumping up to grab my underwear off the doorknob where he'd thrown it. "I can't vanish into the city! I'm about to default on four hundred units. I have to finish Cleaning them!"

"Or what?" he asked, settling back on the mattress. "We're about to quit Cleaning and go on the lam anyway, so it's not like it matters if the DFZ takes your Master Key. Just let them default."

"I don't want a god pissed at me," I said, hopping on one foot as I put my pants back on. "And I still owe you three months of work for helping me. I guess I can do that anywhere, but how are we going to make money? My curse is still active, and I can't do the gold trick anymore. How are we going to live if every job we take only pays half of what it should?"

"Getting around the curse is easy," he said. "We'll just keep you from working."

I froze. "What?"

Nik sat up and casually began putting his clothes back on. "During the first week we were Cleaning together, before you figured out the gold trick, I did some side jobs while you weren't around to help make ends meet. I didn't tell you at the time because I didn't want you to feel bad, but the jobs I did on my own never had problems, even though I was giving the money to you."

My eyes were now so wide they hurt. "You gave me money that I didn't earn?"

"Come on," he said. "You didn't actually think I was selling all that stuff for double what it was worth every time, did you? I inflated the prices and made up the difference by working extra on the side to make sure you got paid."

I couldn't believe what I was hearing. "*Why would you do that?*"

"Because you were so freaked out about your curse that you couldn't focus on anything else," he said angrily. "You kept going on and on about how you were going to leave. I didn't want you to leave, so I got you the money. Simple as that."

"There's nothing simple about it!" I cried. "You lied to me!"

"Not about anything important!" he snapped. "I lied about where the money came from, yeah, but the only person that lie hurt was me. If I don't care, why should you?"

"Because I don't want to be your charity case!"

"You're not," he said. "Charity implies pity, but I've never pitied you. I wanted to be with you, so I did what was necessary to make that happen. End of story."

"No, it's not," I said, furious. "I appreciate why you did it, okay? But your good intentions don't change how I feel. I don't want to be dependent on you!"

"Why not?" he demanded, his voice insulted. "You don't think I can take care of you?"

"I don't want *anyone* taking care of me! I grew up in a dragon's house. I've *seen* how impossible it is to have a healthy relationship when one party is entirely reliant upon the other!"

"I'm not your dad!" he yelled. "I don't want to own you or lock you up in a vault. I just want to live with you, but living takes money, and since you can't make that, I'll have to. And that's fine. I've always worked. I don't mind working for you. Just let me keep you safe."

"But that's just the problem," I said desperately. "I don't want to be *kept*. The whole reason I did this was so I could be free, and I can't be that if I need someone else's help just to make it day to day."

"Needing help isn't a bad thing, Opal," Nik said quietly, reaching out to smooth my rumpled hair. "You've been working yourself to death for months now, but you don't have to do that anymore. You don't have to fight. I can support us both. It won't even be that hard now that we don't have to worry about your debt. If you don't try to make money, the curse won't trigger, so that's not an issue either. Just come with me. You'll get to live in comfort and safety, and I'll get you. It's a win/win for both of us."

I smacked his hand away. "You don't *get* me," I growled. "No one *gets* me!"

Nik sighed. "That's not what I meant."

"Yes it is!"

"Why are you so mad?" he demanded. "There's nothing wrong with wanting to support someone!"

"I'm mad because you're not listening to me!" I cried. "I told you, I don't want to be your kept woman!"

"What else are you going to do?" Nik yelled. "You can't make money, can't support yourself, can't even go outside without your dad hunting you down. Face it, Opal, you're done. I'm your only option. I'm trying to save you, here. Stop being stubborn and let me!"

"You don't get to tell me what my options are," I snarled, backing away. "Doesn't matter how bleak it gets, my life belongs to *me*. Not to my dad, not to a god, and not to you."

I turned on my heel and marched out, bashing open his door to storm into the living room. Nik caught me a second later, grabbing my arm as I bent down to snatch my bag off his couch.

"Let me go," I said in a cold voice.

"I will in a second," he said, tightening his grip. "But first you have to let me—"

I didn't warn him again. The next time I turned around, my hand was full with one potato's worth of magic. I slammed the first one into his arm, knocking him off me. The next two went on his feet and stuck there, their shapes changing to match the image I was frantically imagining of two iron anvils so heavy even Nik couldn't move them. I wasn't sure if it had worked until Nik tried to come after me again and almost fell on his face, his feet pinned to the ground by two glowing blobs that did, indeed, look exactly like little anvils.

"What the hell is that?" he roared, tugging at his feet.

I looked at him, chest heaving. "Magic," I said, my voice wondrous. For a long heartbeat, I stood and stared at the miracle I'd worked, and then I turned my back on him. "Don't follow me."

"*Opal!*"

But I'd already grabbed my bag and walked out of his apartment, taking the steps outside two at a time back up to the parking lot.

CHAPTER 11

The first thing I did when I reached the sidewalk was reboot Sibyl. I didn't bring her all the way back online—my mind was still chaotic enough to trigger her emergency intervention mode, and I didn't want to deal with it—but I turned on enough of my AR to access my bank account, or what was left of it after I'd foolishly paid my dad for nothing.

I stared at the balance for a long time, then I hit the button to transfer everything to Nik. Not that he deserved it after that fiasco, but I wasn't going to let him say I'd cheated him. The twenty thousand wasn't even close to the amount I'd promised in all our various deals, but at least now I could look at myself in the mirror and know I'd given him all I could. Honesty with yourself was important, especially now that I was all I had left.

With that, I fisted my hands on my bag strap and started walking. To where, I didn't know, and I didn't care. I had no one left to run to, no more clever plans, nothing to do but kill time until my dad inevitably showed up to nab me. I wondered if I'd merit a personal visit this time or if he'd just send a team of goons. Probably goons, I decided, trudging down the trash-littered sidewalk. Dad would have to be stupid to come into the city in his current condition.

I tried to take comfort in the knowledge that at least we were both suffering for this, but I couldn't. There was no good to be found in this situation. It was just the worst. The absolute pits from every angle all the way down.

"Doesn't mean it can't get better."

The sudden voice made me jump, and not just because it had spoken right behind me. I knew that voice. Sure enough, when I whirled around, the DFZ was standing with me on the sidewalk.

The god looked very different from when she'd spoken to me from inside Dr. Kowalski. Her body was much taller this time, with darker skin and a long, sharp-jawed face that was closer to the masculine side of androgynous. Like me, she was dressed in disposable to-the-minute-trendy vending-machine clothes, except she actually made them look good. I didn't know if that was because she'd taken over the body of a younger, hipper priest this time or if she could just summon humans like she summoned buildings, but I was certain it was her. If the voice and the intense magic rolling off her like noise from a traffic jam weren't big enough tipoffs, the inhumanly glowing orange eyes were a dead giveaway.

"Hello, Opal," the god said, giving me a thousand-watt smile. "Surprised to see me?"

I had been, but the more I thought about it, the more I realized I should have known this was coming. "Let me guess," I said, shoving my dirty hair out of my face. "You're here to make your pitch again now that I'm at my lowest."

The DFZ's blinding smile grew even wider. "That's the thing about gods. We always appear when you need us most."

"That doesn't speak as well for you as you think it does."

The city chuckled at my bitterness and stepped forward to take my arm. "Why don't we get some coffee? There's a good place right across the street."

I'd been squatting in Nik's apartment for the last three weeks. I knew for dead certain that there was no decent coffee anywhere inside of five blocks. But sure enough, when I looked across the street, there was a lovely little coffee shop wedged between the VR strip clubs. It even had a patio.

"Wow," I said. "That's convenient."

"Most things are when you can move buildings anywhere you want," the DFZ said, giving my arm a tug. "Let's go have a drink and a chat, hmm?"

I planted my feet on the sidewalk. "What's it going to cost me?"

"My treat," she promised.

I shook my head. "Nothing's free in the DFZ."

"Just give me five minutes of your time," the god pleaded. "Please."

Five minutes was a lot to ask given how long I'd been in this part of town already. I was honestly surprised I hadn't been black bagged and thrown into a trunk already. But my dad's people could grab me just as easily from a coffee shop as they could off the sidewalk, so I let the DFZ pull me across the busy street into the cafe, which really did look like it had been here forever. I didn't know how the DFZ had made that happen, but she'd done a fantastic job. The barista at the counter didn't even look fazed that she was now in what had to be a completely different part of the city than she'd gone to work in this morning. She just took our order with professional indifference, calling out our drinks to the empty shop before walking over to the espresso machine to make them herself.

Since the DFZ was paying, I got the biggest drink on the menu: an extra-large mocha latte with a mountain of chocolate shavings, whipped cream, and so many shots of espresso it was basically rocket fuel. The DFZ got a cup of black coffee with an inch of room at the top. I was wondering why she'd asked for so much space when she grabbed the entire box of sugar packets off the counter and started opening and dumping them into her coffee three at a time.

"Okay," I said when I'd gotten over my horror. "You've bought my time. I'll listen to whatever you have to say until I've finished this." I tapped my fingers against the side of my half-gallon coffee cup.

"It's not even going to take that long," the DFZ promised, dumping another three sugars into her coffee, which was already nearing its solubility limit. "I've already made my offer: become my priest, and I'll save you from your dad."

"No," I said without missing a beat. "I will not be owned."

"You might like it," the god said in a sing-song voice.

I crossed my arms stubbornly on the counter. "If I didn't say yes to Nik, I'm not going to say it to you." At least with Nik I'd get kisses. Thinking about the disaster I'd left in his apartment opened an abyss of feelings I couldn't deal with right now, though, so I turned my attention stubbornly back to my coffee.

"You don't know what you're missing," the DFZ said when I'd drained half my cup. "I've been watching your progress with your magic, especially that spectacular pair of rapid-fire blocks you put on Nikola Kos's feet. Dr. Kowalski is very impressed. She's convinced you'll be an amazing addition to our team."

I shook my head again, and the spirit pouted. Then her orange eyes lit up. "What if I gave you my powers provisionally? You know, let you try them out for a while?"

I snorted. "You mean like a free trial? Fourteen days of divine powers, no obligation!"

That was supposed to be a joke, but the god nodded excitedly. "Exactly! You're being belligerent right now because you're feeling cornered, but I'm confident you'll change your mind once you experience what it's like to serve a higher power who actually appreciates you."

I arched a suspicious eyebrow. "Is this one of those 'the first hit is free' sort of things?"

"That depends," she said innocently. "Are you the sort who gets addicted to power?"

Of course I was. *Everyone* got addicted to power. But even knowing it was a trap…I could do a lot in a week with the strength of a city. It would certainly be nice to have my dad cowering before me for once. But tempted as I was, I shook my head.

"Come on," she pleaded. "Just give me one week. I can take you to safety right now, and if you still don't want to serve me when it's over, I'll toss you right back out onto the sidewalk and you can resume running for your life. You can't say no to that."

"No," I said.

The god huffed and took a slug of her coffee-flavored sugar. "You are a stubborn one, aren't you?" she grumbled into her cup. "So much pride. Are you *sure* you're not a dragon?"

A few days ago, I would have been mortally insulted by that. Now, all I could do was shrug. "I'm culturally draconic."

"Yet another reason we should team up," the DFZ said. "I love dragons."

I smiled appreciatively at her hustle. "You don't give up, do you?"

"Never!" she said, straightening to her full height. "What city do you think I am?"

"Touché," I said, tilting my cup at her so she could see how much was left. "So are there any other pitches you want to roll out? Because you've still got four inches of coffee left."

"I think I've made my point," the DFZ said, dumping the dregs of her syrup-coffee into a trash can I swore hadn't been there a second ago. "I'm the city of freedom. Forcing obedience isn't my style, but you've been living in me for a long time now, Opal Yong-ae. I've never seen you pass up a good deal, and I don't think you'll pass up mine. You know where to find me when you change your mind."

I nodded at the street outside the dusty cafe windows. "Everywhere?"

The god smiled and reached out to tap her finger against my temple. For a second, her touch rested cool and hard as a cement sidewalk against my skin, and then she was gone, leaving me standing alone at the counter with what was left of my coffee and a giant pile of empty sugar packets.

I shook my head and downed the last of my drink. Once I'd licked the last drops of sweetness from the sides of my cup, I went back to the counter to ask the barista for the key to the restroom. I didn't actually have to go, but public bathrooms were as rare as unicorns in this city, and I'd already given Nik all my money. I didn't think it'd be that much time before I got caught, but I'd lived in the DFZ for too long now to pass up any opportunity. I used the restroom, washed out my coffee cup in the sink and filled it with fresh water, dropped the last few coins of change from my pocket into the barista's tip jar, and headed back out into the city.

I walked for what felt like a long time. I'd turned off my AR, so I wasn't sure what time it actually was, but the Underground had that early-morning feel. It was still busy—it was *always* busy—but the bars and casinos were emptying out rather than filling up, and the busses were full of shift workers on their way to the factory part of town. Since I wasn't going anywhere in particular, I didn't bother with maps. I just walked in a straight line, following the cracked sidewalk to see how far it went. "Pretty far" seemed to be the answer. I was starting to wonder if Nik's street went all the way to the Ohio border when I spotted something gleaming in the gutter by my boot heel.

It was a penny. An absolutely filthy one but still remarkable. Pennies had been phased out of the U.S. currency system fifty years ago after a decades-long campaign by David Heartstriker, Senator from New Mexico and the only dragon in Congress. He'd argued that the coins cost more to make than they were worth, which was true. Of course, once the law passed, it came out that he was also on the board of a company that was poised to make millions off government contracts to collect and recycle all those useless pennies, but those were the sort of shenanigans you got when you elected a greedy dragon to be your representative.

Anyway, the important thing was that pennies were rare these days and thus highly collectible. This one looked like it was in good condition, too, once I wiped the road grime off. It was only worth about a dollar, but that was still a great return on investment for something that was supposed to be one cent. I was sliding my lucky find in the front pocket of my bag for safekeeping when it suddenly hit me.

I'd just made money.

I froze, causing the drunk walking behind me to swear and stumble into the carts for the tiny grocery automat I'd stopped in front of. Holy shit. Holy *shit.*

I dug the coin back out and turned it over frantically in my hands, but there was no mistake. It was a penny. Even half a century after being discontinued, it was still technically legal tender. *Money.* The thing I was cursed not to make, and I'd just picked it up off the ground.

A horrible feeling blossomed in my gut. I grabbed the phone out of my bag and dialed the number I still knew by heart after all these years. It was daytime in Korea, but no matter what hour it was, Mom always answered her phone. She was First Mortal, the one who was in charge of keeping the domestic side of Yong's empire running so smoothly he never even noticed it. Even when she was spending the night with my father, *someone* would pick up if only to say she was indisposed. This time, though, there was nothing. The phone just rang and rang.

I left it ringing, switching to a new line to try my dad. I knew full well that I was being an idiot. This was probably just a ploy to freak me out and make me call so I'd be easier to find, but I couldn't shake the horrible sense that something was wrong. *Really* wrong. The Peacemaker had told me just a few hours ago that my curse was tied to my dad's life force. If it wasn't working, then either my dad had finally decided to let me go, or he was dead. It didn't seem possible that Yong had had a change of heart since I'd last spoken to him, so that left "dead." Or a fluke. It could have been a fluke. Pennies were in a weird area between currency and collectibles. Maybe the curse had made a mistake?

It had never let anything remotely like money slide before, though.

"Come on," I whispered, pacing the sidewalk as my dad's phone rang and rang. "Come on, you decrepit old lizard, pick *up*."

Nothing.

Swearing under my breath, I flicked my finger across my phone's screen to bring up my contact list. I was debating waking Sibyl up so she could call everyone at once and save me some time when I heard tires crunch to a stop on the street beside me.

"Opal!"

I looked up in alarm. There was a bright-yellow sports car stopped on the curb to my left, one of the super expensive models that looked more like metal origami than a car. The triangle-shaped windows were so heavily tinted I couldn't even see who was yelling at me until the driver's side door opened, and an intimidatingly stylish, dark-skinned man got out to give me a smile.

"I thought it was you," he said, flashing me a perfect smile as he took off his pair of super-slick AR sunglasses, which he'd apparently been wearing at *night*. "Remember me from earlier?"

Of course I remembered. It was hard to forget someone who'd given you a briefcase full of gold. It was Ainsley, the rich collector who threw money around like confetti. He was still doing it now, leaving his ludicrously overpriced sports car idling with the door open as he jogged over to join me on the sidewalk

"Are you all right?" he asked, his charming voice all concern. "I was driving by when I spotted you. You looked quite upset."

"Personal emergency," I told him tersely, keeping an eye on my calls, which still hadn't been answered.

"Do you need a ride?"

"No thank you," I said, turning away in the hopes he'd get the hint.

"Aw, come on," Ainsley said, putting a hand on my shoulder. "You look like you're in real trouble. Let me give you a lift."

"I said *no*," I growled, yanking out of his grip. Rather, I tried to. Despite me putting my whole body into it, Ainsley's hand didn't budge from my shoulder.

"That wasn't a request," he said, fingers digging into my flesh.

I dropped my phone with a curse and grabbed his wrist with both hands. When I tried to pinch his nerves and make him let go, though, I realized that what I'd assumed was skin wasn't actually flesh at all. It was textured plastic covering an arm that felt just like Nik's.

Crap.

Ainsley smiled down at me, clearly relishing my fear as I realized my situation. I didn't know how much of him was metal under those stylish clothes, but it didn't really matter. That arm alone was enough to overpower a normal flesh-and-bone human like me. I was about to ask him what the hell he thought he was doing—because this felt *seriously* out of left field—when he tapped the side of his fancy AR sunglasses to take my picture. Sunglasses I suddenly realized I'd seen on two other guys just this afternoon. And then it all came together with a crash.

"You're one of White Snake's mortals."

"Took you long enough," Ainsley replied in Korean. "My lady has another job for you."

"I'm not doing anything for her!"

"But you already have," he said with a cruel smile. "You've done more for my beautiful mistress than she ever could have dreamed, but you're not done yet. You see…" He lowered his voice to a whisper. "He's not quite dead."

Ainsley reached into his pocket, pulling out three more of the slender, one-ounce gold bars he'd paid me earlier today. I went still at the sight of the glittering metal, my knees going weak as the full weight of just how badly I'd been played landed on top of me. White Snake knew about the curse. Of course she did. *Everyone* did. The Peacemaker had told me as much this evening. She knew how much it hurt my dad, too, so she'd given me everything I needed. No wonder Ainsley had been so eager to overpay me! He wasn't the one being stupid, *I* was. I'd been so focused on beating my dad that I'd let them play me like a chump. Idiot, idiot, *idiot*.

"Aw, baby, don't look like that," Ainsley said, his deep voice teasing. "You should be happy. You've made no secret how much you hate being the Great Yong's favorite pet. This is your chance to pay him back." He pushed the gold toward my hands, which were still wrapped around his arm. "Take it. It's yours to keep. You need money, right? Don't you want to be free?"

I blew out a long, shaky breath, brain spinning. "Okay," I said after several seconds, looking up at him with my best "innocent-mortal" expression. "But can I get my potato out of my bag first?"

A look of confusion passed over Ainsley's handsome face, and I seized my chance, letting go of his arm to plunge my hands into my bag to grab the tuber Dr. Kowalski had given me. I probably could have done what I was planning without it. I knew its size and weight by heart now, but even after my unexpected success at Nik's, I didn't dare take the training wheels off this time. Not when I was this scared. Even with the potato to guide me, I still grabbed too much, but I didn't have time to try again. Ainsley had already realized what was happening and grabbed my throat, his wired reflexes moving faster than mine ever could. I could already feel his metal fingers digging into my windpipe. It was this or nothing, so I slammed the magic into him, frantically picturing a hammer as I crushed it against his face.

Just like with Nik, the effect was immediate. Ainsley went flying, but so did I, tossed back into the shopping carts behind me by the force of my own magic. It was a pretty small backlash by my usual standard, but I hadn't sucked one up in three weeks now, so it hurt way more than it should have. I collapsed to the ground in a fetal position, sucking air through my clenched teeth as I waited for the pain to fade. It always did, and while this one seemed to be taking forever, it couldn't have actually been that long, because when I lifted my head again, Ainsley was lying unconscious on the ground next to the exploded remains of my potato.

My shoulders slumped at the sight. Aw man, and I thought I'd been doing so well. But I'd have to deal with my backslide later. Right now, I needed to get to my dad.

Hopping over the rats who were already rushing over to gobble baked potato off the sidewalk, I ran around Ainsley's twitching legs and hopped into his car. "Sibyl!" I cried, mashing the button on my earpiece to load her in. "I need you!"

"Is it time for that intervention?" she asked frantically as she came online. Then her voice grew confused. "Wait, whose car is this?"

"Never mind that," I said, running my hands frantically over the smooth, buttonless dash. "Help me figure out how to move it!"

My AI gasped. Purely for dramatic effect since, you know, no lungs. "You're a *car thief* now?! How long was I down?"

"It's not theft," I snapped. Then I frowned. "Well, okay, it is theft. But he just tried to murder me, so that makes it legal!"

"I don't think that's how the law—"

"Sibyl, would you just help me?!"

"All right, all right," my AI said, her icon blipping as she checked in with the car's computer. "The engine's running, but there's an automatic lock on the gears. It won't start driving unless the current registered user is in the vehicle."

I nodded and hopped back out of the car, running over to Ainsley, who was still groaning on the sidewalk. Without missing a beat, I grabbed him by his fancy shoes and hauled him across the pavement to the rear of the car. That arm must have been his big-ticket item, because he wasn't nearly as heavy as Nik. He was still a big guy, but I moved couches for a living, and I was scared to death right now. The combination gave me strength I'd never known I had as I grabbed the man limb by limb and shoved him into the trunk.

"There," I said, slamming the lid down and running back around to the driver's door. "Did that work?"

"Let me check," Sibyl said as I flopped into the driver's seat. Sure enough, the moment my legs brushed up against the mana-contact built into the seat, the car's AR field washed over me, covering what had previously looked like an empty dash in a rainbow of glowing displays.

"User detected," the car said in a voice much more sultry than Sibyl's. "Welcome back, handsome!"

I rolled my eyes and hit mute, bringing up my own map instead as I ordered the car to back out and drive us to Canada.

***

It struck me as I was crossing the New Ambassador Bridge that I didn't actually know if my dad was *in* Canada. That was the last place I'd seen him, but my trip to his new house was hours ago now. For all I knew, he'd come into the city to drag me home, or maybe he was already in the air flying back to Korea. Both would have been good ideas, but neither felt right to me. The Yong I knew wouldn't blindly charge in or run back to safety. He'd stay put in his base of power and start working on his next plot. That's what *I* would have done, so that was where I went, directing my stolen yellow sports car not to my dad's house but to the mansion next door. The one with the murderous boxwoods I'd run through just a few hours before trying to get *away.*

"Isn't this karmic?" Sibyl said as I waded back through the sticky river mud around the stand of bamboo that separated my father's stretch of riverfront from the other houses.

"I don't believe in karma," I informed her, yanking my feet up slowly so I wouldn't lose my boots in the bog. "If universal balance was a real thing, my dad would have gotten his comeuppance ages ago."

"He got you," my AI said. "That's certainly caused him no end of grief."

Couldn't argue there, but, "If I'm *his* karma, why am I suffering for it too?" I griped. "I haven't done anything to deserve this!"

"Haven't you?"

I gave her a mental death glare.

"Hey," Sibyl said. "I'm just a mental health AI. My job is to hold up the mirror. I'm not responsible if you don't like what you see."

"Can we just focus on the task at hand, please?" I said sullenly, ripping my boot out of the last of the mud. "This is hard enough already without you turning it into a therapy session."

"I just want to make sure you're mentally prepared for this," Sibyl said as I crept past the last of the bamboo and entered the perfectly manicured lawn of my father's estate. "You've got a whole dry-cleaning shop full of hang-ups when it comes to your dad. I don't want you to choke at a critical point."

I didn't either, which was why I was determinedly *not* thinking about anything except the job in front of me. Fortunately, this part was pretty simple. Even with the house's floodlights, it was dark down by the water, and my clothes were covered in mud. Both made it easy to sneak across the lawn to the mansion. When I reached the wall, I flipped around, pressing my back against the stone as I eased my way down the house. It was farther than I remembered, but soon I was crouching beneath the large windows of the library-turned-receiving-chamber where my dad and I had fought.

Again, I had no idea if I was in the right place. Like everything else about this, it was just a hunch. That said, I'd never met a dragon who didn't relish drama, and the elegant room with its throne-like seat was by far the most dramatic in the house.

Sure enough, when I peeked over the window ledge, there they were, looking like a scene out of a Renaissance painting. White Snake was sitting on the wooden chair with my father on his knees in front of her. His gaunt face was lowered to the carpet, which had once been a multicolored Persian design but was now stained a solid, uniform shade of deep, deep red. The rest of the floor was painted with the same tell-tale color, but there was so much of it, I didn't actually realize it was blood—*his* blood—until my eyes landed on my father's back.

That was when my heart stopped. Yong's back was torn wide open, his expensive suit ripped clean away to reveal huge, deep gouges on either side of his spine. It was the sort of wound that would have killed a human instantly four times over. Not being mortal, my father was still breathing, but only just. Above him, his sister was sitting with her legs draped over the ornately carved chair arm, casually cleaning the blood out from under her long nails with the tip of one of his antique letter openers. I couldn't hear what she was saying through the double-paned security glass, but I knew gloating when I saw it. She was lording her victory over her fallen foe, and I hated her for it with an intensity even I didn't understand.

It was so strange. If you'd asked me a week ago would I like to see my dad on his knees, my only question would have been how much for the ticket. Now that it was actually happening, though, all I could think was that she'd had no right. That was *my* dad in there. I was the one who'd brought him low. If anyone was going to win tonight, it should be me, not her. She'd swooped in like a damn vulture and *stolen* him. Literally snatched him right out from under me! Like hell was I letting her get away with it.

"Anger is a valid emotion," Sibyl whispered in my ear. "But White Snake is still a dragon. Last I checked, you can't take one of those."

"Then I'll call the Peacemaker," I whispered back. "He doesn't allow bloodsport in his territory."

"Yeah, but his territory stopped at the river," my AI reminded me. "Windsor is neutral ground. It's still murder, so I guess you could call the Mounties, but what are they going to do against a dragon? Especially one who's probably about to become the next Dragon of Korea?"

Nothing. Mortal authorities were useless when it came to stuff like this. But what was I going to do? I normally didn't go into things without a plan, but I'd been running on instinct since I'd escaped from my dad this afternoon, and a fine mess that had turned out to be. I couldn't keep doing this. I had to stop and think. There had to be *something* I could do. Even for a little coward like White Snake, beating a dragon one on one was a pipe dream. Dragon fire was still magic, though, and I had a damn big draw. Maybe I could barge in and suck it all out of her before she burned me to a crisp?

"And kill yourself in the process," Sibyl hissed before I'd even finished the thought. "I don't want to undermine your progress, but you couldn't handle not blowing up a potato on normal city magic. If you try to drain a dragon, you're going to pop yourself."

I wanted to say she was wrong, but that would have been a lie, and I didn't have time for those anymore. My dad was in there *alone,* which I suppose explained why he hadn't come searching for me. I didn't know how long White Snake had been in there, but I bet she'd come straight here after Brohomir had chased her out of the consulate. That meant my dad had been bleeding for two hours at least. Maybe closer to four, which was *way* too long. If any of his mortals had survived White Snake's initial assault, there was no chance anymore they were coming to help. I was all he had left, which *sucked*, because this entire situation was his fault. If he hadn't been so…so *draconic*, none of this would have happened!

But I couldn't just leave him in there.

I bumped my head against the stone wall. Yong was my tyrant and my enemy and my owner and my terror, but before he'd been any of those things, he'd been my dad. My father, who'd picked me up when I cried and called me his treasure. It wasn't as sweet now that I knew he'd meant it literally, but somewhere under that mountain of resentment was a little girl still covered in pumpkin. The girl he'd cradled to his chest even though she got squash guts all over his nice suit. No matter how much had gone wrong between us since then, I couldn't let that man die, not even if it set me free. After all, as I'd said to Nik a month ago, it wasn't winning if you couldn't live with yourself afterward.

Unfortunately, while I now knew what I had to do, I still had no idea as to how. I was stuck between two couldn'ts—couldn't let my dad die, couldn't save him. I was the one who'd hammered him down, but White Snake was delivering the finishing blow, and she was a dragon. A puny one, but still orders of magnitude more powerful than me. I didn't even know what I'd hoped to achieve by coming here. I'd just started running because I couldn't stay away. Now it looked like all I'd managed was to secure a front-row seat for my dad's death.

But just as I started to sink into despair, I remembered there was one thing I had left. Ironically, it was the very thing my dad had weakened himself to win. Now, in a twist usually reserved for Greek tragedies, I'd have to give it away to save him. That should have been depressing as hell, but I actually found it very fitting. After all, no one appreciated irony more than a god.

"Okay," I said quietly, sliding down the wall to sit in the cool grass as I looked across the river at the double-layered city glittering like a neon fairyland in the night. "You win. I'll take the power."

I held my breath when I finished, but all I heard—from my head and my ears—was silence. As it stretched and stretched, my stomach began to sink. I was starting to worry that she'd lost interest when an enormous voice sighed in my head.

You couldn't have made this decision before *you went to Canada?*

"I know, I know, I'm sorry," I said, bowing my head before the DFZ because that seemed like a good thing to do when you were soliciting a god. "This was a hard thing for me, okay? But I'm ready to do whatever you want. Just help me save my dad."

That's a tall request, the DFZ said. *And not part of our original agreement. I offered you fantastic powers in exchange for saving you* from *your dad. Saving him as well is a pretty big Plus One.*

"You're the great and powerful spirit of the DFZ," I cajoled. "If you can't save a dragon, who can?"

The Spirit of Dragons.

"She won't do anything," I argued. "She's the personification of dragon-ness! She'd probably just tell my dad to man up, stop bleeding all over the carpet, and claw his way to freedom."

Technically, she'd be the dragonification of dragon-ness, but you make a good point, the DFZ said. Then her voice grew longing. *It would be nice to get one up on her, though. She's always strutting around working miracles, the drunken showoff.*

I knew nothing about the Spirit of Dragons, so I had no idea if that was a fair criticism. She wasn't the one here helping me right now, though, so I ran with it. "You should absolutely show her up," I said. "You show everyone up! You add five feet to your highest superscraper every time a building outside the DFZ gets named 'Tallest in the World.' Why should you stop now? Let's show that snake spirit who the *real* god is!"

See, I knew you'd be good at this, the DFZ said. *You're already talking like a priest.*

"So you'll help?" I asked nervously, peeking over my shoulder. White Snake was on her feet now, looking down at my father as if she was trying to decide if it would be more entertaining to behead him or skin him alive. "I don't want to rush you, but I think we're running out of time."

I don't know, the spirit said. *I want to help, but I don't like how forced this feels. You only came to me because you had no other choice. That's not how I roll.*

"Oh, come *on,*" I begged her, staring at my father with wild eyes. "You said you'd be there for me at my lowest! This is as low as I get."

I am here for you, the DFZ said. *But I told you, I only take willing servants. Gun-to-the-head situations don't count. I'm not your dad.*

Normally, that would have been a huge point in her favor, but I was seriously backed into a corner here. Selling myself to the DFZ was the last play I had. If she didn't want me, it was over. There *had* to be a way to make her accept. Something I could say to convince her that—

"Wait," I said. "What if we made a deal?"

I always like a deal, she said. *Go on.*

I didn't have any time left, so I started talking as fast as I could. "I'm about to owe you nearly six hundred grand in rent. We both know there's no way I can pay that, so what if I worked it off instead? You know, like a job."

Sounds great! the god said. *I'm always trying to boost employment, and I need priests way more than money. This deal doesn't include your dad, though.*

"No, but it would make me your priest," I said. "You said your people get 'fantastic powers'—your words—and I believe it. You're a god who moves block-sized skyscrapers on a whim! Once I'm working for you, I should be strong enough to save my dad myself."

I see what you're doing, the DFZ said. *But I don't know if I like it. Priests are supposed to come humbly to me.*

"But I'm the one in high demand," I argued. "You've been pitching me every chance you got since we met. You wouldn't fault a worker for negotiating a better deal with an employer who wanted them super bad. It's supply and demand, and you are the poster city for the free market. You can't tell me this isn't right in line with your domain."

No, I cannot, she admitted grumpily. *You really are a dragon's daughter, aren't you? Extorting a god.*

"It's not extortion," I said. "It's economics. We both need what the other has, so let's trade. I'll serve you as a priest until I've worked off what I owe, and you'll give me the power I need to save my dad. That's it. No gun to my head, no dark bargains. Just another deal between two willing parties, same as any other job."

Done, the DFZ said.

I stuck out my hand. It was a silly thing to do. It wasn't as if the DFZ was actually here to shake, but I'd done it instinctively. Good instincts, apparently, because I swore I felt a ghostly hand grab mine. I closed my eyes as it happened, waiting for a surge of divine power, but all I got was the smell of car exhaust.

"Wait," I said, confused. "Is that it?"

It is for now, my new god said. *I already told you, Windsor's not in my service area. That doesn't magically change just because you agreed to a provisional priesthood. If you want my power, you're going to have to come back inside my city limits.*

"But my dad needs help here!" I whispered in a panic. "What am I supposed to do?!"

My priests are resourceful, the DFZ said. *I'm sure you'll figure it out. Just get him across the river and I'll take it from there. Meanwhile, I'll get you a distraction.* The spirit paused. *Uh, you might want to duck.*

I hit the dirt. I didn't know what I was trying to avoid yet, but when a city said duck, you ducked. I was still flat in the grass under the window thirty seconds later when I heard a crash across the water. This was followed by such an incredibly strange grinding noise that I had to lift my head, which was how I saw a huge suspension wire detach itself from the New Ambassador Bridge and drop down to wrap sea-monster-tentacle-style around an automated tractor-trailer that was waiting at the border crossing. The truck's tires squealed as the tree trunk–sized wire lifted it off the asphalt, and then the whole bridge arched back like a slingshot to fling the trapped vehicle across the water.

Straight at me.

I slammed to the ground with a muffled scream. I didn't know if the dragons heard me, but it was too late to care if they did. Not three seconds later, the freight vehicle slammed into the side of the mansion right above my head like a spear, crashing through the window and the stone wall that surrounded it before barreling straight into White Snake herself.

At least, that was what I assumed happened. I didn't actually see it because I was hugging the dirt for dear life. When I looked up a second later, though, the dragoness was gone, along with most of the northern half of my dad's house. It looked as if the stone building had been shot straight through with a giant bullet, and still on his knees at the edge of the hole, completely untouched, was my father.

"*Dad!*"

I scrambled to my feet and raced inside, tripping over the wreckage. "Dad!" I said again, grabbing his shoulders. "Get up! We have to get out of here!"

He stared at my face, uncomprehending. I stared back, trying not to freak out. I'd thought my dad had looked bad before, but the dragon kneeling on the bloody carpet was white as a ghost, his normally sea-colored eyes as dim as ash. If he hadn't been gasping for breath, I wouldn't have known he was still alive.

"Opal," he murmured at last. "What are you doing here?"

"Getting you out," I replied, sliding my arm under his shoulders. I was still figuring out where to put my hand so I could help him up without digging my fingers into his wounds when he jerked away.

"You can't be here," he said, his voice disjointed and more frightened than I'd ever heard. "You have to go."

"We're *both* going," I said firmly.

"Don't be stupid," he hissed, finally sounding a bit more like his old self. "She'll kill you, too! I didn't go through all of this so you could die!"

"No one's dying," I told him stubbornly. "Now come—"

A roar cut me off. Through the hole the truck had left in the house, the wreckage in the lawn across the street began to shudder and shake. Smoke came next, then a flash of flame. I watched it rise through the night, transfixed by mortal terror until my father grabbed my hand.

"Go!" he ordered, pushing me away. "I'll hold her off."

The ridiculousness of that statement was enough to finally snap me out of my dragon-induced daze. "You can't even hold yourself up!" I yelled at him, getting right back into position. "But don't worry, I've got this."

He looked appalled. "How can you possibly—"

"You're not the only one with power," I said, glaring down at him. "If you want to do something helpful, figure out how to get us across the river. I'll handle everything from there."

My father opened his mouth then stopped, his face faltering as he dropped his eyes. My stomach dropped at the same time. I'd known getting to the DFZ would be an issue, but I'd never actually believed until this moment that he might not be able to do it. My dad was always unbeatably strong, the unmovable object I'd banged my head against my entire life. Right now, though, he looked more mortal than I did, and I had no idea how to handle that. I was still scrambling to think up a Plan B when the wreckage across the street exploded, and the dragon emerged.

She wasn't as big as some I'd seen, but all dragons are huge when they're glaring down at you. True to her name, White Snake was a river of pale-white scales. Her body was long and winding, and her wedge-shaped head was framed by a mane of sky-blue hair fine as silk. Her slitted eyes were the same beautiful mix of sea colors as my father's, and while she had no wings like the European dragons did, I knew she could still fly faster than the wind. Right now, though, she was hovering over us like a terrifying storm, fire dripping from her bared fangs as she looked around for what had struck her.

Then her gaze fell on us.

"*You*," she growled in a voice that shook the air. "I'll eat you *alive!*"

I didn't know if that threat was for me or Yong, but it didn't matter. White Snake was diving at both of us, her car door–sized claws extended to slice us into pieces. Keeping tight hold of my dad, I reeled back and lobbed a perfect potato's worth of magic at her face while I held the image of a grenade in my head.

It was one of the best casts I'd ever done. The magic even looked like a glowing grenade as it flew through the air, but it flashed off White Snake's nose without leaving so much as a mark. She didn't even seem to notice as she opened her mouth, and the air around us began to superheat.

I cringed when I felt it. I'd never been in a dragon's direct line of fire before, but I knew what was coming, and this close up, I didn't see any way out. Maybe a better mage could have done something with all the dragon magic shivering in the air around us, but I wasn't a better mage yet. I was a cobbled-together failure who'd screwed up one too many times. Now it looked like my luck was officially out. I just wished I'd thought to call Nik before the end. Not that I knew what to say, but it felt wrong that my last words to him would be angry ones.

Oh well. Add it to the pile of regrets. I was wondering if the DFZ was going to make my ghost work off everything I'd promised her or if she'd let me pass on to the afterlife unmolested when my dad grabbed me around the waist and lurched us backwards.

For a horrible second, I was falling down the riverbank. Then I jerked into the air and up. Way, *way* up, leaving the ground and the blinding fire-blast behind as I was catapulted into the night sky on the back of a giant blue dragon.

I grabbed on with a gasp, fisting my hands in the long, silken hair of his enormous green, gold, and crimson mane. For a blissful moment, fear was overcome by nostalgia. I'd ridden on my father's back many times when I was little, and for a heartbeat, I was back in Korea, flying over the mountains on a dragon who never tired and would never let me fall. Then I felt the wetness seeping under my fingers, and reality came crashing back.

"*Shit!*"

My dad was bleeding like a faucet. His mane and back were slick
with blood. It rolled off his snaking body in bucket-sized waterfalls, falling
in streams to the river below. Behind us, White Snake roared and
launched into the sky as well, bolting after us.

Under any other circumstance, that wouldn't have frightened me.
Now that they were both dragons, the power difference between Yong and
his little sister was painfully obvious. White Snake had the same long body
and curving claws, but she was less than half his size, a literal pale shadow
of my father's magnificence. No wonder she'd had to wait until he was so
weak he couldn't leave his house. She'd never have had a chance otherwise.

For all her cowardice, though, White Snake had planned her strike
well. It wasn't just my father's wounds that were holding him down. Even
in this shape, his body was shrunken and frail. Ribs stood out clearly
beneath his scales, and he wasn't floating effortlessly through the sky like
he normally did. It was more like he was crawling, clawing the air for
every inch. Even worse, he was going the wrong way.

"No!" I shouted, struggling to raise my voice over the wind. "Don't
follow the river! Over the river! Fly into the DFZ!"

"Impossible," my father gasped, his voice rumbling through the
blood beneath my fingers. "That's the Peacemaker's territory. I'm not
running to him!"

This hardly seemed like the time to worry about that, but I knew
better than to challenge a wounded dragon's pride. "You won't be!" I yelled
instead. "I've already got it all arranged! Just get across the water, and I'll
take it from there. *Trust me!*"

The huge dragon heaved a pained sigh, and I gritted my teeth. But
then, just when I was sure he was about to tell me to stop being a silly
mortal, he changed course, turning on a dime to fly straight at the DFZ's
skyline.

"I hope you know what you're doing," he rumbled.

So did I, but there was no turning back now. White Snake was
gaining fast, her claws extended to finish the job before we reached the

Peacemaker's territory and her brilliant *coup d'état* became plain old murder. But then, just when I could feel the first heat of her fire on my back, we flew over the wall of buildings facing the water, and everything changed.

I'd lived in the DFZ for a long time at this point. I'd thought I was used to seeing her move, but I'd never seen *anything* like this. The moment we passed the border of her domain, the city came to meet us, the buildings rising up from the ground like fingers to snatch us out of the air. I could actually see the people freaking out inside the windows, grabbing on to their sliding desks as their building bent sideways to circle around us.

My father tried to dodge—*I* tried to dodge, because it was terrifying—but he was bloody and exhausted and miles too slow. In the end, all he managed was to curl himself into a protective ball with me at the center as the fist of skyscrapers clenched down around us. The last thing I saw through the cracks was a second hand rising up to smack White Snake down into the river like a gnat before the twisting knot of buildings pulled tight, and the light vanished.

***

I woke up on the floor of my empty apartment.

I was in my living room, lying on my back on the hardwood my mom had installed, blinking up at the only light bulb that had survived Nik and my purge of valuables. When I finally managed to sit up, I saw that my dad was lying beside me. He was back in human form and unconscious, his whole body soaked in blood. He was also *very* naked.

I covered my eyes at once. Draconic perfection notwithstanding, there were some things no one wanted to see, and your dad naked was one of them. I was trying to figure out how we'd gotten here when something soft brushed my hand.

"Here."

I jumped and uncovered my eyes to see the DFZ standing over me. Once again, she looked different from the last time I'd seen her. Her face was young and feminine this time, like a teen girl's, and she was holding out a blanket.

"Sorry it took me so long," she said, biting her lip. "I couldn't reach over the water."

"You did fantastic," I told her, taking the blanket and spreading it over my dad as best I could without looking. "You saved us, thank you. And great slap on White Snake, by the way."

The god flashed me a wicked grin. "No one messes with what's mine."

I froze, waiting for those words to grate, but all my anger must have drained out with my dad's blood, because I just felt tired. Tired and confused. "How did we end up in my apartment?"

"It seemed like the safest place," the DFZ said, nodding toward my curtained window. "But we're still in transit, so I wouldn't advise looking outside. Mortal minds don't do well with how I run my mazes."

Seemed like prudent advice to me. "Can you help me move him?" I asked, nodding down at my dad.

That was a bold ask since, technically, I worked for her now. But the DFZ just shrugged and helped me bundle Yong up and carry him to my mattress, the only thing left in my bedroom.

"So what happens now?" I asked when we'd made him as comfortable as we could. My dad had been very firm about not asking the Peacemaker for help, but he still looked awful. I didn't know if he needed a dragon doctor or if such a thing even existed. So far as I knew, dragons were fine or they were dead, nothing in between.

"I don't know," my new god said, shaking her head. "My experience is with living dragons, not...whatever he is." She waved her hand at my dad. "Honestly, if I hadn't just seen him flying around, I wouldn't be able to tell he *was* a dragon. I can't feel his magic at all. He's just...nothing."

I swallowed. Nothing did *not* sound good.

"Anyway, it'll take a while before your apartment settles back into the city," she said, patting my hand. "I've got to go clean up the mess I made saving you. People get so mad when you turn their buildings into a fist! It's nothing you're prepared to handle on your first day, so you just stay here and rest. We'll start your employment tomorrow, okay?"

"Thank you," I said quietly.

The DFZ beamed at me and vanished. Just disappeared without a trace as if she was a light that had been turned off, leaving me alone. I slumped over the moment she was gone, sliding down the wall to land hard on my butt beside my father. My dad didn't even twitch at the sound. He just lay there, cold and still. If he hadn't been breathing, he could have been one of those marble statues they put on top of tombs.

"Come on, Dad," I whispered, reaching out to poke his shoulder. "Wake up. Yell at me. Do *something*."

Nothing.

Pulling back my shaking hand, I tucked my legs against my chest and rested my chin on my knees, determined not to cry. I couldn't afford to be weak. Until I heard from Mom, I was the only household the Great Yong had left. I might not worship him like the others did, but I'd be damned if I let him slip away after all that work. So long as he was here, I'd be here, so I forced myself to stay awake, keeping vigil at his side as we sailed together through a void inside a god toward whatever future my employment had bought.

THANK YOU FOR READING!

Thank you for reading *Part-Time Gods!* If you enjoyed the story, I hope you'll consider leaving a review. Reviews, good and bad, are vital to every author's career, and I would be very grateful if you'd consider writing one for me.

Want to know when I release a new book? Sign up for my New Release Mailing List at *rachelaaron.net*. List members are always first in line for everything I do, *and* they get exclusive bonus content like the list-only Heartstriker short story, *Mother of the Year.* Signing up is free, and I promise never to spam you, so come join us!

Still need more to read? Why not try one of my already completed series? Visit www.rachelaaron.net to see the full list. You can also follow me on Twitter @Rachel_Aaron.

Again, thank you so *so* much for reading! I couldn't do any of this without you!

Yours always,
Rachel Aaron

THE HEARTSTRIKERS SERIES

As the smallest dragon in the Heartstriker clan, Julius survives by a simple code: stay quiet, don't cause trouble, and keep out of the way of bigger dragons. But this meek behavior doesn't cut it in a family of ambitious predators, and his mother, Bethesda the Heartstriker, has finally reached the end of her patience.

Now, sealed in human form and banished to the DFZ--a vertical metropolis built on the ruins of Old Detroit--Julius has one month to prove to his mother that he can be a ruthless dragon or lose his true shape forever. But in a city of modern mages and vengeful spirits where dragons are seen as monsters to be exterminated, he's going to need some serious help to survive this test.

He just hopes humans are more trustworthy than dragons.

"Super fun, fast paced, urban fantasy full of heart, and plenty of magic, charm and humor to spare, this self published gem was one of my favorite discoveries this year!" - **The Midnight Garden**

"A deliriously smart and funny beginning to a new urban fantasy series about dragons in the ruins of Detroit...inventive, uproariously clever, and completely un-put-down-able!" - **SF Signal**

THE LEGEND OF ELI MONPRESS

Eli Monpress is talented. He's charming. And he's the greatest thief in the world.

He's also a wizard, and with the help of his partners in crime--a swordsman with the world's most powerful magic sword (but no magical ability of his own) and a demonseed who can step through shadows and punch through walls--he's getting ready to pull off the heist of his career. To start, though, he'll just steal something small. Something no one will miss. Something like... a king.

"I cannot be less than 110% in love with this book. I loved it. I love it still. Already I sort of want to read it again. Considering my fairly epic Godzilla-sized To Read list, that's just about the highest compliment I can give a book" - **CSI: Librarian**

"Fast and fun, The Spirit Thief *introduces a fascinating new world and a complex magical system based on cooperation with the spirits who reside in all living objects. Aaron's characters are fully fleshed and possess complex personalities, motivations, and backstories that are only gradually revealed. Fans of Scott Lynch's* Lies of Locke Lamora *(2006) will be thrilled with Eli Monpress. Highly recommended for all fantasy readers."* - **Booklist, Starred Review**

Devi Morris isn't your average mercenary. She has plans. Big ones. And a ton of ambition. It's a combination that's going to get her killed one day - but not just yet.

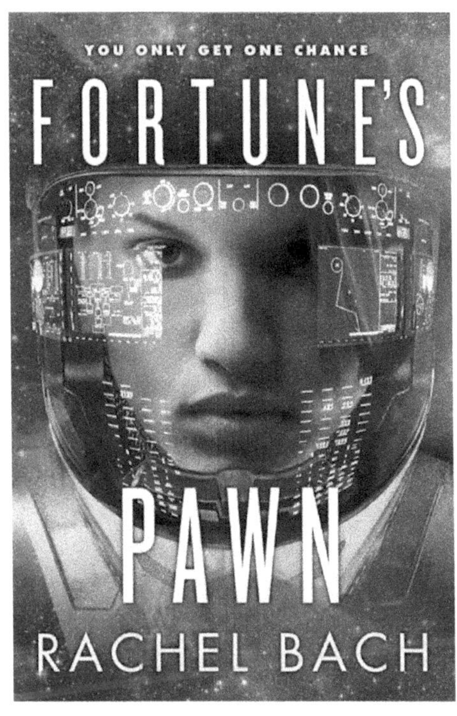

That is, until she just gets a job on a tiny trade ship with a nasty reputation for surprises. The Glorious Fool isn't misnamed: it likes to get into trouble, so much so that one year of security work under its captain is equal to five years everywhere else. With odds like that, Devi knows she's found the perfect way to get the jump on the next part of her Plan. But the Fool doesn't give up its secrets without a fight, and one year on this ship might be more than even Devi can handle.

"Firefly-*esque in its concept of a rogue-ish spaceship family... The narrative never quite goes where you expect it to, in a good way... Devi is a badass with a heart.*" - **Locus Magazine**

"*If you liked* Star Wars, *if you like our books, and if you are waiting for* Guardians of the Galaxy *to hit the theaters, this is your book.*" - **Ilona Andrews**

"*I JUST LOVED IT! Perfect light sci-fi. If you like space stuff that isn't that complicated but highly entertaining, I give two thumbs up!*" - **Felicia Day**

FOREVER FANTASY ONLINE

In the real world, twenty-one-year-old library sciences student Tina Anderson is invisible and under-appreciated, but in the VR-game Forever Fantasy Online she's Roxxy--the respected leader and main tank of a top-tier raiding guild. In the real world, her brother James Anderson is a college drop-out struggling under debt, but in FFO he's famous--an explorer who's gotten every achievement, done every quest, and collected all the rarest items.

Both Tina and James need the game more than they'd like to admit, but their favorite escape turns into a trap when FFO becomes a living world. Wounds are no longer virtual, stupid monsters become cunning, NPCs start acting like actual people, and death might be forever.

In the real world, everyone said being good at video games was a waste of time. Now, stranded and separated across thousands of miles of new, deadly terrain, Tina and James's skill at FFO is the only thing keeping them alive. It's going to take every bit of their expertise--and hoarded loot--to find each other and get back home, but as the stakes get higher and the damage adds up, being the best in the game may no longer be enough.

"Rachel Aaron and Travis Bach have written an amazing story and a realistic LitRPG."
- The Fantasy Inn

"Excellent characters, an engaging story, and geek humor. What more can one ask for?"
- TS Chan

The first in a new gamer/fantasy collaboration from Rachel Aaron and Travis Bach!

2,000 TO 10,000: WRITING BETTER, WRITING FASTER, AND WRITING MORE OF WHAT YOU LOVE
(nonfiction)

"Have you ever wanted to double your daily word counts? Do you sometimes feel like you're crawling through your story? Do you want to write more every day without increasing the time you spend writing or sacrificing quality? It's not impossible; it's not even that hard. This is the book explaining how, with a few simple changes, I boosted my daily writing from 2000 words to over 10k a day, and how you can too."

Expanding on Rachel's viral blog post about how she doubled her daily word counts, this book offers practical writing advice for anyone who's ever longed to increase their daily writing output. In addition to updated information for the popular 2k to 10k writing efficiency process, 5 step plotting method, and easy editing tips, the book includes all new chapters on creating characters who write their own stories, plot structure, and learning to love your daily writing. Full of easy to follow, practical advice from a professional author who doesn't eat if she doesn't produce good books on a regular basis, 2k to 10k focuses not just on writing faster, but writing better, and having more fun while you do it!

"I loved this book! So helpful!" - **Courtney Milan, NYT Bestselling Author**

"This. Is. Amazing. You are telling my story RIGHT NOW. Book is due in 2 weeks, and I'm behind--woefully, painfully behind--because I've been stuck...writing in circles and unenthused. Yet here--here is a FANTASTIC solution. I am printing this post out, and I'm setting out to make my triangle. Thank you, thank you, THANK YOU!" - **Bestselling YA Author Susan Dennard**

ABOUT THE AUTHOR

Rachel Aaron is the author of sixteen novels and the bestselling nonfiction writing book, *2k to 10k: Writing Faster, Writing Better, and Writing More of What You Love,* which has helped thousands of authors double their daily word counts. When she's not holed up in her writing cave, Rachel lives a nerdy, bookish life in Broomfield, CO, with her perpetual-motion son, long-suffering husband, and grumpy old lady dog. To learn more about Rachel, read samples of all her books, or to find a complete list of her interviews and podcasts, please visit rachelaaron.net!

As always, this book would not have been nearly as good without my
amazing beta readers. Thank you so, so much to Michele Fry, Jodie
Martin, Eva Bunge, Christina Vlinder, Kevin Swearington, Lindsay
Simms, and the ever amazing Laligin.

Y'all are the BEST!

www.ingramcontent.com/pod-product-compliance
Lightning Source LLC
Chambersburg PA
CBHW071232190726
48292CB00007B/2254